Also by Ann Aguirre

CORINE SOLOMON NOVELS
Blue Diablo
Hell Fire
Shady Lady

SIRANTHA JAX NOVELS
Grimspace
Wanderlust
Doubleblind
Killbox
Aftermath

D0187003

ANN AGUIRRE

DEVIL'S PUNCH

A CORINE SOLOMON NOVEL

A ROC BOOK

ROC
Published by New American Library, a division of
Penguin Group (USA) Inc., 375 Hudson Street,
New York, New York 10014, USA
Penguin Group (Canada), 90 Eglinton Avenue East, Suite 700, Toronto,
Ontario M4P 2Y3, Canada (a division of Pearson Penguin Canada Inc.)
Penguin Books Ltd., 80 Strand, London WC2R 0RL, England
Penguin Ireland, 25 St. Stephen's Green, Dublin 2,
Ireland (a division of Penguin Books Ltd.)
Penguin Group (Australia), 250 Camberwell Road, Camberwell, Victoria 3124,
Australia (a division of Pearson Australia Group Pty. Ltd.)
Penguin Books India Pvt. Ltd., 11 Community Centre, Panchsheel Park,
New Delhi - 110 017, India
Penguin Group (NZ), 67 Apollo Drive, Rosedale, Auckland 0632,
New Zealand (a division of Pearson New Zealand Ltd.)
Penguin Books (South Africa) (Pty.) Ltd., 24 Sturdee Avenue,
Rosebank, Johannesburg 2196, South Africa

Penguin Books Ltd., Registered Offices:
80 Strand, London WC2R 0RL, England

First published by Roc, an imprint of New American Library,
a division of Penguin Group (USA) Inc.

First Printing, April 2012
10 9 8 7 6 5 4 3 2 1

Copyright © Ann Aguirre, 2012
All rights reserved

ROC REGISTERED TRADEMARK — MARCA REGISTRADA

Printed in the United States of America

For Jen, who saw the beauty in the bones

ACKNOWLEDGMENTS

Thanks to Laura Bradford, my shiny agent, who never tells me an idea is terrible. I also doff my hat to Anne Sowards, Kat Sherbo, and the Penguin team. (I don't actually wear hats, but it's an awesome image, right? Thought so.)

Jen, Bree, Lauren . . . and the PoP loop, of course. You're my go-to crew. You never let me down. *fist bump*

Next, there's my family. I love you guys so much. Thanks for everything. I feel like there are no words, which sucks, considering what I do for a living. Just know that every pot of veggie chili is chock-full of love. And beans.

Thumbs up to my fabulous proofreaders, Fedora Chen and Katy Sprinkel, and to my copy editor, Jan McInroy, who a did a terrific job on this book.

Finally, I thank caffeine, liquor, and chocolate — without which none of this would be possible.

And as always, I offer utmost appreciation to my readers. Y'all rock. Please keep writing; that's ann.aguirre@gmail.com. I love hearing from you.

New Beginnings

I carried the last of Chance's boxes up to the flat.

Mexico agreed with my ex, physically speaking. The constant sun was similar to Florida, though the weather was milder and more temperate in the mountains, the humidity lower, and so his skin glowed golden, a fine contrast to his inky hair. His features were sharp, feline, but sculpted in a way that you could stare for hours and never tire of marveling at the cut of his cheekbones or the curve of his mouth.

Looking at his impossible beauty, I was reminded again that he wasn't human. He didn't sweat or grow facial hair. Once I'd written that off as a unique genetic boon, but it was unquestionably more. While his mother, Min, was human, I was positive his father had been something else. I had no idea what.

Smiling at me, Chance was confident again, and I'd always loved that about him. Generally speaking, he didn't indulge in long moments of self-doubt. He brushed past me on the stairs, carrying a carton of linens; he smelled of lemon, carambola, and rosewood, top notes from his cologne, Versace Man Eau Fraîche. Less familiar than the Burberry he'd once sworn by, but I didn't smell of frangipani anymore either. By tacit agreement, we'd decided on a fresh start all the way.

My ex had been serious when he said he'd do whatever it took to be with me, including moving south of the border and starting a new life. The two of us had a complicated history, fraught with old mistakes and regret. But maybe this time our relationship had a real shot.

His building was simple stucco, painted canary yellow with azure trim, a bold color scheme typical of the neighborhood. Down the block, there was a house painted lavender and mint green. His new place had a fantastic view of the mountains instead of the crowded streets below. I stood by the window, lost in thought. Chance was lucky to find something close to Tia's house. In Spanish, *tía* meant *aunt*, and I'd never been clear if people had been calling her Auntie so long it had supplanted her proper name. At any rate, she'd adopted me as part of her family; I felt like a favored niece with her. In recent days, she'd become my mentor as well.

After we'd returned to find my store in ruins, Tia let Chance sleep on the couch while he sought a place of his own; it took three weeks for him to locate a one-bedroom in the neighborhood. During his search, I sorted out the paperwork and paid the workmen with Escobar's money; he was the rival drug lord with whom I'd allied to take out the Montoya cartel before they could kill me. The Montoyas put me on their hit list over the part I'd played in liberating Chance's mother from their clutches. So maybe joining forces with Escobar wasn't the smartest thing I ever did, but it felt like my only viable choice for survival at the time. Ergo, I made a pact with Escobar to destroy the Montoyas, and when we succeeded, I walked out with a briefcase full of money—well, enough to rebuild my pawnshop.

It would be better than before, once it was finished, and I'd still have a nest egg in case of future disasters. With Chance around, such events became more likely. Oh, he had his own money, and he'd help, if he felt responsible, but I didn't want to depend on him—or anyone—again. I'd learned how well I like self-reliance.

After Chance shook hands on a rental agreement, he'd offered to let me room with him, no strings, but I didn't want to start our relationship that way. Living together right off? *Uh-uh.* I'd meant it when I told him I wanted to go slow.

When Tia offered to let me stay with her while I rebuilt, it seemed like the ideal solution. I got a place to live; she benefited from my help around the house and I could drive her around more easily. Plus she was training me to the extent that she knew spells and charms. No matter how inept I proved, she never lost patience.

Any other *curandera* wouldn't touch me with a ten-foot pole. By dealing with Maury and summoning his mate, Dumah, to solve my problems, I'd marked myself as a black witch, one who trafficked in demons. Maury was the entropy demon I'd set free in Kilmer; he saved my life when one of the elders stabbed me that horrible night in the forest. When that debt came due, he had me summon his mate in repayment. I managed to trick him on the letter of the agreement, so while Dumah writhed inside the circle, I renegotiated our terms. In the end, I wound up with his reluctant acquiescence to use his mate as backup against the Montoyas. When push came to shove, I did. I fed those men to a demon to save my own life.

That decision made me anathema to those who worked on the side of right and light, though I was hardly a witch at all, having just realized I could access my mother's magick, along with the awful touch that once comprised my sole skill. When my mother died saving my life, I gained the ability to read objects with a touch, known among the gifted as psychometry, but my talent wasn't natural and painless; it carried the pain of the fire that claimed my mother. In the dark Georgia woods where I found her necklace, I touched the metal and unlocked the rest of her abilities. From that point, I felt the difference in my blood and bone. I knew that spells would respond as they never had before.

Fortunately, Tia had studied the darkness of my choices, and then she shook her head. "What I see you've done, that's not your heart," she'd said. "I *know* you."

Most wouldn't be so kind or understanding. Already,

I'd noticed a few people crossing the street to avoid me. As in the U.S., there were gifted in Mexico, but because of my crippled abilities—and the limitation of the touch— I could never ID them unless we made contact and our talents sparked. Now, with my witch sight, I could spot them from a distance, not an aura but a halo of dark or light, depending on their gift and how they used it. My own was a grimy mixture of bright and shadow, mottled from my contact with Maury and Dumah. I tried not to look at it any more than I had to. If there was a way to scrub off those choices, I didn't know what it would be. No, the consequences would remain with me forever. Even if I spent my lifetime doing good deeds, practicing white magick, at best I would be—to others—a nether witch who denied her fundamental nature.

Even if the viper doesn't bite, it's still a snake.

Despite ostracism from some of her friends and colleagues, Tia had taken me into her home. I'd asked, "Don't you mind? They won't speak to you anymore. You're an outcast now . . . like me."

She'd given me a fleeting smile. "I'm too old to care about such things, child. I don't have much longer, and I choose to spend those days helping you. At least you're willing to do my shopping when my legs hurt. That's more than I can say for Juanita Lopez."

I'd laughed, because Juanita was one of the worst; she'd hated me since my return. Before, she'd paid no attention to me at all. Apparently, my mother's magick made me register on their visual radars well, whereas the touch had permitted me to run silent. Now I was a marked target.

With effort, I put the dark thoughts aside. Tia had been kind to me. I would make sure she didn't suffer. She'd helped me with the grimoires I inherited from my mother, explaining various techniques. And she teased me mercilessly about Chance. He was good with her from experience with his own mother, Min.

"You should keep this one," Tia would say. "You'll make beautiful babies."

I always laughed. It was almost—almost—enough to make me forget other pain. But I'd lost so much. Jesse, my almost-boyfriend, who didn't remember me. My best friend, Shannon, who I missed even more than the man I'd thought I might love. In Laredo, I'd cast a forget spell—and screwed it up, giving the charm too much power—and fogged myself right out of their minds. Deep down I hoped the phone would ring soon. That the effect would wear off, and they'd both yell at me, and then everything could go back to the way it was.

But we don't always get what we wish for. So far, my cell phone had been silent. No Shannon. No Jesse. And for obvious reasons, no Kel. He wasn't—couldn't—be here. It was awful that I wanted him to be, even a little bit, with Chance craving my attention. Kel wasn't for me; rationally, I knew that. He was Nephilim, committed to fighting for all eternity. He didn't have a life apart from his orders, and so there was nothing for me with him. It had been around two months since I'd seen him, three weeks since I'd come home. I shouldn't be thinking of him. I should file our brief connection under MISTAKES I'VE MADE, or more accurately, THINGS I WANT BUT CAN'T HAVE.

Yet I found myself looking for him. Searching the crowd for him. Sure, I could call him, but what would I say? *Hi. Missed you. Killed anybody amusing lately?* You just didn't trifle with someone who reported to archangels. So I remembered and I missed him and tried to put the pieces back together. Too bad they'd all been broken into jagged shapes that cut when I tried to connect the edges.

"You all right?" Chance asked, coming up beside me.

The mountains were beautiful, dark green and pointed like weapons against the darkening sky. Where I'd grown up, it was relatively flat and the countryside tended toward swampland. Until coming here, I'd never lived at high altitude. It changed everything from cooking to taking a walk. Everything felt like more of an achievement at seven thousand feet.

Including moving day.

I nodded. "Just tired. You fit a lot of boxes in the Mustang."

"I'm a good packer. We used to move around a lot."

"You and Min?"

His silence felt like an affirmative. Then I wondered why I didn't know more about him, why I'd permitted his reticence. A woman more confident of her self-worth wouldn't; she'd insist on learning about her lover. And if he didn't care to share, she'd move on, looking for someone who wanted to be a partner, not a manager. The mistakes in our rearview didn't all belong to Chance.

At length, he offered, "I think she was hiding from someone."

"Your father . . . or the Montoyas?"

"Both? Min doesn't talk about the past much."

"And you didn't press her."

He shook his head. "I never wanted to disappoint her. She'd get this look, like I should know better than to ask. Like it was . . . impolite."

"Maybe it's a cultural thing?"

"What I've read suggests that it is. Which is weird— that I'm reading what it's like to be Korean, but I'm American . . . and I've learned what I know about relating to people from my mom."

"Did she ever have a boyfriend when you were growing up?"

Chance laughed. "Never. Not that they didn't try. But she always seemed like she was waiting."

"For your dad to come back?"

"I don't know. I'm sorry if this is frustrating, but some of it I really don't know. She tried to give me a normal American childhood, as much as she could, as much as we could afford."

"Well, at least you're telling me straight out that you don't have the answers," I said, smiling. "That's more than I got before."

"True."

"Let's unpack a little more, and then I'll get us something to eat."

The nice thing about the neighborhood, there were several *tortillerias* and taquerias within a couple of blocks, where I could buy rice and beans. The taco joints stayed open super-late, too, as they were a favorite of the college drinking crowd.

"Will you sleep over?" he asked.

I laughed. "You don't even have a bed. But nice try." In truth, he had little furniture. The Mustang carried his personal belongings, his books and clothes, but it couldn't hold a sofa. "I'll take you shopping tomorrow in the El Camino. I should be able to fit what you need, if we make multiple trips."

"Thank you, Corine."

I didn't know what he was thanking me for—the offer of help or the second chance between us—but when he leaned down to kiss me, I forgot to wonder. His mouth tasted of tea and lemon with a hint of salt. It was a sweet nothing of a kiss, full of hope and expectation. Happiness swirled through me, despite everything I'd lost.

I forced myself to sound brisk. "If you had your way, we'd make out on the floor all night. Get to work."

He grinned, shameless and beautiful, and my heart fluttered. The last of the light shone on his raven-dark hair, limning it blue. In profile, he was still the best thing I'd ever seen. I didn't want to love him again; I feared it, but he had a siren's call bound up in his tiger eyes and tawny skin. With Chance, I suspected—in the end—I would walk into the water, smiling, and let it close over my head.

An hour later I finished putting away his kitchen things, so at least we'd have cups and plates. The previous tenant had left some rusty wrought-iron patio furniture on the balcony, so we'd eat there, watching the sunset. I let myself out while Chance hung clothing in the bedroom. I ran lightly down the stairs; the hundred pesos in my pocket would more than buy our dinner.

The taqueria was two blocks down the hill. After passing the gate, I jogged them easily; thanks to my time in the jungle with Kel, passing Escobar's test, I was fitter than I had been in years.

Because the food was good, there were a few people waiting outside. The man at the counter took my order and then I joined the queue. I got tacos al pastor, rice, and beans. Takeaway came in simple containers and wrapped in paper. I cradled the bag against my chest and retraced my steps. The security guy recognized me and didn't demand my ID this time. He opened the gate just wide enough for me to slip through and then I headed for Chance's flat. He met me at the door and relieved me of our repast, carrying it out to the balcony without being asked.

I guessed he realized there was nowhere else to eat. But in my absence, he'd fixed up the area with a couple of potted plants, cushions Min had embroidered, and candles. With the sun setting over the mountains, it was breathtaking.

"You approve?"

"Absolutely. I can't believe you managed all this so fast."

He winked. "Not a problem. I just unpacked the box labeled 'seduction.' "

"And you were doing so well too." But I was smiling as I laid out the meal on dishes I remembered picking out with Chance.

Oh, goddess. When I agreed to a second try, I didn't realize how hard it would be to keep from falling into his arms, without being sure we'd changed old patterns.

To my relief, he accepted the implicit request to back off. "So, what are you doing tomorrow?"

"In the morning I'm meeting with the project foreman to go over progress they've made on the reconstruction. Then I'll practice my spells with Tia."

"She's a slave driver."

"I have to master the magick." It wasn't open to debate.

"Are you free in the afternoon? Shopping?" he reminded me.

"Yeah, absolutely. I'll pick you up at three?" There were a number of furniture stores in the area, and some had cash-and-carry availability. "Let's see if we can get a mattress first, and then a sofa and a table."

"Sounds good."

After dinner he spread some bigger pillows on the

balcony and we curled up together. He'd truly given up everything for me. Started over. The night passed in sweet conversation and tentative plans. There was kissing too, of course, but I backed off before it got too intense. That didn't seem fair to either of us when I would return to Tia's place at the end of the night. At eleven, Chance walked me to her door, kissed me again, and I went inside.

My mentor had left a lamp on for me, but she'd gone to sleep an hour before; she rarely stayed up past ten. The woman followed the light, working during the day, reading a little at night. We had no television, but I didn't miss it. *Chance would want one,* I thought as I put my purse on the bed. I hadn't put my mark on this space—a simple room decorated in colonial style—because I wouldn't be here long, if the weather held and the work crew remained reliable. I'd hired an excellent foreman named Armando who was opposed to physical labor on his own behalf but excelled at making others buckle down.

Butch trotted to meet me, his nails clicking on the tile floor. He'd gotten a little pudgy since our return. He preferred staying with Tia while I worked at Chance's place, as she had a nice courtyard where he could nap in the sun or chase birds. Usually it was the former—hence the Chihuahua spare tire.

"Anything exciting happen?" I asked, kneeling to scoop him into my arms.

He snuggled in with two quiet, negative yaps. It might not be normal for me to talk to my dog and get an answer, but it had been going on long enough that it didn't seem odd to me anymore. I'd considered asking *why* he could understand me, but I'd decided some mysteries were better left alone.

"Did you keep Tia company?"

An affirmative bark.

I stroked his head, then scratched behind his ears, just as he liked. "Good boy. Did she remember to feed you?"

Yap. *Yes.* But Butch stared up at me with sad eyes, despite the fact that everything seemed to be okay in his world. I thought I knew what it was. "You miss Shannon, huh?"

Me too.

Shannon had been my best friend ever since I rescued her in Kilmer. She'd become my roommate and my closest confidante. Before the shit went down in Laredo, we'd discussed opening a consignment store in the new building, becoming true partners. The girl had been the closest I had to a sister.

With Butch in my arms, I curled up on the bed and remembered.

Witchy Business

Laredo. A summoning spell had gone wrong due to my ignorance and lack of training, and Shannon was injured. The memory and regret swallowed me.

I had to stop putting her at risk. Maybe I should put her on a bus, even if she didn't want to go. Before it was too late. "Look, Shan, I really think—"

"No." *She slammed the first door open and stomped to the apartment.* "If you want to get rid of me, I'll go. But you're* not *sending me to my dad. I'm not a little kid. . . . I can get a job. Maybe I'll try Cali. I hear it's pretty there."* She glared, as if daring me to object. "You *did fine on your own."*

"Not really," I said softly. I'd never told anyone this. I didn't like thinking about it. "*I landed well at first. I found a job in a used-book store, and I had a room in a boardinghouse. But when the store went under, I couldn't find anything else. Pretty soon I had no money and I had no place to stay. I don't make friends easily, so I had nobody to turn to. I moved on with only enough money in my pocket to get to the next town. I found myself sleeping in the bus station. I did things I'm not proud of."*

I'd taken insane risks, and it was lucky I wasn't diseased or dead. It would break my heart if I drove Shannon to that with my good intentions.

"*Like what?*"

She wouldn't be satisfied unless I told her. I wouldn't reveal my past to anyone else, for any other reason—only to keep Shan from repeating my mistakes. I was over it, mostly. I'd learned to deal. But she needed to know how much I trusted her.

So while I wrapped an ice pack, fixed a glass of water, and set out two pills, I revealed the whole story. Nobody knew this much about me—I'd picked up men for food and shelter, using serial monogamy as a means of survival. Those relationships never lasted long, because I chose men who wouldn't reject me, ones who'd take me home and were lonely enough not to complain if I stayed. But I always moved on, feeling worse each time, because I lived with them out of desperation, not desire.

My past left me with such low self-esteem that I didn't demand to be an equal partner with Chance when he came along. I didn't feel worthy of him, and I did anything to please him; I spurned my old identity because it was awful and tawdry, and I wanted to forget that woman, the sad, desperate Corine. It would kill me if Shan ever thought she wasn't equal to any man who wanted her.

I went on. "By the time I met Chance, I had gotten myself together. I had a place of my own and a job at a dry cleaner's. But you know how hard it is to get work if you don't have an address? How hard it is to keep clean in public restrooms so people's eyes don't slide away from you? It's easier if you're young. But if you're old and homeless, it's the next thing to an invisibility spell. I knew people who died on the street, people who froze to death and nobody noticed. Nobody cared. The city just removed the bodies like they were leaves in the street." *I bit my lip against the burn of tears and the throbbing in my head.* "So if you think I'm letting you leave with nothing, you're out of your mind. I want better than that for you."

And that was part of the reason I couldn't turn down Escobar's money. I wanted her to have a future brighter than I could provide alone. Having a place of our own mattered desperately, and now maybe she'd understand why. If Chance knew, he might get why my pawnshop had meant everything to me, and with it blown to shit, why I felt as if someone I loved had died. I needed a home, damn it.

"I had no idea," she whispered.

"Nobody does." I exhaled shakily and got my own *Aleve* and *agua.*

Her expression said she understood; we didn't need to speak of this again. Thank God. *Though I'd come to terms with my mistakes, I didn't enjoy reliving them, even for Shan's benefit.*

But she had her own point to make as well. "Look, I'll stop threatening to leave if you stop talking about sending me away. I know it's dangerous. I'm not an idiot. But for the first time I feel like I belong and I'm not giving that up. Okay?"

I downed my water like it was a shot of something stronger. "Fair enough."

Now, she didn't remember me. Part of me—the selfish part—wanted desperately to cast something to negate what I'd done, but with my lack of control, I couldn't risk making Shan and Jesse worse or hurting them again. So I lived with the consequences and missed my best friend. I'd do pretty much anything to have her back in my life, but my options were limited.

I went to bed that night and dreamt of old mistakes. In the morning I had some fruit for breakfast, showered, and dressed. Tia was cleaning this morning, so the house was empty when I left. I left her a note saying what time I'd be home and headed to my meeting, where I argued with Armando, the foreman, about his projected date of completion.

"If you don't step it up," I said in Spanish, "rainy season will set in, and there won't be time to finish."

"We're doing the best we can, *señorita.* There have been delays. Materials—"

"Let me make this simple. You will have the building finished by"—I named a date—"or I will hire someone else to take your place. Understood?"

"*Sí, claro.* I'll get the work done."

Tia was waiting when I got back. She greeted me by demanding I cast a blindness spell.

I protested, "What if I blind you permanently?"

She cackled. "I'm mostly blind already, *nena*. So get to work!"

Under her supervision, I spent four hours drilling the five spells she insisted would be most useful: Blind, Trip, Steam, Freeze, and Open. I'd mastered Blind by the time we knocked off for the day. Trip and Steam, I executed successfully 75 percent of the time. I had less luck with Freeze and Open. Those were more complicated, requiring complete focus. I had perfected Light weeks ago and no longer needed practice. At the end of the day, she added a new spell, Truth-sense. That one wasn't complicated, but it required a fair amount of focus. I failed it the first couple of times, but then, once I fell into the correct pattern, I understood it instinctively.

"A good day's work," Tia said. "Soon you'll be casting like a proper witch."

"*Gracias*." I kissed her cheek and grabbed my purse. "I'm going shopping, Butch. Interested?"

He shot me an *as-if* look, but followed me as far as the courtyard. I refilled his water dish at the outside spigot and then went out to the El Camino. Fortunately it wasn't market day, so traffic on the narrow road wasn't heavy. I drove down and hung a left, then a right, and then another right. Roads were weird, with odd round-abouts called *glorietas*, but I didn't mind because the medians were always so green, full of trees and flowers and beautifully landscaped. I turned around and went back down the mountain a few blocks to the gated community where Chance lived. The guard greeted me with a raised hand and let me in. This was a small complex with one- and two-bedroom flats, up the hill from an expensive private school, no more than twelve buildings, two units each, but there was ample parking. I didn't wait long for Chance, who bounded down the stairs to meet me.

He swung into the car and kissed my cheek as I backed out. "I thought we'd go to Soriana first."

"That's nearby, right?" Chance still didn't know where everything was, even in this neighborhood, but that wasn't so bad. I'd lived here for two years before I could find the nearest mall on my own.

Now I could find five different ones—without GPS.

"Yep."

"I went grocery shopping today. I'll cook dinner when we're done tonight."

That was an interesting offer. The Chance from my memory preferred takeout menus to working the stove. In his new place, he had a nice kitchen with pretty white ceramic tile and pristine counters, so it was good he intended to make use of the space.

"What're we having?" I asked as I nudged out into traffic. Between the bodyguards blocking the right lane, waiting to pick up the ambassadors' kids, and the delivery trucks that didn't want to let me in on the left, the merge took longer than it should have.

"*Chapchae* noodles. Or as close as I can get, anyway. I doubt there's a Korean grocery around here."

"Superama has a small Asian foods section, but it's eclectic." I glanced over at him. "It's been a big adjustment, huh?"

"I like the energy. And it's . . . different."

No arguing that.

I didn't say more until I parked at Plaza Jardines, a small shopping center with one anchor store—Soriana—a couple of midsize places, like DormiMundo, where you could buy mattresses, and Altimus, which had furniture. But those places both took a week or more for delivery. I didn't want Chance sleeping on the floor that long. Soriana would let you carry anything out that you could buy and fit into your vehicle.

Chance followed me past several vet clinics, beauty salons, and a dry cleaner's. Inside Soriana, it was kind of a mess, but I threaded through women looking at glassware to where the mattresses were stacked up in stalls. It didn't take long to pick out a reasonably priced set. Fortunately, he'd brought his own linens because I could only think of one store that sold thread counts high enough to content him.

Then Chance and I wrestled the mattresses out to the

El Camino. I'd been canny enough to bring rope, so once we got the set situated, I helped him secure it. Though we weren't going far, it wouldn't help afternoon traffic if the box springs bounced out onto the road. I navigated the parking lot carefully, leaving via the Sanborns exit and driving up the hill, then back down and into his lot. The afternoon passed in shopping, hauling, delivery, and more shopping. Three hours and four trips later, he had enough furniture in his apartment for it to be functional. I helped him put the shelves together so we could unpack his books. By the time he started dinner, I was exhausted. I slumped onto the cushions on the floor, which we'd moved in from the balcony.

He'd bought an odd assortment of stuff. No living room or dining room furniture, but candles and shelves and a flat-screen TV. From my vantage point on the floor, I watched him cook for a while, and then I went to put expensive sheets on his mattress. I found his comforter neatly folded in the closet. I guessed he'd used a pile of blankets for a makeshift pallet last night. When I finished arranging his bed, it looked inviting.

After dinner, we sat together, bent over his laptop, and I showed him a site where he could order all his furniture online. Mercado Libre was similar to eBay, only it served Latin American countries. Ingenia Muebles offered elegant, minimalist designs, which I felt sure would appeal to Chance. And I did know him that well at least. An hour later, he'd ordered stuff for bedroom, living room, and kitchen. The flat would be lovely, once it all arrived.

That took a week, during which time I hounded the builders and Armando, then took lessons with Tia. Chance and I—our nights fell into a comfortable routine. Sometimes we ate at home; he was a better cook than me. Some nights we went out and had dinner at some unlikely American chain, like Applebee's or P.F. Chang's. He was always surprised at how American influence had permeated Mexico, but if you turned down another road, some neighborhoods felt as exotic as the jungles of Peru. Once a week we went to the VIP cinema, which had spoiled me for regular showings. On Fridays we visited the farmers' market and bought produce and fresh cheese. From what I could tell, Chance enjoyed it all. I fought the bad memories and dared to hope we could build a life here. I also wondered if we should be sleeping together. With an ex, it was hard to be sure of the pace. Butch had no answers for me, and Tia counseled that sex should wait until he put a ring on my finger.

I didn't even know if I *wanted* jewelry with such strings attached.

"Are you bored yet?" I asked Chance one night.

He shook his head. "I'm considering my options."

"Do you want to work in the shop with me?"

"Doing what?"

"Appraising items? Customer service? Inventory? Bookkeeping? Financial—"

"Bookkeeping," he said at once. "I can handle that for you, and I'll probably do some online trading. Advise you on good investments."

I wasn't averse to increasing my nest egg, and Chance had a knack. "Of course."

"I won't be at the store full-time, though. Just as needed to keep the books balanced."

At some point I needed to replace Señor Alvarez, who perished when the Montoyas firebombed the pawnshop, but that was a raw spot, and I couldn't bear to consider it yet. There would be time once the workers finished the new building. Assembling the pieces of a broken life couldn't happen overnight.

"Then I should ask a different question, a more important one. Are you happy here?"

Chance considered, delving into his pocket for his silver coin as he always did when he was thinking. He spun it along his knuckles until he decided what to say. The silence didn't worry me. I'd rather have the truth than a polite lie.

"I'd be happier with you," he admitted finally. "*Really* with you. Because that would mean you trust me. But I enjoy figuring things out. It's an adventure, though I do feel a bit *Stranger in a Strange Land* at times."

"It took me a year to acclimate. You'd do better if you took some Spanish classes."

"Can't you tutor me?" He arched his elegant brows. "The fringe benefits are exceptional."

"I'll take a class with you," I offered.

My Spanish was good, but not perfect. It couldn't hurt to learn more. Gratification spilled through me when Chance nodded. His willingness to try made me believe, more than anything, that he wasn't just screwing with me, trying to even the scales or something so he could be the one to leave me this time. Yeah, my ego was fragile enough to wonder, but only a lunatic would uproot his life this way for such a petty revenge. Chance was many things—obsessive among them—but I didn't believe he was nuts.

"How much longer are you going to live with Tia?" he asked, nuzzling my neck. "It makes sense for you to move in here."

Mmm. He remembered perfectly what to do with the side of my neck—wandering lips, gentle scrape of teeth. I contemplated his soft bed and tried to recall why I wanted to go slow.

"Does it?" I breathed.

"Mm-hmm. Even after your property's rebuilt you still have to furnish the upstairs apartment. Whereas mine's ready for you, and you helped decorate it." He pressed a trail of kisses down my throat, nuzzled my collarbone. "It's a smart business decision. You could rent the flat above the shop. That's more income."

"So you're only thinking of my financial future?"

He flashed me a wicked grin. "Well, I didn't say I had no personal stake in the matter."

The kisses grew more heated. Chance drew me down on top of him, so I could feel how much he wanted me. I teased him a little, and he groaned.

Eventually I said, "If things are still . . . this way between us when construction's complete, I'll give your proposal serious thought."

It wouldn't be as convenient, living here, but it wouldn't hurt me to walk six blocks to work instead of running downstairs with my hair wet. At the least, the sun and the wind would dry it a little by the time I arrived. And the exercise would be good for me.

"Until then, you'll go back to Tia's every night?" His disappointment rang like cathedral bells.

"It seems prudent."

He muttered something that sounded like *Fuck prudent*, but I just grinned. "Speaking of which, it's time for me to head out."

"I'll walk you home."

Dating Chance was turning out to be unexpectedly sweet.

Bad News Travels Fast

Like berries fermenting on the bush, that sweetness couldn't last, of course. But it wasn't Chance's fault.

With disbelieving eyes, I read the words:

Save the girl or claim your crown. Either way, you'll come to us.

Whoever had sent this must be talking about Shannon. Visceral fear crackled like lightning in my veins. *Please let this be someone's idea of a joke.* But since it was in English, not Spanish, it probably hadn't been written by one of Tia's *bruja* friends. Those witches didn't like me, but they weren't pranksters, either.

Shannon had a new life in Laredo. The crown . . . This was a guess at best, but when I'd defeated the Knight of Hell, Caim, he'd called me *my queen.* So maybe it had to do with that. Demons. Leaving a note. But they wanted a meeting, or wanted to lure me somewhere. If they had Shannon, this was a damn effective strategy. Even knowing it was a trap, knowing it would be stupid and suicidal, I'd go for her. I'd go.

I read the note a second time and then glanced down the street both ways. There was little through traffic this way; the streets climbed higher and higher, until they just . . . stopped. I'd discovered that the hard way. After backing down a narrow mountain road for half a mile,

I figured my skills behind the wheel were better than average. But today there were no drivers at all, bad or otherwise. The sidewalk, cracked and uneven, stood empty.

A chill wind blew over me, and I fancied it carried a hint of brimstone. Telling myself I was being stupid, I plucked the parchment from Tia's front gate and studied it. Expensive paper. It had a thick, quality feel, like the posh stationery someone who came from money would use. The ink, too, wasn't simple ballpoint or even gel tip. From the swoops and curves, it had an old-fashioned look, calligraphy more than simple cursive. I flipped it over and found a set of coordinates. Longitude and latitude? Or maybe GPS. I couldn't tell where somebody wanted me to go just by looking at the numbers, but it occurred to me I should get off the street. Though I'd taken care of the problems with Montoya, it didn't mean I had no enemies left. They could find me.

Obviously, someone had.

It unnerved me to think of unseen eyes, watching, but that was a fact of life once you accepted magick was real. I unlocked Tia's front gate and stepped into her courtyard. Immediately, I felt safer, though it was a psychological response at best. As I knew, magick could get behind walls to strike you if the practitioner was determined. There were ways to undermine the wards. With that in mind, I checked Tia's protections. I didn't touch them, as that would weaken the runes, but they yielded a strong, satisfactory glow to my trained eye.

But there were always loopholes. Hell, *I* could do it with simple spells, given sufficient time and planning. That knowledge unsettled me. Around me, the courtyard shivered with life, wind rippling gently over leaves and petals. Flashes of color—vert and crimson—reassured me. There was still a faint, mossy crack in the clay. Nothing had changed, even if someone had left me an inexplicable note on the door. Though it couldn't mean anything good, I would deal with whatever new problem was about to level my life.

I let myself in and found Tia in the kitchen, making

homemade corn tortillas. She greeted me with a smile and a lift of one gnarled hand. "*¿Tienes hambre?*"

Well, I had been hungry. Not so much anymore. I had a coiled thing in my stomach that belched and swelled like a toad. Certainly, it was dread. Everything had consequences. To wit, Newton's Third Law: *To every action there is always an equal and opposite reaction.* So I'd known there would be a cost, but it wasn't right that Shannon should pay it in my stead.

When I found Min—helped save her from her past—I incurred the wrath of the Montoya cartel. I'd resolved that threat, but in doing so, I crossed a Knight of Hell. That didn't come without cost; demons weren't known for forgetting. When he'd crawled back through the gate I opened, he must've carried a grudge with him. I'd vanquished him. Stolen his true name. A note, therefore, seemed like pretty small payback. There was no doubt it heralded more horrendous things.

Her smile faded at my silence. "What happened?"

"I'm not sure." I showed her the note, then translated it aloud.

"You don't know what this means?"

"I have some ideas. Nothing certain."

Tia nodded and returned to the tortillas while I went to my room to see if I could get some answers. Which meant getting out my athame. I searched both grimoires, blue and crimson, until I found the necessary spell; then I read it twice to be sure I understood the steps. This wasn't one I had practiced with Tia. Divination didn't seem to be my thing; I'd had more success during our training with more proactive spells and charms.

Fighting a rising tide of worry, I dug out my magick chest. Constructed on Tia's orders, it was a small, warded box a foot long and just as wide. Made of good cherrywood, banded with willow, it was an elegant piece, but more important, it protected my spell components, kept them fresh and prevented people from meddling with them. I'd inlaid it with a strong avoidance spell, more powerful than the one on the store where I'd bought my chalice and athame with Shannon.

To be cautious, I copied the coordinates before I got started, and then the message itself, just in case something went wrong. Though my control was better, it still wasn't perfect. Next I set the note in the center of my desk and then arranged four white candles around the edges. Taking a deep breath, I lit them. After sprinkling a powder of sage, bay, and mugwort—commonly used in divination spells—around the outer edge, I whispered the words that encapsulated my intent. With my athame, I pricked the tip of my finger and drizzled my blood across the powerful herbs. And then I traced the athame through it. I fixed my desire in my mind—unshakable, immutable. There was a pull, painful, some resistance, but it wasn't a block. Just . . . residual strength left from the last person who had touched the note. I might've tried to read it with a touch, but it was unlikely that the person had held it long enough to imprint it, and I needed the practice with my spells. This wasn't dangerous. At worst, I would destroy the paper, and I had a copy of what it said.

More resistance. But this wasn't a spell that changed anything. It didn't do anything complicated; it was only meant to show traces of magick. Darklight kindled in shadowy swaths, streaking the paper. The stench of sulfur and brimstone whispered at the edge of my senses. That was confirmation enough. I dropped concentration. Demons had definitely had a hand in creating this thing, maybe even possessing the person who delivered it.

Feeling ever worse, I packed my arcane things. I took care in sealing up my magickal chest, and then I wrapped my athame in red satin. I gazed up at the ceiling, simple white plaster. Cobweb in the corner. Maybe the demons were screwing with me, but they weren't known for being practical jokers.

Butch padded into the room, his nails clicking on the tile floor. He grumbled at me, so I picked him up. "Should I?" I asked him.

He yapped. Which was affirmative. I didn't doubt he knew something was going on, and his opinions had saved my ass before, crazy as that sounded.

"And so it's come to this, taking advice from my dog again."

He wagged his tail as I stroked his head. I decided it wouldn't be a bad idea to call Shannon; I still had her number. If she picked up, I'd just disconnect, knowing she was fine. No need to torture myself with the future I'd lost, though I was building a shop that could accommodate her desire for us to do vintage clothing as well as trinkets. Just in case. That meant I hadn't entirely given up hope.

My heart pounded unpleasantly as I hit speed dial. She was my first contact. Best friend. Kid sister. Apprentice. All those words applied to how I felt about Shannon Cheney, but none was quite big enough. Losing her hurt worse than anything ever had, even my breakup with Chance. And I'd loved *him* like a madness.

International cell calls took a while to connect, and then it rang. And rang. Five times, then it kicked to voice mail. Unease stole over me. *Maybe she didn't answer because she didn't recognize your number. The note isn't talking about her. It can't be.*

Jesse came next on my phone. It had been that way from before, and so Chance was further down the speed dial, like number seven. I hadn't changed it, full of superstitious fear that if I moved Shannon, it would be the same as accepting she wouldn't ever remember me. It'd be like giving up on her—on our friendship and our plans—and that I would *not* do.

So she was one. Jesse, two. I wrestled with indecision, but before I could make up my mind, my phone rang back. Shannon's number. *Thank you.* I shouldn't answer it, but on the off chance that things were starting to come back to her, I had to.

"Hello?"

Silence on the line, for a beat too long. And then: "You just called my girlfriend's phone. Who is this?"

Jesse. The revelation felt like a fist in the heart. Maybe I shouldn't have been so surprised. She was young for him, but ten years or so wasn't the end of the world in terms of age difference. *What did you expect? You left*

*them together with no memory of you, no recollection of
why they mattered to each other. It was natural for them
to fill in the blanks.*

Shannon had just enough issues to hit Jesse's white
knight complex . . . and she was alone in the world, apart
from the dad she didn't want to see. She needed him.
There was no way he could resist. Still, it hurt, though
things were good with Chance. The pain existed because
their hookup made me feel . . . replaceable. I squeezed
my eyes shut, listening to Jesse breathe.

"Well?" he demanded. He sounded odd. Angry.

Finally, I answered, "She was a friend. I haven't talked
to her in a while."

Hoping that would be enough. I couldn't drag this out.
Couldn't.

"Have we met? Your voice sounds . . . familiar." Now
he seemed unsettled. I pictured him raking his hand
through his tawny hair.

"Yeah." No point in lying.

But that reply opened the door to more questions,
answers he wouldn't believe—or maybe he would.
Maybe the fog was finally lifting. Too late. Too damn late.
They'd moved on without me. I felt cheated and hurt but
not angry. And not even surprised, really. Back in Kilmer,
I'd seen the beginnings of a crush forming on Shannon's
end, though I'd never thought it would go anywhere. Under normal circumstances, they wouldn't have done this.
Fuck. I had to get off the phone.

"Just have her call me, I guess, when she gets a
chance."

"I'd love to." But his tight tone caught me, and it left
so many questions. He was too upset to wonder when
he'd met me, this mysterious friend of Shannon's, and
that meant the bad things promised by the note on Tia's
front gate had come true.

"But?" *Why don't you hang up? Idiot.*

"I don't know where she is."

Sweet Lethe

My fingers tightened on the phone until I felt them going white. The hard edges bit into my palm. "How long has she been gone?"

"I saw her yesterday. She left her phone at my place, but I didn't worry about it because we were supposed to meet for lunch today. When she didn't show—"

"You decided something must be wrong because that's not like her."

"Sounds like you know her pretty well."

"I did. Jesse, can you feel her?" He'd sensed I was in trouble from Texas, when I was investigating my mother's death in Georgia. His empathy had a powerful range, and it extended to those he cared about.

"No." His anguish came across the line clearly. "It's like she's dead. Or . . . gone. So far, I can't sense anything. But she wouldn't just leave . . ." Then he seemed to recall I was a stranger. "Shan *told* you about me? Who are you again?"

"Corine Solomon." I paused, wondering if my name meant anything to him.

A sharp intake of breath. "I feel like I should know you. Like I *do* know you."

Poor Jesse. He exuded bewilderment.

"It's . . . complicated. But don't worry—I won't say anything. I'm gifted, too."

"Ah. Corine." He repeated the word like a talisman. "My parents mentioned you once. Asked me where you'd gone, and since I didn't know what they were talking about, I just shrugged. And my boss, Glencannon," he added in a tone of realization. "He assumed you'd left because of my job. Who the hell *are* you?"

Chuch and Eva knew everything; they were old friends, not gifted themselves, though some of their family had been. So they knew the score with regard to spooky happenings. They both had a shady, interesting past—Eva had dabbled in forgery, and Chuch used to run weapons, but they'd settled into suburban bliss in Texas.

Chance and I stayed in Laredo long enough to see their baby daughter, Camelia, christened. Eva's mother was religious, and she insisted on having the rite performed as soon as possible. Afterward, I'd explained to Chuch why Shannon wouldn't be returning to Mexico with me. I offered money for her room and board, but he'd refused, as I had known he would. He said Shan was welcome to stay as long as she needed, and that Eva appreciated her help. He'd also promised not to say anything until the forget spell wore off because I didn't know what the effects would be if magic ran up against human interference. I'd heard it could be traumatic to force people to recall something they were blocking, so if this was similar, then we had to err on the side of caution. I hadn't wanted to hurt Shannon and Jesse, only protect them.

"Well?" he prompted in his sweet drawl.

"The important thing is finding Shannon," I said softly. "You start the search on your end. I'll do what I can here, and if I locate her, I'll call you."

"That's not good enough—" But I did then what I should've done earlier, and cut the call.

He rang back, but I let it go to voice mail. Jesse was Shannon's boyfriend, which meant she was all that connected us. I'd made my choices. Even if he remembered everything down the line when the spell wore off, as it seemed he might, I'd never be with him. Some things you just don't do, and hooking up with your best friend's ex sat at the top of the list. For me, Jesse Saldana was now an untouchable.

It seemed I had to go to the rendezvous point on the back of the note if I intended to save the girl. And obviously, I did. I couldn't bear to consider what she might be suffering; I had to focus on the here and now. After tucking my cell phone in my pocket, I got a backpack and started filling it with provisions for a road trip. When Chance arrived a little later, I was still at it. Tia must have let him in; I didn't hear the bell, but my room had thick walls and was near the back of the house. So, not surprising.

He tapped on the door and then came in before I answered. Because he knew me so well, he took one look, drew me against him, and said, "Tell me."

It felt good to be in his arms, familiar, even with the differences. I was slimmer than I had been at any point in our relationship. Rubbing my cheek against the smooth fabric of his shirt, I explained the situation succinctly. He let go of me then, but not in rejection. He picked up the note to examine it, and studied the writing.

"So you think demons have Shannon?"

"The spell suggested as much. Certainly they're involved on some level."

"What do they mean, 'claim the crown'?"

He knew I'd handled my business with Montoya, but he didn't know the particulars. And this wasn't the time to tell him.

"I'm not sure," I prevaricated. "But I *am* sure demons took Shan."

Chance nodded. "Let me get my laptop. I'll input the coordinates and figure out where we're going. It's a good thing the shop isn't finished yet."

Gratitude warmed my smile by ten degrees. I wasn't ready to sleep with him, or move in with him, but I remembered why I'd been with him in the first place, before everything went wrong. Maybe second chances made more sense than I thought. By and large, I'd thought that if something failed, it was best to put it in the rearview mirror and try not to think about it. I cut ties like a professional swordsman, and only Chance refused to let me go. Maybe that meant something after all.

He dropped a quick kiss on my upturned mouth and then loped off. His smooth grace captured my eye, as it ever had, and I finished packing while waiting for him to return. Twenty minutes later, he was back in my room, laptop in hand. Tia didn't have Internet, so he had a USB wireless card, convenient for travel. Chance took the note and brought up a program. A few keystrokes and clicks later, he had a map on the screen.

"They want you in the Sierra de Juárez in Oaxaca."

I studied the topography. "That's about five hundred miles southeast of here."

"I could drive that in less than eight hours," he said confidently.

While I had the utmost confidence in Chance's maniacal skill behind the wheel, the roads might not be good enough to support the speed he preferred. I said so politely, and he laughed.

"Don't worry. I won't get you killed."

"I wasn't worried about that at all."

At least not since I started getting regular cleansings. It wasn't a perfect solution to his infernal luck, but as long as I had the bad karma scraped off on a regular basis, we rubbed along well. Tia was happy to do it, if I bought the eggs. Maybe one day we'd figure out a permanent fix, but until then, this kept me alive. Chance's unique ability gave him the best possible luck in all circumstances, but since the universe liked to keep things in balance, the person closest to him got whacked with the most terrible shit imaginable. He could use it in the most interesting ways, dowsing for the sense of what direction would solve any given problem. It reminded me of focused coincidence; Chance's luck could make the most improbable factors come into alignment.

"If the roads get bad, I'll slow down," he promised. "Chuch would kill me if I broke the Mustang's axle."

"Where we're going, we might need a truck or an SUV."

"It's remote, I take it?"

"Incredibly."

"Is the El Camino reliable enough?" He didn't love the idea of driving my car, but it made more sense for a trip like this.

"I had a friend go over it after we got home. It doesn't look fabulous, but he's got it running like a Swiss watch."

"He?" His brow rose.

Surely Chance wasn't jealous of my mechanic friend. But I could tell by his steady look, he really wanted to know who I had fixing my ride. My nights since we got home had belonged to him. Apart from the errands I ran during the day and my studies with Tia, there hadn't been time to date anyone else.

"Julio lives four blocks over. He's fifty years old, married, and has four kids."

His expression eased from tension to sheepish relief, and he lifted his shoulders in a half shrug. "It's like you said in Laredo. . . I don't know you that well anymore. I don't know your friends. I want to, but you're different that way too. You don't share like you did."

Yeah, I'd learned to be closed, self-contained—and the irony of that? I'd gotten those tendencies from him. Now it felt oddly like he was an open book, and I had figured out how to hide the lines that revealed everything about me.

"I got good at being alone," I said softly. In the old days, I'd have called him first thing instead of packing a bag on my own, ready to handle whatever came my way without asking for help.

"I know." Awkward silence.

He needed me to make a move. So I added, "But I'm remembering how to be half of a couple. I thought we were doing all right."

He'd promised to tell me about his dead ex. Maybe this road trip would be a good time for that. Since our return, we'd danced around the edges of intimacy, two steps forward, one step back, a particularly self-conscious waltz.

So far, Chance wasn't rushing me. He didn't push for sex or commitment. Emotionally, he was more accessible than he had been when we were together. From the vantage point of hindsight, I suspected he shouldn't have been with me so soon after Lily died. I'd been a light against the loneliness, a body in the dark, and our jobs kept him from having to think or grieve or heal. But I hadn't known about her. Or his loss.

If I'd had more experience with relationships, I'd have known something was wrong sooner. Before Chance, I had only hookups, nothing real. I hadn't understood how it should be, and I'd so desperately wanted it to work, had needed him to love me, that I hadn't seen the problems staring me in the face. I don't think he loved me at all in the beginning; maybe he did in the end, or he realized how he felt too late, after I'd gone. Now, I *wanted* to believe in his feelings, but I feared them too. I had such a collection of scars carved on my heart, and many of them carried his initials.

For him to be willing to dodge out on a rescue mission at the drop of a hat, no questions asked? That boded well for our future together.

"Tia," I called.

"Is Chance staying for dinner?" she yelled back in Spanish.

"No. Neither am I." I went into the kitchen, and in a few words summarized where I was going and why.

She listened with no judgment, and then she shuffled into her bedroom. I was used to her ways, so I waited. When she returned, she had a charm bracelet in one hand. It was dull and tarnished, didn't look special at all, but when she wrapped it around my wrist to fasten it, I felt the thrum of magick emanating from the trinket.

"It is the best charm I ever made," she said softly. "Wear it well."

"I can't take this. You could sell it at the market—"

"Corine." Her tone was dangerous, and though she came only to my shoulder, I knew not to cross her.

So I yielded gracefully, thanked and hugged her. Chance joined us with my things in his hand. In short order, he stowed my backpack in the El Camino parked in front while I prepped Butch for travel. Most dogs would be excited at the prospect of a road trip, but this Chihuahua was not a normal animal; he'd saved my life more than once with his warnings. He whined his misgivings at me, and he tried to tell Tia that this trip was a bad, bad idea, but she only laughed and scratched behind his ears. With a final whine, Butch settled in my purse, heaving a despondent doggy sigh. It was funny how well he could express his thoughts, even without Scrabble tiles. I had packed those too. Just in case. I had been astonished to learn he could use the letters to communicate with me when the matter was too crucial to trust simple yes/no questions.

"Let me cleanse you," Tia said.

Though I'd had a cleansing the previous week, it was a good safety precaution, as I didn't know how long I'd be gone. So I stood quiescent while she fetched her supplies: candles, a stout switch to lash me with, and of course, the eggs. She whispered the blessings as she rubbed the egg over my chakras. As usual, it took two to rid me of the bad luck Chance had deflected my way. His mouth twisted when he saw the darkness staining the center of the first one.

"I'm sorry," he whispered.

"It's fine now that I know how to deal with it."

Haunted eyes, tiger striated in rich shades of amber, watched me while Tia wrapped up the brief ritual. I could tell he was thinking that Lily might have lived if he'd known to tell her how to protect herself. It occurred to me then that he didn't have much experience with relationships either; otherwise, he'd have known this already. In his way, he was as confused as I was. And that made a difference.

"*Ya termine,*" Tia said. "*Buena suerte, nena.*" *I'm done. Good luck, child.*

We said our farewells quickly—no point in lingering. From my bag came a soft whimper, Butch making a last-ditch effort to persuade me to stay home.

But I couldn't. The demons knew I cared about Shannon, so they'd taken her for leverage. Whatever horrors awaited me, she was suffering them already, and it made my skin feel too tight. But I couldn't let myself go there. Too much imagination would paralyze me. The only way I could do Shannon any good was to contain my anxiety and focus on something else. I strode out to the car.

Chance didn't like being a passenger, so I tossed him my keys. Instead of getting in, he asked, "Would you prefer to drive the first leg of the trip?"

It wasn't a matter of whether I wanted to; it was the fact that he thought to ask. Once, he'd made decisions for me. He did what he thought was best for me, and kept information from me. His question showed me that he'd really changed. He saw me as stronger and more capable, someone who *should* have choices.

Smiling, I shook my head. "It's fine. Just let me know if you get tired and we'll switch. Do you have a bag in the car?"

In answer, he indicated the backpack behind the seat in the El Camino. "I guessed we'd be traveling. Just a change of clothes and protein bars, but with you, I've learned it pays to be prepared."

"Clever man."

The Mustang was nowhere in sight; he must've left it at his apartment. It would be safer there anyway. Tia had opted for a front garden instead of a garage, but nobody thought my El Camino was nice enough to steal. Looks could be deceiving.

I let Butch pee in the grass, and then I climbed into the car. It smelled faintly of the piña colada air freshener I'd bought, and the interior was pristine. I'd never owned a car before; I took care of this one.

It was almost dark when we took off, which meant heavy traffic as we came down the mountain. Chance had been here long enough that he wasn't surprised by the way the *periférico* choked up, and he bitched like a native as we inched along, exhaust creeping in the windows. Since it was a cool night, it seemed wasteful to run the air conditioner. Buses clogged the right-hand lane, stopping every four feet.

In the evening, it looked magical here, even with the traffic. Mountains rose in the distance as we crept along. Lights sparkled from faraway houses; neon blurred into red and yellow lines from shops set along the highway. The sky above was gray, not black, so that even night felt mutable here, like shadows held no sway.

Once we passed what used to be the *toreo*—bullfighting ring, although it had been torn down a while ago—the traffic cleared somewhat, permitting him to drive faster. He drove like he'd learned in Italy, whipping in and out, throwing the car at spaces that seemed too small. Horns sounded in our wake, but he was smiling, and so was I.

Despite my worry over Shannon, it felt good to set out with him. This wasn't a job he needed me for, and yet Chance was here beside me. He'd come to Texas because he wanted me. Missed me. Maybe even loved me. I entertained the possibility without suspicion whispering in my ear.

The city stretched before us, an endless monument to human ambition. It took two hours to cross onto the *cuota*—toll road—that led toward Oaxaca. At this speed the wind whipped my hair about my face, and I rolled the glass up halfway. That was better. Out here it was darker too, a black velvet sky and stars shining down on the hulks of mountains sleeping in the distance.

He drove halfway, and then he pulled over so I could take a turn. To the best of my recollection, he'd never done that. I smiled at him, silhouetted against the headlights of a passing car.

"You can nap if you want. I'll wake you if I get tired."

"Thanks." He tilted his head against the window and went to sleep. That demonstrated a level of trust we hadn't achieved before. In the past, he'd been tense the whole time, as if giving me that much control proved problematic for him. The El Camino had an old AM/FM radio in lieu of a more expensive stereo, but that was good, as it eliminated any interest in jacking it. I listened to ranchero music all the way to keep my mind off Shannon's plight, but when I got off the highway, I woke

Chance. GPS could be unreliable in the mountains, and the coordinates were remote.

"I think we're getting close."

He rubbed his eyes and studied our surroundings: nothing but trees and mountains and bright, indifferent stars shining down. Pretty soon we were on a dirt track that became downright impassable. When we hit a deep rut, I parked the car in what was meant as an overlook, just rocks and dusty soil. Chance climbed out and grabbed his rucksack. The night air smelled of pine resin and distant smoke, possibly from a campfire. This looked like a good place if you were trying to get back to nature. Terribly remote, in fact.

He offered a half smile. "My backpack has plenty of room. Is yours full?"

I shook my head.

"Get the minimum of what you need and wedge it in with my stuff."

"Athame. Chalice. Grimoires." I wished he had room for my magickal chest, but it was heavy. I had to make do with the touch and spells powered by will alone. Fortunately, the five spells I had practiced with Tia fell into that category. This meant leaving my clothes behind, but the arcane items were more critical.

After we arranged my things, he said, "It's pretty dark. We can set off on foot, or we can wait until light to see if it's safe to drive on."

"I can fix that." It was a simple charm, but Chance hadn't seen me cast it before. Maybe I was showing off a little.

With my athame, I etched the air with the symbol for magnesium, coiled the power within me, and then whispered, "*Fiat lux.*"

I used Latin when possible because it *sounded* more impressive, but so long as I had the willpower to drive the desired result, I could say *Clap on, clap off*, for all it mattered. This spell I had practiced often because we lost power a lot, and so it flared to life smoothly. The result was a white-hot glow at the top of my knife, far brighter and more piercing than anything technology could kindle. The pain I ignored and swallowed, like a large pill down my throat. I'd gotten good at pretending magick didn't burn me from the inside out like a live coal. This was a small price to pay for using it, and Tia had said it didn't seem to be doing me any harm. She'd worked at first to see if there was a way to mitigate it, but eventually she just shook her head and said, *Everything comes at a cost.*

Chance drew in a breath. "Wow."

"I have a few tricks up my sleeve these days."

"So I see."

I still hadn't told him about the demon summoning. I *should.* God, after my lectures about transparency, and how people should have the right to choose, I should be ashamed. He needed to know what I'd done to survive and how it had changed the way the world reacted to me. Then he could make an informed decision about whether he still wanted to be with me.

Soon, I promised myself.

The path lay before us, rocky and uncertain. Farther on, it narrowed and became impossible for a car to pass. I'd stopped, in fact, at the last point where a vehicle could turn around and head back. The whole area gave off an *abandon all hope* vibe. The light made us easier to track, which set my nerves on edge, but I wouldn't dare move without it. One wrong step could send us tumbling down the side of the mountain. Good thing Butch was opposed to nature hikes; he dozed uneasily in my handbag, as usual.

To make matters worse, I was stiff from driving, exhausted, and worried. Not in top fighting form. Maybe it wouldn't come to that.

"We're heading the right way?"

Chance closed his eyes, and the air around him crackled as if with heavy static electricity. When he turned his luck to a problem, he received a sense of whether the set course intersected with the desired result. "Yes. It's not far. Less than a mile."

He took my hand then, interlacing our fingers, and he led the way, sensing that fear and weariness made it hard for me to act decisive. If we took turns leading, as true partners, that'd make me very happy. I focused on walking, picking my steps with care. When we approached the rendezvous point, I had five spells locked in my head. I'd prefer if we arrived first so I'd have time to lay a circle, but from the smell of sulfur and brimstone, I could tell I wouldn't be so lucky.

Chance sniffed the air and glanced at me with a raised brow. "Seems like we have company. What do you want to do?"

"Go forward. We have to, for Shannon."

"Do you have any idea what they want with you, Corine?"

"In Peru I fought a demon. A Knight of Hell, actually. I wounded him pretty bad, stole his true name, and banished him. If I had to guess, I'd say revenge."

"A Knight of Hell," he repeated. "Like the ones my mom summoned to witness her pact with the Montoyas."

"Yep."

"And you fought one?"

I flashed him a smile. "I didn't just fight. I won."

His muscles coiled as if in protest of that revelation, but he let me take the lead. I went up the path the last few steps, and found a single demon waiting. It was unlike any I'd seen before, with an odd, marine-animal look. It had gray, scaly skin, side-set eyes, and a tremendously narrow skull with two rows of teeth. The thing was naked and showed no genitals, but its chest moved, breathing the air. I saw no gill slits. Its hands were elongated like paddles, tipped with wider fingers. I couldn't imagine what purpose that design served.

The demon offered its hand, evidently knowing that much of our customs, but when it registered my repulsed fascination, it drew back. The face did not change. "You are familiar with our lore, then? I would take nothing uninvited."

"Where's Shannon?" I demanded.

On second glance, I saw that the broad pads of its fingertips were curved, almost like little suckers. They appeared perfectly suited for draining . . . something. Best I'd opted not to touch it.

"I am Greydusk, here as guide only. To survive the descent, you must do precisely as I instruct."

The . . . descent? That did not sound healthy. I glanced at Chance, who stepped forward, both fists clenched. "Where's our friend? I won't ask again."

"Sheol," Greydusk answered. At my blank look, it added, "The other side of the gate, where you must also go, if you would ever see her again."

The Descent

"You want me to cross over?" Fear clamored in my head.

As if in response, Butch whined. I knew the feeling. I should've left him with Tia, but there was no chance he'd behave himself. For good or ill, he was *my* dog. If he couldn't talk me out of an adventure, then he always accompanied me. So I settled him in my purse and crossed the strap over my body.

"What I want is irrelevant," the creature said. "But if you mean to save the girl, you must follow me."

I remembered how Jesse said Shannon was so far gone as to be beyond his range entirely. Or dead. If they'd taken her to Sheol, that explained why he couldn't sense her. That seemed to bear out their claim, but I needed proof it wasn't a wild-goose chase.

"How do I know you have her . . . or that she's still alive?"

The demon offered me a small circular object. "This token will function but once. Are you certain you wish to use it now?"

On closer inspection, I saw it was a mirror. "Yes, show me Shannon."

He whispered a word in an unfamiliar language I guessed was demontongue and a magickal glow kindled within the glass. It was dark and shadowed; I couldn't see where she was being held, but that was definitely Shannon. Her breath sounded quick, distressed with fear, and she was curled up, arms about her knees.

"You bastard."

"I am not responsible for my employer's actions, Ms. Solomon. Will you come or not?"

"Let's go," I said.

Greydusk turned and climbed a few steps, its movements too limber and loose, but when Chance followed me, the demon stopped. "My contract provides only for the Binder."

That was a name Kel had given me, and then the Knight of Hell I'd defeated in Peru had echoed it. Supposedly, I came from King Solomon's lineage, which gave me power over demons. I didn't scoff at that notion as much as I once did. Too much had happened to make me believe.

"It's not negotiable," Chance said before I could reply. "You take both of us."

In the glow from my witchlight, his features were fixed, determined. It would come to violence if I tried to hand him my keys and send him away. And with his luck, there was no telling what might happen. If the demon was more ferocious than it looked, and Chance's life was in danger, we might trigger an earthquake.

Greydusk considered, weighing factors to which I wasn't privy. At last, it replied, "The godling may come. I agree to the new terms."

Godling? Wide-eyed, I stared at Chance. He lifted a shoulder in a shrug that claimed he didn't know either. But it opened the book on all kinds of questions, the one foremost in my mind: *Who the hell* was *your father?* Stunned, I hurried to keep up with the demon already moving up the mountainside.

It was a long, steep climb, with less oxygen as we went up. Eventually Greydusk reached a plateau that ended in a sheer rock wall. Above, the trees grew spindly, thinning with the altitude. Below, everything was lush and green, with a blue thread of a brook running through it — or I imagined it would be, if I could've glimpsed the view during the day. At this time of night, it was all darkness, with stars glimmering just enough light to render the mountain spooky, and the glow from my athame only added to the eerie atmosphere.

"This way." As the demon pressed forward, I saw the gaping maw between two giant stones.

This cave mouth yawned so that my witchlight couldn't penetrate the shadows within; it had to be two hundred feet wide by one hundred feet high, and I couldn't tell how deep it was. I'd read that Mexico had some of the deepest caverns in North America, and that many of the systems hadn't been fully explored yet. For obvious reasons, this chilled my blood.

I asked, "How far is it?"

"Let's see . . . how to parse it so you'll understand." This made me think demons used something other than the metric system. "Ten kilometers horizontally, and one kilometer down. There we shall find the entrance to Sheol."

Chance appeared to weigh the information. "And what dangers will we face?"

"Darkness. Terror. The odd hungry beast." If demons had a sense of humor, and from Maury I rather thought they did, this one was joking with us. *Ha ha.* "The closer we get, the more likely it is that something may . . . pass through."

"Are there other portals?" I asked.

"Certainly. Weak places between the planes offer the potential for two-way passage. They also constructed magickal gates at various locales that offer one-way transit. And no, I will not tell you where."

I didn't expect it to. "Let's get moving, then."

The mouth of the cave swallowed us, but my light pushed the darkness back. The demon didn't ask me to put it out, which was just as well. There was no way I trusted the creature enough to proceed otherwise. Greydusk led, I followed close behind, and Chance walked at my back. I was relieved to have him there because without him, my nerve might not have been sufficient to go on, even for Shannon. Butch squirmed in my bag, no happier than I was, but he didn't protest. I suspected he understood the importance of the mission.

In the entrance chamber I shined my light around, finding shamanistic paintings on the walls, shards of broken pottery, and chunks of bone. The floor felt precarious beneath me because it wasn't one smooth surface; instead it was formed of large rocks wedged together, leaving dangerous gaps where I could see myself getting my foot stuck or breaking an ankle, all too easily. *No bad luck,* I told myself. *Not this time.* The passage sloped downward, as I picked a careful path behind Greydusk.

We walked for half an hour; I amused myself looking at the ceremonial markings that adorned the walls. The longer we hiked, the colder it got. I couldn't think about what was waiting for me on the other side. I'd focus on this. Right now. By tacit agreement, we didn't talk. There was nothing Chance and I cared to discuss in front of our guide, and it kept its dark, creepy eyes on the lookout for potential danger ahead.

It's for Shannon, I told myself.

Memories flashed in rapid succession: of meeting her in Kilmer, her riding the bike out to the spooky house we'd rented, and then later begging me not to leave her behind. I'd never done so. Not once, even against my best judgment. I had done unspeakable things to keep both of us safe. To no avail, it seemed.

Ten kilometers deep, one kilometer down. It was hard to imagine what we'd find, maybe wonders out of H. G. Wells. Logically I knew that was impossible, but what did that word mean when your boyfriend was a genuine lucky charm and you were pressing into the dark with a demon that had eyes on the side of its head?

Exactly. We had been hiking for a while when Chance touched me to get my attention. "Are you sure about this?" he asked softly. "We can still turn back."

For a second, I was tempted. One didn't travel to Sheol casually. It wasn't a trip to the mall, and there *would* be consequences. But I couldn't give up on Shannon Cheney. I couldn't. I hadn't saved her in Kilmer only to lose her now. If I had to die to get her out of Sheol, I would. It was that simple, and by the way Chance's lips compressed in pain, he knew. He'd always been good at reading me. To my relief, he didn't argue; he just set his shoulders and went on. He trusted me enough to let me do as I thought best—and it meant everything.

In the stories, the heroine was always told not to look back or there would be dire repercussions. So no matter what I heard creeping along in the shadows behind us, I didn't. After a while, though, it became difficult to ignore the flap of leathery wings. Bats lived in caves. Intellectually I knew there were worse things that I ought to worry about, but bats freaked me out. Sometimes it was easier to fixate on small things than to deal with the enormous ones.

The dark passage widened into a large cavern with a high ceiling. From the artifacts lying around, it looked like this might have been used for religious purposes at some point. More telling, this appeared to be the end of the path.

"Our first drop," Greydusk said. "Only seven meters."

That sounded like a lot. I took a breath while it made the preparations. Fortunately, it had a rope; it glimmered golden in the witchlight. The demon went first, sliding deftly down.

"It's a bit damp, but safe enough. Come along!"

Chance touched my cheek. "Now you, love. I'm not leaving you alone here."

"Don't move," I ordered the dog.

"Why don't you let me take him?"

Since he was more athletic and coordinated, that was a good idea. I unlooped my bag and handed it over, which left him with both the backpack and my purse. If I hadn't been so scared, I'd have laughed over using Chance as a pack mule. He was far too elegant for that.

I mustered my courage and sank to my knees, then tucked my glowing athame into the back of my pants. *That's fantastic luck, I'm sure.* I had no idea if my upper-body strength could handle this. It took all my willpower to edge back off the rock and start inching down. I wanted to wrap the cord around my waist, but Greydusk held the other end.

We should have belts and straps and pulleys and things, shouldn't we? Shit. Don't think about falling.

I was halfway down when the bats appeared. At least they seemed to be, only they were more aggressive than any I'd heard about on National Geographic. They dived at my head, my hair, biting and scratching. My hands slipped on the rope, and I cried out as I slid down. Rock crumbled away against my feet.

Above me, I heard Chance cursing. "I'm not sure the rope will hold us both. Keep moving. You can do it."

They're small. They can't actually hurt you. Only a fall can do that. My hands were shaking by the time I got to solid ground again. As the demon had mentioned, a thin stream of water trickled down the rock, leaving the stone where we stood slick and dangerous. It was so dark that I couldn't see without the witchlight. I held it up for Chance, not daring to say a word until he hit the ledge beside me.

Thank you.

I threw myself into his arms. He rubbed my back and brushed a kiss against my hair. "I'm fine. You know I always land on my feet."

Just like a cat. And so he did. But it would kill me if anything happened to him. Maybe we were still figuring out how we fit together, but he mattered.

He cupped my face in his hands and kissed me: leashed passion, restrained desire, and tenderness too. I knew him now in ways I hadn't before. I could read between the lines of that kiss: *I'm here, and I care. I want you.* Butch poked his head out of my bag—I didn't think I'd ever seen the little dog so worried, and we had been in some dire situations. The Chihuahua whined a little, but he settled. Chance kept him for me, which was probably just as well.

"We must press on," Greydusk said. I couldn't read its face, but I thought I heard amusement in the tone.

"Is the route like this all the way down?" I asked.

"Uncharted and dangerous? Indeed."

I swallowed a sigh. "Awesome. What's with the bats?"

"They're demon-touched. Pay them no heed."

Demon-touched. Obviously. I should've thought of that.

I realized then that we stood on more a ledge than a proper path, which meant we had to descend again. The demon whispered a word, too faint for me to catch, and then the golden rope uncoiled above us, drifting down to him in a glimmer of light.

"Would the rope react if we lose our grip?" Chance asked.

Greydusk nodded. "It offers better safety than all the mundane climbing gear."

That was something at least. The reassurance that magick might catch me if I plummeted gave me the guts to approach the edge while the demon tied the rope off again. His knots were impressive, complex and intricate. This time, the drop was deeper, double what we'd done before. Fourteen meters, and I couldn't see the bottom. Below us, the darkness was absolute.

Shannon. I built her face in my mind's eye. Dyed-black hair with colorful streaks. She liked to tip the ends in blue. She had a pretty face, but she always wore makeup to make the most of her pallor and a thick coating of kohl, along with three or four coats of mascara. It made her striking, for sure, and she liked dressing in Lolita-style Goth gear. Her panache made men who should know better take a second look.

For her, I could press forward. I could. The rope felt cool in my palms and I decided to try the demon's trick. Magick would catch me if I failed, so . . . I let myself slide down, and the cord slid smoothly through my hands with an unnatural friction. No rope burns on my palms when I hit bottom, and it was way less terrifying than trying to brace my feet on the rough rock face.

"Well done," Greydusk said.

Chance followed my example, with more alacrity and grace. He was smiling when I aimed my witchlight at his face. This probably felt like an adventure to him, bigger than any job we ever took when we were together. Usually it was pretty mundane stuff—missing persons and belongings, or occasionally somebody wanted to use me as a lie detector, like Escobar had done. Since I could view things as they'd really happened, provided an object with sufficient charge had witnessed the scene, I had done that more than once. Seen a few things I wished I hadn't too.

This was something else entirely.

In this fashion, I clambered down two more drops. These were like stairs cut by a giant inside the mountain, made more difficult to navigate by that trickle that was growing into a cascade the farther down we went. Water streamed from cracks in the rock, rendering them slippery, but the rope simplified our passage.

The next level was downright wet. I tried to stay out of the downpour, but my movement swung me into the stream. I lost my grip on the rope and plummeted, slamming into the rock face, but the cord twined around my waist before I dropped more than a few feet. My heart pounded wildly as I hung there, swaying halfway between up and down.

Magick. Yeah, magick's good. I didn't have a spell in my head. Fear drove them all out until I could only dangle upside down and helpless, listening to Butch yap above me. He knew I was in trouble. *Good dog.*

"Are you hurt?" Chance asked, his voice taut with worry.

"Fine." Mostly. Bruises and scrapes on my right side, but without the demon rope, it would've been worse.

Greydusk called, "Are you ready to resume?" like nothing had happened.

Gripping the cord in preparation for the positional shift, I answered in the affirmative, and it spoke a command. The rope straightened, and I slid the rest of the way down, where the demon caught me. It set me on my feet without comment, and then Chance followed.

"How much more of this?" he asked.

I wondered too. It felt like we had already come that kilometer downward, but it might just be that I wasn't used to such activity. Clearly I wasn't. At the best of times, I didn't like heights, and the dark made it worse. So much worse.

In answer, Greydusk set off along a path that had become proper flat ground again, not just a slippery ledge. I strode after him, using the witchlight to assess the area. The primitive markings higher up had given way to more disturbing décor; I recognized some of the symbols from the harness that belonged to Caim. Which meant they were demonic sigils.

"What do they say?" I whispered to Greydusk. The heaviness of the dark made it feel wrong to speak in a normal tone of voice. Plus the weird acoustics stole your voice and sent it echoing down distant passageways. Not a good idea, under the circumstances.

The demon's reply didn't help. "Nothing you want to know, I promise."

On second glance, I noted the faint flicker of magick emanating from the runes. The air was cold as a freezer as we passed through, a dark and silent stream running beside us. Some distance along, the river expanded into a shallow underground lake, broad enough that I couldn't see the opposite shore.

Butch whined then, and Chance put him down so he could stretch his legs and christen the ground. The demon was patient with the dog's needs, which was a surprising kindness, I thought. Then it knelt and touched the animal on the head with its long, strange fingers. Butch quivered, but didn't flee, his big, bulging eyes fixed on the creature before him. He didn't growl, either. Interesting.

"A most intriguing creature," Greydusk said as it rose. "Shall we move on?"

I was tired, but didn't want to camp down here; that was for sure. The sooner we got to the gate, the better I'd like it. So I nodded, Chance grabbed the tiny dog, and we set off.

Here There Be Demons

This time we marched for hours. The path led subtly downward, following the lake, wherein . . . things splashed. Just beyond the range of my witchlight, movement stirred, the hint of fins and tentacles bestirring the water, and that uncertainty was worse than knowing what danger I faced. I hastened my step as Greydusk diverged from the lake, charting a course across more uneven rocks that led to a natural archway painted in more demonic sigils. I hoped this would be the homestretch. Surely we'd almost covered the distance the demon had mentioned.

Earlier we had paused for protein bars, rest, and bottled water. My thighs burned from all the climbing. I concentrated on Shannon. It didn't matter how much this hurt me; I'd get her back.

This is your fault. Her involvement with me led to her abduction. Yet if I'd left her in Kilmer, she'd be dead. And if I'd taken her away and then found somewhere else for her to stay, I had no guarantee that would've ended better. Sometimes there were no good choices.

"What's Sheol like?" I asked eventually.

The demon answered without turning. "Darker than your world. Colder."

That didn't tell me as much as I'd hoped. "Anything else?"

"You'll see when we reach Xibalba."

"I thought we were going to—"

"Xibalba is a city." By its tone, I could tell Greydusk wished I would stop pestering it.

Since my questions could distract from important matters, such as our safety, I shut up, but we hadn't been walking long when that faint flutter of wings got louder. The demon's reaction told me that wasn't good. Not just bats like I had been telling myself for half a kilometer. This wasn't the small flutter of many leather-winged creatures, but a deep and powerful *snap-snap-snap*. For reasons I couldn't articulate, the sound chilled the marrow in my bones.

"It appears we shall encounter heavy resistance," Greydusk observed. "Prepare to fight."

The passage had a high ceiling, which wasn't good. It gave whatever was coming too much room to maneuver. I had five spells swirling in my head, and one of them made light. *Not* helpful. So really I had four spells at my command, plus the touch, and unless the monster coming for us was wearing some article of clothing, like the knight had been, it probably wouldn't help. Beside me, Chance crouched in a fighting stance; he had knuckle knives on both hands. Before, I'd always seen him fight without weapons, but a demon's hide wouldn't take damage from a human fist.

Even if he's only half *human.*

The creature shrieked and dive-bombed us from the shadows, moving too fast for me to get a good look at it. I had a fleeting impression of a monstrously female face grafted onto the body of a humanoid pterodactyl, and I saw claws that shone like diamonds as it dove a second time. Chance slashed at the wings, trying to bring it down, and I mustered my resolve, firming hands that shook as I raised my athame. While this spell might not save us, it wouldn't hurt either.

The power swelled inside me, burning, hurting, but I let it center me. *Pain means I'm still here, fighting.* I envisioned it swelling in my hand in a seething rush, gathering, gathering, and then I sent it out on my resolve like a dark and winged thing riding the magickal wind as I whispered, "*Hostes hostium caecus.*"

The enemy sightless.

I knew nothing about this demon, but it would help if the monster couldn't see us. Its face looked so hideous that I wondered if this thing might have inspired the Harpy legends, thousands of years ago, but its skull didn't seem shaped for sonar. A second later, it proved it had no special neural navigation when it screamed and slammed into a wall. The collision stunned it, and the thing dropped. Chance sprang to finish it before it could recover, but Greydusk raised a long, unsettling hand.

"Please. Allow me. Its death can serve us in two fashions if I do it."

Though I didn't know if this was a good idea, I nodded, mostly because I wanted to see firsthand what it could do. That might save our lives later, if it gave me time to prepare some defense. My spells weren't super-blow-the-door-off-the-hinges powerful, but properly deployed, they might save us.

Greydusk strode in, dodged a blind and desperate strike, and slammed both hands—with sucker pads—on either side of the misshapen skull. The creature seized, grand mal tremors rocking it from head to toe. Steam hissed from the point of contact, and an awful purple light ran up our guide's spindly arms. An orange glow sparked in Greydusk's skull and then the attacker went limp.

"You killed it?" Chance asked.

It had done more than that, but I waited to see how it would reply.

"I drained it," the demon corrected. "Its knowledge, memories, and skills are now mine. Sadly, in this form, I cannot use some of them."

A joke, I thought, if not a funny one. It reminded me of the way a cat licked its whiskers after a mouse. I smiled uneasily.

Chanced stared down at the still-smoking corpse. It was smaller, withered, as if Greydusk had taken more than information, terrabytes of data streaming in magickal light. The exchange set my teeth on edge. I wanted to blind Greydusk, and then let Chance kill it, but then I'd leave Shannon stranded in Sheol. I couldn't do that, so once again I proved myself willing to work with the devil in order to achieve my own ends. *Is this what evil feels like? How it begins?* You started with a slippery slide down the slope of good intentions until you were mired in the blood and mud at the bottom, unable to see any light no matter which way you turned. Heart dark and heavy, I wondered how far I would go, and what I would become when I got there.

If you care for no one, a little voice whispered, *if you remain firm and steadfast and will not act to save the ones you love, in the name of some abstract good, is* inaction *not the same as evil?* I couldn't fashion an answer; it was too much, too confusing, but I did, unfortunately, see how good and evil were almost like a wheel, and that if you went far enough down one road, the two became virtually indistinguishable. People had done terrible things in heaven's name, too.

"What happens to demons when they die?"

"Nothing," it said.

"There's no afterlife? No hell?"

It flashed its teeth. "According to your lore, Binder, we're already there."

"But Maury told me—"

"Ah, yes." Its tone became disapproving. "You have . . . contacts, do you not?"

"I guess. What kind of demon is Maury?"

"He is of the Birsael caste, the bargainers. They are easy for practitioners of your world to call because they long to cross over. They are . . . playful?"

"Playful?" I thought about what Maury had done in Kilmer, and shivered. I did not want to meet a non-playful demon, but I was on my way to a city full of them.

"Over time—and many summonings—they become attuned to a certain human . . . trait." That hadn't been the word it meant to use at first. "And then they hunger for more of the same."

"An acquired taste," Chance put in.

"Just so."

Maury's thing was stagnation, as I recalled. Entropy.

"What is Dumah's affinity?"

"Hunger," it replied. "Greed. Need."

Shit. And I'd unloosed her on the world. Hopefully, the way I'd crafted the bargain would keep them from wreaking too much havoc. Guilt plagued me, but Greydusk was saying, "I have no doubt that Maury told you that Sheol is another world. The fact that our citizens enjoy playing in yours has given rise to interesting stories over the eons."

"You view people as toys?" I was indignant, even if I couldn't afford to be.

"Entertainment, certainly. To us, it is no different from how human children toy with insects or set anthills on fire."

"Only *bad* kids do that," I muttered.

"Yet I am not here to argue with you."

"How come it attacked us? I thought the demons *wanted* me in Sheol."

"Some do," Greydusk replied. "But there are ... factions in play, and others want different things."

"Such as?"

"Power. Or to preserve the status quo."

"What did you learn from that?" Chance nudged the corpse.

"Many things, but the most important? Who hired it. You have enemies, Binder, and some of them prefer you never reach Xibalba at all."

"Why?" God, it was too much. I just wanted to rescue Shannon.

"Because you presage change, no matter what you decide. The caste structure has been etched in blood and bone for thousands of years, and you could topple it."

"I don't plan to topple anything."

Secretly, I thought I might die, and if that meant saving Shan, then I was okay with that. It was a peaceful thought that she could go back to Jesse, and have the life I'd wanted—holidays with his family, nieces and nephews, maybe children someday, although she was so young that the relationship might not last. At the least, she had to live. I'd settle for nothing less, even if I had to level Sheol to make it happen.

Greydusk watched my face, guessing my thoughts, I half suspected, from the tightness of my mouth and the set of my jaw. "Intentions seldom match results."

"Maybe not. What is that thing?"

"Aronesti." It spat the word like a curse. "They are the snatchers, and they have no honor."

The snatchers. Of what?

Chance asked, so I didn't have to.

"Flesh. They crave it from the dead. Carrion feeders, the lot of them."

"Do they ever cross over? I mean, obviously this one did . . ." But we killed it before it could go out and swoop around the battlefields in a ghastly feast.

Greydusk nodded. "From time to time. It is my understanding that the Nephilim hunt them down."

Among other things. So Kel might be out there right now, hunting demons, along with killing people he was told would start the apocalypse. How the hell did you trust in orders like that? I wanted to see him, talk to him, *shake* him. Everything I learned about his world made me understand him less.

"Can they be summoned?" Chance asked.

"Most demons can be called by a practitioner of sufficient skill and power. Aronesti are sometimes found in the bodies of cannibal killers."

What a horrible thought, but also better, if I could believe many of the ghastly things humans did came from demons. Unfortunately, I didn't think so. People could be evil without any help at all.

Chance sounded thoughtful. "Is that because they sense a sympathetic hunger in the host or because the demon drives the person to it?"

A shrug. "That I do not know."

This frank discussion of flesh-feasting demons and cannibal killers in a scary cave with a dead thing at my feet? Not. Helping. I decided to get us back on track, stepping over the monster and moving farther down the passage.

"But you're contracted to make sure I reach Xibalba in one piece." It was my way of saying *let's go already*, but without meaning to, my word choice apparently questioned its integrity.

Its eyes gleamed like onyx. "I will ignore the affront, this one time, but ignorance of our ways does *not* excuse your discourtesy."

"Explain," Chance said.

"Very well," the demon replied. Stiffly. Its movements were jerkier than they had been. Anger? I guessed so. "As we move, I shall."

Good going. You pissed off your protection. Given how I'd needled Kel while he guarded me, it appeared I had a knack for it. We started down the passage, leaving the corpse behind us. It was more than a little creepy that everything that had been in the demon's head, Greydusk now knew. How powerful did that make it, exactly? Not something I cared to fight, if it could unmake me with a touch.

"I am Imaron," Greydusk said, like I should know what that meant. At my obvious confusion, it added, "That is my caste."

Ah. It had mentioned castes earlier, how I could break the whole social structure of Sheol. That wasn't on my to-do list.

"Would you tell us about the castes?" Chance was still looking to increase his knowledge base, and he would use everything he gleaned from Greydusk to prepare for whatever we'd face in Xibalba.

"There is no reason I cannot," the demon replied. "It is information freely available in the archives."

Booke would love the sound of that. He was a friend and a research specialist in the UK. I'd never met him in person, but maybe one day that would change. And if we didn't get back soon, he'd worry when I missed our weekly chat. Then he might call Chuch and Eva. Maybe I should have e-mailed them, but a message like *Going to play demon bait, back soon*, would only make the situation worse.

"Thanks," Chance said. "Start with your caste?"

"The Imaron are known as the soul-stealers, but we abide by our contracts. It is death to act otherwise."

Soul-stealers. Awesome. But at least they were all lawyerly about it. Somehow that didn't make it better; no wonder humans thought Sheol was hell.

Chance spoke again, sounding pensive; his puzzle-solving brain would help so much on this venture. "Death? Is breaking the contract fatal or is the offending behavior punished?"

It was a good question. Greydusk angled its slender neck in an unnatural fashion to give Chance an approving look. "The former. When we sign a contract, we do so in blood, and there is a magickal ritual. Should I break my word, the blood turns to poison in my veins, and I will perish instantly."

Wow. The Imaron took their promises seriously. I felt bad for doubting him. Treachery would kill this creature, so I had nothing to fear for sure. While I might question its intentions and its abilities, self-preservation ranked pretty high on the list of things I felt sure of. I thought about that in silence for a little while, listening to our steps scrape over the stone.

And then I asked, "What happens if you fail? I mean, not through a breach of contract, but just . . . overwhelming odds? Do they hold that against you?"

"Then I am already dead," it said simply.

It walked on.

If I had a thousand dollars for every time I followed a demon down a dark and terrifying tunnel, well . . . I'd have a thousand dollars. Because this was a first, even for me, in a weird and unlikely life. Greydusk lost its interest in talking, though it had promised to explain the caste system to us. It wouldn't happen right now, anyway, as it appeared to be listening as we moved.

Finally I had to ask, "Is something coming?"

That wouldn't surprise me. I just had to get ready for it.

"I don't think so."

"Is it hard to pass the portal?" Chance asked.

"Yes. It requires power and sacrifice."

Good to know. I hated the thought of anything like

the weight-sensitive doors at most major shopping centers, where the minute you approached, they slid open, linking our world to Sheol. But it made sense that these natural portals required opening. Otherwise, the demons would've overrun us ages ago. Wouldn't they? Some of them might be perfectly happy at home, despite what Maury had said. After all, not everybody loved to travel.

"So the more our enemies try to send something through to strike at us, the weaker they'll be when we arrive?" I guessed.

Greydusk nodded. "Most will be prudent enough to wait until you cross to send their best assassins. It is a calculated risk, of course. Should you choose to ascend, once you reach Sheol—"

"Ascend?"

"It is not my place to explain your choices, Binder."

Bullshit. Greydusk was just tired of answering my endless questions. I took the hint and trudged on in silence. The deeper we went into the mountain, the more it felt like a subterranean forest with exotic stone trees. My witchlight kept the dark from becoming oppressive, and I ignored the burn in my thighs. It was a lengthy hike, but not one that required an overnight rest, thankfully.

We didn't speak more. I traveled down, down, down, until the air puffed from my lips in smoky whorls. That wasn't normal in the caves I had visited before, yet another sign that these weren't normal caverns. Witch sight revealed shimmers of magick in various crystals, glowing red and blue and silver. The stones would be good for various spells, I knew instinctively. I resisted the urge to dig them out of the walls.

The path became steeper, nearly vertical in places, and I braced my hands against the wall as I fell. Greydusk caught me with a careless arm, demonstrating unnatural strength; its gangly limb shouldn't have possessed that kind of tensile power. The demon lifted me down in an easy gesture, and I stepped away before my unease could insult the creature further. It had dealt with us in good faith; I had no cause to distrust it other than its obviously alien nature.

"We must climb from here. There will be no more easy path."

Greydusk tied the trusty rope around a rock formation and indicated the yawning chasm before us. Straight down then, no more path. The sound of water greeted my ears, distant and filtered through the tunnels.

This time, it wasn't ledges, just an endless slide. I zipped Butch all the way into my purse and then handed it to Chance. It was hardest thing I'd ever done to step off the wall into darkness and just let myself fall. That meant trusting the rope was long enough to reach the bottom, even though I couldn't see it. Butch whined as I went down, a canine study in misgiving.

When I landed, the demon said, "Not much farther now."

Chance followed with my purse looped around his neck, and Greydusk reclaimed the rope. With one long arm, it indicated the last leg of the journey. Then he gave me back my handbag, still containing a nervous dog.

We went toward the water we could no longer see; it was almost as if we had passed under the river, descending to the point that I expected to see molten lava at the next turn. To my surprise, massive boulders blocked our progress. I'd expected the gate to look more . . . gatelike, but this was just impassable rock with a stream bubbling beneath it.

Greydusk produced a shimmering red jewel from his pack; it was enormous and unlike anything I'd ever seen, more luminous than a maharajah's ruby. I considered asking what it was, but then he whispered an incantation in demontongue, a language that lent itself to quiet sibilance. He set the gem in a small niche on the rocks, and a glow sprang up, radiating outward from the gem to encompass us. It arced down into the water like a laser, drawing a path in the air with each movement. Down below, the water gained a bloody glow, swirling up to fill the space between the scarlet streaks that split the dark.

"Now!" Greydusk ordered. "Dive now!"

Maelstrom of Doom

Into that? Seriously?

Before I could think better of it, I took a running leap and flung myself toward the water, expecting to smash on the rocks, but instead, the sparkling curtain of water caught me as if it were something else, and I passed through it like a doorway. The magick screamed through me, sparking my own gift, and it was like being boiled in oil. I landed, gasping, and I was somewhere else.

Not in the caverns.

I peered into my purse to check on Butch. He popped up and shook himself all over, ears flying wildly. As far as I could tell, he seemed fine.

"You okay, boy?"

He yapped in the affirmative.

I laughed. "Wanna do it again?"

Butch cocked his head as if to say, *Are you crazy, lady?*

Well, yeah. Maybe. Probably.

A sickly sun shone overhead, but the whole world seemed bathed in ash, sullen and gray, a universe done in charcoal and chiaroscuro. A thin trickle of a stream flowed over rocky ground, and on the bank above grew a tree barren of greenery. In its spindly boughs perched a thing that wasn't a bird, but might have been their evil cousin. It had skin instead of feathers, like a hairless cat, leathern wings, a small red beak, which was full of tiny, sharp teeth, and beady, nosy eyes that tracked my movements as I pushed to my feet. I stepped out of the river, wringing out the bottom of my pants. From a magickal perspective, it made sense water would be used in transitions like this one, given it was symbolically linked to journeys.

Overhead, the evil avian chirred with unsettling interest.

"Shit," I said.

Before I could worry about bird-thing's curiosity, Chance tumbled out of a rent in reality, similar to the one I'd seen in Peru when the sorcerer gated the demon knight in to slay me. It happened a third time, permitting Greydusk to join us. Then the magick diffused on a dank breeze, carrying remnants of light as the only brightness in this otherwise wretched vista.

"You all right?" I asked, offering Chance my hand.

"That was ..." He shook his head.

"Right?" There was just no adjective to describe that trip.

"What was the deal with the ruby?" I added to Greydusk.

"It was a soulstone," the demon replied.

Chance raised a brow. "Did it have an actual soul in it?" *Please say no. Please.*

Greydusk inclined its head. "I did say that passage between realms required power and sacrifice."

"So you destroyed somebody's soul to get us here?" Horror overwhelmed me. Whatever religion you followed, destruction of a soul meant the end of that path. No more rebirths, no afterlife. Just ... gone.

Fuck.

The demon offered a cold smile. "No, Binder. *You* chose this path. I am merely the guide."

Chance objected, "But you'd have burned the soulstone to get home, wouldn't you? If she'd declined your offer."

"Would I?"

Maybe Greydusk would've chosen to go sightseeing in the human world for a few hundred years. *Damn it.* Then I recalled the terms of his employment: If he failed to guide me to Xibalba, as agreed, if I'd refused to come with him, he died. The person captured in that stone wouldn't have been destroyed. This was another sin that I hadn't anticipated, but unintentional harm didn't make it better or more forgivable. I closed my eyes, sick.

"You didn't realize," Chance whispered.

Thing was — and it made me worse than he knew — I'd have gone ahead, even if Greydusk had warned me. I'd choose to sacrifice some unknown soul to save Shannon. That was the kind of person I'd become, or maybe always had been. Certainly, I wasn't a gentle white witch like my mother had been. I really had to talk to Chance. *Damn.* First chance I got, I'd tell him everything, before we went back.

"Take me to Shannon," I said quietly.

"Those are not my orders."

I froze. Magick flared from my fingertips in a wild rush. It felt different here in Sheol, darker, almost viscous, as if I could drip it through my fingers like molasses. The energy clung to me like a dark cloak, sizzling beneath my skin in silent threat. Sure, it hurt me too, but if this thing tried to double-cross us, I would fry it. Somehow. Before it could touch either one of us. I gauged the distance and calculated how many seconds I'd have before it reached me.

"That will not be necessary, Binder." The neutral tone was back, a sure sign I had offended it. "I will convey you to my employer, as I was instructed. Where you go from there is between you and her."

Her?

"Do we have allies?" Chance asked.

"In a manner of speaking. The Luren want to see you. Speak with you. They are . . . amenable to the idea of a shift in the power structure."

I pondered; I wasn't without resources, so I etched a sigil in the air with my athame, whispered a word, then asked, "Did the Luren have anything to do with taking Shannon?"

"No," the demon answered. "But they did not strive to prevent it either."

Truth echoed in my head. The spell wouldn't last long, so I needed to get as much info as I could.

"Who are they?"

"They mean you no harm," Greydusk said impatiently. "Which is more than I might say for any other caste. You imperil yourselves by arguing here. It's imperative that you permit me to complete my contract."

Half truth. The whispered judgment from the spell didn't shock me. Unfortunately, it couldn't tell me which part was less than honest. Maybe the last bit, because the consequences would be terrible for Greydusk if we balked. *He'll die,* a skeptical voice reminded me. That meant it was doubtful we could trust him. He'd say anything to get us to cooperate. Yet it wasn't like I had a demonic version of Chuch hanging around Sheol, waiting for my call. There were no better offers on the table.

"What do you think?" I asked Chance.

He lifted one shoulder in a graceful shrug. "I don't know where the hell we are. We could die here before we find Shannon without some help, so it seems better to let him take us to the demons who *don't* immediately intend to kill us."

That summed up the situation nicely. Greydusk had us over a barrel. So I muttered, "Let's get on with it."

The Imaron set a small, intricately graven box on the ground. Then it whispered a word in demontongue, and the item responded with an agitated rattle. It unfolded rapidly, assembling into something larger, and when the pieces stopped unfolding and turning, the tiny article had turned into what looked like a mechanical coach. I shared a glance with Chance, brow raised. In reply, he shook his head: *Nope, never saw anything like that before.*

Next, Greydusk uncapped a vial, and blacklight poured out. I recognized it from Lake Catemaco, even if I hadn't been able to identify the smell. Panicked, I drew, so that magick sparkled on my fingertips, burning like ten small suns. My spells slipped, so that I couldn't remember which sigils matched what effects; I was that scared, and without an outlet for the power I'd drawn, I would cook myself alive.

"Calm down," Greydusk said impatiently. "The Klothod won't hurt you."

Except when they possess a bunch of angry monkeys, who then try to eat your face. They killed the boatman in Catemaco without breaking a sweat. "Since *when*?"

"Since I command them."

Chance took my hand, even with the energy crackling from it, and it burst away from him, lancing the air in a wild bolt that shook the tree. Overhead, the bird-thing uttered a raucous cry in protest. As I watched, Greydusk whispered orders to the Klothod, and they infused the carriage he'd called. The thing shuddered to life, fed on demonic energies. I swallowed my misgivings, climbed up, and then we were off.

The smell lingered around us, tingeing the air. I couldn't forget that some of these things had tried to murder me; they had killed Ernesto, an honest boatman from Veracruz. In my heart, I knew Kel wouldn't approve of this. He'd said I held both heaven and hell in me, and that I had yet to choose my course. But this? No. There was no paradise waiting for me after this. So I'd better make my mortal life count because it was straight down in a handbasket thereafter.

A lonely road stretched before us; there was no other traffic. No signs of indigenous life either. No native flora and fauna. "What is this place?"

"The Ashen Plain. On its other side, we will cross the River of Lethe, and come through the Chasm of Despair."

"Seriously?"

It ignored my sarcasm. "Once past, we will see the city walls."

"Xibalba," Chance said.

"Just so."

"From there, you're taking us to the Luren. Tell me about them?" Since Greydusk didn't seem to be guiding the carriage—the enslaved, formless Klothod appeared to be doing the work—it seemed safe to ask.

"They are the tempters," the demon said. "Beautiful. Seductive. Deadly. They are . . . difficult to resist."

"Is that how you wound up guiding us, against your better judgment?" Chance wanted to know.

Greydusk offered a curt nod. *Interesting.* So these Luren had incredible powers of persuasion, even over other demons. I'd have to be on my guard. I wished I had some spell to make me proof against mental shenanigans, but off the top of my head, I couldn't remember anything in either grimoire that would help. Chance's luck should keep him safe to some degree, but the longer I stayed close to him without a cleansing, the more danger I'd encounter.

"You mentioned taking us to *her*?" I prompted, hoping the demon would take the hint.

"Sybella," Greydusk supplied. "She is the patroness of the Luren caste, holding the rank of Ruling Knight."

Like Caim, I guessed. Time to learn a little more.

"Do you know of a demon named Caim?" I asked.

Greydusk cut me a sharp look. "The Ruling Knight of the Hazo?"

"I guess?"

"They are the warriors, not to be trifled with."

Shit. What I had done to the demon knight in Peru was way worse than that. I imagined he'd want to impale me on something sharp and rusty, as soon as I hit the city. The news just kept getting better and better. I mean, I'd known Caim was scary as hell, but the fear that laced Greydusk's expression made my dread worse.

Chance cut in, "Back to the Luren. Do the others take orders from Sybella?"

"Nothing so brutish," Greydusk replied bitterly. "It is all much more smooth and civilized among the Luren. More accurate to say she has seduced them to the point that most would rather die than displease her."

More shit. I preferred free will.

"Is there anything we can do to protect ourselves from her?"

The demon considered, and I could tell it was weighing the advantages of helping us. I wished I hadn't pissed it off so often. "Don't look her in the eyes. Stay at least two meters away at all times. Above all, don't let her touch you."

"Touching is bad?" Chance looked worried.

"For you, yes. If you consent to sexual contact, she'll steal a year of your life, and once you start down that road, you'll find it impossible to stop. The Luren are a . . . lethal addiction."

Yeah. Bad. Really bad.

"No sex with the Luren. Got it." I narrowed my eyes. "I thought you said they mean us no harm."

The Imaron laughed softly. "They need not intend harm to inflict it . . . as you well know, Binder."

Ouch. Direct hit.

"I take your point. And we'll be careful."

"It is nothing to me either way, once I complete my contract." But a hint in the demon's expression told me that wasn't entirely accurate—or maybe it was a flicker of response from the truth spell I'd cast a while back.

So I called its bluff. "So no matter what we do in Xibalba, it won't affect your world at all?"

Greydusk angled a cold look at me. "You have the power to *level* my world, Binder, but I am no kingmaker. I am Imaron—I honor my contracts. And that is all."

"Would you like to be more?" I asked.

"That's like asking an *eyreet* if it wants to fly. Some things can never be."

I had no clue what an *eyreet* was, but I recognized stifled ambition when I saw it. "Let me offer you a new deal. Keep your contract with the Luren, but once you deliver us, you come to work for me. I need someone who can explain how things work and keep us from making stupid, terrible mistakes."

"That could be dangerous—and unwise," Greydusk said.

"You said I have influence here, whether I want it or not. And it's always better to have powerful friends."

"Will you force me to submit to the ritual?" Its tension and word choice gave me insight into its preferences.

I recalled the demon had mentioned how it was compelled to complete its contracts via a blood ceremony—with death as the penalty for failure. So I shook my head. "No. Your word is good enough for me. It isn't right to force you to keep an agreement in such a way when you have no assurance that I will deal faithfully with you in return."

Greydusk shifted and offered me its hand, long fingers with those soul-stealing sucker pads. The first time, I'd refused to touch it. This time, I gambled—and as Chance drew in a sharp breath in protest, I clasped the demon's palm in mine, sealing the bargain. I didn't know if this was the right move, but it had to be better to have some notion of how to behave and what dangers we might face.

I didn't expect our mission to be as simple as demanding to see Shannon and being taken to her. The fact that I'd been brought to Sheol was a power play, pure and simple, and the ones responsible for her kidnapping would try to make sure I did as they wanted—whatever that action might be. *My* goal was to survive, keep Chance safe, rescue my friend, and get the hell out.

The ride continued in silence from there. Beside me, Chance seethed. He hadn't changed so much that he enjoyed seeing me take foolish risks. But this one was calculated more than stupid. Killing and draining me to a husk didn't serve Greydusk's interests at all at this juncture. That move, in fact, would've killed the Imaron, as it had an obligation to take me to Sybella. So with minimal risk, I made inroads into its good nature, such as demons might possess, and gave it reason to think well of me. I was a sentient being who had dealt honestly and kindly with it and who trusted its honor enough to make a pact that wasn't rooted in death magick. That had to be significant.

I understood why this was called the Ashen Plain. It looked as if volcanoes had erupted for eons, before the lava cooled, leaving a dark, ashy earth that churned as our diabolic carriage clanked along. It plumed out in our wake like a macabre banner, and the bird-things swooped along behind us. There were more of them, singing our arrival in a cacophony that reminded me of tortured cats.

Greydusk threw a nervous look over its shoulder. "I do not like the interest the quasits have taken in our arrival."

So that was what they were called. I asked, "Do they work for someone?"

"Perhaps."

"They're spying on us, then." Chance firmed his mouth into a tight line.

"Indeed. We can expect trouble at the river, if not sooner."

I sighed and shook my head. "Bring on the next assassination attempt."

"I'm glad you're amused," Chance muttered.

"Better to laugh than cry." Or I'd never stop.

I was in over my head here and scrambling for purchase on a slippery shore. *Oh, Kel,* I thought. *Save me.* But he wouldn't. Not here. Maybe never again—he'd made that clear the last time I saw him. He didn't have a life; he had a calling. And I had to save myself. Good thing I'd had some practice.

With the Klothod-powered carriage stinking up the area, it was impossible to smell trouble coming, like I usually did with demons. The plain grew darker as we approached the river, which doubtless fed the tiny tributary at the natural gate, and even that didn't look like normal water. It had an unnatural blue tint, like it was full of dye. Overhead, the sun looked peculiarly broken, as if it hung in two halves with a dark rift in between them, and that darkness was full of blood. Shadows on the ground moved as the quasits chased us, their raucous cries telling anything that might be nearby where we were.

"I'd love to kill those things," Greydusk muttered.

Chance asked, "Why can't you?"

"Because if they're indentured to a demon's house, then I've injured him and will owe reparations."

I thought about that. "Historically, it's kind of like harming a man's servant?"

I remembered something from my history lessons about when the lower classes weren't seen to have much value, and so if you killed a maid or something, you had to pay her master for the inconvenience. I was pretty indignant over that law, as I recalled. Not so oddly, I cared less about the fate of weird winged monsters that were probably reporting on my whereabouts to those who intended to execute me.

"Close enough," the demon replied.

Which meant we had to leave the quasits alone, no matter how annoying they were. I didn't care to end up in debt before I worked out a game plan. So like Greydusk, I ignored the creatures flying in our wake and focused on the crossing ahead. A stone bridge arched over roiling water, but it wasn't in good repair. Chunks of stone had dropped away, leaving a rock-lattice that didn't look strong enough for the carriage to cross.

"Should we get down?" I asked.

Greydusk shook its head. "Just hold on."

The Deadliest Desire

In response I grabbed onto the metal bar before me; Chance wrapped both his arms around me. I leaned against him and shut my eyes. The loud bang of the wheels striking the stonework made my stomach clench. More rock broke away and the demon coach shuddered; the Klothod strained to heave us across the gap.

"Whatever you do, don't fall in the water," Greydusk shouted.

I didn't need to ask why. *Lethe* meant *forgetting*. Oblivion. Therefore, it followed that if we were submerged in the river, it would erase everything that made us who we were. Which was almost like death—and unlike the forget fog I'd cast on Shannon and Jesse, this wouldn't wear off. Demon magick was always stronger; that was why practitioners craved it. Killed for it.

Nodding, I hung on for dear life as the carriage went airborne. It was an aerodynamic impossibility, but we weren't relying on the laws of nature anymore. The Klothod used their power to carry us across the bridge, and another piece fell away behind us as the coach clattered onto the rocky shore. And so, at full speed, we hit an invisible wall. If not for Chance's arms around me, I would've been flung against it, breaking all my bones in the process. He held me tight, face against my neck, and the Klothod hissed out of the infernal mechanism, dissipating into smoky tendrils all around us.

"What's the deal?" I asked.

Greydusk held up a hand as it leapt from the vehicle. Watching it explore the edges of our unseen prison was a nightmare, mimery in hell. Expression grim, the demon felt its way around the edges. In the end, the Imaron shook its head. It seemed we were seriously encased in an invisible box. I tried to ignore the Klothod swirling around us. They whispered in my ears, so faint I couldn't make out the words, but they sounded . . . hungry. Not. Good. For obvious reasons, the Imaron focused on getting the Klothod back in their vial, which required an incantation and more than a little magick. I recognized the signs of casting, though demon spells looked much different.

I climbed down and checked on Butch. He was cowering at the bottom of my purse, looking as miserable as I'd ever seen him. He didn't even lick my hand when I picked him up. This was one traumatized dog.

"Sorry."

Butch stared up at me with limpid, despondent eyes, and when I said, "Don't worry—we'll figure it out," he didn't even dispute me. Which was really, really bad. When your Chihuahua stops arguing with you, you know you're in trouble.

"Magus trap," Greydusk said finally.

"How does it work?" Chance joined the Imaron, unwilling to take the demon's word that there was no way out. So I watched him mime his way around the square too. God, this really *was* hell. No wonder Maury wanted out so bad.

Greydusk explained, "Magical lines are drawn, and when the desired target crosses, they snap together, creating an unbreakable casement."

"Shit," I said. "So we just sit here, waiting for whoever to collect us?"

If possible, its gray skin went paler, sickly green, as if it contemplated the surety of its own death. "I know of no way to break this enchantment."

For sure, mime-craft wasn't doing it. "Cut it out," I said to Chance. "There are four walls . . . we get it."

Expression sheepish, he returned to my side and slid an arm around my shoulders. "Unbelievable, right?"

"Yep." I pointed at the carriage. "You might want to put that back in the box. It's taking up a lot of room. I figure the spell goes both ways?"

Greydusk nodded. Having something to do seemed to help it. I held out my hand for Chance's backpack. Once he handed it over, I dug for grimoires. If we had limited time to figure out a way out of this before our captors arrived, I wanted to be ready. I flipped open the blue book and started reading.

Most of the spells weren't helpful. My mother had been a white witch, one who believed in getting back to nature, so there were lots of charms for growing plants and discouraging animals from rummaging around in your garden. If I wanted a life like that, I'd never have to worry about gophers eating my veggies. Unfortunately, I didn't see a damn thing that could get us out of a magus trap.

"Balls," I muttered.

Chance knelt beside me. "No luck?"

It was fantastic that he sounded surprised, as if he thought enough of my abilities that I could cast something that would help. Min's abilities were quieter, though I did believe her salves and creams had magickal healing properties. His mother went more for result than special effects, and Lily's ability hadn't been flashy either. I mean, when she went astral, she just laid there. Not exactly ostentatious.

"Would you mind skimming the red one for me?" In my bones I knew we had to hurry.

"Of course." He took it and sank down beside me. "Can you cast all of these?"

"More or less."

I didn't admit I hadn't practiced them all. Especially not the gopher spells. Glancing up, I had an idea, so I plucked a small stone from the ground, stood, and threw it upward as hard as I could. At twenty feet or so, it plinked into an invisible ceiling and came back down.

That was probably why the quasits weren't inside with us and instead had to content themselves with taunting from outside.

Then it hit me. I'd touched the ground. Picked up a rock. Which meant this thing had no floor. Chewing my lip in delighted inspiration, I ripped the red grimoire out of Chance's hands with an apologetic look. I flipped the pages madly until I found the spell I wanted . . . and then sighed in relief when I saw it had no herbal components. *Thank you, Mom.* I read it four times, memorizing the related sigils.

It was risky as hell, but I might be able to reverse-engineer this. Her spell was designed to drive away go-phers. If I tweaked it and cast it backward, I might be able to attract tunneling creatures. And that would give us a way out, provided whatever I summoned didn't eat us. Chance knew I'd figured something out, but he didn't ask. He just made room. Greydusk watched me with hope dawning in its expression, like it believed I might be able to break us out of the indestructible snare. *Watch me try.*

I drew my athame and brought my magick up, so that it flared in sparks from my fingertips. In the air, I etched one symbol in reverse order while the energy swirled around me in dark circles. Casting felt different in Sheol, darker and more dire. Would my halo show my trip to the underworld as well? I'd be lucky if I didn't become *kill on sight* to all other gifted humans hereafter, but I couldn't worry about that now. The spell swelled to a crescendo, pain boiled up from my belly, through my hips, and down my arms to flash from my fingertips.

"*Advenio*," I shouted as I released it.

Arrive.

And something did. The ground rumbled beneath our feet, starting far away and closing the distance with ter-rible speed. Rocks trembled as the creature came, frantic to answer my call. The impact shook me to my knees when a yawning hole opened up in the earth. An enor-mous thing rose before me; it had a lizard's body and a worm's head, and no eyes, but instead, its mouth ran all

the way across its face. It turned its blind head toward
me and a white forked tongue licked out. I froze, staring
at the creature I'd called.

"The Gorder awaits your orders," Greydusk said
softly.

In some ways, it reminded me of ancient renderings of
Chinese dragons, only with a more reptilian body. I had
no idea if I had any control over this beast. By reversing
the charm, I'd called it, but my mother hadn't written
command spells. Therefore, I could only guess how to
proceed. Magick had drawn it to me, and something was
keeping it from attacking.

I summoned just enough power to lend my words
weight, pushing it out as I spoke. "Lead us to safety."

Its head tilted this way and that, and I feared it had
decided to eat us, but then its gigantic body twisted in the
tunnel, and it scrambled out of sight. Shocked out of my
stillness, I charged after it. Greydusk followed me. Chance
paused to grab his backpack and my Butch-filled purse;
afterward, he slid down into the burrow. It looked like the
Gorder had chewed its way to us, and if it lived on rock
and dirt, maybe it didn't crave flesh after all. That would
be a nice surprise. I ran along the rocky channel; it was
more than large enough for us to move upright, but the
least movement caused dirt to crumble down, giving me
some fear that we'd end up buried alive. But that might
be better than waiting for whoever had trapped us. I felt
sure they didn't have friendly intentions.

Every now and then, the Gorder angled its neck to
ensure that I was still with it. We ran I don't know how
long, until the space widened into what I'd call a lair. Interesting things lay scattered around the ground—shiny
objects, old weapons, gemstones, gold, and sadly . . .
bones. So it didn't eat rocks. Bummer.

The Gorder trilled. *Shit. Yeah.* This qualified as one
of those *out of the frying pan* moments. For the time being, the demons hunting us wouldn't be able to find us
and if they did, I suspected my new pet lizard-worm
would eat them. But this wasn't what I had in mind as a
final destination.

"What now?" Chance asked.

God, I wished I knew.

While I watched in alarm, it curled into a ball on top of its treasure pile. This was how I imagined a dragon would behave, but this thing wasn't *exactly* a dragon. They always wanted virgins in the stories, but the Gorder didn't appear to hold my experience against me.

"There are other tunnels," Greydusk said. "Perhaps one of them leads to the surface?"

"I'm willing to try, provided Scary doesn't object to us leaving. Chance, can you find a way out?"

"Already on it."

The air around him gained a subtle charge, as if each particle had a little lightning in it. It raised the hair on the nape of my neck, and the Gorder cocked its sightless head as if it sensed the change in the atmosphere. It trilled deep in its throat, followed by a growl. It showed teeth, aiming its head at Chance, and I motioned for him to stop.

"I guess it wants to keep us," I said tiredly.

"When they arrive, your would-be captors will be able to follow the tunnels," Greydusk said. "Therefore, time is of the essence."

I frowned at him. "Yeah, but Dragonface doesn't want us to go!"

"Talk about a rock and a hard place," Chance muttered.

Since we were surrounded by tons of the stuff, I wondered if that was supposed to be funny. I moved closer to the Gorder. "Could you seal the tunnel behind us? Bad demons might come and try to steal your stuff."

The monster perked up with a disapproving roar and I scrambled backward. "Hey, not me. I'm a good guy. See? This is me, not stealing your hoard. I won't touch anything, I swear, but if you go block the tunnel, that should keep them away from your gold."

The Gorder snuffled as if considering. Eventually, it slid off the pile and scrambled the way we'd come. It left long enough for Chance to locate the path, but before we could dash for the exit, the underground warren trembled. Impact was strong enough to throw me to the ground, and chunks of rock broke away from the ceiling, bombarding us. I dove clear, but a good-size stone clipped Greydusk on the shoulder.

As the dust settled, I crawled toward it. "How badly are you hurt?"

"I'm fine," the demon said, as if surprised that I'd even ask.

I offered a hand to pull Greydusk to its feet, and that was when the Gorder returned. It trumpeted a celebratory sound, obviously expecting praise for a job well done. So I said, "Great work. Now they can't steal your treasure."

It growled.

At that moment, Butch came out of his stupor at last. He popped his head out of the bag; I expected him to disappear again with a whimper, but instead, the crazy dog came out and took a couple of tiny steps toward the dragon-beast. Ordinarily, Butch would be barking, trying to assert his dominance when he had no hope in hell of doing so, but this time his stance was almost playful; he pranced one step closer, two steps back, while he held his tail high, wagging like mad.

"It's going to *eat* you," I whispered to the dog.

The Gorder reared, its blind face turning to follow Butch's movements. Its tongue licked out to taste the air.

"That's how they see," Greydusk said quietly.

I watched, astonished, as Butch went all the way over to the Gorder's tail and then hopped up. The little dog ran along the curve of the creature's spine and found a place to snuggle in. The beast let out a trill. Though I didn't speak dragon-thing, I suspected trills were good; growls were bad. The Gorder coiled its body, showing every sign of going to sleep, though it was kind of hard to tell without eyes.

"Huh," Chance said. "It likes dogs."

"Let's see if it will let us leave," I murmured.

If it was asleep, we could slip past and call Butch once we were safe. Making no sudden movements, I edged in the direction Chance had specified earlier, but as I drew closer to the hoard, the Gorder growled at me. I backed away. Unfortunately, there was no way to reach the tunnel without passing the treasure pile.

"Thoughts?" I said, retreating to a safe distance.

"It doesn't mind our company," Chance mused, "but it doesn't trust us yet."

"How do we gain its confidence?" I asked Greydusk.

The demon lifted a shoulder. "I've no idea. If you'd asked, I wouldn't have imagined we could escape the magus trap."

"But you're our guide."

"To the *city*. I can't be expected to know the solution to every obstacle."

"Fair enough. Then would you check how thoroughly it blocked the path?" I asked the demon.

"Certainly."

The Gorder didn't object when Greydusk left the lair, going back the way we'd come. So it definitely was a hoard issue. Somehow, we had to befriend it. While I thought about that, Chance sank down against the opposite rock wall.

At my inquiring look, he shrugged. "What? I'm tired."

"Yeah, it's been a hell of a day."

When the demon came back, it reported, "The collapse closed the passage completely. It would take magickal intervention to clear it."

"Is that a possibility?" I asked.

Greydusk nodded. "But not all demons would be able to cast such a spell."

"Who could?"

"The Saremon."

"Could they also create a magus trap?"

"Yes, but that spell can also be bound in a trigger object and released."

"So any demon could have bought one." I tapped my fingers on my knee, thoughtful.

"Basically," Greydusk confirmed.

Chance sighed. "That doesn't help us figure out who's after us."

"That's not the immediate problem anyway. We have

to get out of here." I tried the approach again, but the Gorder roused at once and made a warning sound.

"You called it," Greydusk said thoughtfully. "That implies a certain level of control. Can you try commanding it?"

I laughed at the notion. Why would this beast listen to me? But it was worth a shot. In fact, it was the only idea we had.

Chasm of Despair

I moved toward the tunnel. The Gorder roused, ready to snarl, but I drew on my full power. Magick snapped through me like a live current, and when I spoke, it gave my voice an odd burr. "You trust me. You love me. You know I would never hurt you or your hoard."

It gave a questioning trill, and Butch yapped. The effort of holding the charm hurt. The magick burned deeper as I edged backward. I motioned for the others to follow me. *Come on, I don't know how much longer I can do this.*

To my vast relief, Chance and Greydusk slid past. Butch followed.

"Stay," I told the lizard-worm as I exited.

To my astonishment, it listened to me. The creature didn't budge as I led the way through the channel, which sloped up toward the surface. I shook all over in reaction. I let the magick drain out of me as I saw the gray light of Sheol. I scrambled out of the hole and waited while Greydusk summoned the carriage.

"We must hurry," it said.

Well, obviously. I cast the demon an evil look as it filled our ride with Klothod. Shudder. I'd never get used to that.

In short order, we got moving again. The plain descended into a valley that was framed on two sides by rocky bluffs. Dark, red-veined rock didn't resemble anything I'd ever seen on earth; it was like diabolic marble.

Greydusk followed my gaze and said quietly, "Don't let it touch your skin."

Since the carriage was whizzing along at a crazy, jarring speed, that wasn't probable. But still, I asked, "Why not?"

"This is called the Chasm of Despair for a reason."

At those words I took a closer look over the side and saw that bones littered the ground here. Their posture was . . . disturbing, as if someone had leaned up against the cliff for a rest, and then just never mustered the will to move. *Despair,* I thought, and a chill rolled through me. There was an insidious power in this place, one that sapped inner strength and hope and made you feel as though it was too much trouble to try.

Chance wrapped an arm around me, his expression grim. By the look in his eyes, he felt it too. I leaned into him, more frightened than I cared to admit. Even the demon knight in Peru had been a foe I could fight. How do you combat cursed demon rock? Yeah, exactly.

I squeezed my eyes shut and ignored the rising impulse to throw myself out of the moving vehicle. Because clearly we were doomed. We couldn't save Shannon. In the end, nothing I did mattered. My mother had died, and I couldn't help her. I'd hidden like a coward. My father, shit, he left ages ago, probably because he saw I was worthless. I should've let Shannon perish in Kilmer because at least it would have been faster than what awaited her in the hands of the demons.

Heaviness spilled through me, dark as blackberry wine, and I listed, ready for everything to stop. The futility, the struggle, the failure—I wanted it all over. There was no hope. No purpose. No point. I threw myself toward the edge of the carriage, but Chance was there. He caught me.

His arms went around me, tight as steel bands, and he put his face against mine. "Fight it, damn you. You're stronger than this."

Stronger than what?

"You don't know anything," I said wearily. "I'm a fake and a liar, Chance. Which you'd already know if I wasn't both those things."

"Corine—"

"You think I'm a good person, but a good person doesn't do deals with demons, even to save her own skin, maybe *especially* then. You remember the demon from Kilmer? In Laredo, I did business with it. I summoned its mate in return for help against the Montoyas."

Shock tightened his features, but he recovered. "You wouldn't have done that if you'd had a better choice."

"Wouldn't I? After I summoned Dumah, I forced Maury to give me a better bargain. And then, later, I used her true name to summon her. She's how I defeated Montoya and his sorcerous brother. I *fed* them to her." I heard myself saying these things, and I couldn't stop. The words were poison that had to be lanced, right then, or I would die.

"Do you feel better?" he asked.

But I wasn't done with my confession. "While you were trying to find a way to win me back, I was with someone else. I slept with Kel in Peru, and—"

He kissed me. It was a time-tested way to shut a woman up, I supposed. Afterward, he held me. Argued with me. Distracted me. Before I could fight him in earnest, we cleared the chasm, and the effects faded. Just enough for me to realize how stupid I'd been, how much I'd told him, and hot color flooded my face. I had meant to come clean with Chance, but not like that. I could've chosen my moment and my words better. Greydusk sat like a statue beside me, carefully not looking at either of us.

Gods and goddesses.

"How do you not hate me?" I asked.

He pulled away slowly, and I missed his warmth, his comfort. "This isn't the time to talk."

Chance couldn't be happy about the demon summoning or the destruction of human souls, even bad ones. Who would be? Especially since we were in Sheol, the demon capital of the universe.

"But Kel . . . ?"

His jaw tightened. "Obviously I'm unhappy about that. It's a knife in my gut, imagining you with him."

Embarrassment kept my cheeks hot; I shouldn't have crumbled so fast. Maybe that spoke to my lack of fortitude—or it might be the unholy rock still at work in my head. Surely, though, he couldn't have imagined I'd abstain. I mean, I never expected to *see* Chance again, let alone have him devoted to winning me back.

In silence, I linked my fingers together and studied the incredible vista rising before us. The city was . . . immense. Imagine the biggest human metropolis, like Mexico City or Tokyo, and then multiply it times two. Or four. A sense of spatial relationships wasn't my strong suit. The point being, Xibalba was an enormous urban sprawl. The demon city looked like a baroque painting with round, classical lines, but a little too vivid, as if it was realer than anything else around it. That impression made me distrust my eyes.

Tall stone towers rose up from the city center, and a dark, sooty pall hung over everything. It might come from industry, I supposed, though that was an odd thought. Demons, working in factories, demon teamsters—and that sent my brain to places I'd better not go. If I started seeing demons as like humans, who had daily lives and went about them the best way they could, I'd lose the only surety I possessed—that they were the evil, the enemy, and must be vanquished at all costs. *Shit.* The possibility that all demons weren't one hundred percent wicked was already lodged too deep to shake out. I was in *so* far over my head.

The carriage took us to the walls, where a guard stopped us. A magickal glow swirled around the stone, layers of protection when glimpsed through my witch sight. I cocked a brow at Greydusk while we waited our turn. There were numerous conveyances ahead of us, many of them Gothic or unlikely, straight out of a Tim Burton movie, and the denizens of said coaches were more exotic still.

"Do you see anything interesting about the fortifications?" the demon asked.

I squinted. The walls *were* really tall. I shrugged.

"No?" But the question made me wonder what I wasn't seeing, so I switched to witch sight, and the walls glowed with scintillant color. "What's that?"

"The light?" it asked.

I nodded.

"The Vortex. It keeps undesirables out."

By which he meant monsters like the Gorder. I pointed. "And over there?"

It looked like a shantytown, shacks built out of scrap wood and stone. I glimpsed shambling figures, but they were too far away to make out details. *Please don't let that be a human slave labor camp.*

"Those are the Xaraz, demons who have been convicted of a crime and stripped of caste status."

"You don't have prisons?" Chance wanted to know.

Greydusk seemed puzzled. "What is the purpose of feeding and housing our criminals? Outside the walls, they will fight to live or die. Some perish. What punishment could be worse than that?"

"Our prisons claim they're striving toward rehabilitation," I offered.

"And how's that working out?" The demon scoffed.

I had to admit, I took his point. "Aren't you worried they'll get back in?"

"They cannot. The Vortex requires each vehicle or pedestrian to possess a rune of passage, or the energy field destroys them."

"This one does, right?" I leaned over to look at the front, as if there would be magickal license plate on it.

"Of course."

Then it was our turn at the gate.

The guard asked something in demontongue; he looked more or less human, except for his tail. It twitched in impatience while he discussed our entry with Greydusk. I could only guess at what they were saying, but the language grated on my ears, simultaneously harsh and sibilant. Then our demon produced some documents and the guard waved us through.

"What did you say?" I asked, once we passed into Xibalba proper.

"That I am an Imaron guide in service to Sybella of the Luren. And here are my contracts, providing provenance for the arrival of two specimens."

Chance laughed. "I don't think I've ever been called that before."

Me either. But I was too weary to take offense.

In exhaustion, I felt unable to take in all the wonders; the city blurred before my eyes as we clattered over rough stone streets, which seemed to be laid out in concentric circles. After we passed through another set of gates, we were ushered inside a magnificent estate. We waited a while, and then a silent, gorgeous male Luren guided us into a sumptuous chamber to confront Greydusk's boss.

Sybella wasn't just beautiful. She was . . . I didn't have a word. Her hair was black silk; her skin gleamed like a pearl. Her eyes shimmered like tropical waters, and her mouth was lush and succulent like dew on a perfect red rose. *Shit.* I was only looking at her out of the corner of my eye, and I already had an uncontrollable urge to the throw myself at her feet and lick them.

Double shit.

Beside me, Chance studied the patterns on the floor.

Sybella was speaking, but I found it hard to focus on her words. She smelled luscious, cinnamon and candied apples with the richness of a caramel slightly burned, a sugar-sweet scent that made me step toward her, before Chance grabbed my arm. Even her toes, which I was studying intently, were lovely. Her feet were slim and high-arched, alabaster pale and smooth as marble. A layer of polish gleamed in a surprisingly innocent shade of pink, and the effect was . . . disarming.

"And so, I am pleased to make you welcome in my home," the Knight of the Luren caste concluded.

Unfortunately, I had no idea what words had come before. Not an auspicious beginning. But maybe if I admitted I had been distracted, she might be flattered. Then again, she must be used to affecting people that way, and so it would merely reveal me as a weak link. *Damn it.* I cast a sideways glance at Greydusk, but its impassive expression gave me no sign as to how I ought to proceed.

"When would you like to get down to business?" I asked.

It was a bluff, of course. For all I knew, she might've already offered me a deal, but I suspected Sybella wasn't the type. Such efficiency would strike her as uncouth.

"You need rest," she said smoothly, "before you can be expected to begin complex negotiations. I give my word that you will be safe in my house."

At this, Greydusk inclined its head slightly. I could trust Sybella to keep her promise. Like most demons, I imagined she would twist any agreement to her advantage, but this was a simple matter.

So I nodded. "I'd appreciate an opportunity to freshen up and sleep. Chance will share my quarters."

"You're dismissed, Imaron." The scorn in Sybella's voice raised my hackles, but I didn't dare meet her eyes to express my reaction with a dirty look.

Greydusk planted its feet beside me. "With all due respect, mistress, you lack the authority to discharge me."

Sybella went arctic. "Pardon me?"

"I have completed my contract with you in good faith, and the Binder now employs me."

"I . . . see," the knight said quietly. She stepped toward me as if to take my arm to guide me somewhere, and I darted out of range. "And you've been busy, filling her ears with tales, I see. Not necessarily with an eye toward my best interests, Imaron. I will not forget this."

"Indeed." The demon sounded like it didn't give a damn.

Not nearly soon enough, Sybella summoned a lesser Luren to show us where we would stay for the time being. This one smelled delicious too, like nutmeg and allspice; he was golden like a lion, with tawny hair and gilded skin and eyes like layered topaz. He shot me a lazy, gleaming smile as if he sensed my rebellious hormones. I didn't want any demon to affect me like this, but at least I wasn't alone.

This was sort of their purview, after all.

Balls to the Wall

The hallways were palatial yet other. On the floor, patterns looked alien, laid in black and bloodred tiles. It seemed like a preternatural path the longer I studied it, but before I could unlock the riddle of where it led, the Luren paused outside an ornate basalt door, etched with peculiar symbols. Greydusk studied them and then gave me a half nod.

"They are protective sigils."

"I am Gilder," the minion went on. "And I will be stationed outside your quarters for your own protection. In the event our people grow . . . curious."

That wasn't why. Well, at least not entirely. But I already knew that demons could tell partial truths. He was in charge of making sure I didn't escape this complex before Sybella got whatever she wanted from me. I pretended I didn't realize the difference because it couldn't hurt if they underestimated my intelligence.

Greydusk leveled a flat, black gaze on the other demon. "And *I* will be guarding the inside of the door. So be warned." That was all it said, but the tone sent shivers down my spine.

By this point, I was so tired that I was swaying on my feet. Chance opened the door and we stepped through to a suite that would charm a Turkish potentate. Everything was gold and scarlet, not restful colors but opulent ones. And the furnishings were baroque in the extreme, as if I'd wandered into an old pleasure house. Yet everything gleamed, showing no signs of age.

"Thank you," I said to Greydusk.

It paused in the midst of securing the door. I thought I had surprised the Imaron. "Knights do not thank their servants, Binder."

"I'm not a knight."

"No," it agreed. "You are she who could be queen." It settled on the sofa near the door, guarding me.

I didn't have the heart to start the argument over again. It would be fruitless to claim I had no interest in ascending—whatever the hell that meant—and it might undermine the demon's loyalty. Right now, Greydusk thought it was getting in on the ground floor of my regime. So I inclined my head in what felt like a laughable manner, but the Imaron didn't react with mockery, as I half expected. Instead, it bowed.

"The bedroom's through here," Chance said.

I followed, needing sleep in the worst way. It had surely been more than one day in the real world, but it wasn't like I had a watch that could convert from Sheol to Mexico time. However, my body felt as it had during the worst moments of my life, when I didn't have a bed for the night and would try to snatch some rest in the bus station while keeping one eye out for cops, terminal employees, and people who had bad things on their minds. The result back then had been this same dry-eyed, bleary exhaustion, so I guessed it had been two days.

Our room had an enormous bed with heavy red velvet drapes; it was worthy of Henry VIII. Expensive tapestries with disturbing characters woven into patterns made me dizzy, mostly because they seemed to dance before my eyes, as if they wanted to assemble into forms I could understand. Chance closed the door and went around the room, looking for trouble. I could tell he was dowsing from the low-grade crackle in the air that raised the hair on the nape of my neck.

"All clear?" I asked when he stopped by a set of double doors.

He lifted a shoulder in a familiar half shrug. "Seems to be."

Chance flung open the doors, revealing an other-worldly garden. I had no words for the shape of the plants that grew here, but they were dark and twisted, thick with thorns. Their stems shone like coppery metal with a patina of green; each leaf was a sculpted marvel, and the flowers exuded a siren smell, so that I wanted to step onto the stones and bury my face in the petals. At the thought, the foliage shivered around me as if it *craved* that—needed to slice my skin and drink my blood.

I stepped back at once, my flesh crawling. The beauty was unearthly, but it was dangerous too. "Butch can use the bathroom out here, but let's keep a close watch on him. I don't trust this place."

"Me either," he muttered.

When I peered into my purse, which Chance had been carrying, I found Butch sound asleep, and despite my best efforts, I could not wake him. He had been fine, af-ter the crossing, but this didn't look natural. Come to think of it, he should have reacted to Sybella, yapped a warning or something, because she had been a threat. Which meant he'd been out ever since we entered her compound.

I shared a worried look with Chance. "What do you think?"

"Not good."

Though it was futile, I tried a little longer to rouse the dog. Maybe I had a spell that could wake him, but I was too tired to risk Butch's safety by trying to cast. *Look at how I screwed up the forget fog.*

Quietly worried, I crossed to the other door and flung it open to reveal a bathroom. It was ridiculously posh, even more so than the one I'd used at Escobar's estate. Even the fixtures were gilt. *Whatever.* I didn't care what the place looked like, as long as it had running water. And it did. I thought it might come out stinking like sul-fur, but it was smooth and soft, falling over my body in a hot rush.

I didn't let the pleasure seduce my senses. I kept myself on task and used the soap and shampoo provided—so odd to think of demons like Gilder bathing. That made them too relatable. Shaking my head at the additional correlation, I stepped out of the tub and dried off. I had no thought to teasing Chance, as I'd done at the old house we rented in Kilmer.

He greeted me with one of his spare T-shirts. I hadn't packed any underwear when I moved my stuff to his backpack, but that was the least of my worries. The tee was long enough, and I'd get covered up soon. Gods and goddesses, I was tired.

Chance headed toward the bathroom, and then paused. "Where should I sleep?"

Valid question. But I believed he'd changed. I trusted that he had, in fact, loved me at the end, and he'd been coping with his own shit and hadn't meant to hurt me. Those were enormous leaps of faith.

"With me," I said quietly. "The bed's huge."

He might not want to, though. We hadn't talked about my confession yet.

"You sure?" he asked.

"Yeah. Well, unless you'd rather not. I can take the floor."

Closing his eyes, he leaned his head wearily against the doorjamb; I took advantage of his momentary lapse of focus to swap my towel for his shirt, and then I slid between the covers. The sheets felt like the most expensive Egyptian cotton, all buttery soft, and I immediately wondered if this room was actually all dust and rags, whether the Luren could spin illusions like that. A shudder worked through me. I couldn't trust anything here, not even my own mind. The Chasm of Despair had proven that.

"There's no reason for either of us to be a martyr," he said finally. "I'm shocked . . . and angry. But mostly I'm exhausted."

"You think I should've told you this stuff before we came to Sheol."

"I feel somewhat misled," he admitted.

"You didn't ask how I dealt with Montoya." After the words came out, I wished I could take them back.

Chance stiffened. "And *you* didn't ask whether I had anything to do with my girlfriend's death. But that lack of curiosity didn't stop you from blaming me later, after you ended up in the hospital."

"That's true," I said softly. "There's no defense. I should've told you what you were getting into, so you could make an honest decision. I'm sorry."

"Was it revenge?"

"No," I said miserably. "I just . . . I didn't think you'd want to be with me if you knew the truth."

"That was always our problem. Too much thinking, not enough trusting."

"I do trust you." *Now.* I wasn't sure when it had happened, but at some point during the weeks, rebuilding together, he had become a different person in my mind. Not the same man who hurt me.

"You *can*," he said. "But it goes both ways. And that means talking to me, even when you'd rather not."

That stung, as he'd turned my own sentiments against me. "Yeah, you're definitely mad."

"Obviously. But I'm too tired to fight." He smiled in a way that pierced my heart and pinned it to the back of my rib cage, where it fluttered, caught and helpless.

Our gazes clung, and everything I felt for him swamped me a torrential rush. *Please don't break my heart again,* I thought.

Since I'd confessed all my secrets, it seemed fair he should do the same. If he froze me out, the rejection might mean he was more than just angry. "Will you tell me about Lily?"

He stilled, just a few seconds; then he came toward me and perched on the edge of the bed. "Of course."

"Where did you meet her?"

"In college."

That much was news to me. I hadn't known that Chance had gone, although I wasn't surprised, come to think of it. He had a certain polish that came from education, although I suspected he'd grown up poor. It was

the only thing that explained his obsession with money—
or rather, the fact that no amount could ever be enough.
I still found it tough to credit that he'd stopped doing
business to be with me.

I'd caught him researching investments, but he was
secretive about why he was looking up tablets produced
in Taiwan or Japanese technical innovations. Everyone
needed a purpose. I didn't think he was trying to keep
me out of the loop, however; this time, I suspected he
wanted to have all his ducks in a row before explaining
the premise.

I prompted with a small, encouraging sound. "Uh-
huh?"

"Lily was a music major. Beautiful voice."

If I knew anything about Chance, she had a lovely
face too. The first time around, I felt like a consolation
prize or that he secretly believed he didn't deserve better. Obviously that could've been my old self-esteem issues. I didn't feel that way about myself anymore.

"What did you study?"

He shot me a grateful look. "I majored in finance.
Didn't graduate."

"Why not?"

"Money," he said flatly.

From his tone, I shouldn't ask. There were limits to
how much he could open up, and I couldn't just dig out
all his secrets with a conversational backhoe. This was
supposed to be about Lily, so I'd stay on topic.

"What was she like?" *And did you love her?* I didn't
ask the second question out loud for obvious reasons.

"Her voice was a smoky alto . . . like a torch singer." By
the way he produced the words in staccato increments, it
hurt him to talk about her. "She joked a lot. Made me
laugh. She came from money, but she never . . ."

"Flaunted it?" I guessed.

"Yeah. Or made me feel bad because I couldn't take
her to the places her previous boyfriends could."

Expensive jewelry, fine restaurants— check. It occurred
to me then that while we were together, Chance had
used me to get rich enough to please a dead girl. I'm sure

he wouldn't have thought of it in those terms because she was gone, but sometimes we grieve in odd ways and do things that don't rationally make sense. Pain clamped around my heart.

"And she was gifted?"

He nodded. "Like I already told you, astral projection was her thing. I had no idea I was dangerous then." Chance hesitated, and I heard the pain tightening his tone. "Before Lily, I hadn't gotten serious with anyone. A few months, and I was bored. Ready to move on."

"But she was special," I said softly.

"Yeah. She stuck by me through some tough times."

"Oh?" Sometimes, I thought, it was better not to know. Right then I imagined a different Chance, bright and wild in love. Not the quiet, closed-off man whom I had been so desperate to please. Maybe this was a terrible idea, after all, because no matter what he felt for me, I'd never be Lily, and that hurt me all over again.

Fortunately, some happier memories put a smile on his face and he didn't notice my reaction. "We lived in this awful apartment because I couldn't afford half the rent on anything better. At one point, her father tried to buy me off. Offered me a hundred grand to walk away and not look back."

"You told him to fuck off?"

"More or less."

"If you weren't in college, what were you doing?"

"Dealing blackjack in a casino."

That was something I hadn't known either. He was already self-employed when I met him. "And Min?"

Funny, but until now I didn't realize how little he'd shared about his life. When we first got together, I had been so dazzled, so awestruck, that he wanted to be with me, that I hadn't asked too many questions. I'd respected the DO NOT DISTURB sign posted in his eyes. Chance had wanted to live in the moment, and since I had my own ghosts, I was happy not to think about the future . . . or the past.

"She was working in an herbal remedies shop. I hadn't saved enough for her to open her own store yet."

"So when you and I went into business together—"

"We were working on my mom's behalf. At least, that's what I did with my share. She deserved to be her own boss. . . . She sacrificed a lot bringing me up. I know she went without so the other kids wouldn't make fun of me at school."

Another new thought, Chance as an underprivileged kid. If they'd scrimped and saved to put food on the table, that, too, probably explained his fixation on making money. *But back to Lily.* Provided I could handle more revelations. At least getting to know Chance took my mind off what might be going on with Shannon.

"Did Lily graduate?"

"Summa cum laude."

Impressive. I only knew that meant she'd gotten really good grades. The education I'd gotten since high school, I'd acquired myself, and I did a lot of reading on my own—various fiction and nonfiction. I was partial to John D. MacDonald. None of that eclectic reading constituted a degree, but I didn't let it make me feel bad. He'd come after me, given up everything for me. Surely that meant something, more than just that he didn't want to be alone. A guy like Chance never had trouble finding company; he could crook his finger and summon a date. He wanted a partner. He wanted *me.*

"What did she want to do, music-wise?"

"I thought she was good enough to sign with a major label," he said, "but she wanted to get her master's and go into music therapy. She intended to do good works instead of get rich."

Wow. That might've been a bone of contention. I could see the trouble brewing in my mind's eye. If Lily grew up with money, and just wanted to help people, she might not understand Chance's need to prove himself by putting lots of zeroes in a bank account. She wouldn't have understood that particular drive, even if she loved him. Since I'd been dirt-poor, I got it. I had the same compulsive need about having a home.

"How long were you together?"

"Five years, until I was twenty-four."

Longer than I'd expected—sometimes answers didn't offer all the solutions; they just created more doubt. How could I *compete* with this? Yet he was doing as I'd requested, so it didn't seem fair to punish him because he'd loved someone else first.

"And how long until you started dating me?"

"It had been a year when I met you."

I was twenty-one then, and I'd been on my own for three hard years since leaving Kilmer. I'd hit rock bottom, but by the time we started dating I had a job in Tampa at a dry cleaner's and a crappy studio apartment. He had been twenty-five, though he'd seemed older in terms of sophistication. Those basic facts I'd known before, but they felt different, now that I saw the context of his loss. We had been together for over three years, until I nearly died, until I couldn't take the emotional distance anymore. However, at least I understood why he'd behaved that way. In all honesty, I'd been his rebound girl, and so it was a wonder our relationship lasted as long as it did, a testament to how desperate I had been to please him.

He was thirty-two now, and I was twenty-eight. Our footing had changed.

"Ah," I said, and he heard something in my voice.

"I know I was wrong in the way I handled . . . us. I thought I could I could protect you, if I could just control everything."

"Even me."

"Yes, even you. I managed you. Or I tried to. And I just *couldn't* let myself be vulnerable the way you wanted, especially toward the end."

"I understand." I did, now. It didn't lessen the damage he'd inflicted on me, but it helped me to comprehend it. "Did you mean to marry her?"

"I wanted to be able to provide for her first."

"You were saving for a ring . . . or a down payment on a house?"

"Both. I had no idea what I was doing to her," he went on brokenly. I'd never heard this tone from Chance, and a fist curled around my spine. His shaking hands clenched on his thighs. "After she died, I didn't even know . . ." He took a couple of steadying breaths, and I reached for him.

He didn't cry in my arms because that wouldn't be a Chance thing to do, but he trembled, and he let me comfort him. *Not* a Chance thing to do, but I'd realized the Chance I'd known was the broken version. I'd very much like to get to know the man who loved a woman as fiercely as he'd loved Lily . . . and maybe me, now.

"How did you find out?" I asked when he eased away.

"I overheard my mom discussing how to break the news. She said she hated to hurt me, but that I had to know so I could take suitable precautions going forward."

"Did she realize your gift could kill?" If she had, then it was criminal of her not to tell him sooner, even if her intentions had been good. For the first time, I felt a flicker of anger at Min. Before, I'd always blamed Chance, but she guarded her own secrets as tightly. Like his father's identity.

He shook his head. "She knew the bad luck could be deflected, but she thought there were limits. So did I. But it makes sense—if the luck can save my life, then it can take someone else's. After that, Mom looked for ways to compensate, but I wasn't interested. I decided I wouldn't get close to anyone else again."

In his way, Chance had been every bit as messed up as I was. He probably still was, but I wouldn't hold it against him. "So then . . . why did you—"

"Ask you out?" he finished. "It was the oddest thing. I tried to explain it to you once before, that click. I heard your drawl, saw your smile, and everything in my head went fuzzy. It was like *I know this girl*, or I felt like I should. I had to see you again. I told myself I'd be careful."

"So you were trying to protect me."

He nodded. "Later, I thought if I kept the emotional walls up, it would keep you from getting hurt."

"I don't condone how you handled things, but I understand."

"That's the best I could hope for."

"And I guess my accident proves you did love me, after all. By the end."

He closed his eyes. "I tried so hard not to. My love kills, Corine. But you were so sweet, so . . ."

"Gullible?"

"Irresistible. I couldn't help myself. And the luck compensated when I stopped fighting, when I fell headlong for you—"

"I fell too. Literally."

"I'm so sorry."

"It's okay," I said.

And it was. The past was no longer a thorn in my soul.

I had a lot to think about, but everything made sense now. From my perspective, he should have told me the risks after we got serious—my opinion on that didn't change—but he hadn't acted out of malice. His head was all fucked up at the time, and he was trying to do what was best. And maybe, just maybe, he'd seen a glimpse of my past—a suggestion that I needed somebody to take care of me for a while. I certainly hadn't fought at first. It was only later that I wanted more.

Now I'd given him reason to doubt me. Did that make us even?

Then I added, "I won't make you talk about her again if you'd rather not."

"It's not Lily, per se. Just how badly I failed her."

Yeah. He wouldn't be here, if he'd known the risks, if she'd gotten regular cleansings. Such a small thing, but for want of the horseshoe nail, and all that. Most likely, he'd be married with a kid or two, working as a stockbroker or a day trader, while his wife with the beautiful singing voice ministered to the unfortunate. Instead, he had an inert Chihuahua and me. That illustrated perfectly how unfair life could be.

Sweetness and Light

"It's pretty clear neither one of us is perfect," Chance said. "We've both screwed up. At this point, we have to decide what to do about it."

"Do you believe I can do better?"

"Do you think *I* can?"

"Yes," I said without hesitation.

"Then let's start there." He pushed to his feet, weariness in every movement. "If I can stay awake, I'm taking a shower." He paused. "You're lucky, you know. If I had more energy, I'd have bitched you out good."

"Let's hear it for exhaustion." I listened to the water running in the bathroom, and the next thing I knew, it was a long time later. I knew that because Greydusk was rapping politely on the door, and it wouldn't wake me without a good reason.

"Sybella grows impatient," it said.

"Any trouble?"

"It was quiet until the summons."

"Awesome."

"I am to inform you there is clothing suitable to your station in the wardrobe."

Suitable to my station. Fabulous. No doubt it would be elegant and uncomfortable as hell.

"I need time to get ready."

"I will pass the message to Gilder." Its footsteps trailed away.

I raised up on one elbow and found Chance gazing at me with lambent, sleep-lidded eyes. The bed was big enough that I couldn't remember running up against him in the night. Or day. Whatever we'd slept through.

I made a conscious choice to move toward him. He met me halfway and his arms slipped around me, as they had so many times before. I didn't stifle the memories this time. I let them come, and some were beautiful. Once, I'd thought he was the best thing ever to happen to me. Maybe I would again.

"You feel so good," he whispered.

"You too."

He buried his face in my tousled hair, rubbing his cheek slowly side to side. I wondered then: *Did love ever truly die?* I stroked his back and held him, savoring the moment.

"Sad as it sounds, this is the happiest I've been since you left me."

I eased back to stare at him. "That's . . . pretty messed up."

"I know," he said.

I wasn't sure how I felt about that revelation. I mean, on the surface, it was flattering. But I'd moved on. Put my life back together and grown stronger. Chance had fixated on getting me back. I asked myself if that was healthy or if it was a sign of how much he'd come to love me. Maybe I didn't know shit about relationships and I was looking for an excuse to wig out and run.

Right now, none of it mattered.

I leaned in and touched my lips to his. His fingers tangled in my hair, his mouth an endless sweetness on mine. He'd always kissed like a god. Our breathing was ragged when I pulled back.

"Time to get up."

But before we did, he brought me breakfast in the form of another protein bar and water. After I ate, I got out of bed and went to the wardrobe, where I found clothing suitable for the circus. Seriously.

Apparently, Greydusk wanted me to wear a satin brocade gown with a jeweled belt and a formal headdress. It looked like a combo of the shit they made Amidala wear in those awful *Star Wars* prequels and crazy Ren Faire garb run amok. *Yeah, there's no way. Over my dead body, I put one of those on.* Chance came to stand behind me, wearing nothing but his boxers.

Damn.

He really was breathtakingly beautiful. His hair was long and shaggy, gleaming like a raven's wing. It looked like my hands had been in it. His face? Well, that had always been sculpted to splendor beyond human limits. Since I'd left, he'd spent more time working out, more time sparring, and the result was a body that could make me stop and stare. I'd never seen anyone with an eight-pack before. When he caught me looking, he ducked his head, inexplicably shy, and it delighted me.

"You're gorgeous," I said. "I mean, you always were, but in a more *GQ*, impervious way."

"Now?"

"I can't look at you without wanting to touch."

His eyes widened, but so did his smile. I never would've been so honest about my desire before; my confidence wasn't up to the mark. Back in the day, I'd worried that he'd feel like he had to lie if I said something like that, because clearly I wasn't his physical equal, and I avoided the subject instead of addressing it. I pretended the looks we got from other women, the *oh my God, you're seriously a couple* stares, the *she must be a freak in bed* speculation, didn't bother me. This time it really didn't.

Yet I stopped myself from going to him. With Sybella breathing down my neck and a comatose dog to worry about, I couldn't be making out with Chance. Even though I wanted to. And that was a little worrisome. Not that he wasn't totally kissable, but when in Sheol, I had to wonder if the demons were fucking with my libido. I wasn't going to dance to their tune.

So with a faint, regretful sigh, I hauled the least offensive garment out of the wardrobe. In side drawers, I discovered their idea of underpants suitable to my station. Chance's jaw dropped. And I stifled a scream of frustration.

"Seriously?" I said out loud.

"That's so . . ." He was grinning.

"I hate you. Go take a cold shower or something."

While he mercifully did as I ordered, I scrambled into the ridiculous contraption. The undergarment was all one piece, designed to pinch and push up, and give me a demon-style body with impossible curves. It was a little hard to breathe after I got it on, and then I pulled the dress on. The fabric slithered in a disconcerting manner as I smoothed it down. Then, to my horror, I saw it . . . moving. Tightening. I went to yank it off, suspecting it would try to kill me, and then I realized it was shaping itself perfectly to my demon-enhanced silhouette.

Holy shit.

Light as air, it felt like wearing nothing at all. There had to be magick involved, because with the dress on, even the horrible corset-thing didn't bind like it had. Naturally demons would think of something like this since they lived for temptation. And what better way to drive men crazy? I was eyeing the headdress when Chance stepped out of the bathroom. He stopped in his tracks, towel in hand.

"Dear God." His voice went hoarse.

I admit his expression gave me a purely adrenal thrill, like if I offered him the slightest encouragement, he'd back me up against the wall and do me hard with my elegant gown around my waist. And what woman didn't love that feeling?

Focus, I told myself.

"There are clothes for you, too." I broke the spell over him by using my words.

He exhaled and gave himself a slow shake before crossing to get dressed. Then I went to check on Butch. The dog still couldn't be roused.

Heartsick, I paged through the blue grimoire, muttering to myself. Chance skimmed the other one alongside me. I wanted to believe he cared as much as I did. After all, he'd been there when we adopted the dog. Together, we almost constituted a family. Maybe we *were* if the rules were generous in their definitions of such things.

A tear slipped down my cheek, and that made me mad. My dog lay like a tiny statue, unresponsive. Even his flesh had gone cold.

He's not dead. He can't be.

But *if* he was, I would ascend and level this place.

Without much hope, I tried a couple of spells, but Greydusk pounded on the door again and worry laced the impatience of its tone. "We truly should not keep Sybella waiting."

Well, Chance was ready—and he looked like a prince. No shit, he really did. He wore black trousers, a white shirt edged in silver, and a sleeveless surcoat, which wasn't exactly what I'd call a vest. With a sword belt and a couple of rapiers, he could have starred in an adventure movie.

"Butch will be okay," he said, soothing me with hands on my shoulders.

I squared them. Sure. Just like Shannon would be. With me at the helm and his luck staining me as we went along, there was *no way* this could go bad. I kept the thoughts to myself as I stepped out into the antechamber, where Greydusk was waiting for us. Not surprisingly, the demon looked the same as the day before.

"It's about time," it muttered.

But that didn't prevent the Imaron from sweeping me a surprisingly elegant bow. Court manners, I knew instinctively, though why I'd recognize them as such when I'd grown up in a cursed Southern town so small you could blink and miss it, I had no clue. *Movies,* I thought. Or maybe it was more inborn knowledge that Kel had mentioned, bred in my blood and bone from the genes I carried.

"Shall we?" I ignored the obeisance.

With unpracticed hands, I lifted my skirts and followed Greydusk. Gilder had gone at some point, leaving another hauntingly exquisite Luren in his place. This one was darkness with an inky river of hair and eyes that shone like polished obsidian in his dusky face. I swept past with less than half a glance; that was the way I had to roll here. In Sheol, I might find land mines everywhere.

Greydusk did not greet him, so I passed down the hall in silence. When we reached the imposing double doors, the demon paused. "Remember my warnings. Agree to nothing. You must bargain with her for sufficient freedom to investigate the city and find your friend or she will hold you as her benign hostage."

"For how long?"

The Imaron replied gravely, "Until your will is no longer your own."

That was an insidious thought. Sybella didn't need to move against me. She could just keep me here, close to her, gradually becoming seduced by the constant exposure to heady demon magick. Eventually, my will would falter, and given my performance at the Chasm of Despair, I imagined it wouldn't take long.

Our time's limited. Good to know.

I puffed out a fortifying breath and gestured for the demon to show me in. Instead, Greydusk threw open the doors and boomed in an impressive voice, "To the assembled august personages of the Luren court, I present to you Her Highness, Corine Solomon, the Once and Future Queen, now and forever more, the Binder!"

What. The. Fuck.

With an introduction like that, I had no choice but to put some swagger in my step. I entered the room bareheaded, chin high, and I was thunderstruck to find myself surrounded by Luren. The aura was dizzying, so strong I almost blacked out from the collective sensual overload, but the charm bracelet Tia had given me pulsed on my arm. Pain lashed up to my elbow, but it also settled my head. Likely it wasn't supposed to work that way, but magick never hit dead center where I was concerned. Things went wrong or backward; at the moment, I was grateful I could think.

This was Sybella's version of an ambush, then. In confronting me with the assembled might of her court, she'd calculated that I would buckle and I'd be her slave — one way or another — by the time I left this room. And without Tia's help, it might've gone down like that.

Beside me, Chance collapsed. My heart twisted with fear, but I couldn't show too much concern or they would realize how much he meant to me.

Instead, I offered a wintry smile. "It is a pleasure." Most of the Luren knew I meant I'd rather eat glass than make nice with them, but they did seem impressed by my fortitude. Who the hell knew how long it would last? I skimmed the room instead of approaching Sybella. "But do you truly mean to conduct our business amid such a multitude? How . . . egalitarian of you."

By her sharp sound, she knew precisely what I meant. "Guards, clear the room, save for Gilder and Lash."

In short order, the minions carried out her command. When the influence dulled, Chance stirred at my feet. Greydusk helped him up. I held myself stiff and still, conscious of Chance swaying at my shoulder. It had to be weird for him, hearing me described this way, even stranger that I'd stood against their charms. He'd found me clerking at a dry cleaners for fuck's sake, but it was no less bizarre for me, remembering that Greydusk had called him a godling. And maybe that was why he'd felt that "click" he tried to explain; it had been our mutually odd heritages perking up.

Greydusk stepped up on my other side, so that I had an honor guard of my own. I felt pretty sure he wouldn't let Sybella get within touching distance, and I wouldn't look into her eyes.

Fixing my gaze over her left shoulder, I said softly, "You did something to my pet. Not one day, and you've already broken your promise."

She hissed out a breath at the boldness of my sally. "You dare to call me oathbreaker, here in the heart of my strength?"

"Only because it's true. You promised no harm would come to me in your house, and yet my dog won't wake up. I *love* my dog. Therefore, I am upset. Worried. Hurt, even. And that is harm, by any definition."

Greydusk made a soft sound. I heard approval in it. Strength surged through me, surety. I knew how to talk to demons. I knew how to push them and twist them, manipulate and force them to my desires. It wasn't something I had ever learned, but I *knew* it, like the curve of my own cheek or how to breathe as I slept.

Shit. I really *was* the Binder. I had the old king's magick, along with my mother's. What that meant for the future, I couldn't guess. I could only steer with one unshakable goal in mind.

Save Shannon.

Or die trying.

"You are owed recompense," Sybella muttered. "You may ask one boon before our true negotiations begin."

The knowledge came to me in a barely heard whisper, like there was someone else in my head. *She wants your loyalty to the Luren, above all others, and your promise to raise them high when you break the castes wide open.* Alarmed, I searched for the knowing presence, but it fell quiet, leaving me with a pervasive sense of dread. Well, creepy whispers aside, I understood what Sybella wanted. And she wasn't getting it. I just had to buy some time.

"You will grant me one week's grace, as the time runs in this realm, to see the sights in the city and take Xibalba's measure. Greydusk will stand as my guard and guide. You will not interfere by means direct or indirect with him *or* me, which includes those under my protection." With a gesture, I indicated Chance. "That also extends to my dog, of course, whose health and awareness you will restore *at once*."

"Well said," Greydusk whispered with approval.

By his tone, I gathered I had made the agreement sufficiently watertight. I didn't need to keep her from scheming. I just needed this week before I made a true enemy of her. Right now, I thought she respected me. She'd expected a weaker opponent, more susceptible to her particular allure.

"It shall be done. Gilder and Lash stand witness." Sybella whispered then in demontongue, a spell that made my skin try to crawl off my bones.

"What—"

But before I could complete the question, Greydusk reassured me in a low voice. "She's removing the ensnarement spell on your mammal."

"Why did she mess with him anyway?"

"She may have thought you intended to use the creature as food and believed she was assisting you in rendering it docile."

"Oh." *Gross*. "I guess the Luren don't meet too many humans."

"Not unless they're summoned in sex rituals and those lucky few tend not to return to Sheol."

"Our business is tabled . . . for the nonce." Sybella's voice indicated she'd like to give me to her minions and let them do terrible, degrading things to me.

"See you next week."

Somehow I made it out of the room without revealing how much the encounter had taken out of me. Once the doors shut behind me, I stumbled, reached for the wall, but Chance was there. He was shaky, but together we kept our footing.

His expression was all confusion and raw wonder. "I've never seen you like that. You were . . . magnificent."

I leveled a shaky gaze on him. "If you say 'regal,' I'll punch you in the junk."

"You're sexy when you threaten me. But how did you keep them from putting you on your ass?"

Holding up my wrist, I said, "Tia's charm."

"Handy. I should've had her make me one."

I shook my head. "I don't think she can just whip them out. It's powerful."

Greydusk emitted a sigh. "Can we move along, please?"

"Absolutely," I said. "Your first mission is to locate me some decent street clothes. I assume people don't dress like this all the time?"

The Imaron looked amused. "Indeed, no. The lesser castes would be put to death for donning royal silks . . . and many of my brethren don't wear clothing at all." It gestured at its own form.

"Right. Well." This time I led the way. I'd marked the route he took, and the floor tiles made it easy to remember.

Greydusk excused itself to carry out my request. And I decided I could get used to this. When I stepped back into our chambers, Butch greeted me with a noisy yap and a lot of prancing in circles and whining. Then he got a good look at me and cocked his head, ears flapping. He growled.

"I *know*," I said. "I'm working on it."

Muttering about ungrateful dogs, I hunted up Chance's backpack and set out Butch's collapsible food and water dishes, then filled them. He set to with a vengeance. I guessed being enscorcelled made animals work up quite an appetite. When I glanced up from tending the Chihuahua, Chance was eyeing me with barely concealed amusement, tiger's eyes gleaming like topaz.

"What?" Then I realized.

Yeah, it was pretty incongruous for me to be doing chores dressed like this. I tugged at the gown that fit me like a second skin and was relieved when it gave. Otherwise, I didn't see how I could get it off. Under Chance's intent gaze, I stretched the fabric and then pulled until it slithered over my head in a sinuous motion that seemed . . . sentient to my jangled nerves. That left me standing in the demon-corset.

"Could you get my laces?"

He came toward me, dreamy-eyed with lust, with the easy grace that once rendered me boneless with desire. It still did, I realized, as he turned me. His fingers lingered on my skin as he loosened, loosened, until my breasts fell free in front. Then he cupped my waist between his palms, stroking the indent of skin, slowly gliding down to the flare of my hips.

I listed back toward him and his arms went around me. He canted forward, his pelvis nudging the curve of my back, and grazed my bare shoulder with lips that left a trail of fire tingling in their wake. It was exquisite. Unforgettable. He'd always been a slow, careful lover, but there was a leashed wildness in him too, a side he'd never

shown me. Now he did, his hands hard, as he pushed
against me from behind. It wouldn't take much for him
to bend me over.

He wanted to. I felt it in every particle of his body, and
I wanted it too.

"You've been teasing me for weeks," he growled into
my neck. "And seeing you that way . . . radiating power.
Christ, Corine."

I puffed out a shuddering breath. Maybe it didn't have
to be sex. Relief would clear both our heads. I couldn't
be sure it wasn't demon magick sparking our libidos, but
I'd always desired him, and it would be cruel to leave
him hanging again. I'd teased him in Kilmer, and if he'd
told me the truth, he hadn't been with *anyone* else since
I left him. For me, there had been a few men in Mexico . . .
and Kel, of course.

"We'll have to be quick," I whispered.

He never had been, and at first I hadn't minded his
measured lovemaking, the way he applied himself to my
pleasure like a science. At first I'd screamed and thrashed
and assumed he went as wild as I did. Only he didn't. He
never had. He watched and pushed me and he let go
when he was damn well good and ready.

Not this time.

"I don't think I could be anything else."

I spun in his arms, half naked, every inch a seductress
in these exotic rooms. I felt disconnected from my customary fears, as if the power that turned him on still
streamed in my veins. I was Circe and Aphrodite and my
will was absolute. He proved just how eager he was when
I unbuttoned the flat of his trousers. His shaft leapt into
my hands, and I took him in my hands with bold demand, tugging, stroking. Arching, he watched my face, his
gaze laser-focused on my mouth. I rose up to kiss him,
hotly, endlessly. Chance gasped into my mouth and his
heart slammed against mine, racing in time to his thrusts.
There was no careful judgment now. His harsh breaths
melted into groans, and then he peaked in my hands.
Lost to everything but me. He gave himself completely,
and I went wild with the surrender.

We fell together onto the bed, and he wrapped his arms around me. Fast and frantic, I came over him and worked to a quick finish against his trembling thigh. He petted my back with clumsy hands, his eyes dazed. His lashes fluttered toward his cheeks. Once, twice. I'd never seen him so utterly undone.

This Chance could destroy me. And he was irresistible.

By the time Greydusk came back, we had tidied up, Butch was done eating and taking his stroll around the patio, and I was decently covered in Chance's shirt.

The demon paused on the threshold, sniffed, and sighed. "It reeks of copulation in here."

Fire washed my cheeks. "Hi to you too."

"I suppose one must be thankful you have one another with whom to sate these urges. It would be disastrous if you succumbed to a Luren. Gilder or Lash, for instance."

"Disastrous for whom?"

"Everyone. If you take any native as your lover, you make him—or her—your consort here in Sheol, should you ascend."

"Anyone who tries to touch her comes through me," Chance bit out. "I need better weapons, demon."

His eyes were scary-fierce, primal in intensity; I'd seen the last of my hypercontrolled, calculating ex. That genie was out of the bottle for good. I suspected he'd always had these tendencies, carefully leashed, but something in Sheol—demon magick maybe—seemed to draw it out of him. Neither of us might be entirely ourselves, but I didn't regret what we'd done. Not when I felt so good.

Greydusk studied us for a moment longer and then shook its head. "I was afraid of this."

"What's wrong?"

"You've chosen him as your consort. That will affect his thinking. He can't help but respond to the ancient magick."

"Is there anything I can do to stop it?" I asked.

"No. Once chosen, the consort belongs to the queen until death."

"But I'm not the queen."

"Near enough." Greydusk thrust a package toward me. "Clothing for both of you. I'll wait in the next room." It turned with precision for such long limbs and went out.

"Are you all right?"

"Fine," Chance answered in reflex, and then he gazed at his curled fist as if surprised. "No. I'm *not*. Tell me you're mine. To guard and keep and protect. Please." The last word came from him on a pained groan.

I sensed it wasn't the time for questions or exceptions. Quietly worried, I took his hands in mine, stilling them. Unfurling the tight fingers. "I'm yours."

A heavy sigh slid out of him. "I don't know what's wrong with me. This place fucks with my head."

Just like Greydusk warned.

"I know. But we have a week to find Shannon and get out. I'll keep you safe if you do the same for me."

"I promise," he whispered.

Dark City

Before we left, Greydusk took us to the armory.

The guards at either side of the door were beautiful, like all Luren, but at this point, the effect was starting to wear off. I imagined our sojourn here was sort of like a supermodel convention. At first you're totally overwhelmed by the sheer amount of physical perfection surrounding you, and then slowly you build up immunity. You started wondering if any of them could sing or hold a decent conversation. And these demons looked like the answer was no to both questions; their eyes were pretty blank.

They let us pass because they had orders not to impede us, I supposed, or maybe Greydusk had some pull. Either way, I stood marveling at the range of weapons—not that I knew how to use any of them. But Chance was in his element. He tested several blades before choosing a set of gloves that glimmered faintly with magick. Since he usually fought bare-handed, the gloves would help. They weighted his blows with knuckle guards, and I was sure the spell would make his strikes more effective.

"Can you tell what these do?" he asked the demon.

Greydusk took them and whispered in demontongue. In response, the gloves spat fire and then ice. *How cool.*

"They augment your strikes with elemental strength. There are two effects on the gloves, but you choose which to use with a command word. Only one can be active at a time." The demon set the gloves down, and then whispered to Chance, I guessed to prevent activating the magic.

"I don't need a weapon," I said.

"Perhaps not. But what about an athame?"

Those generally weren't used for stabbing or fighting; they were ceremonial blades used in rituals, though some witches kept them sharp in case a spell called for a small blood sacrifice. I had the one I'd purchased in Laredo, but one from Sheol might help with my casting. It might also come with a price.

"Will it show in the human realm if I cast spells here?"

Greydusk cocked its head. "You mean will it be evident you've been using demon magick?"

"Yeah."

"Of course, Binder. The only energy you can access at this time belongs to *us*—and you shape it through your father's lineage."

"Wait—so I'm casting my mother's spells via dear old Dad?"

"Essentially, yes."

Crazy. But it was also making a mess of my halo. By the time I got out of here, the other practitioners in Mexico City would put me on the Most Wanted List. I shoved that worry aside and joined the demon where it stood before a polished, lacquered shelf. Blue velvet sheathed this athame; it was carved of smooth obsidian with ominous sigils etched all the way down the blade. The handle shone like sanded bone—I hoped it was ivory—and the symbols circled the hilt as well, which was banded in shining platinum. The whole knife looked old, well preserved, and priceless; it was also razor sharp.

"Sybella would allow me to take this?"

"Perhaps *allow* is the wrong word," Greydusk said.

I grinned. "She doesn't even know we're in here, does she?"

"Not as such. She did not expressly forbid it, however."

Which just went to prove how careful one had to be in

dealing with demons. If they did this to each other, imagine how much more thoroughly they could screw humans, who weren't used to crossing all the t's and dotting all the i's in a verbal agreement. I resolved to be on my guard.

Before I could talk myself out of it, considering the damage I might do to my spirit, I forced myself to think of Shannon. If this magical athame could help me save her, I couldn't afford to be squeamish. It would be selfish not to grasp every advantage. And that brought me right back to making evil choices for the right reasons. Stomach churning with dread, I snatched the artifact off the shelf. It seemed to nuzzle into my palm, not exactly a movement, but a vibration, eerily in sync with my heartbeat.

"The more you use it," Greydusk told me, "the more it will attune to you, and the more powerful your spells will become."

"I wonder why the magick still hurts here, if it's different than the energy I use in the other world." The human one. Which was already starting to feel far away.

I didn't ask in expectation of an answer, more musing aloud, but Greydusk gave it real thought. "Since I don't know why it hurts you to cast, I can't be sure, but I'd speculate it's because those channels—neural pathways—are already cut."

"What's done cannot be undone," Chance murmured, easing into his gloves.

Between the gauntlets and the black clothing he'd donned earlier, he looked like a beautiful enforcer, capable of the most delicious mayhem. Before, I'd always thought him elegant, not brutish, but his expression held traces of the latter. He wanted to hurt someone, and I wasn't sure why.

It's Sheol, a small voice whispered. *It's turning him. He doesn't belong here.*

This sounded like the same person who had explained about Sybella's motives. *Who are you?* I asked. But the voice didn't reply. Maybe I was going crazy.

With nod at Greydusk to acknowledge the explanation, which made as much sense as anything, I tucked the athame into the back of my pants. Fortunately, my cloth-

ing was nondescript, black as well, which—along with
brown—lower-ranked demons wore a lot. Darker colors
didn't show dirt and blood.

And that ought to indicate just how I foresaw the day
going.

Greydusk led us unerringly to the exit, and true to
Sybella's word, her people did not interfere. I wouldn't
come back here before my week was out. There must be
someplace safe for us to hole up while we searched for
Shannon. I'm sure the Luren knight expected us to make
use of her lavish hospitality, but I preferred staying out
of her reach as much as possible.

Sometimes I sensed eyes on us, though. We were definitely being watched. I whispered to Greydusk, "Can
you lose her spies?"

"I'll see what I can do."

Outside the Luren compound, my tension eased a
little. The whole way I'd thought Gilder or Lash would
pop out to restrict our passage or to scream "THIEF."
They hadn't. At least we'd cleared the first hurdle.

Our demon guide chose the most circuitous path I'd
ever seen, applying itself to my instructions. Soon, I was
hopelessly lost—and so were our pursuers. I hoped. Traffic teemed around us. In this way, it was a city like any
other. But the citizens—they were strange and shocking.
I didn't let my eyes linger long, as staring had to be rude
even in Sheol. Oddities gnawed at my senses, reminding
me forcibly just how far from home we were.

As if he sensed my unease, Chance twined his fingers
with mine. "Where to?"

At first I thought he was asking me, but then I saw his
gaze fixed on Greydusk. Who set the pace as it considered. I had no resources here, except the Imaron's knowledge and willingness to help. *Some queen.* But as Kel
had told me, the mark of strong leadership wasn't the
ability to do everything yourself; it was being capable of
recruiting key personnel, and I was doing okay for my
first day on the job.

"You could probably tell us," I said, as the idea
struck me.

Chance's expression brightened. "You want me to turn my luck to it?"

"If you can." He'd managed it in the tunnel, but we were in the city, surrounded by demon magick. In Kilmer, due to the demon magick that sealed the rest of the town away from reality, Chance had trouble with his luck. That shouldn't be the case here, though, unless those who took Shannon had known to shield her. Since Chance's ability wasn't one I'd encountered before, it was safe to guess they wouldn't have planned for him.

"I'll try."

The air crackled with power, and he closed his eyes. Greydusk watched with apparent fascination as Chance spun in place. It took several moments, but he eventually said, "That way, pretty far, I think."

"Still in the city?" the demon asked.

Chance shrugged. "How would I know?"

"What's the fastest way to travel?" I asked.

Please tell me it's not that Klothod-fueled carriage.

In reply, Greydusk summoned something like a pedicab, but it was pulled by a hulking, red-skinned demon. I noted the resemblance between this cabbie and Caim, which made it Hazo caste, lower in rank than the knight.

It growled, "Where to?" as we slid onto the box seat.

The Imaron thought for a second. "Toward the Barrens. I'll let you know when."

"People usually give me an address," the cabbie muttered.

"You'll earn your tip," I put in.

Redskin sniffed the air appreciatively, and said in a bass rumble of a voice, "Mmmm. Human. Lost, pretty thing? Want to—"

"Drive," Chance said softly. That was all.

That was all he needed to say. Something had shifted in him; and even though he didn't alter in appearance, he gave the impression of being larger and more menacing, as if he held power enough to snap the cabbie's spine.

"Yes, boss."

Greydusk regarded Chance with new respect. "What did you do?"

"Nothing."

It wasn't, but I didn't press. Neither did the demon, which spoke volumes on how much scary Chance was channeling. In a way I couldn't nail down, he was different here in Sheol. Not himself. From what Greydusk had said, he was becoming less Chance and more the consort. I didn't like the idea of him losing himself, but hopefully, we'd be in and out before he yielded everything that made him Chance. Once we got out of Sheol, he should return to normal.

Shouldering the poles, the Hazo took off, weaving into traffic with kamikaze intent. The other vehicles weren't like those in the human world. Some were obviously Klothod-powered, and others were pulled by demons. Yet others ran in a disconcertingly magic/mechanical fashion. The carriage next to us had a pair of spindly legs that didn't look strong enough to bear the weight, but they clattered on, running, running. It and reminded me of the legend of Baba Yaga's house.

We passed by a market with vendors hawking and customers haggling. I would've liked to have taken a look, as I could imagine the kind of items for sale in Sheol. But at Chance's direction, the Hazo ran on. It was incredibly strong and fast, and I remembered the terror of facing down Caim in Peru. More of the beasts I'd first glimpsed outside the city circled in the air above us. Greydusk had called them quasits.

"Left."

The turn carried us into a narrow alley between buildings. On the other side, the neighborhood deteriorated swiftly. In big cities, it was often like that. Two or three blocks could mean entering a different world. How odd that it would be the same in Xibalba. More twists, until I was hopelessly lost. These small thoroughfares were a warren of crumbling stone and dangerous characters. And you'd get a lot worse than mugged if you wandered off alone.

"Stop," Chance said at last. "She's nearby, I think. I should get a better fix if we walk from here."

Elated, I slipped from the pedicab while Greydusk

paid the Hazo. Into his shovel-size palm, the Imaron counted out a number of ivory disks. I guessed those were coins, but they didn't look like any I'd ever seen. The cabbie growled a farewell, leaving us in the Barrens. As he lumbered off, we drew some interest, but Greydusk discouraged it with a gesture.

"Who runs this part of the city?" I asked, noting its influence.

"It's neutral ground. Each caste controls its own territory with the exception of the Mhizul. We came from the Luren sector, which is called the Mirror."

"Because they're obsessed with them or because everything is shiny?" I asked.

The demon bared its teeth at me in an appreciative smile. "Both."

Chance had his eyes closed, circling. It wasn't exactly like the dowsing that witches did to find water. Instead the luck drew him in the right direction, which would in turn put us onto something that would help us in the case. For the first time, I wondered why he hadn't just done that to find his mother, why he'd needed my help at all. So I asked.

"I can't effectively turn it on people I love," he answered. "I tried when my mom first went missing. But it was erratic and my emotions got in the way."

"Would you be able to use it to find me if I was in trouble?"

"Not a chance."

Crazy, but his reply sent a thrill through me. Time to focus on the big picture, though. Chance got a fix and I trailed after him, keeping my purse tight to my side. Butch stared out the top of it warily, eyeing one demon that looked like it might be considering us for a snack. The Chihuahua growled and then graduated to yapping; his ferocity wouldn't deter this creature, which had the look of a deformed child with a big head and green skin. Through thin lips, it licked sharp teeth and took a step toward us.

"Do not interfere, Noit."

Was that the thing's name or caste? I waited to see

what the other demon would do. Beside me, Chance was ready for a fight. Since our arrival, he had become steadily more aggressive ... and it worried me. He'd never been the alpha-dog type, at least not in this way; it made me wonder if something in his heritage was reacting to the pervasive presence of demon magick. What would he turn into if we stayed?

"Not interfering. I sees things. Knows things." The Noit did a little jig at our feet, edging closer.

Greydusk took a step forward. "Be advised that you bargain with your life. Do you still wish to trade?"

Shit, it was going to kill the Noit if it didn't go away. That shouldn't bother me. It was a demon, after all, even if it was short and had a crazy-playful look in its muddy eyes. Without understanding my reasons, I put myself between them.

"Wait. Let's hear what it has to say."

"That may prove a mistake, Binder. The Noit are notorious for their mischief."

I ignored the advice. "Speak your piece, but stay away from my dog."

"Mmm, dog ..." The Noit stared at Butch for a few seconds, and then tilted its head back to meet my gaze. "Binder, binder, never find 'er. She's gone, gone, for a song, into the heart of where it's dark, and nevermore, forevermore."

Before I could ask any sensible questions, the Noit scampered off, cackling madly. Greydusk heaved a sigh. "I told you."

"Let's check out Chance's lead."

The split and bloody sun threw a queer, scattered light over the broken stones. I pictured Shannon here, as I had avoided doing up until now. She must be so terrified. If I knew her at all, she would cover it with bravado, but deep down she must be wondering if she'd ever get out alive.

You will, I promised.

It was my fault. I'd make it right.

Chance led us to a building constructed of strange red stone. It looked almost like blood and dirt, baked into bricks, but surely not. Even demons weren't that awful. Were they?

I cast a questioning glance at Greydusk. "What's this made of?"

"You don't want to know."

Oh, man. I imagined I could make out glimmers of bone in the mortar, and my flesh crawled. *I can't go in here.* Chance shoved open the door, less squeamish, and I fixed my gaze on his back. *It's for Shannon.* I'd gone through the caves and the portal, and followed a lizard-dragon-worm through the earth. What was an apartment building made of blood and bone?

Inside, it smelled. Nothing I could pin down, but it was . . . unpleasant. It made me think of dark things, musty rooms, foreboding whispers and cold fingers on the spine. I'd never encountered an odor that carried so many feelings before. But it was more than just the scent of the place—it was like moments had burned themselves into the walls, flashes immortalized in the chipped and peeling paint. The furnishings had mostly been broken or carted away. They lay in bits of wood and scraps of cloth, mementos of another time.

"What is this place?" Chance asked.

"Hard telling now. It used to be a club, but that was a long time ago."

I raised a brow. "A club . . . like with music and dancing?"

"Not so much. More of a special-interest group."

By the way this room felt, I had some idea what that might have been. I made a mental note not to let my focus slip while we prowled around inside. The revelations might scar me for life.

Shadows moved on the far walls—without a light source. Cold darkness stalked toward us. There was no time to think, only react. I'd fought these creatures in Laredo. Shades. They hated all life, human or demon. Once, I thought they must come from Sheol. Either way, someone had left these for us as a surprise. That likely meant we wouldn't find Shannon here at all; it was a trap.

And it was time to fight.

Burn It Down

Chance whispered a word—the command Greydusk had taught him—and flames flowered around his fists. The glow showed clearly how many we were up against, but it didn't faze him. He grinned in pure delight and then ran at the shades.

"Careful! If they touch you—"

"Don't worry. I'm fast."

And he was. That edge I'd been noticing translated to speed. As I watched, he danced around, just outside their range, burning them down with the power of his demon-fueled fists. Each blow sizzled and ate into the size of the shadow. Each time, he wheeled away, sometimes spinning, flipping, sweeping low. I'd never seen anything like it, and he'd kicked some ass with me before.

"Can you help him?" I asked Greydusk, racking my brain for a spell that would have any effect on these things.

Freeze wasn't cold-based; it stopped physical, kinetic motion, and these creatures were energy. So really, I needed some kind of drain or absorption spell, and I didn't have one. Even with Chance's startling prowess, we were outnumbered, and if he got hurt or tired, one lucky strike—

Fortunately, Greydusk did not seem worried. "These creatures are an inconvenience. We shall prevail."

That's right; he's a soul-stealer. So he might've absorbed some ability that would kick some tail right now. We needed it, as I still couldn't think a single spell that would turn the tide one way or another. They had no eyes, so blindness was out. In Laredo, they seemed to track us by heat—

Genius. I had a plan.

Beside me, the demon's skin boiled. Bone crackled. Joints popped. Shape-shifting looked horrendous . . . and painful. It wasn't an ability I would want, but if it could help Chance, well, I looked away. Accepted it. And pretended I didn't care at all what the Imaron did in our names.

Needs must. Devil drives.

I whipped out my demon athame and it responded with an excited buzz. The spell I wanted was deceptively simple and not one I'd expected to find useful. It was one of the five I committed to memory because I thought it might help us elude pursuers. I'd never envisioned deploying it like this. Bracing myself for the burn, I dropped my blocks and let the power come. It fell on me like a dark rush, a swarm of locusts chewing through my veins, and my head went dark and heavy.

Nausea rose in equal measure to the energy. Yeah, no question, this wasn't good for me. I pushed on, bringing the magick to my fingertips. As I cast, Chance destroyed one. Or banished it. A second managed to brush up against him, and he cried out. I knew all too well how that numbness spread, how fast the cold could pull you down. He stumbled back, clumsy.

I fought the tremor in my hand as I etched the sigil in the air. Fear would make me careless; worry would kill us all. I had to be resolute. I whispered the Latin word for steam and released the demon magick in a devastating rush. My whole body went weak, and I almost blacked out. Staggering, I rested my trembling body against the wall. *Shit, I'm not ready for this. I'm not trained. I don't know how much power to use or how much to give each spell. It's a wonder I didn't cook us.*

But my intent had been clear, so I produced excess

volume, not heat, and the room filled like a sauna. I'd hoped the shades would have a hard time finding us if we blended with the ambient temperature of the room, giving Chance an opportunity to recover and Greydusk the time to finish its transformation and wade into the fight.

For my part, I scrambled back toward the door. The steam made it impossible for me to tell what was happening, and it would be the height of stupidity to wander into it, giving a shade a chance at me. Better to hold still and trust in my people. My men would win this war for me. They existed to serve me, after all.

The moment I registered the thought, I froze, despite the heat washing over my skin. Damp heat. Sticky. And I was cold as ice. That couldn't have come from me. I didn't feel that way. I *didn't*. There was no war. I wasn't trying to win anything.

Just to find Shannon and go home.

When we had a free minute, I really needed to talk to the Imaron about what the hell it meant by "ascending." Clearly it was some kind of transformation, but would I become a demon or what? It was a little too murky for my peace of mind how the Old King had gotten his power over demons. The stories weren't clear. Kel had told me it came from the archangels, which meant it wasn't a bad thing, but if the demons were on board with my arrival—*some* of them, at least—then that seemed to call everything I knew into question.

Muffled noises reached me, but I resisted the urge to investigate. It took every iota of self-restraint, and it felt like forever before Chance stumbled out of the cloud and toward me. I reached for him since he was cradling his right arm against his chest.

"Numb?" I guessed.

He nodded.

"It wears off." I raised my voice. "Are you all right, Greydusk?"

An enormous shape lumbered into sight. Horrible. Monstrous, even, but the arms like swords gleamed with magick, darklight capable of destroying even shades. Whatever this creature was, clearly the demon had drained it at some point and gained the ability to take its form. And its power. Beneath my weary gaze, it slipped into its own form. It looked easier this time around, as if its body sighed a little with relief at being permitted to resume its natural lines.

"Well enough. The hide on this Swordwraith was thick enough that the drain takes longer. I told you all would be well."

Though I wasn't sure this would work, I gave it a shot. Not a spell whose forms and rituals I'd memorized. My mother's charms shouldn't work anyway, so clearly I was driving without a license, practicing demon magick here. Best to see what I could accomplish when our life didn't depend on it. Clutching the athame, I called the power to me again. It enveloped me, still cloying and unpleasant, and it tried to smother my head. I forced it down and out to my fingertips, where I held the blade. Then I whispered a single word and let it go. More delicately, as if it were a silken rope lowering an inch at a time. In response, a puff of wind swept the room, blowing away the remaining steam. This time I felt a little sick, but not on the verge of puking or passing out, as I had when I'd summoned the steam.

Greydusk nodded. "Better control. Do you lack training, Binder?"

Since it was on my side, I figured I could be straight with the Imaron. "Precious little. I haven't been able to access my mother's magick for very long."

"Interesting. There was a block?"

"No. I think her power was held in reserve for me in her pendant, but she died, and Maury had the necklace in his lair, so I didn't get witchy right away."

"So you came into the power late. I understand."

"We should wrap up," Chance said. "And take a look around before something else pops up."

"Agreed." I turned to Chance, waiting for him to find the path.

There had to be something of Shannon's here. Maybe she had been held nearby at first, and then they moved her. Or . . . *maybe* the shades had been posted as guards. She could still be captive in the building somewhere.

Spurred by that unlikely possibility, I prodded Chance, who still looked dazed. "Can you work?"

The chill effect just about froze your brain, so maybe he couldn't.

He closed his eyes and turned, but eventually he sighed and shook his head. "I'm not getting much of anything now."

"Because of the shade? Or because what was here isn't anymore?"

"Not sure. The feeling is fuzzy now and . . . far. Like it's moving."

"You mean they moved Shannon while we fought the shades?" My heart dropped all the way to the pit of my stomach.

If they knew to watch out for us now, it would be ten times harder to find her next time. They could ward off Chance's abilities, maybe. They'd move her and set monsters on us every time we got close. I saw the week going by in a flash of heartbreaking near misses, and I curled my hand into an impotent fist.

"Oh, Shan, I'm so sorry." The whisper slipped out before I could stop it, and I hung my head.

"Even without his gift, I believe we may find something useful here," Greydusk said. "Let's check."

It had a good point. Our enemies might have overlooked some clue that would lead us to them, directly or otherwise. So I cast the spell that turned my athame into a serviceable flashlight, and held it ready. It wasn't a weapon, but it would hurt if I shoved the blade in a monster—and I had no clue how the magickal glow would affect a demon if it was burning inside its chest. Maybe before the end of the day I'd find out.

With my light on, I could see that we were in the foyer of what might have been a magnificent structure long ago, albeit in definite creepy diabolic style. If demons had built their version of White's in the nineteenth century and then abandoned it to the roaches and rats for a hundred years, this would be the end result. I led the way toward a bigger room, passing through a tall archway into a shadowy chamber. But these were harmless shadows, created by my light and our movement. The familiar chill was absent. Some of the furniture remained: a chewed-up chair, a decrepit table.

"There were private rooms upstairs," Greydusk said. "If there's anything of note, we'll find it there."

"Have you been here before?" Chance asked.

"Yes."

Interesting. But I didn't ask why. I figured I probably didn't want to know, if the meetings had been as gruesome and depraved as I imagined. I crossed the debris-littered floor to the stairs, which were partially blocked with fallen stones. A dust-and-copper smell deluged me, making me wonder again about these bricks.

There was enough room for me to slip past if I turned sideways and took care with my footing. My companions were likewise slim enough to get by. Kel would've been too broad in the chest, I thought, even turned. My time with him felt like something I'd made up, a story or a wistful fancy. It was probably better if I let it keep slipping, though the loss felt sharp as icicles and just as chilling.

From above came the sounds of small creeping things. No threat to us, just pests or scavengers, but I couldn't *wait* to meet the wildlife that filled those niches in Sheol. Actually, not so much.

"Is the feeling coming back?" I asked Chance over my shoulder.

"Yeah."

Relieved, I paused to take stock. The second-floor hallway stretched before us, with six doors on either side. Meeting rooms, my ass. This had been a brothel, I was pretty damn sure. The open room below would've served as the lounge, where demon dudes picked up demon hookers, and then took them upstairs for a good time. Whatever the hell *that* entailed.

"Left or right?" I asked.

"Left." Chance sounded so sure that I just turned and opened the door closest to us.

And a wee angry thing tried to eat my face.

Fortunately, since it *was* small, I knocked it aside and

then crushed it under my boot. A wet squelch greeted my stomp, and then I shone the light to see what I'd killed. The animal was too squished for me to tell anything about it, but Greydusk just shrugged.

"It's a tuali. They're territorial."

Stepping over the tiny corpse, I moved into the room, where the wrecked furniture confirmed my earlier guess. There was a bed, sunken in the middle. It smelled like something had been nesting in it, probably the tuali. *Hmm.* Unlikely we'd find anything there, except stuff the tuali thought was cool.

So I turned to the bureau while Greydusk went over to the closet. Chance stood watch in the doorway to make sure nothing tried to whack us from behind. In each drawer, I found scraps of paper that might've been receipts at some point but now were just shreds, dry pellets that looked like droppings, and a few stray articles of clothing.

From the last one, I pulled out a whip. I knew it didn't belong to Shannon, but something like that could come in handy. Okay, so maybe I just wanted to tease Chance with it later. The situation was all kinds of fucked up, but if I didn't keep my sense of humor, I'd fall into a black hole of despair and never save Shan.

Greydusk turned from the closet, shaking his head. "Nothing."

The rest of the rooms went likewise, until we came to the last room on the left. Chance had been quiet up until this point, massaging his arm and maintaining a brooding silence. Greydusk opened the door and a host of spiders poured out. Only they weren't normal, household spiders. Which would've been bad enough.

No, these were the size of small dogs, like, say, the one cowering in my handbag, and they had long, excessively hairy legs, and the purple wizened faces of human babies that had been dead for four or five days. They chattered as they rushed us. I sprang back with a stifled scream and slashed at the ones surging at my feet.

Chance growled the command word and ice crackled around the dark leather of his gloves. He pounded them with lightning strikes and the guts spattered all over my boots. When Greydusk attacked, it was cleaner, as these animals could be drained.

I impaled one with my athame, and the light burned it up from within. It was horrifying yet fascinating to watch; the flesh cooked and shriveled. I danced away from the fangs as the dark, dried flesh dropped off my obsidian blade. The demon fighting beside me was slow in his absorption, and after taking one that way, it lifted its large foot and went with a more direct approach. I slid back to get out of the way.

As I moved, I stumbled over something. *Shit.* That one sank its fangs deep into my boot, far enough to pierce the leather, and the tooth grazed my ankle. It stung more than the slight wound merited, which told me I was in trouble. How much so remained to be seen.

In short order, Chance and Greydusk eradicated the infestation. Meanwhile, my ankle swelled and felt like it was on fire.

"Hey," I said. "How bad is it if you get bitten?"

Greydusk and Chance must not have heard me, as they'd started searching. Since the room was clear, I limped inside to see if there was anything noteworthy. My expectations weren't high by that point, but there was nothing lost by being thorough. Pain lanced through my left calf with every step. The boot felt like it might be cutting off my circulation.

Hang in there. For Shannon. How dangerous can those things be?

My eyesight sparkled. Dark streaks, as if I were peering through a filthy window. Worried, I leaned up against the wall and left the rummaging to Chance and Greydusk. They were fast but careful, leaving no inch of the room unexplored, as we'd done eleven times before. I had little hope it would be different this time.

Until Greydusk opened the closet door—and what I saw took my focus off the bite. Through wavering vision, I recognized it at once: a black backpack with colorful, feminine skulls. Shannon had been here. They'd held her in this room. Oh, gods and goddesses, with those spiders?

Was she even alive any longer? The way I felt, she might not be, if they'd bitten her. Even worse, maybe she'd been kept in the closet, in the dark, listening to those hideous things scuttle with the endless and permanent threat that someone could come—for no reason at all—and open the door.

"It's hers," I said. "Grab it."

I tried to take a step toward the pack, toward that link to Shannon, because I could read something in there, maybe get a clue. Find her. Save her.

But the stupid words the Noit had babbled echoed in my head instead: *Binder, binder, never find 'er. She's gone, gone, for a song, into the heart of where it's dark, and nevermore, forevermore.*

My leg buckled. I hit the dirty floor with it twisted beneath me, and I couldn't see. I heard Chance's voice cast in worried tones, and Greydusk's calmer reply, and then it all went away, as if through the water gate, and I became a thing spun in so many directions that I lost all cohesion, and went sailing into nothing at all.

I'm Not Quite Dead Yet

Pain.

Darkness.

Someone's hurting me.

My throat was too tight and dry to scream, but I heard it in my head. Echoes of voices chattered above me. Noise, not words. One of them was familiar. I wanted to reach for him. I couldn't. A fire blazed in my leg, eating into my muscles and bones. It stretched up from ankle to thigh, nibbling toward my hip, and my face felt parched and swollen. My eyes wouldn't open.

"Will she be all right?"

"I don't know."

More nothing.

The pain lessened after the poking and jabbing. I sighed in relief as cool hands stroked my cheeks. Whimpering, I turned.

"Does she know I'm here?"

"Hard to say. I'd guess yes, though."

I know, I tried to say, through lips as solid as wax. *I know you, demon prince with the tiger's eyes.*

Slow fade.

The next time I came back to my head, I could move it. A few seconds later, I unsealed my eyelids and blinked against the low light. Chance was asleep beside me, and I had *no idea* where we were. My dirty clothes were piled on the floor beside us, along with my wrecked boots. The room was small but neat, serviceable rather than ostentatious. Our bed had been built into the wall—or rather, it was a stone ledge with a mattress on it. Cunning design, I thought, and cozy with Chance spooned up against me. I touched his arm where it rested across my waist and his eyes snapped open instantly. He'd always been a light sleeper.

"Corine," he rasped.

I turned into his arms, and even that small motion made me dizzy. "What happened?" It was all a blur, and then before he could answer, it came rushing back. The former demon brothel, the spiders with dead baby faces, Shannon's backpack. "How long was I out?"

"After Greydusk administered the antidote, almost a full day."

"And how long did it take him to find it?"

"Eight hours."

So it had been over twenty-four hours, in demon time, since we found her pack. *Damn it.* My injury had cost us a day we might not have to spare. Angry with myself, I strangled a curse.

Gathering my resolve, I tried to sit up and failed. *Still too weak.* "How long will it take me to recover?"

"Do you not understand you almost died?" His features were tight with exhaustion and worry.

"I get it," I said. "I also know that Shannon may not have much time left."

If she has any at all.

"Corine," he said. "I know you love her. But *I* don't. You're the one I care about, and it kills me to see you go down this road." He stroked a hand through my tangled hair. "You're ready to sacrifice anything for her."

"Yeah. But I'd do it for you too." That shut him up, as I'd known it would. "Where are we?"

"Greydusk's place."

"Wow, he took us home with him?" Talk about going above and beyond the call of duty. Suddenly, it didn't feel right to think of the Imaron as "it" as if he wasn't a person. "Sybella must be furious."

Chance shrugged. "I haven't been out of this room."

"I'm sorry I scared you," I said quietly.

"It wasn't the first time. I doubt it'll be the last." A ghost of a smile chased across his face.

"I didn't do it on purpose." In fact, just the opposite. I had been trying to get out of the way, but in the confusion of combat, shit happened. Chance knew it as well as I did. "You didn't answer my question."

"Soon," Greydusk answered from the doorway.

"Seriously—" Chance began, but the demon didn't give him an opportunity to complete the objection.

"I can give you a tisane to hasten your recovery if you wish."

"If? Why would you even ask? Let me guess—there's some hideous side effect, like I grow horns or bark like a dog for the rest of my life." Butch raised his head from the pillow on a nearby chair and gave me a look. "Sorry, bud. No offense."

He heaved a particularly eloquent sigh.

"There are consequences for every action," the demon said. "As you well know, Binder."

"Lay it on me."

"The cost for a swift recovery of your strength is a year of your life, should you ingest this potion." The demon held a slim vial in one long-fingered hand. When he held it to the light, it swirled in shades of red.

Chance tensed. "How long will it take her to heal naturally?"

"Nine of your months."

I pushed out a slow breath, thinking. It made sense. If I used sufficient energy in one pass to heal that much damage, there had to be a cost. Nine months' time couldn't just magickally disappear; it had to come from somewhere. Whatever. In the end, I could make only one choice. The same one I'd been making all along, no matter how shitty the path before me. But . . .

"What's the catch?" I asked. "What you said doesn't guarantee I knock a year off my life span. It could also mean that I lose a year of my past—when something important happens—or I might wind up in indentured servitude."

"I cannot offer any warranty," Greydusk said. "All of the above are possible side effects. The ultimate payment results from the will of the potion's creator."

Which I have to deal with later. I often took actions that would cost me down the line in order to survive present circumstances. So be it.

"I understand." I reached for the tisane.

Chance caught my hand. "Are you crazy? Isn't there any way to narrow down the potential costs?"

"He's right," the demon said. "You should give this more consideration."

Implacably, I turned my arm so my palm faced up. Silently demanding. There was no merit in arguing with either of them. Words were no use after a certain point. I would not be gainsaid or advised by my men when I had not sought their counsel. Greydusk yielded to my stare without further objection, delivering the vial. Chance turned his face away as I broke the wax seal and downed it. It tasted of blood and heartbreak, burning all the way down my throat. My stomach roiled as the demon magick streamed into my veins, lacing my system with black wildfire.

At first it hurt, and then it spun me around, almost as powerful as the Nephilim blood, only instead of colors I saw darkness. Shadows and layers and whispers of gray, marking the demon, and Chance's hair, which had once only been raven black to my human eyes. Now I saw the hidden glimmer, like the sheen of oil in the sunlight, too subtle and deep for my formerly limited senses to discern.

I felt strong and fast and damn near invincible. Laughing, giddy, I leapt from the bed and demanded, "Where the hell are my clothes?"

Wordless, almost subservient, Greydusk fetched them for me. It was only afterward that I caught myself, a long way past the euphoria, and some part of me shook her head and worried and choked on words of caution. *This isn't you. You don't think of people as your servants. You don't give orders. You grew up* poor, *and you're not the queen of anything.* But that voice was small and boring, and I squashed it. Chance had a grave look about him, and I thought I might need a new consort if he couldn't learn to be more obedient.

That was a difficult and thorny issue, however, as I didn't want to ally with any one caste. I would raise no demon higher than another. That way led to unrest and eventual civil war. No, I would be better off with Chance beside me, even if his behavior became tiresome. He offered precisely the measure of presence and charisma I required in a mate. On my arm, he added consequence, as others would certainly know he was no mere human. I liked the fact that I had ensnared a godling; I dropped a careless kiss on his quiet mouth and dressed quickly.

"Bring me her bag."

"She's not herself," Chance said sharply to Greydusk.

"It was a risk of the tisane."

"*What* was?"

Outrage built inside me. Were they talking about me like I wasn't here? *Do they not know who I am?*

"What's happening to her?"

In another minute, I was going to blast one of them. The power gathered, and it didn't feel wrong anymore. It was dark and luscious in my bloodstream, like a black velvet throw, just the right weight to show I meant business. Magick flowed to my fingertips as my rage burned as bright as a falling star.

"She's starting to ascend."

Good. All this fucking around made no sense. Skulking? Hiding? I'd level this city, find Shannon, and then run the place properly. These demons knew nothing about fear as of yet, but so help me, I would *teach* them.

"What does that mean?"

I held the black fire, burning in the palm of my hand. Enough curiosity stirred that I wanted to hear the answer before I smote them for their impertinence. Greydusk turned to watch me, expression unreadable. And then he sank to his knees. Chance turned his head, his brow furrowed in disbelief. The demon used his unnatural strength to drag my consort down into a reluctant obeisance.

"It means the demonic part of her soul is on the rise."

"Explain," I demanded, letting the fire die. This seemed like something the Once and Future Queen should know. And since they'd abased themselves before me, my ire was appeased. After I heard the explanation, I would dispense an appropriate punishment for their defiance.

"You have doubtless been told that the Old King's power over demons came as a gift from the archangels," Greydusk said softly.

I inclined my head.

"What your source did not reveal, I suspect, is how they imbued the first Binder with that power."

"My patience wears thin."

"Long ago, there was a true queen of Sheol, named Ninlil. She ruled over the castes and all owed her fealty. Then the greatest of the archangels called her forth. On the steps of the temple, after a great battle, he slew the demon queen and bound her power to the Old King's soul. The angels gave Solomon other gifts, such as the ring of Aandaleeb, known to most as the Seal of Solomon. He used it to summon and bind Asmodeus, who had been Ninlil's consort, at which time we bestowed upon him the title Binder. Your line has carried it ever since."

"So . . . the more she uses demon magick, drinks potions fueled by it, the more she'll change. Become less herself and more the demon queen."

Since it was more or less what I'd have asked, I didn't reprimand the male. Yet. But he had to learn subservience if he was to remain with me. And under me.

"Rise," I said. "And bring me the bag. We need to find the girl. She's one of mine, and those who stole from me will suffer."

Greydusk obeyed with alacrity, as it should be. Once I had the pack in my hands, a wave of . . . something swept over me. It was soft and warm, aching, and I had no name for this feeling. The scene replayed in my head; it was a young girl—the one we were searching for—and me in a store, shopping, laughing over nothing in particular. She nudged me gently, grinning, and a lock of dyed-black hair flopped into her eyes. We'd picked out this bag together. All at once, I wanted to weep, but demon queens did not. Obviously the girl was mine, and that was why I wanted her back.

I ignored their stares as I unzipped the backpack. It had her things in it: a change of clothes, a toothbrush, some books, her netbook, and iPod. Oddly, they both still had power. I clicked through her playlist, wondering if she'd cowered in the dark listening to the music that drowned out her terror: "Fear of the Dark" by Iron Maiden, "Trains" by Porcupine Tree, "Don't Fear the Reaper" by Blue Öyster Cult, "Drumming Song" by Florence and the Machine, "The Weeping Song" by Nick Cave and the Bad Seeds, "Wretches & Kings" by Linkin Park, "On My Own" by Three Days Grace, "I'm Not Okay" by My Chemical Romance, "Cryin' Like a Bitch" by Godsmack, and "Last Man Standing" by Pop Evil.

At that point I stopped scrolling. Her music told me so much about her—or rather, it reminded me. A lot of it was old, a hallmark of her stunted childhood in Kilmer. Other bands were those she'd discovered since I freed her, and they reflected more of her personality.

Steeling myself, I curled my palms around the iPod, which I knew she loved. There would be a charge. If her time in this room had been as traumatic as I expected, I'd learn something. Sufficiently braced, I let my concentration drop and the pictures screamed into my head, and I became Shannon Cheney.

I'm bound, hand and foot. Someone shoves me roughly from behind. My iPod clutched in one hand, I tighten my fist so I don't drop it. This is my one link to safety. What the hell am I doing here? What do they want? These things don't talk to me. They don't tell me anything. Oh, God, I'm so scared.
　　Jesse.

I want him so much I ache with it. He's my first love, and he doesn't know where I am. And maybe to him, I'm just another weird, gifted girl who wigged out because I have a less-than-stable background. He thinks maybe I'm too young for him, like he's a dirty old man for being with me, but I'm not a kid. I'm not.

I wanted him from the first moment I saw him. But now I'm here in a nightmare I can't wake up from. Where is here?

Monsters skitter at my feet. Hideous things that are like spiders, only they're not; it's like they ate a baby's head or something, and they're so hungry. I wish I had my radio. Surely there are dead things even here. I'd wreck them all.

The bastard behind me whispers low in a language I don't understand, calming the spider things. They back off, permitting my faceless captors to shove me toward the closet. They've kept me blindfolded until now, and I still haven't seen anything. Stop talking about me.

A hard push launches me inside, and then the door shuts behind me. I land hard, slamming into the far wall. My face is bruised. Blood drips down my chin. Chains rattle as they fasten me in here. My hands are bound, but not my arms. With some careful maneuvering, I get my earbuds in so I don't have to listen to the monsters scrabbling at the door. I won't let them break me. I won't.

Maybe the music can take away this awful, endless pain—because I remember now. Passing through that water gate burned all the cobwebs out of my mind. Something was done to me—it made me forget. I don't understand it, but somehow, I lost all my memories of my best friend. And then I stole her boyfriend. So I probably deserve to be here. Whatever happens next, I've got it coming.

I fell out of her thoughts then. Maybe the music calmed her so that her mood leveled out, stopping the imprint. Whatever the reason, I lost connection. Tears caught me by surprise, burst out in a noisy rush. *Oh, God, Shan, it's not your fault. It's my fault. Everything is.* I couldn't shut off my grief. The sobs felt endless, and I couldn't resist when Chance pulled me to him. He rubbed my back, whispering in low, worried tones to Greydusk, but with so much of Shannon's terror and anguish in my head, it was impossible to do anything but weep.

It took long moments for me to cry it out. Chance pressed little kisses against my hair, holding me close. Eventually I mustered the self-control to explain what I'd seen. I didn't share Shannon's private thoughts, her guilt. That was my burden to bear alone, until I could find her and explain. She had to know I didn't blame her for anything that had happened with Jesse. In fact, I was happy for them. My own relationship with him hadn't progressed far enough for me to want anything but his happiness—and if he could find it with Shannon, then they had my blessing. But it tore me up to hear her beating herself up for the spell I cast on them, against their will. I accepted full responsibility for the fallout.

"Unfortunate," Greydusk said when I finished.

"What is?" Chance was still holding me, but he had a look like he was handling a crate of C-4 instead of the woman he professed to love.

Then I remember how I'd acted before I handled the iPod. Cringed. "God, I'm sorry. The potion—"

"Then you didn't see anything that could aid us in tracking Shannon?" the demon interrupted.

The remnants of Ninlil's power, passed down through the ages, flared at his presumption, but I stamped her down. I didn't intend to let her take over my head again. Now that I was forewarned, I'd be stronger. I wouldn't ascend and rule over Sheol. I would *not*. *I'm Corine Solomon. I run a pawnshop. And I'm going home.*

At least I knew the identity of the whisperer in my skull. I wasn't losing it.

"I'm sorry," I whispered to Chance again.

"It's all right. That wasn't you." But he still seemed . . . unsettled, as if I'd become way more than he bargained for.

I swallowed hard. "That was who I could become."

"That was . . . scary as hell. You didn't even see me. And the fact that I couldn't bring you out of it . . ."

Yeah, I got where he was going with that. It had taken Shannon's fear, Shannon's pain, to shock me back to myself. Yet I had been *immersed* in it. That was more powerful than someone talking to you, no matter how much you cared about that person. But I understood why he felt worried.

"You're faster than me," I said then. "And you've got the gloves. If you see me going darkside, knock my ass out."

He laughed then. "You say that like I *could* hit you."

"And there's no guarantee it would fix the problem," Greydusk put in. "You might only wake up in demon queen mode, three times as enraged."

"Okay, so maybe that's not the solution. Let's head downstairs so I can sort through the rest of her stuff."

"As you wish, Binder."

After having Ninlil in my head, the Imaron's instant obedience didn't feel wrong anymore. And that bothered me. Chance still wore a troubled expression, and when he let go of me, I got the feeling he'd love to put some space between us so he could do some thinking. I didn't blame him.

God knew I'd like some distance from myself. Only it wasn't possible. I had to live with everything I'd done and everything I was. Until the end.

Rock Steady

I trudged downstairs in silence, clutching Shan's back-pack. There were other items, the laptop, books, and articles of clothing. I'd handle everything, just in case, but it didn't make sense to sit in bed while I did it; I had to recover quickly. With any luck, I'd find a clue that would tell us what our next move should be.

Less than five days before I had to return to Sybella.

My one consolation was that Shannon had been alive in my vision, listening to her iPod, and the music player still had power. So it couldn't have been too long since they took her to the new location. There had to be *something* that could lead us to her. I'd find it.

Chance took off. Not into the city, but he stayed upstairs, making clear through his body language that I should give him some space. Though I regretted hurting him, there was nothing I could do. I *wished* his concern had been enough to drive the demon queen out of my head, but he could either accept me or he couldn't. I had no energy to spare for reassuring him.

Clearly I had been here for a while, but I didn't remember, so I took stock of my surroundings, inside and out. In Mexico City, I'd call this a town house, as it didn't touch the other homes nearby and there was a small courtyard out back. It was similar in design, in fact, to Tia's home.

Otherwise, in furnishings, design, and building materials, they were nothing alike. Not surprisingly. The Imaron favored neutral colors, tan and brown, and odd sculptures. I couldn't really be hanging out in a demon's house. Soooo surreal. But after everything that had happened to me, my brain didn't balk as much as one might expect.

Greydusk had a padded bench in the central sitting room, so I dropped down on it, opening Shannon's backpack. I pulled out each item and laid it beside me.

Toothbrush. She would've carried this with her for overnight stays at Jesse's, which meant they were sleeping together. The thought didn't even give me a pang; that door was closed in my head for good. Unlikely it would tell me anything useful, but I'd leave no stone unturned.

"Do you require anything, Binder?" The demon stood at the edge of the room, watching me.

From behind him, Butch padded into view. He tended not to want me out of his sight during adventures like this one. I picked him up for a cuddle and he rested in the crook of my arm, licking my cheek.

"Were you worried about me?" I addressed the dog first, not the demon.

Affirmative yap.

"Things are pretty fucked up, huh. Any advice?"

Another *yes* yap.

"Want me to get the Scrabble tiles?" Those should be in Chance's bag.

The dog wagged so hard he almost fell over. Another single bark. *Yes.*

"I guess I do need something," I answered the Imaron. "Do you know where Chance's bag ended up?"

While I had a better athame, it would break my heart to lose my mother's spellbooks. Until now, those grimoires hadn't been out of my sight since they survived the explosion at the store. They were, literally, all I had left of her. That old T-shirt of hers, along with everything else I owned, went in the firebomb.

"I'll fetch it for you." On returning, Greydusk handed me Chance's pack, and went on, "With your permission, I'll pursue some leads on my own. There are sources I

dare not trust in your actual presence but who might be
moved to part with information."

"Are we safe here?"

The Imaron considered. "The protections should be
sufficient against most would-be intruders. Don't answer
the door. Don't invite anyone in."

"That matters? I thought it was only for vampires."

Greydusk flashed a mouthful of sharp teeth. "Ah, but
the legends take their lore from us. It does, indeed, matter to the Dohan, the Drinkers."

Drinkers. There was no question it meant what I
thought. But apparently I had to be dumb enough to say,
C'mon in and crack open some A-positive. Of course, the
way I'd been going, I understood why the demon would
warn me against the obvious.

"Go on. I'll be careful," I promised.

Once he left, I felt relieved. I didn't want a witness to
my bizarre conversation with my genius dog. Some
things were too weird even for demons. I set Butch
down, alongside the scrambled tiles. He pawed at them
with adorable concentration, fumbling the letters with
his tiny paws. When he finished, I read:

Theres a bad spirit in you

Hmm. "Do you mean the demon queen?" He had
been in the room when Greydusk had explained how the
Old King gained his gifts, but who knew if Butch had
been paying attention?

Positive yap.

"Could you see her in me before?" God, I felt dumb,
though you'd imagine I would be used to this by now.

Two barks equaled *no.*

"So coming to Sheol changed everything. Awesome."

He went to work on the tiles again. New message. *Its
growing*

My blood chilled. "When? If I use demon magick?"

All the time

Every moment I spent in the demon realm, the more
power the queen gained over me. Soon it might be her in
charge all the time and me screaming helplessly in my
own head. Likely the demons had known—or at least

suspected—it would come to this. So the ones who
wanted me to do something to wreck the natural order?
They only had to get me here. It was an insidious scheme,
worthy of a cunning mind. If they could delay me long
enough, they won.

There was nothing I could do about it now, though.

"Thanks for the warning, bud." My expression must
have been hopeless because Butch nuzzled my leg until
I picked him up.

Then he licked my cheek. He only did that when
things got impressively awful. I stroked his spine in deliberate, dragging motions, and then scratched behind his
ears, which he loved. He forgot he was supposed to be
consoling me and rolled over to demand a belly rub. I
obliged for long moments, trying not to look too far
down the dark path ahead of me. When I stopped, Butch
stepped off my lap to curl up next to me. Being such a
smart dog, he knew I had work to do.

I put away the letter tiles and then applied myself to
the next order of business. I hoped Chance would brood
for a while. Once I started handling Shannon's things,
well, any wild emotional reactions I preferred to keep to
myself. Maybe I could salvage whatever dignity I had
left. I didn't brace hard; I just wrapped my fingers around
her blue toothbrush and let the images come. This time
the charge wasn't strong enough to pull me in.

Instead, it showed a fleeting moment, sparkling bright,
like a sunny day at the beach. Shannon leaned over the sink
in Jesse's bathroom in one of his shirts. As she brushed her
teeth, he came up behind her and wrapped his arms around
her waist. Nuzzled her neck, and she turned, smiling. The
toothbrush clattered to the sink and I lost the thread.

Nothing that can help me. But it was good seeing them
both happy. It offset some of the pain still swirling from
earlier.

Next, I tried the clothing, but there was nothing. Likewise with Shan's laptop. It wasn't the sort of personal
possession that lent itself to emotional resonance. Nudging faint guilt aside, I skimmed her e-mails and browser
history, hoping to feel closer to her. I wanted to know

what I'd missed about her life these past months. Pretty quickly, I formed a picture.

Chuch and Eva had helped her find a place while they rebuilt. One of his many cousins needed a roommate, and Shan fit the bill. She'd gotten a job selling clothes at the mall, which she didn't love, but it paid the rent. At night, she studied for her GED, and two weeks ago, she'd passed the test. She had an e-mail from Eva, congratulating her. In her DOWNLOADS folder I found a couple of PDFs from Laredo Community College. One contained fee info and the other was an admissions application.

Wow. I was *so* fucking proud of her.

And there were random notes from Jesse, too, showing the evolution of their relationship. At first just short and quick, uncertain almost, as if he didn't understand why she was on his mind. They got gradually longer, and then I read, *Dinner was amazing. And breakfast was even better.* That had to be their first night together. I felt like a spy then, and I closed the computer.

Where are you, Shan?

I wished I had the ability to connect with her, mind to mind, but I knew no spells that permitted it, only natural gifts. Some people were born telepaths, but I wasn't. Which meant I had to do this the hard way. *Fine.* With a faint sigh, I packed up her things and zipped the backpack we'd bought together. Afterward, I sat with my eyes closed, thinking, hoping Greydusk returned with a vital lead, as I had nothing, a galling admission.

Later, Chance came down to join me. I heard his steps but I didn't open my eyes. What he had to say wouldn't be fun to hear, but there was no point in putting it off. I steeled myself for a twist on the breakup speech. This time, accurately, it would be *It's not me, it's you.*

"Corine." His tone throbbed a demand: *Look at me.*

So I did. I owed him that much, even if he broke my heart again. This time, I didn't blame him.

"Yeah?"

"I don't care about the demon stuff."

I froze. Ran my fingers through my hair in stunned reaction.

He went on. "I don't even know who my father is. And it's clear something's happening to me here too. I love you. And I'll stand by you, even in this." His charming, disarming smile flashed. "If the worst comes to pass, if you ascend as the demon queen, I'll figure out some way to keep you happy, because there's no way in hell I'm letting anybody else take my place as your consort."

"Holy shit," I breathed. "You'd do that? Why?"

"Because I've seen what life is like without you."

"But you'd meet someone else—"

"Don't you think I tried? You were gone eighteen months before I came looking that first time. Until Min vanished, I had decided to let you go."

"For my own good," I muttered.

"Well, yeah. I dated. But never more than once with the same woman. I was empty. Broken. When I had a reason to find you, I did. I was so glad to see you, even under the circumstances. Because in that time, I never found anyone who clicked with me like you. Now that we're together again, I'm not leaving you. Ever."

"It won't come to that. I'll do better at reining her in . . . and I won't drink any more weird potions against your advice."

"I understand why you did," he said. "But your recklessness scares the shit out of me, love. Sometimes I think you don't care if you live or die. You play chicken with the universe."

I didn't—couldn't—deny it. Instead, I reached for him and when his arms went around me, I luxuriated in his familiar, comforting heat, the lovely cadence of a heartbeat that had lulled me to sleep in years past. "What's your last name?" I asked.

Like he would tell me.

But his tiger's eyes glimmered with amusement. "Yi, of course."

"That's your *mother's* name."

"She never married my father." He cocked his head. "I can't believe you didn't know we were teasing you. I mean, she hasn't told me who he is. That much is true. But I don't have a secret name."

So ridiculously simple.

"It was a running joke?" I ventured.

"I thought you were in on it too. Mom and I both did."

Heat suffused my cheeks. God, my naïveté when I started dating him had been painful. "Oh."

"We need to communicate better this time around."

I smiled. "We're working on it."

He kissed me then, but before I fell into the pleasure, an idea struck me like a lightning bolt. *The backpack. Shan had it with her when she was taken, and they let her keep it until they moved her that last time. If she saw anything at all during the kidnapping, the bag might know about it.* I broke away from Chance.

"I've got an idea," I explained, giving him a quick consolation kiss.

She always wore it lopsided, hanging on her right shoulder. So I went for that strap with an incoherent prayer. *Please, please let this work.* The charge was fierce enough to thrust me into her head, and I lost myself.

I'm walking to work. It's pretty far, but I don't have enough money for a car yet. Sometimes a girl from the store gives me a ride home, but I don't know her well enough to ask if she'll come pick me up. I'd totally kick in for gas. But car pool stuff can wait. It's just fucking awesome that I'm self-sufficient.

Jesse's coming to take me to lunch. A happy starburst, remembering. We've been together a whole month now. Which doesn't seem like that long, but the boyfriends I had before were such children compared to him. I love how he supports me. He wants me to go to college.

A dark van passes. I don't worry until it fishtails to a stop, blocking my path. I know how trouble starts, so I turn to run. They're on me in four steps. Pain wracks me as I'm stuffed into the vehicle. Bound. They look like ordinary men, except for their eyes. Those are dead. Bloodred. As the van starts, I tip over. Hit the floor hard. One of them smashes a fist into my temple, and that's the last thing I see.

*   *   *

I became Corine again, my head throbbing with Shannon's phantom pain. Chance stroked my cheek. "How bad was it?"

"Bad enough."

"Did you get anything?"

"I think, maybe. We'll have to ask Greydusk if he knows of any demons that manifest in possessing a human host by showing red eyes."

"It could point us to the right caste," he said with rising hope in his voice.

"Then he can start threatening to suck the life out of those who don't cooperate. I'm pretty sure that's what he's doing now, in fact. With less direction." Because he'd been willing to support me, I owed him complete honesty. And so I shared Butch's warning. I concluded, "If we don't find Shannon soon, this might be irrevocable. I'd understand if you changed your mind."

"I'm not going to. I fucked things up with you before. I failed Lily. I'll do it right this time."

I cracked a reluctant smile. "I don't think the relationship manuals cover this kind of thing."

"Since when did *normal* ever apply to us?" Chance rubbed his cheek against mine, and then nuzzled my jaw with his lips.

A pleasurable thrill trembled through me. The demon queen wanted to push him down and force him to serve. Demand immediate sexual satisfaction. I strangled her, but Butch whined, as if he could see the dark tendrils wrapping tighter about me. Before I could kiss Chance back or thank him or any number of interesting options, Greydusk slammed through the front door. By the demon's expression, one of great excitement, his errand had not been in vain.

"You learned something?"

"How astute of you. But before I go into detail, I must ask your help."

"What's wrong?" After pulling the gloves from his pocket, Chance drew them on and pushed to his feet.

The Imaron gestured toward the window. "Well. There seems to be a mob gathering outside."

Club Hell

"Come out now, or we carry you out in pieces!" By the roar that followed, this demon meant business. And it spoke so I could understand it, though the thick accent sounded Slavic.

More shouts followed—threats in English and demontongue—and unfortunately, I could understand the former. Something crashed against the house, and then a small boom followed. The door thumped inward, bowing on the hinges. We had little time.

"I guess some demons don't need an invitation?" I backed away.

Greydusk shook his head, making frantic preparations for our escape. I hoped.

"Who *are* they?" Chance demanded.

"They're minions, working for the castes who want to use you, Binder. Some would take you captive. Others would kill you."

"How did they find out you're working for me?" I asked.

"If Sybella has kept her end of the bargain, then I suspect it was the informant I spoke with earlier. He must have put the pieces together from street whispers and my rather pointed questions."

About Shannon.

"He wasted no time selling that info," Chance muttered.

That didn't matter. "How many?"

"Twenty or so. More will come."

"Do you have a back door?" I asked.

"I do, but there's no escape from it. The courtyard dead-ends in walls from the other houses nearby."

Chance thought for a moment, then said, "Can we go up and over?"

None of us wanted to fight twenty—or more—demons. Well, except the evil queen in my head. She was sick of running. She was ready to march out and smite them all. The queen whispered of lost and ancient knowledge, demon magick she could teach me.

Join with me, she whispered. *I can end this. You shouldn't be forced to flee like a fugitive. You carry royalty in your fragile human skin.*

For a moment I was tempted. But if I let her fight this battle for me, it would make her stronger. I'd fade even more. It was happening without my cooperation, so I sure as hell wouldn't embrace my own annihilation.

"Does the demon rope we used in the caves work in the opposite direction?" Like, could we slide up or would it make it easier for us to climb?

Greydusk seemed much struck by this idea. "It might, if I reverse the command."

Something smashed into the side of the house. That spurred me into motion. I grabbed Shannon's backpack while Chance shouldered his. Then I snagged my purse and stuffed Butch into it. "Let's get out of here."

The Imaron ran for the rope and met us at the back door that led out from the kitchen. Demons cooked. Ate. Tended gardens. *Oh, man.* I puffed out an exasperated breath; I didn't want to find kinship in them. But everything I learned about their world made me view them in a different light.

Out back, Greydusk had a tidy plot of land with weird, exotic flowers. The surrounding walls were of chipped gray stone. He had tied one end of the cord to a grappling hook and I backed up as he swung it in a tight arc before slinging it toward the top of the wall. It clattered and struck, then the tines reacted like claws, burrowing into the wall. Magickal, no doubt.

A whispered word and then, "Test it out, Binder."

Shouts came from close-by. Our pursuers had broken into the house. Fear proved a powerful motivator, so I launched myself at the rope. I'd never had the upperbody strength for climbing, but as soon as I touched the cord, it felt like I'd dropped a hundred pounds. I hauled myself up as if I weighed nothing. Reaching the top of the wall, I scrambled over into someone else's backyard. The lots were terraced here, which made sense as the city was built in the mountains. We'd passed through a chasm to get here, after all. The other two followed me and Greydusk whispered the word that let him reclaim his rope. On deactivation, the crablike grappling hook folded into a package the size of a large coin. Handy.

"Who can we trust in the city?" I asked.

"No one," Greydusk answered.

If I unleashed the queen, I could command anyone to render aid. And then enforce their loyalty. Eager to begin her quest for Sheol domination, she pushed at the box that caged her in my head. I whispered *no* again and she howled in rage. The chaos in my brain could drive me crazy if I let it.

"Well, let's move," Chance said. "There are demons who look humanoid, like the Luren. We should find a crowd and try to blend in."

"You could pass for Luren," the demon admitted, after a cursory inspection.

That was a backhanded compliment if ever I heard one. Chance's mouth tightened, but he didn't protest as I hurried alongside the neighbor's house and out the unlocked courtyard door. I emerged onto a different street. From here, I looked to Greydusk for leadership. He could decide where it would be best for us to hide in plain sight and plot our next move.

"One thing." The demon touched the corner of each of my eyes, and it stung. The feeling spread, leaving my irises prickly.

Chance drew in a sharp breath. "What did you do?"

"Camouflage. While you can pass on your own, she needs a little help."

"What?" I demanded, seeing the anxiety he couldn't hide.

"Your eyes are bloodred."

"Like the Dohan," Greydusk said, unconcerned. "It will wear off in time."

The Dohan were the Drinkers, if I recalled correctly. Which meant I had to feign a yen for human blood. *Awesome.*

"Thanks." I meant it.

"It falls within the agreement, Binder. I pledged to serve your interests. It does not benefit you to be captured by your enemies." He turned to Butch, just barely peeking over the edge of my bag. "Now something must be done about your mammal."

"Like what?"

By his worried yip, Butch shared my concern and curiosity.

Greydusk didn't reply. He merely whispered in demontongue until my ears burned with it. Magick built around us and Butch tried to hide. But he couldn't. Because in a swirl of darklight, he turned into something else.

And he had wings.

After a moment, I recognized what the demon had done. He'd turned Butch into a quasit. It was a revolting but sensible choice, as an imp might serve a demon, but any self-respecting Dohan would eat a Chihuahua, not lug it around and pet it. Butch couldn't even whine over his fate; his vocal cords were shaped differently now. A muted *chir* came from his throat. He flapped his wings in agitation.

"Don't be dramatic," the demon told the dog/quasit. "This wears off too. It is best for your mistress. Be brave."

That actually seemed to work, as the quasit settled, still in my purse, but you know, you couldn't build Rome in a day. *Time for us to move.* It was odd because we didn't gather a second look from passersby. Well, Chance did, from time to time, but that was due to his beauty, not anyone's suspicion. Some glimpsed my red eyes and gave us a wide berth. Apparently the Drinkers didn't limit themselves to human sources. Which made sense. So they could live on the blood of other demons, but maybe humans tasted like a really nice Shiraz, a treat they couldn't pass up.

Greydusk led us through winding city streets. In place of the split-faced sun rose a breathtaking moon. It was whole and haunting, larger than any moon I'd ever seen on earth; the edges burned with silver, softening all the ugly lines and imbuing Xibalba with alien beauty. For the first time, this land was not merely strange and terrible, and the dark queen in my head rejoiced.

"Is it not lovely?" Greydusk whispered, following the trajectory of my gaze.

"Gorgeous," I admitted.

"There was a well-known poet here who wrote, *Night in Sheol steals the soul.* I have forgotten the rest, but each time I see the moon, I remember that one line."

"For obvious reasons," Chance said softly.

I put my hand in his. For long moments, I just stared up. I didn't care about finding Shannon. I felt warm and languid, as if my skin soaked up that lunar light. I wanted to take Chance somewhere dark and private and spend hours— No, that wasn't me. The demon queen craved those things. The flavor of her desire differed from mine; it was deep and sharp, like a rapier lodged in my rib cage.

"I understand the land was not always so dark and cold. Barren," Greydusk observed.

Raising a brow, I prompted, "Oh?"

"There was a civil war. Our records are incomplete. . . . It was so long ago. But I imagine how majestic it must have been, before our forebears broke the world."

Damn. I'd assumed—wrongly—that Sheol was ugly because it was full of evil beings, but that involved a logical disconnect. Places weren't inherently bad; sometimes people populated them who did terrible things and it scarred the land.

"You have a destination in mind," I said to the Imaron, making a mental note to consider the implications later.

He nodded. "I know of a club where we won't draw attention. Mixed-caste parties often venture there for a night of carousing."

Demons, carousing. My spirit recoiled, and my instincts screamed this couldn't end well. "Take us there."

Greydusk did.

The walk took a while. I felt we couldn't afford to flag a cab and leave someone with a clear memory of us. I chose not to use my forget fog again because I didn't intend to use more demon magick than I absolutely must. Each spell gave the demon queen more purchase in my head, and she was already fighting me for control. Though I hadn't confessed as much to Chance, I feared how this would end.

I could lose myself here, forever. There might be no avoiding it.

The club was nothing like I'd expected. For one, the building was made of metal, which must create a hellacious echo inside. The segments looked to have been fused together with incredible heat; other plates had been riveted in place. It looked like a drunken remodel of a battleship, turned on its side so the stern pointed straight in the air. Over the door, someone had scored CLUB HELL into the rusty steel.

"Seriously?" I said.

"What?" Greydusk shrugged. "The locals like it. They think it's kitschy."

Well, it was that. Shaking my head, I followed the demon to the door, where he paid the cover charge for all of us with more of those ivory disks. Inside, it wasn't as noisy as I'd expected. Sure, there was music, but it was more the torch variety. An enormous red-skinned Hazo female crooned from the stage in a surprisingly lovely voice. Which went to prove, you shouldn't judge by appearances.

Just inside, the demon whispered with the host, and then he showed us to a private room. More accurately, it was a round niche with a booth in it, covered by a folding screen. I slid inside and Chance flanked me. The Imaron chose to slide in the other way, leaving plenty of room between us. In contrast, Chance settled against my side, an arm around me, and Butch flapped his brand-new wings. He made a delighted noise when he discovered they would, in fact, lift him off the ground. Soon we had a quasit-Chihuahua swooping around our heads. Which was just what the day needed.

"Come here often?" I joked.

"Sometimes," Greydusk replied. "This is a good place to do business."

That didn't make a lot of sense. At first. But when the demon lit the taper on the table, all sound from the outside ceased, one of the coolest tricks I'd ever seen.

"Magickal?" I turned the fat white candle in my hands. "How's it made?" Then I read his expression and supplied, "Let me guess—I don't want to know."

"You catch on quick."

The demon ordered drinks using a magickal panel on the wall. By tacit consensus, we waited until the server had come and gone. It hit me then. With this illusion, Greydusk had answered the question I had about the caste with red eyes. I looked like one of them. Quickly, I filled the Imaron in on what I'd learned from handling Shannon's things, including the detail about her red-eyed captors.

"This helps immeasurably," the demon said, once I finished.

Chance frowned. "Were they manifested Dohan who took Shannon or—"

"Spirits who had been summoned in a blood ritual?" Greydusk completed the question. "Since the Drinkers look human in their natural form, it's hard to say. It would take a soulstone to transport them, and those take an incredibly long time to manufacture."

"In a *factory*?" Chance asked, aghast.

The demon shook its head. "In a magickal lab, though we have factories for mundane goods. At one point, the Birsael owners tried to enslave the Noit to work in them, but they only broke the machines and ran amok."

"So they were probably humans, possessed by Dohan?" I guessed, steering us back on track before Chance pursued the idea of that goblin creature working an assembly line. I sympathized; I was intrigued too.

Pondering, I remembered that Greydusk had said Maury was Birsael, of the Bargainer caste. Coupled with this new information about factory ownership, did that mean he came from the merchant class? And perhaps, despite parental objections, he'd run away from home to lead a more glamorous life. Despite myself, I smiled at the irony. Some things were constant, even between disparate species.

"I suspect so. They would have taken her to the nearest natural nexus."

I nodded. "To draw me here." —

"Precisely so."

"At least we have a place to start," Chance put in. "If the Dohan took Shannon, you can check into their holdings, places they'd hide a hostage."

I flashed him a grateful look, glad that his methodical mind was still ticking over the angles. He'd always been good at that.

"That presumes they still have her," Greydusk replied.

Toying with my drink, I asked, "Why wouldn't they?"

"I wonder if when they moved her, it was more along the lines of trade."

"Someone else has her now?" Chance asked.

"Perhaps. The lead that I ran down this evening suggests as much. If the Dohan took Shannon, they received a better offer today and handed her off."

"To whom?" Panic clutched at me with spidery fingers.

Greydusk looked grave. "The Hazo."

That struck me as a worst-case scenario. Their knight had reason to hate me more than most. Caim was nursing a grudge, and now he had my best friend. Squaring my shoulders, I told myself, *You beat him once. You can do it again.*

But this is his home ground. I recognized the voice, so

smooth and seductive. The demon queen had found a way to get her thoughts outside the mental prison I'd built for her. *Free me, so I may raze your enemies. We are one, Binder. The Knights of Sheol have been permitted too much freedom for too long. They grow impetuous and insolent. They need a queen.*

"But not me," I said aloud.

Chance and Greydusk glanced at me, but neither asked what I meant. They both seemed to realize I was talking to the bitch in my head. Chance's mouth tightened, but the demon acted as if it was natural to converse with long-dead demon queens. *Only in Sheol.*

Join with me, Binder. Your companions will die if you do not.

"I can protect them," I protested.

Chance touched my hand lightly, drawing me out of the argument of which he could hear only my half. I'd be lucky as hell if we lasted another day at the rate I was going.

"So the Hazo traded the Dohan for Shannon." Chance reminded me where we'd been before I wandered off mentally.

The Imaron inclined his head. "Or so my informant led me to believe."

"Could it be a trap, a play from Caim to draw me out?"

Greydusk shrugged. "Possible but unlikely. The Hazo are not known to be strategists. They prefer to resolve their grievances in direct confrontation."

I thought about that. "Which means getting his hands on Shannon and putting word on the street is how Caim would proceed if he wants a rematch with me."

Greydusk nodded. "Exactly."

"Do we have to worry about him tracking us?" I asked.

The Hazo Knight had tasted my blood back in Peru. I wasn't sure what that meant in relation to demon magick. For all I knew, he might be able to use that memory of my taste to dispatch a goon squad to our location.

"Does he have samples of your hair, blood, or . . . other bodily effluvia?"

I shook my head. "Not that I know of. Unless blood, once tasted, stays in the demonic digestive system?"

"Er, no. It would be quite difficult for him to home in on your location. Xibalba teems with magick, which will retard efforts to find you."

That was good news. The mob who appeared at his house ran us down on regular street gossip. If we laid low and kept moving, they couldn't track us.

"And Shannon," Chance said grimly.

"That's why I didn't suggest it," Greydusk said, in agreement. "While the Binder has considerable power, brute force cannot winnow out a minute trace from the swirling morass of magickal energy that makes up the Vortex."

"You mentioned that in passing before. I saw it . . . but what the hell is it?" I propped my chin on the table and drank . . . whatever he'd ordered. It tasted like lemonade with a bit of a kick.

Greydusk put on his lecturing face. "Every demon has some ability to work magick. His position in the caste determines how powerful he is. The amount of magick done inside the city limits contributes to the protective field that prevents monsters from attacking the walls. It also keeps the outcast Xaraz from attempting to return, once they've been exiled."

"It's like a force field?"

"Rather."

"How does it work?" Chance asked.

"For every spell cast in Xibalba, the Vortex steals a small portion of the energy to sustain itself. Not enough to affect the outcome of the casting."

"And split among so many demons, nobody notices the drain," I guessed.

Chance said, "So it's kind of like a toll."

"Near enough. But what protects us also makes it all but impossible to successfully use scrying or seeking spells within the city limits."

"But my luck still works," Chance murmured. "Sort of."

Greydusk pondered for a moment, likely remembering how we'd tracked Shannon. "I'll wager you get some interference from the Vortex, but since what you do isn't magick per se, there's no cost."

"We need a plan," I said then.

"Agreed. Caim will be fortified and ready for you." Greydusk drummed long fingers on the table, thinking.

"A frontal assault against the warrior caste sounds like suicide," Chance muttered.

"Perhaps we can deal with the Dohan first," the demon suggested. "And turn them against their allies."

Sitting forward, I rested my elbows on the table. "Tell me more."

Hungry Like the Wolf

"The Dohan prize one thing above all else." When Grey-dusk paused significantly, I knew I wasn't going to like where the conversation went. "They rarely get to experience it, however. The number who are permitted to respond to blood rituals are few. It's only the honored, the chosen."

Chance tensed. "What are you suggesting?"

"A simple commodity exchange."

"That's our blood you're talking about," I snapped.

The demon shook its head. "Not yours, Binder. His."

"Why not mine?"

The Imaron sighed as if I were dense. "Blood rituals comprise the most powerful spells in Sheol. You can't risk that the Dohan would use yours to enslave you, rather than drink it. All the castes want you to align with them, elevate theirs above the others. Ninlil would sometimes pick a favorite and that caste had dominion. She did it because she was mercurial and cruel and it amused her to see them clamor for her favor."

Those were good days, the demon queen whispered wistfully in my head.

"Which means you want Chance to feed them. No."

"What else do you have to offer as payment?" Greydusk asked coolly. "Thus far, I have spent my own money on this endeavor with no guarantee of recompense."

Before I could stop her, the queen snapped, "You are honored to serve me, Imaron. You are fortunate I do not remove your head for such impertinence."

"Ah. I am reminded, now, why I serve."

"I'll do it," Chance said.

I touched him on the thigh. "Not happening. Nobody's bleeding for me. If I give my blood, they'll drink it in my presence. I'm *not* letting them store it for later use. And if they try to double-cross me, I'll set the queen on them."

She growled in anticipation, pressing against her bonds, and this time it was all I could do to contain her. The mere promise of freedom and my body for her use? Her excitement pounded in my head like tribal drums.

"Are you sure you wish to pursue this path, Binder?"

"It's the only currency I have."

"The Dohan may claim to own your especial favor later," Greydusk warned, "if you choose to feed them from your own veins."

"They can claim whatever they wish. Let them try to enforce it." I didn't realize it until the icy words left my lips, but the dark lady was whispering them along with me in my head.

Now I wasn't sure where the sentiment had come from, where I ended and she began. *Oh, Shannon. What have I done?*

I finished my drink. Afterward I remembered Greydusk telling me that food and drink consumed here would strengthen her hold on me. But we hadn't packed much from the human world, so I hoped my self-control was sufficient for the time it would take to get the information we required from the Dohan, maneuver on what they told us about the Hazo plans and their stronghold, and then execute our final move by liberating Shannon from the warrior caste. Oh, and then there would be Sybella and the Luren to deal with, and then I needed to devise an exit strategy.

No problem.

Okay, maybe a few.

The Imaron blew out the candle and led the way out of Club Hell. He wove a neat path through the writhing bodies. Butch flapped in our wake; the pseudo-quasit flew like a drunken bat and nearly slammed into the top of a demon's head several times, but he appeared to be having fun for the first time since our arrival. That counted for something, so I didn't yell at him to get down. Of course, if the spell wore off in midflight, I'd have a very sad dog on my hands.

On the street, the night had gotten colder as the moon rose, as if it streamed icy breath down toward us. I shivered and Chance drew me against his side. He laid a gentle kiss against my hair.

"Why wouldn't you let me help you?"

I knew what he meant. And it was complicated. I mean, I'd let Kel give his blood to the witch in Catemaco. But it felt different with Chance. I could accept it from Kel because it was his job. He'd been assigned to protect me, and he'd chosen a compact with the witch as part of his orders. I also thought Kel could protect himself from harmful spells. So maybe that was it. Chance seemed more vulnerable, even less at home in this fucked-up world than I was. I had to look out for him.

Greydusk pulled a little ahead of us as he walked, scouting, I suspected. If there was trouble, he would loop back and let us know. In the meantime, it permitted us to talk on the way to meet the Dohan. I wondered what they'd make of my eyes.

"I don't want you hurt because of me," I answered at last. "You know how you said it kills you to see me taking crazy risks? I feel the same way about you."

"You do?" Some of the tight, injured pride faded from his face.

"Yeah. God, Chance, you were the first guy I ever loved. You'll probably be the last."

"I want to be," he whispered.

A dark feeling came over me then. Like I could wrap him up in my arms, but it wouldn't be forever. No matter how much I wanted it, or how much I believed in his feelings. He was one man I couldn't keep.

Somehow, I pushed past the foreboding and blamed it on the demon queen fucking with me. I found the strength to tease. "You want it all with me, huh? House. Kids. The whole nine?"

Honestly, I expected him to panic. Instead, he stepped closer and in instinctive response I pressed into his chest. He wrapped his arms around me. Demons surged around us, muttering about uncontrollable Luren urges, but half of their ire contained an edge of envy. At least that many wished they were in Chance's arms instead of me, even here, where beauty came in forms so powerful that it doubled as a weapon.

He brushed my lips gently with his and said, "Yes." Another kiss. "Yes." Yet one more, this the deepest and longest of all. "And again, yes."

"Did you just propose?"

He smiled. "Technically, I think you did."

"But I was kidding."

"Then I'll have to do it right . . . at a better time."

If we made it out of Sheol, I looked forward to that day.

He went on. "Is that what you want too? A future with me?"

The old Chance had never been so direct with his questions or so plain in his intentions. I believed that he'd changed—or maybe it was more accurate to say he'd come back to the way he'd been with Lily, instead of the broken, guarded man he had been with me. On a street in Sheol wasn't where I'd have chosen to have this conversation, but a throwaway remark got us here. I wouldn't blow him off when he'd put himself out there.

"Yes. I love you, Chance." It was time to say the words because he'd done what he set out to do—win my heart again. I was his, as much as I ever had been. Hell, the guy had stuck by me through this, through some super-crazy shit. It couldn't have been awesome to learn I had a demon queen rattling around in my head, but he wasn't running. He could've. Not home, maybe, but he could've said, *Okay, this is just too weird. This is where I get off the crazy train.* But no, he took some time to process and then came back for more.

With more than a little regret, I broke away, as I wanted to make out with Chance for about an hour, but I didn't trust those urges. They might not belong entirely to me. The queen cackled quietly. *Can you trust your feelings at all, Binder? Maybe I'm making you love him too.*

"That's bullshit," I said aloud.

Chance glanced at me, but he knew what was going on. His mouth tightened, but he didn't complain. *How much of his patient understanding belongs to him,* the queen wondered, *and how much to my consort?* This time I ignored her. Sighing, I hurried to catch up with Greydusk. Chance followed, his steps quick and light.

"All clear?" I asked quietly.

The Imaron nodded. "So far, so good. We have a clean run to the Dohan complex."

As I recalled, each caste had territory in the city. "Where are we now?" Presumably his house sat within the boundaries of the Imaron sector, but Club Hell had been open to all castes, so it made sense that it would lie in neutral ground, so this must be . . . "The Barrens?"

"Very good," he approved.

Chance asked, "How far?"

"About an hour's walk from here. There won't be much foot traffic once we leave the Barrens."

"Will we be crossing through other caste territories on the way?" Man, I wished like hell I had a map. Or a guidebook. Or both.

"So we shall."

"Is it dangerous?" Chance had his hands in his pockets, no doubt readying his gloves.

"Best to be on your guard."

And so he slipped them on, flexing his fingers to ensure the perfect fit. I watched him, aching with regret, and I didn't know why. The demon queen laughed softly, mockingly, but she didn't speak. For the first time, I wished she would. Her insights might help us. Or destroy me.

Probably both.

"There will be checkpoints at each border," Greydusk explained as we walked. "If we were in a sanctioned cab, we'd slip right past because for good or ill, people with the money to pay avoid scrutiny. It's assumed that if you can afford the fare, you have business in that zone."

I thought of how homeless people got hassled in up-scale neighborhoods. "Demons have that in common with us."

"I imagine that's an uncomfortable realization," Greydusk observed.

"To say the least."

"Would it be smarter to take a cab?" Chance asked.

"It would be faster."

I noticed the demon didn't say safer. There was a risk that instead of taking us to our destination, the cabbie would deliver us to someone who had put a price on our heads, if he saw through our makeshift disguises. So really it came down to speed versus caution and by the way they looked at me, I needed to make the decision.

"Call a cab," I said. "The faster we reach the Dohan, the quicker we get Shannon."

"I have a better idea," Greydusk said. "If we care more about speed than running unnoticed—"

"We can take the Klothod carriage," I finished.

The demon was already setting down the cube in the street, whispering the control words, and then whipped the vial out. In another couple of seconds, we clambered in. My skin didn't crawl this time. And that bothered me. A lot.

Greydusk said, "This conveyance is conspicuous. But we won't be stopped. And I suspect you want to reach the Dohan more than you wish to be discreet."

"You got that right," I muttered.

"Then we're off."

The ride was . . . memorable. At this time of night, there was little traffic, and the pedestrians stopped to stare. Anyone who questioned them would get a detailed answer, I thought, but no matter now. I was committed. I had a blurred impression of the checkpoints, where demons watched us pass but did not attempt to interfere with our progress. As Greydusk had said, anyone who could afford such a contraption was obviously powerful and not to be crossed.

At the Dohan compound, he spoke the command word again and the vehicle stopped. I hopped down, impatient, as the demon put away his unnerving toys. Pain surged in my head, a break, and then . . .

Shaking my hair out of my face, I decided it was not suitable that I should wear it loose. It decreased my dignity to have it flapping in the wind. Yet the Dohan would give me the information I needed. Or I would leave this place a smoking ruin.

I turned my gaze on my consort. Despite his lack of proper training, he stepped forward and offered his arm. I did not thank him, but I made a mental note not to whip him today.

Greydusk strode toward the front gate. He showed no trepidation, which made him a worthy minion. In the new regime, I would permit him a place at my feet. I might even raise him up as the Knight of the Imaron caste. Such things had been done, of course, but never without the support of the queen.

The demon touched a glowing panel. A voice responded, "Who seeks an audience with the Dohan?"

"Her Highness, Corine Solomon, the Once and Future Queen, now and forevermore, the Binder."

That was a proper introduction. I offered an approving nod, and the Imaron swelled with pride. In so many ways, my kin were like helpless children, desperately in need of a firm hand. Fortunately for them, I had returned at long last. Soon enough, I would set my realm to rights.

To their credit, the Dohan did not keep us waiting. While I might not wear a crown—yet—they knew better than to alienate me. Despite their appetites, the Drinkers were cowards when it came to confrontation. Even trapped in this human vessel, I could still wreak a most satisfying havoc. They wouldn't risk my anger.

The gate swung open, and within awaited an honor guard. They fell in around me, but they were not a threat. We all knew it. I permitted them to encircle me because

I could have killed them all. I half wanted to make an example of the nearest Dohan foot soldier, but sometimes it was better to leave the danger as potential to be realized.

They escorted me through a dark and exotic garden and down the gilded hallways to the receiving room, where the Knight of the Dohan awaited. He was a slight male with a goatee, long nails, and bloodred eyes. He dressed for effect, all in black. And when he saw me, he fell to his knees. The rest followed suit, including the six who had escorted me from the front gate. I let the silence build. Left them on their knees. Let them remember the taste of terror thickening their tongues. Let them remember what it meant to displease me.

Then, when the fear had reached paralyzing levels, I said coolly, "Rise."

The Dohan failed to do so with their customary grace, limbs stiff from kneeling on the hard stone floor. A smile curled my lips, and one took a step back. I lifted a brow. The knight cleared his throat and then gestured for the room to be vacated. It was reassuring to learn they had not lost all wisdom, or the lessons I'd taught in ages past.

"My queen," Azon whispered. "So the stories are true. You are risen."

I inclined my head. "Long have I been bound to the Solomon line, and at last it comes full circle. I return. Choose your course, Knight of the Dohan caste. You may follow me . . . and receive my favor. Or I will crush you here and now."

It was not a choice. I never gave true choices. That would offer my subjects the erroneous idea that they had any control over their futile, wretched lives. And in Sheol, I held all the power.

Behind me, the Imaron and my consort kept silent. Their behavior pleased me. If either one dared put himself forward, I'd have executed him on the spot. They had gotten away with such behavior in private because I needed them for the time being. In public, my response to presumption never varied.

"There is only one answer," Azon said reverently.

"You own us, my queen. Simply tell me what you would have and I shall see it done."

The human girl scrabbled weakly, but I pressed her to silence. She'd had some ridiculous plan of offering her blood to gain their cooperation. I would never stoop to bribery. My will was sufficient to get what I wanted. It always had been. Like a worm, she squirmed at the back of my mind, too weak to wrest control from me.

"You will tell me everything about your business with the Hazo."

The Demon Queen

It was a beautifully illuminating discussion. Afterward, I demanded accommodations suitable to my station, and I loved watching them scramble to please me. The Dohan had a style all their own, pretentious but elegant. The reason I had never favored them, however, came clear to me as I passed through a corridor swarming with quasits. The Drinkers were all too fond of the little pests.

"I suspect we have an answer to the question as to who was spying on us," the Imaron said to my consort.

The idea of anyone daring to invade my privacy made me want to have everyone in the compound whipped. I was appeased when they put me in a grand suite, the nicest the complex had to offer. As ever, Greydusk guarded the doors while I explored the bedchamber.

Shortly after I retired to organize my schemes, my quasit turned into a small mammal. I stared at it, wondering what I was doing with such a creature. I approached with interest, but it snarled and tried to bite my fingers. I drew my hand back to kill it, darklight coiling in my palm, but my consort drew my attention with a soft clearing of his throat.

"Is there some way I can serve you, Highness?" The proper subservience in his tone soothed me.

I skimmed him from head to toe. He was . . . beautiful.

I understood why I kept him close; even the Luren lacked such pure physical perfection. And that made me ... curious. He wasn't fully human. Of that I was sure. I flicked my vision over to the astral and surveyed him. His corona possessed the most intriguing edge.

A blink restored my normal sight, and I stalked toward him. To his credit, he stood his ground, head bowed. He didn't make eye contact, which would've enraged me. He was everything I wanted in a male. I would keep this one ... forever.

"Are you mine?" I asked, low, knowing the answer already.

"Completely." His voice thrummed with conviction.

And oh, I liked it.

"So I may do anything I wish with you?"

"Anything."

I didn't need his invitation, of course. He belonged to me, like everything in Sheol, but there was more pleasure in a willing slave. I withdrew my athame and took his hand. He shuddered at my touch because I put a thread of power in it, pulled it through him in a flicker of the darkest pleasure. Soon enough he'd beg for this, unable to perform with anyone else. I knew how to enthrall my lovers. With a faint smile, I pricked the tip of his finger. Not as much pain as he expected, I think, but I drew blood. His gasp aroused me. His blood welled like a crimson jewel and I took his fingertip between my lips, tasting him. Learning his secrets.

The revelation was *stunning*. Delightful. This one was worthy of me.

I sucked a little longer than I had to, after I possessed the knowledge I sought. And he reacted with all of the alacrity I could wish. His lean, lovely body tensed and I scented the heat of his arousal. He wanted to be taken in every manner I could devise.

When I freed his hand from my lips, he reclaimed it slowly. Reluctantly.

"You don't know what you are," I said softly. "Do you?"

Mute, dazed with desire, he shook his head.

"What will you give me if I tell you?"

I knew his response before he spoke it. But it pleased me nonetheless.

"Anything," he whispered.

"Come, sit with me."

Other lovers would know to be wary of gentleness. But he was so deliciously brand-new that he came without hesitation. It almost made me decide not to break him. We sat on the large bed with him at my feet. He obviously wanted to touch me, but he wouldn't dare without an invitation. I could keep him ready and aching for hours. My power washed over him, and he groaned, his eyes going hazy.

"Please," he whispered.

"Then let me tell you a story. There was a girl from Korea who spent a year studying in Japan. She was special, this girl. She had great healing gifts. There, she met a young man. He seemed to be a simple fisherman. They courted. And eventually, beneath the cherry blossoms, they made a child."

"Me?" The question meant he wasn't totally lost to the urges coursing through his veins.

"Yes, my darling. Are you ready to find out who your father is?"

"Please," he said again.

"In Japan, they know him as the Laughing God. Ebisu. The god of fishermen and . . . luck."

He seemed starstruck by the revelation. "What does that mean?"

"You're a demigod. Not immortal precisely, but divine blood, even that of a small god, is enough to guarantee half a millennium. Longer here, of course, as time runs differently." I smiled at him. "That makes me happy for obvious reasons."

"My mom never told me."

Bored with the topic, I hit him with another trill of power, skimming his whole body in the addictive snare. I didn't want to talk about his intriguing heritage. Divine blood or not, he existed to please me. His breath came faster, his hands curling into fists. I realized then that he was trying to resist. How . . . delightful.

"Disrobe," I ordered.

He trembled when he stood, but I didn't see the beauty of his naked form. Agony lashed through me. *Curse this puny human shell.* Darkness filled my head.

I had the mother of all hangovers.

But it seemed way wrong that I'd have gone on a bender while I was supposed to be finding a way to save Shannon. Sitting up, I glanced around, taking stock. The room was lush. Opulent. And I was sure I'd never been here before.

There was also a gaping hole in my memory. I cast back and found myself in the Klothod-driven carriage with Chance and Greydusk. Beyond that, nothing. Bile rose into my throat from my churning stomach. I forced my breath out of its panicked rhythm and sought something familiar in this strange chamber. It was reassuring to find Butch in the corner. And he wasn't a quasit anymore. Even as a kid, I hadn't drunk enough to have blackouts or lost time. So this was disturbing as hell.

The door opened, and I looked for a weapon. *Nothing nearby, damn it.* I relaxed when I spotted Chance. He canted his head, studying me.

"You're . . . you."

"Shit. It happened again?"

"Yeah," he said softly.

"How long was I out?"

The days I'd bargained from Sybella kept vanishing, thanks to this bitch queen in my head. That might even be part of her plan. Each time she helped me, she also stole time. I *hated* her. If I could cut her out with a knife, I would. Unfortunately, that would result in a self-lobotomy. She was bonded to me in a way no surgery could remove, the ultimate conjoined twin.

"About eight hours, I think."

A night's sleep.

He went on. "The queen took over after we left Club

Hell. She managed the meeting with the Dohan. Eventually you passed out. Greydusk has been making excuses as to why nobody can see you, hiding the fact that the queen is not herself."

Fuck.

"I didn't even know . . ." I dug my knuckles into my eyes, fighting the urge to cry.

How could I check her when I couldn't even see her coming? Hopeless. I was never going to get Shannon out of here. Worse, Chance and I would be stuck. He didn't love the demon queen, and he'd end up her slave.

He perched on the edge of the bed and reached for me. I resisted at first because I couldn't doubt I was bad for him. But he persisted, and I was weak. I curled into his arms, rested my head on his chest.

"I can see it," he said. "Now that I know what to look for. Your eyes change."

"Change how?"

"They go black, like your pupils expand until there's no more iris."

"Freaky?"

"Fuck, yes."

"I'm sorry about all of this," I whispered. "I wish you hadn't come."

"You didn't know what would happen when you came through the gate. And I'm not sorry at all. It's kind of nice that you need me again."

I choked out a laugh. "Even if it means I'm possessed?"

He offered a wry half smile. "It's a . . . challenge. But at least I can tell how I should act, depending on your eyes. The queen likes the submissive stuff."

My stomach knotted. If he told me I'd tied him up and whipped him and then fucked him with the queen driving, I might be sick. Not because that wouldn't be okay under other circumstances, but the idea of my body being used without my consent? The churning started up again.

"Did we—"

"No." He reassured me. "The royal aura she uses to scare the shit out of everyone takes a lot out of you."

"So we're inside the Dohan compound and they don't know I'm not . . . her."

That could pose complications. The Drinkers would know immediately that I was just a human, not their scary demon queen. Which meant we needed to sneak out, provided we'd learned what we came for. Otherwise they'd hold me hostage, like Sybella had intended, and I couldn't count on them fucking with Butch again to give me some leverage. In those circumstances, I'd have to petition for her help, and the more I let her drive, the less chance she'd ever go away. With each possession, I felt as though I lost a little of myself, like I was more hers and less mine.

"It's not a wash," Chance said then. "You got the info we came for."

"That would help if I remembered any of it," I muttered.

"I'll fill you in."

He did.

As it turned out, the Dohan had taken Shannon because they wanted Sheol to change. They wanted greater access to the human realm due to their particular appetites. Demon blood permitted them to survive, but it was like eating wheatgrass when you wanted chocolate cake. The Drinkers had thought if they brought my best friend here, I would follow. And then the queen would ascend, taking her place ruling over the castes, and she would regulate gate use, as she had done in ages past. Being the favored children who had been instrumental in drawing her back to Sheol, they would, of course, benefit from her triumphant return.

"At least," Chance went on, "that was the initial plan. But the Hazo threw a wrench in the works."

"Yeah, I was wondering why they gave Shannon away." I wrapped my arms around him, desperate to warm the chill inside me. "I mean, maybe they just wanted to get me here and they didn't care what hap-

pened to her after that. And so they gave her to the
Hazo to play with?"

The tears came. I felt so weak right then, so *broken*. It
seemed like it'd be par for the course if Shan was suffering in my stead, if Caim tortured her with all the anger
I'd instilled. He couldn't expect to get revenge on the
demon queen, after all.

"That's not why." He stroked my back in soothing
strokes while I cried. I'd never done it gracefully or pret-
tily, but we were so far past any of that at this point.

"Then tell me!"

"Apparently there was some old debt between the
castes. The Hazo demanded Shannon in payment."

"Because Caim wanted to be sure he got to see me
again," I said bitterly.

"That's what Azon thinks anyway."

I nodded and managed to stop the waterworks. "We
have unfinished business. But I wonder why the Dohan kept her in the Barrens instead of bringing her
here."

Chance smiled, but it was a little unnerving, full of
love, but also . . . fear. "She asked that question too."

The bile rose again. This time I couldn't stop it. I
puked into a decorative urn. He didn't approach me, a
fact for which I felt thankful. Afterward, I staggered to
the bathroom and rinsed my mouth repeatedly. Above
the basin, I stared at the woman in the mirror. She had
dyed red hair with tawny streaks and a pale, thin face.
Below her eyes, she had deep bruises, as if she hadn't
slept in weeks. This looked like a woman on the edge, as
if she were about to break for the last time. And maybe
I wouldn't have minded so much if the final fracture
didn't mean losing myself forever.

"Tell me the truth," I said, coming to the lavatory
threshold. "Are you hanging in because you promised
you would? Because you don't want to let me down?"

He laughed softly. "Do you think I'm the kind of guy
who keeps a promise beyond all common sense?"

"Maybe."

"Uh-uh. My mama didn't raise a fool. I believe we can

save Shannon, keep you from going all demon queen
forever, and get the hell out of Dodge."

"Nothing like dreaming big." But his optimism was
contagious. "No matter how long the odds."

He flashed his beautiful smile. "Hey, I'm the king of
long odds, baby."

*Yeah, you are. I'm not. I'm the queen of coming up
snake eyes.*

"That's certainly true."

"Once, I'm sure you would've said there was no way
in hell you'd ever give me a second chance. Yet here we
are."

I grinned back. "In hell. Yeah, you're a funny guy."

The love in his tiger's eyes wrecked me. "I'll play the
clown if it keeps you smiling. I'll even be the queen's
jester." There was a shadow in his face that made me
wonder just what the hell had passed between him and
the queen while I was locked in an airtight box in my
own head.

"Don't *say* that."

"Can't help it," he whispered. "Haven't you figured it
out yet? There's nothing I wouldn't do for you."

Hearing that should have felt amazing. I should've
been on top of the world and flinging myself into his arms.
Instead, a chill ran down my spine. *Don't love me like that,*
I wanted to scream at him. *It's not safe. It's not wise.*

"Something's different," I said. "What did she say to
you?"

Before Chance could reply, Greydusk tapped on the
door.

"Come in," I called.

It wasn't until after I spoke that I realized I shouldn't
have known. But I *felt* him, as if his essence were bonded
to mine . . . like a queen who monitored her minions. The
realization sickened me. Her dark tendrils sank deep
into my spirit, undercutting my personality and resolve.
Soon there would be nothing but echoes where Corine
Solomon had been.

"You're human again." Disappointment flavored the
demon's tone, and that rocked me.

I had started counting on Greydusk as a true ally, but he served me only because he wanted the dark queen's favor when she ascended. Destroying me. That meant Greydusk wasn't mine. He was *hers*. Much more of this and I'd go crazy.

"If I said I'll stay, after we save Shannon, how would you feel?"

"Relieved," Greydusk said at once. "Sheol needs you."

"Needs her, you mean."

The demon gave me a unsettling, toothy smile. "That's semantics, Binder. At this point, you're as much hers as your own."

Unwelcome truth, but he was correct. *I'm losing this fight.*

I glanced at Chance; he was meant for brighter, better things. I wished he hadn't come back for me with his healed spirit and his grand gesture, ready to love me like I deserved. I wished I'd had the courage to send him away in Laredo, but I had been so hurt that I couldn't bear the thought of being alone. And now my weakness might destroy him too. With a deep breath, I firmed my faltering resolve.

"Well, guys, how do we deal with the Hazo?"

Best-Laid Plans

"The first question you must ask, Binder, is what Caim wants of you."

Once, I'd have said revenge. No question. But I'd realized that demons didn't always react as I expected. I had friends where I'd anticipated persecution and hidden enemies who didn't dare move openly against me, in case I did ascend. Beyond that, a faction had been spying on me for reasons I didn't understand, and now I was inside their compound.

"I have no idea," I admitted after a moment's thought.

"Would you like me to present a likely theory?" Greydusk asked.

"Go for it."

"Given what you told me of your prior interaction, Caim is worried that the Hazo will suffer for his role in that debacle. Though he had little control over what the caster forced him to do, the queen is not known for being reasonable or forgiving. I believe he wishes to present your friend as a gift. Amends, if you will."

"Seriously?" After all this, could it be that easy?

We could walk up to the front gate and get her back? Every nerve in my body insisted that was bullshit. Caim would know I wasn't the queen—unless I let her drive.

Again. I recoiled from the thought, but I wondered if it even mattered now.

It doesn't have to be like that, the queen whispered. *We could bond. Some of me, enough to convince them. And some of you, so you don't lose everything. It's a fair deal, your most likely chance of survival.*

I stilled. *Why would you offer that? Aren't you going to wipe me out?*

There's a small chance you could win. Smother me forever. This way, I don't lose everything. It's a limited-time offer, human. Don't think about it too long.

When I looked up again, I found Chance and Greydusk regarding me with an odd expression. "Did I zone?"

"For ten minutes," Chance answered.

"You were with her last night." Not a question.

But he nodded as if it had been.

"Did she hurt you?"

He replied carefully. "*Hurt* is the wrong word."

"Pick the right one."

Chance cast a nervous glance at Greydusk. He didn't want to talk about this in front of the demon.

I responded to the cue. "Could you give us a few minutes? I'll know what I intend to do by then. Go make the arrangements to get us out of here. If Azon asks for another audience, tell him he risks pissing me off."

The demon inclined his head and backed from the room. *Good. He respects you,* the queen said with satisfaction. *You have made a good beginning even with all the bumbling, human. Your court will not be such a wretched thing after all.*

"You said she didn't hurt you, but . . ." He was clearly holding something back.

"I don't have much self-control. She does this thing with her magick, and I respond. I stop being me. Stop caring about anything but pleasing her."

God, but it was weird hearing that. Because she was me, essentially, and I hated knowing I'd done that to him. "Are you all right?"

He nodded. "I was glad when she passed out. It took more power than she expected to subjugate me."

"Why?"

Chance hesitated. And then he told me his deepest secret, a truth his mom hadn't shared. When he finished his quiet summary, I sat back, eyes wide. Greydusk had known Chance carried divine blood, I thought. But I'd imagined he was fucking with us.

"Wow," I breathed. "Does that change everything?"

"Like what?"

"I dunno, how about your whole worldview?"

Chance lifted a shoulder in a bewildered shrug. "It explains my luck, but I don't feel any different. I'm still my mother's son. She's the one who gave up everything to see me raised right."

That was why I'd fallen in love with him in the first place. I couldn't imagine any other guy finding out he was a demigod and not having it impact his self-esteem. But Chance had always been confident, solid in his sense of self. Once I found that certainty comforting . . . and then upsetting because I couldn't match it.

"Are you going to try to contact him?"

"If he'd wanted to be part of my life, he would've been."

I smiled up at him. "This takes the deadbeat dad thing to new levels, huh?"

"*God*, I want you." The fervor came from nowhere, at least from my perspective, until I remembered that the demon queen had tormented him last night, wearing my face.

I regretted that, but there wasn't time to rectify the situation.

And why not? she asked. *Anything of import waits on our pleasure.*

There was seduction—and evil—in such complete self-absorption. I fought her lazy desire, rolling over me in waves. When I made love with Chance again, it would be because we both wanted it more than anything—with no help from outside stimulation. Something about Sheol stirred his sex drive, making him more primitive, and she didn't help with her teasing.

"Do you think your divine blood might be reacting to

the demon magick, in addition to the compulsion as consort?" No wonder he wasn't himself.

"Probably," he said, still looking at me as if he wanted to bend me over.

"Dial it down. We have work to do."

My sharpness returned him to himself and he regained his composure, but his eyes retained that hungry edge. "I'll find Greydusk."

While they were gone, I used the facilities, freshened up, and found a change of clothes. These fell between my ornate robes from the Luren and the simple street garb the demon procured for me later. Though this outfit was all black, it had a satiny pattern imprinted on it so that it showed in each flicker of the light. I liked the knee boots that came with it. I almost felt like a queen, dressed like this.

Only if you intend on doing some killing, little human girl. Otherwise you're not nearly elegant enough. Because I suspected it would irk Ninlil, I ignored her. Pretended I couldn't feel her like a cancer in my brain or hear her insidious voice.

By the time the others returned, I had a headache from her shrieks.

For now, *I* was in control.

"How sure are you that the Hazo aim to make amends?" I asked Greydusk.

The demon's gray skin paled, as if he couldn't bear the thought of disappointing me. *Her.* "I could send a messenger. Discover their intentions."

"That might be best."

"We can't spend too much longer here," Chance said. "Or the other castes will get jealous."

"An astute observation."

I couldn't believe I hadn't thought of this before. "Is there a palace somewhere? Or a royal residence the castes weren't allowed to claim?"

"There is," Greydusk replied slowly. "Likely to be in rags and ruins, however. It's been . . . uninhabited since Ninlil left us."

I was murdered, the demon queen raged. *Murdered!*

And what did you fools do to avenge me after the angel ripped my power away? Nothing! You cowered in Xibalba and squabbled over scraps like this pitiful animal. She wrested enough control from me to cut her eyes at Butch, whom she wanted to kill for some reason.

"Then let's make our intentions clear. I'm tired of running. Tired of hiding. Take me there." The crack of demand in my voice, well, it came partly from me and partly from her.

Maybe that fusion she'd mentioned was already under way. Even as I loathed her, it was better than losing myself entirely. I would dig in and cling to it as long as possible, fight tooth and nail. I'd never resign myself to captivity in my own head. Power over demons ran on my father's side of the family; that must count for something.

We marched out of the Dohan stronghold as we'd come. I kept my eyes straight ahead, and none of the lesser demons dared look at me long enough to detect a difference from the day before. I ignored them all, and that seemed to suffice.

Finally, I had a handle on the situation. I'd use my power, such as it was, to get the Hazo to set Shannon free. That was smarter than attacking the warrior caste. If I fought them, that would indicate that I saw them as a worthy foe. If I *commanded* them, they would kneel, especially if Greydusk read our circumstances correctly.

Outside the Dohan compound, we didn't have a chance to arm up before they pounced. A flash of magick fell on me like a net. The queen howled her bootless fury, but I was already caught, an insect in amber. All around me, the air felt thick and slow. I couldn't move so much as my fingertips.

"Corine!" That strangled cry was the last I heard from Chance.

I couldn't even turn my head to see how he fared.

Complacent. I had listened too much to the dark lady in my head. To my detriment, I had forgotten the one lesson I'd learned as a child. *There are always enemies.* And now they had me. Greydusk had warned me there were factions who didn't want to see the queen return. I had chosen speed over caution in reaching the Drinkers, and now my true foe had us.

A magician stepped forward, clad in midnight robes etched in bloodred sigils. His hair was long, twined in complicated plaits, and vestigial horns sprouted from his forehead. "Load them up quickly, before the snare wears off."

This is the one who set the magus trap, the queen said. *I recognize the stink of his magick. I will enjoy skinning him when I get free.*

For once, I didn't disagree. Too bad about the Vortex Greydusk had mentioned. Otherwise, I could call the Gorder to save us again once the spell failed. They couldn't keep the snare alive forever with the queen working to dismantle it. I gave her the lead, knowing I had no hope of setting us free. But this time my world didn't go dark. It was like I sat at her shoulder, watching. Still here. Still me.

I told you, she said. *It needn't be all or nothing. We can become . . . symbiotic.*

My body and your magick?

Precisely.

I wasn't ready to accede, but I was closer, and she had to know that. How many times had she made this offer? How many times could I be strong enough to decline? I tasted her triumph on the tip of my tongue. *Do you know who's got us?*

Her displeasure flashed through me. *No. These beasts belong to a new caste. No wonder they oppose my return.*

I racked my brain—and then I made the connection. Greydusk had said only the Saremon could have created the magus trap; now the queen recognized the smell of their magick. Which meant they had tried to capture us once already. That knowledge didn't help at the moment, but it might down the line. While I waited, helpless, a minion loaded my frozen body into the back of a cart. There, they bound me and sealed my mouth with a foul-tasting mixture. Then they stole my athame and the packs containing all my worldly goods . . . and Shannon's.

Just in case, I supposed. When the paralyzing spell wore off, I would kill them *all* for this.

And though the dark queen approved, it was my thought.

All mine.

They have Butch. The realization terrified me. He was small and helpless, despite his big heart. *If anything happens to my dog—*

Vengeance, Ninlil promised, though it was cold comfort.

At this angle, I couldn't see anything but the sky. No way to judge how Chance fared, Greydusk or Butch, either. I just had Ninlil raging in my head, and for the first time, I understood her position perfectly. I took a mental step closer to the union she wanted. This life might not be so bad.

Whoever they are, they'll pay.

The journey passed in a haze of white-hot rage. In time, the spell weakened, but not enough for me to do more than wiggle my fingers and toes. I was still helpless when more goons dragged me out. Adding to my sense of vulnerability, they blindfolded me and towed me like a statue for a while. I had no sense of direction, only the idea that we'd gone inside, from the cessation of the wind. A door shut somewhere behind us, reinforcing that impression.

At last, they removed the cloth from my eyes. I couldn't speak with my lips sealed, and I had the horrible fear they intended to stuff and mount me. First, they would cut out my insides, fill me with sawdust, replace my eyes with blue glass, and then sew my mouth together for all eternity.

See the demon queen? I bagged her myself.

"You must be wondering about my intentions," said a deep voice behind me.

For obvious reasons, I held still. I couldn't speak. Couldn't turn to face him. I'd never felt so powerless in my life. Doubtless, that was exactly what they intended. So I waited for him to tell me more. Even Ninlil quieted, listening with a silence that burned with hate and the promise of awful retribution.

"The Saremon care nothing for politics. Nothing for the human realm either. But arcane power? We care a great deal about that. So we will use you in our experiments, of course." The magician paused significantly.

I couldn't respond. If I could have, he'd have died in a fountain of blood. I'd never wanted anything that much in my life, but I had no way to make it happen.

Not yet, Ninlil purred.

"You will serve us, Binder." He gave the title a mocking inflection, probably because I was the one bound here. Then the Saremon spoke the words that nearly stopped my heart. "Just like your father."

Death Match

The demon mage was lying. He had to be. *My dad left us.* Albie Solomon was probably selling used cars in Des Moines. The man who sang off-key in the shower, loved Panama hats and bowling shirts had no place in this world. None.

His blood runs in your veins, Ninlil whispered. *That is his value. He too carries the Binder's power.*

"I imagine you have many questions," the mage went on.

In fact, I did. Too bad my captor was a sadist and unlikely to sate my curiosity. I tried to melt his face with my mind, but it didn't work. He circled in front of me then.

He smiled. "I shall not tell you my name, Binder, as that would give you too much influence over me."

Yeah, the minute I learn your true name, asshole, I own you.

"But you can call me Oz."

As in the great and powerful? I wondered if he knew that the real Oz turned out to be a weakling who hid behind a curtain. I'd thought my dad was that kind of guy, someone who couldn't deal with his responsibilities, so he'd bailed. My mind touched on and skittered away from the idea that he was here somewhere, held hostage by the Saremon. Gods and goddesses, he had been gone since I was a kid—twenty years. Was it possible someone could survive that long in demon hands?

All my life, I'd blamed him for deserting us. I'd told myself it didn't matter. My mother seldom talked about him after he left, but sometimes I'd found her staring out the front door with a wistful air, as if she expected him to come walking down the lane, years later. She'd loved him deeply; that much I knew.

Twila, a vodun priestess who ran most of the supernatural business in Texas, had told me, *By the way, you've carried the weight of a lie your whole life. Your father didn't leave. He was taken.* At the time, I didn't believe her. I hadn't seen enough of the wider paranormal world then. I'd done my best to stay away from it. I didn't want to learn or explore; I wanted to be normal.

Given my heritage and history, I understood now how impossible that was.

As if he saw my inner turmoil, Oz laughed. "Soon I'll take you to the arena."

Arena? My eyes must have asked the question, because he answered it. "You'll choose which of your companions fights to the death for you. According to our records, Ninlil was fond of such spectacles."

The Imaron, the dark queen counseled immediately. *He has centuries of stolen skill to call upon and his drain will immobilize almost anything.*

"Which one?" The mage mused. "Either way, it will erode loyalty, as your designated champion cannot help but realize you deemed him expendable."

"But I'm not your queen," I protested.

The mage whispered a spell in demontongue and energy sparked against my skin. "No. You're not. I don't even sense her. Has she not awakened, then? Did the Dohan get it wrong?"

"Duh. They're not geniuses."

"Alas, no. The Drinkers are not known for their mental acuity."

Neither are you, I thought.

Oz cut the conversation then, as he held all the power. He murmured to his minions, and then one hauled me

away like a statue. I doubted any effigy ever boiled with
hate quite like this, though. As the goon dragged me, the
pressure on my skin waned. I wriggled the tips of my
fingers, but I couldn't move my hands, and even if I could
have, they were bound at the wrists.

Did you hide from Oz? I asked her silently.

*Surprise offers our only advantage. He must believe
I'm dormant, sleeping. Now focus on regaining your
voice,* Ninlil urged. *I don't need to move. Only speak.*

The paralysis was easing on my throat, but I still
couldn't feel my tongue, which meant any words would
come out wrong. But there were no magick words, just
the will behind them. I was unsure how that translated in
the demon realm, however. Maybe Ninlil needed her
voice to shape the spells.

I do, she told me.

The minion dumped me in a holding cell. Chance and
Greydusk fell on either side of me. I guessed this was
where they caged the gladiators. And I couldn't turn my
head to see if they were injured. I lay there, helpless, as
the Saremon thug loomed over me. He showed a mouthful of sharp teeth.

"Boss said to put this on you." The demon bent and
snapped a cuff around my wrist. Afterward, the Saremon
left and closed the door. It was made of heavy wood with
bars across the small window at the top, too close together to permit escape that way.

A dampener, Ninlil whispered, seeming cowed for the
first time since she'd awakened in my head.

What is it? It couldn't be good; I knew that much.

*It restricts my magick. As long as I'm wearing it, I can-
not cast.*

Shit. I wished I could scream, but I only managed a
gurgle. Beside me, Chance made a sound in response, but
it wasn't a word, just a moan, seething with anger and
fear. In increments, the feeling returned to my body.
Eventually, I squirmed upright, then I concentrated on
working my lips free of the disgusting resin they'd used
to seal them. It was like glue, only more acrid.

"Chance?"

"Yeah?" His speech still sounded muffled, as if he hadn't quite unstuck his lips completely.

"Did he put a manacle on your wrist?"

"No."

"Greydusk?"

"Yes, I have one." The demon sounded remarkably composed. "I can't touch any of my extra skills."

So that was the catch. If I chose Greydusk, he would be au naturel. Since I didn't know who or what he'd be fighting, it might be the same as a death sentence. Knowing I'd as good as executed my only ally would certainly work on my state of mind, making it easier to break me down the line. I understood the Saremon mage's thought process all too well.

"Let me fight," Chance said.

"You don't even know what you'll be up against."

"It doesn't matter."

"You're that confident in your skills?" I asked.

"I'll fight for you as well," Greydust put in, before Chance could answer me.

Great. So they were both willing to die on my orders. And that made up my mind. I sat bound, in silence, until the minion returned a long while later. Outside the door, I heard Oz's voice, murmuring instructions in demon-tongue, but I couldn't understand the words.

I could translate, the demon queen offered.

Go for it.

It was like she slipped the soundtrack into my head because the conversation cut in right away, midstream. ". . . and under no circumstances permit any of them to leave the compound alive."

"Yes, sir."

"After her companions die, take her to the labs and bind her beside her father."

It took all my self-control not to react. I cut a look at Greydusk, and he inclined his head, indicating he understood. Both he and Chance were doomed unless we came up with an alternate plan.

Then the door swung inward, revealing Oz and his chief lackey. The mage grinned in delight, as if I were a clever monkey for maneuvering into a sitting position with my arms bound behind my back. Truth be told, it hadn't been the easiest thing I ever did.

Oz rubbed his hands together in anticipation of the great show to come. "Tell me, then, have you decided?"

"I have."

"Who will stand as your champion?"

Chance leaned into me, demanding my favor. Greydusk sat still and quiet. *Ready,* I thought.

I smiled. "I'll fight for my own honor."

"Corine!"

Ignoring Chance, I waited to see how the mage would respond. "This is . . . highly irregular. Do you not wish to enjoy the entertainment I've provided before we get down to grimmer business?"

By which I had no doubt he meant drilling my brain or making me drink more weird potions. "I'll pass."

"You are a most unusual queen."

I like *this,* Ninlil said.

"Remove the cuff."

Oz shook his head. "No, I won't be doing that until you're safely in the arena, where protective wards prevent you from smiting any of the spectators."

"I had to try."

"Understood."

"You won't touch my people," I said with deceptive calm. "If you do, you'll regret it. Not for a minute or for an hour, but you'll pay for an eternity."

"As your father has," Oz returned in a conversational tone.

I didn't let the implication rattle me. "Then you know precisely what I mean and I needn't spell it out for you."

The mage cocked his head, considering my sincerity, and I let a fraction of Ninlil's malice slip. He took a reflexive step back before replying, "I do, yes." He turned to his lackey. "Confine the males here. The door is to be secured and none are to tamper with them in the Binder's absence."

"Corine, no." Chance gazed at me, eyes imploring.

I smiled at him and let the guard haul me to my feet.

I love you, I mouthed. And it was true. He had claimed my heart first and now he had it in his keeping again.

As they led me away, he thrashed against his bonds and screamed for me in such raw, agonized tones that it nearly broke my resolve. Greydusk tried to calm him, but we were too far away for me to make out the words. I heard the turmoil until the mincing steps of my chained feet carried me out of earshot.

That's not normal, I thought.

It's a combination of love and compulsion, Ninlil told me.

Compulsion?

I didn't do it on purpose. It's part of the royal aura.

So he's . . . bound to you?

Us, she corrected. *He is our consort. Part of that bond means he'd die to keep us from harm. As first male, he is imprinted with the imperative to protect.*

Greydusk had tried to explain, but I hadn't understood the depth and breadth of it. Before I could process what the hell this meant in normal relationship terms—if I was ever to have such a thing again—Oz stopped outside a set of double doors. They were crafted of a dark, scarred metal that looked like it would be impervious to fire, acid, and frost. The outward dents said unspeakable things had attacked from the other side and never broken them.

"This is where we part company. My aide, Craven, will escort you from here." Oz touched two fingers to his brow just beneath the vestigial horns, in a mocking salute. "I will be cheering for you, Binder. I'd prefer a live specimen to a postmortem dissection, but these little wagers make life interesting, don't you agree?"

"Indisputably," I purred.

The queen surged forth as the mage hurried away. I laughed lightly, mockingly, and then turned to Craven, arching an aristocratic brow. It was odd thinking of my face in those terms, watching as if I were a little bird on her shoulder.

Craven grabbed my arm again, and the queen shook him off. "I *will* flay you alive if you touch me again without permission."

The goon swallowed, his throat working visibly, and then he said quietly, "This way, Your Majesty. Please pardon my disrespect."

Damn. I could get used to this.

He unlocked the double doors, waited for me to step inside, and then added, "With your permission, I'll remove the dampener cuff and your bonds."

"Go ahead."

With tentative hands, he did so, and then shut the door between us, as if I would slam a lethal spell into his skull the first chance I got. And Ninlil was thinking about it, but she decided to save her energy for the coming battle. I rubbed my wrists, bent and massaged my ankles to get full circulation back. You never knew when coordination would come in handy.

Thus warmed up, I strode down the narrow, sloping corridor. It was dark and quiet as I went toward the light ahead, where the space widened into the arena. Once I emerged, I saw that *arena* was, perhaps, an overstatement. This was more of a pit with stone stadium seating above and around it. The sunken fighting area spanned twenty by twenty meters, not too much space in which to run.

We won't need to, Ninlil told me.

As I spun in a slow circle to take stock of my surroundings, people—or I should say demons—filed into the chamber above. They spoke in low whispers, and they were all Saremon. Good to know the other castes weren't involved in this.

I will destroy them, the queen said. *They will not profit. They will not* survive *this day's work.*

It was easy to sling vengeful promises when we couldn't do a damn thing but what we were told. She settled then, her anger chilling to an icy resolve that fortified my own. With her help, I opened to my witch sight to assess the wards Oz had sworn would prevent me from striking the audience. They wove in dark, beautiful patterns along the walls.

For a moment, Ninlil admired their artistry and then her sigh filled my head. *We must fight—and win. Then*

*strike as they come to release us. If we lie in wait outside
the doors, we can take a whole squadron.*

Will you have enough in reserve after the match? I
wondered.

Certainty filled my head and lent me confidence. I
squared my shoulders and waited for the enemy.

On the other side of the pit, another set of doors
opened. The ground trembled beneath the weight of
whatever was chugging down the tunnel toward me. My
opponent stormed into sight, and while I assessed it,
Ninlil whispered in demontongue, sparking a handful of
darklight as if it were a snowball. This thing was easily
twice the height of a Hazo and half again as wide. It had
scaly black hide, thick enough to excite admiration in a
rhino, and its teeth jutted through its thin lower lip.
Extra-long arms gave it an apelike appearance, but its
fingers ended in razor-sharp talons.

There was no announcement; the monster just
charged. As it ran for us, Ninlil unleashed her first spell.
The darklight slammed the creature full in the chest,
rocking it, but the magick rippled away without effect.
Magick resistance, Ninlil said. *This could be bad.* Since I
didn't have a weapon and I had little combat experience,
yeah, that would be an understatement.

The beast swung its arm like a crossbeam. My reaction
time wouldn't have been fast enough to avoid decapita-
tion, but the demon queen took over, rolling me smoothly
beneath the raking claws. I came up behind it in a half
crouch, shaking from head to toe. I stepped back then,
because if we were going to win this—if I was to survive
to wreak havoc in this compound—I had to trust her.

In the time it took for the monster to come about, Ninlil readied another spell. This time, whispering her command words, she coiled the darkness into what looked like
a snare, and it snapped tight around the thing's calves as
it took a step toward me. The magick didn't dissipate, and
the beast overbalanced. It caught itself on its overlong
arms, claws digging into the stone, but I was already running. There wasn't room to kite, but I had no chance close
up. Which meant the longer I stayed away from it, the

longer I kept breathing. I might have a demon queen in my head, throwing spells, but my body was all too mortal.

I whirled, darklight flaring from my fingertips as Ninlil voiced the words of power. She was casting so fast I didn't even know what she was doing until the magick hit. A patch of black slammed into the creature's head, wreathing it in shadow. Belatedly, I realized this was my mother's blindness spell, adapted for demonic use. The monster roared in outrage and spun—rather, it tried. With its legs bound, it could only hop.

We need a weapon.

She conveyed to me that her spells couldn't kill it, only immobilize it, and they wouldn't last forever. I skimmed the walls and found a spear with a broken haft at the far corner, presumably left from another match. There were bloodstains in here and bits of debris. Urgency sent me sprinting across as the monster struggled with the dispersing magick. With a scream of rage, it chased me blindly. I zigzagged as much as the small space permitted, and it couldn't hear or smell well enough to place me.

I snagged the weapon on the run, and splintered wood gouged my palms. Ignoring the pain, I doubled back and came in low. As Ninlil chanted up another blindness spell, I struck, stabbing the thing up through the groin. Its claws came down, and only the demon queen saved me from complete evisceration. With her preternatural reflexes, I twirled and took the blow down my right side. Blood gushed from both wounds, the monster's and mine, but I hadn't killed it.

Join with me, she whispered. *Some of yours, some of mine. We are stronger together. If you fall here, Binder, your companions die as well.*

No. But the refusal felt shaky. The demon queen withdrew, leaving me to my own devices. Fear streamed through me like whitewater rapids, drowning me. My wound throbbed twice as hard, twice as hot, and my whole body trembled.

I slid sideways, but not in time to avoid a blow on the backswing. She made me absorb the full impact, and I tumbled backward ten feet, landing hard on my injured side. The Saremon crowd shrieked, scenting blood. They thought I was done.

We'll both die, she said. *Is that what you want?*

Do something about those claws. I'll . . . think about it.

Ninlil's agreement came at once. *Cloudbind.*

Then she was speaking the words, driving the magick, as I surged to my feet with renewed energy. Lowering my head to charge, I wheeled toward the beast with a feint and wrested my broken weapon from its crotch. I screamed as I pulled because the motion wrenched my wounded side, and the monster raked at me, but its claws were covered in darklight that offered a magickal buffer. The blunt trauma hurt like hell and I saw stars, but at least it didn't take my head off. Another hit like that, though, and I was done.

Let me in, or we both fall. Last chance, Corine Solomon. Even my power is not infinite. Will you let them die of your fear, your weakness?

Oh, no. Chance. Greydusk. Shannon. At last, my will chipped away, I accepted the unthinkable bargain. *Yes. Do it.*

The queen threw her strength into mine, and we merged. I had all her experience, all her power at my fingertips, and the spear pulled free in a bloody fountain. Ichor spewed from the wound. *Again,* I thought, and I drove the weapon into the vein on the creature's thigh. It could die. It *would* die. Even with my wounds, riding the royal aura, I spun away from the injured beast. I came up behind it and stabbed twice more. Back of the thigh. Hamstring. Its chest was too armored for me to penetrate, but it was softer down low. Its sight came back too late. I stabbed. Again. Again. Until it bled from ten separate wounds. The audience was screaming, but it sounded distant, as if through a wall of glass. I didn't care. All that mattered was that this thing died.

Final thrust.

I hit a vein and the black blood spurted like oil, slicking the stone beneath my feet. The monster staggered, moaning, a piteous sound, but there was no kindness in me. I was the demon queen, and I had risen.

No Mercy

There was no time to rest.

They'd arrive soon to escort me back to my cell and then kill my companions. That meant I had to be ready to fight. I had magick to spare; it coiled, lustrous, around my hands like a drowsy snake. I didn't posture for the surprised crowd, most of whom had expected to watch me die. Instead I ran like hell for the doors where I'd come in. I didn't expect to break them down. But they had to come and get me, didn't they? I smiled in delicious anticipation. I whispered the words in demontongue that cloaked me in living darkness, a shield against the suckerpunch of a spell Oz had dropped on me before.

He wouldn't get lucky again.

The Saremon were weak. They'd relied on lazy tricks for too many centuries, being too much mage and not enough demon. I would destroy them all.

A voice boomed. "Stand back from the doors."

Like that's going to work.

When they banged open, ten Saremon grunts awaited me. Unfortunately, they couldn't find me for the dark fog filling the corridor with every step I took. I laughed softly, seductively, and they spun. I whispered and trailed another spell into the air as gracefully as if I had been born for this moment.

The mania set in at once. One guard grabbed another, and the second retaliated. They swung their weapons in a blood-frenzied madness. I picked a path through the carnage like the ballerina of death, and then paused on the other side to watch. Perfect. They fought until one by one, they all hit the ground. Smiling, I twirled my broken spear and retraced my steps toward the cell where they'd put my people.

Darkness drifted in my wake as the spell died away. Footsteps pounded the halls, but they came from some distance away, guards from the other entrance. It would be too late for them to catch me and once I had reinforcements, we would level this place. There would be nothing left of the Saremon caste when I finished here. For good reason, they'd feared my coming, but when they interfered with my destiny and harmed one of my blood, they sealed their fate. Excitement quickened my steps. The sooner I released Chance and Greydusk, the sooner my vengeance could begin.

I passed a number of cells; some held occupants. With a flick of my wrist, I called the sleepy demon magick that sang in my ears like ocean. It was . . . lovely. For the first time in my life, I felt whole. The darklight drifted into the locks and turned the tumblers. Beautiful sound, freedom. The doors popped open and the prisoners of the Saremon stepped out into the hallways, some injured, some fearful, others bristling with wrath. As one, they stopped. Stared. And they fell to their knees en masse. It was good they recognized me, for I had been gone a long while.

"You know me?" I said.

"Yes, my queen." The awed chorus sent a pleased shiver down my spine.

"You have my leave to demolish this place. Your enemy is the Saremon. Their whole caste has become Xaraz." In those words, I exiled the mages of Saremon, stripped them of rights and rank. Henceforth, they would be reviled and driven beyond the Vortex to cower in the shantytown with the other wretches. "Kill as many as you please, so long as they are Saremon. Touch no others inside these walls. If they are not Saremon, they belong to me."

The assembled host whispered, reverently, "Yes, my queen."

"Afterward, carry the message to the rest of Xibalba that I am ascended. Go. Do my will."

And they did.

I continued down the hall to where they had confined Chance and Greydusk. The door stood open, but they did not emerge. If Oz had kept his word, they had not been tampered with, which meant they were still bound. I stepped into the cell.

"You're alive," Chance breathed. And then he froze, cocking his head. Sorrow surged from him in a tangible wave, so thick I could taste it. "You—you're—"

"My queen," Greydusk supplied in an awed whisper.

I inclined my head. It was not the time to talk about such things. I knelt and cut their bonds. With a whispered command, I made the dampener drop off the Imaron's wrist. The demon rubbed his arm in quiet gratitude.

"We should get the hell out of here," Chance said, low.

I smiled. "After." He cut me a sharp look, and the echo of the human woman I had been stayed my hand. When I said, *some of you, some of me*, I hadn't told her that as the stronger, older personality, my will would often be dominant. She wasn't destroyed in our merger, but it would take her a long time to fight back to the surface again, apart from the occasional impulse.

"I must burn their stink from my city, First," I went on.

"First? Why're you calling me that?"

"First male," Greydusk explained. "You're her consort. Be honored that she explained herself this once and did not take your head for the insolence. She is . . . not the woman you knew."

Chance swallowed and then nodded. His silence hurt me because it cradled heartbreak in its depths, but beneath my need for retribution, it was a distant pain, a torch flickering in gale-force winds. With a practiced gesture, I called them to battle, and the males flanked me. I handed my makeshift weapon to Chance, still slick with demon blood, and he stared at the evidence of my conquest with a set expression.

"It was my first kill upon coming home," I said dreamily. "I shall have that blade set in a proper haft when we finish here."

Neither of them spoke. There was nothing they could add.

The hallway was dark and quiet; my minions had gone to do to my bidding with flattering alacrity. It wasn't in delight at my return, however. Some of them were merely angry at the Saremon and wanted to make them bleed. So long as they touched nothing I had claimed for my own, the arrangement worked to our mutual benefit.

"We need to find our belongings and then my father," I said.

Those words sounded odd to my ears. Part of me scoffed at the idea of a human male siring any creature so glorious as myself, but I could not permit anyone else to use him as Oz had done. Harm done against my blood was the same as injury to myself, and if I could not defend my line, then I deserved the damage.

"Can you find the creature you call Butch?" Greydusk asked.

It was an excellent suggestion; the Saremon compound had protections in place to prevent interference from the Vortex, and I was familiar enough with the dog's life energies that I could easily seek for him. If they had left him with our things, then it would be a two-for-one solution. Closing my eyes, I built the animal in my mind's eye, and then coiled the dark energy around the image. I whispered the right words in demontongue and then set the spell free. It soared from my brow like a raven, dipping and swooping on the shadows, rebounding off the walls, and then flitting almost out of sight. Belatedly, I signaled them to move and I ran.

The spell tried on several occasions to pass through solid walls, only to be stymied by various runes. They sparked in warning and the air stank of fresh lightning where the light died. Those moments gave me a chance to catch up and to find more passages where we could turn. This chase culminated at a storage closet near the front of the building. From inside, as we approached, came the frantic yapping of a confined animal.

Still alive. For the life of me, I couldn't understand why this filled me with ambivalence. Part of me wished the creature to the pit, and the other half felt suffused in ridiculous, impossible joy. I ignored the schizophrenic reaction as I popped the lock with a burst of magick.

Butch lunged out the door at me, growling, but his tail started to wag, and then he drew up short. His barks grew more hysterical when he sniffed at me, and then he scrambled away toward Chance, who picked him up without a word. With graceful hands, he soothed the small creature, and I spared a thought for how lovely it would be to recline in his arms later and receive that same treatment.

But first we had work to do.

"Greydusk, our bags."

The demon complied with a small sound. He radiated pleasure, as if he had been waiting a lifetime to hear my commands. And the Imaron was, unquestionably, male — one with submissive tendencies, which made him an ideal servant. I wondered why I hadn't been sure of that before; it seemed so obvious now.

I reclaimed my athame. The demon slung one bag over his shoulder, the colorful one that belonged to the girl I'd come to save. At the moment, I didn't remember why I had been so alarmed at finding that she'd been taken to Sheol. My home was no more dangerous than the human realm, and even less so for the queen's companions. Here, she would be well. Safe. Protected. Yet the same lesson must be taught to those who had stolen her. The Drinkers would be humbled too.

Chance took the other bag and stashed the dog in it. I was pleased he'd taken charge without being asked. As first male, it was his role to find ways to satisfy my needs, whatever they might be. This was a good start.

As I closed the closet door, shouts came from down the hall. Chance pulled his gloves from the bag and donned them, then he handed me back the broken spear. "This is yours," he said softly.

I nodded.

Greydusk took a defensive position on my other side. As soon as I saw the enemy coming, I crooned their death in demontongue. The magick flowed in me like blood. I could pull it from the endless flowing river of energy beneath our feet. Here in their stronghold, the Saremon had done something impossible . . . and clever. They were leaching power from the Vortex and had built up a private supply that flooded the foundation itself. The rock had channels cut into it with microscopic precision, so when I gazed into the astral, I saw the dark tracery swimming through the stone.

This time Oz had sent more grunts to kill us . . . or capture us. Twenty, instead of ten. Unfortunately, they were low-ranking Saremon, so they didn't have much magick. The leaders, like Oz, kept them stupid and feeble, good for nothing but frontline fodder. I watched them struggle for minor charms and fail to connect to the energy surging beneath our feet.

This will be . . . delightful.

"Kill them all," I said softly.

Chance whispered and flames formed around his fists. Greydusk shifted forms, as he had done in another fight, and whirled into motion with threshing claws. My consort stayed clear, and with each blow, he set the Saremon soldiers alight. They screamed and slapped at their own clothing, their skin, and in their distraction, Greydusk gutted them. It shouldn't have been such a slaughter.

When there were twenty corpses, I stepped lightly through the pile. "Where do you suppose they're keeping my father?"

Greydusk considered. "Hard to say. Oz said they had been experimenting on him, so the labs would seem an obvious place to start." He paused, as if weighing whether to warn me. "They'll send spell casters from this point."

"I am aware."

"We'll kill them even quicker," Chance said.

"You are worthy." Surprised and pleased, I leaned over to kiss him. He must know how favored that made him, for me to show affection before witnesses. The queens of Sheol had never been known for their softness.

In another part of the complex, the released prisoners were rioting; they would thin the resistance we faced. Distant noises hinted at marvelous destruction—booms and thumps and shudders and the faint, delicate scent of smoke. *Perfection.*

"I'm surprised they let you fight," he said as we pushed deeper into the compound. "I mean, you're such a powerful sorceress that they should have suspected it would be hard to restrain you afterward."

"I suspect Oz didn't know I could tap their secret well. He imagined I would be spent after the battle and subduing me would prove no challenge."

"Secret well?" Greydusk asked.

Which answered my next question. The Imaron couldn't sense it, apparently. "Tell me about the Saremon," I ordered.

"They're descended from Solomon's line, as you are, Your Majesty, through scions who interbred with demons. In time, they organized sufficiently to form their own caste. They focus on events in Sheol over the human realm and are concerned with increasing their own arcane powers. They maintain an occult library which is the envy of the other castes."

I thought about that. "That's probably why I can sense their source."

"And I cannot."

After that, I fell silent. At length, I passed from the arena complex into the main compound, where the sounds of fighting became sharper. I joined the battle from the flank, throwing another cloud of chaos at my enemies with a whispered shaping in demontongue. The darkness drifted and maddened everyone it touched. They fought like wild things, screaming as they died, then Greydusk and Chance whirled into the fray like twin dervishes, born for death.

When the screaming stopped, four slaves were still standing. "Go," I told them. "Spread the word of my coming."

Though one was too injured to walk, the demon pulled itself along at a crawl, leaving smears of blood on the ornate tile. The other three ran toward the doors at the other side of the courtyard. I watched their obedience for a few seconds more and then turned toward the broken doors that led into the compound proper. The Saremon had guarded the egress to the best of their abilities, but it had been insufficient.

Instead, I found more wreckage. It was sad that the angry captives had been so thorough; there was little left for us to kill. But they'd had my permission, and so I swallowed the tang of disappointment and pushed on. They wouldn't have gotten to the most powerful mages; those would be holed up somewhere, seeking a spell strong enough to kill the queen.

I went room by room, clearing each. A couple of times, we killed survivors who had hidden from the fight. Their cowardice did not earn them mercy. There *was* none for what their leaders had done. Should any Saremon be outside the caste compound on the day of reckoning, they would be sent from the city to shelter among the Xaraz, whose ranks they joined when they moved against me. A whisper in my head said it wasn't fair to judge everyone the same way for the actions of a few, but I banished it like a buzzing insect.

At no point in my long and storied reign had I ever cared about "fair."

Several rooms smoldered as I passed through, the result of spells gone awry, I guessed, before the mages went into hiding. *As if that can save them.*

Eventually I came to a tall, imposing door that didn't open. I opened my gaze to the astral and examined the runes etched over it; the wards sealed it against all comers. Nobody was meant to get inside. Which only increased my desire to see what the Saremon prized so highly.

"This is the entrance to the library," Greydusk said. "I have been here for research a few times."

"Excellent. Stand back."

The two males did as I requested, and I found the

source running beneath my feet, boiling the rock. With a mental touch, I stole the magick in a smooth, sweet rush. Part of me realized, somewhat belatedly, that it didn't hurt anymore, but instead of being relieved and thankful, that portion of my soul wept as if it had lost something precious. I ignored it; that was weak and would distract from my mission.

It took infinite patience, but I unpicked each rune, thread by thread. The unraveling took ages and more energy than I could've called on my own, without the Saremon spring that fueled their whole fortress. It was quite deliciously ironic that I could turn their assets against them. When the last ward puffed away in smoke, I withdrew from my working to find a pile of corpses. Both Greydusk and Chance were bloody; my consort's face was battered and drawn with exhaustion.

"It took me some while?" I asked.

"Six hours," Greydusk replied.

"Thank you for your protection." I didn't need to speak the words, but I could tell they meant a great deal to my two defenders. "Now let's go see what the library's got to offer."

Chance opened the doors, and I could see in his movements that he was at the ragged edge of exhaustion. We all needed food and rest, and after I finished what I'd started, I would take care of my own. I became aware of my own weariness then, a burning dryness at eyes and mouth.

Regardless, I pressed on. Inside, rows on rows of shelves spread out as far as the eye could see. They were filled with books in all shapes and sizes, some bound in scales, others in what looked like tanned human skin. In the astral, the whole chamber glowed with magick, blazing from some tomes more than others. But no question, each volume in this magnificent library was valuable and powerful.

"Do you know how to get to the labs from here?" I asked Greydusk.

We had explored the rest of the complex. The spell casters had retreated, leaving the weak to fend for themselves. I'd expected to find them cowering in the library, but I was relieved that the mages had gone further still because I would have hated to fight in a room full of priceless grimoires. It seemed ... barbaric. This way, I could seize the books and have them brought to the palace when we finished here.

He cocked his head, as if listening. "I drained a Saremon once. In his memories, there's a story of a hidden entrance."

"Then let's search this place, top to bottom."

Make It Quick

The library smelled of old books and musty paper. I wished I had time to examine the tomes, but that could wait until I confiscated them. Once they were delivered to the palace, I could research advances in the arcane arts to my heart's content. Well, such as governmental duties permitted. It would take a while to get the city running in a respectable, orderly fashion again. The castes had been autonomous too long for me to see my reign beginning bloodlessly.

After a fair amount of investigation, Greydusk found the hidden exit. A row of shelving slid away from the wall, revealing the door. It was dark and cool within, eerily quiet as well. I peered into the astral and saw a shield of silence rune laid on the threshold, so whatever they did behind this door wouldn't alarm the rest of the complex. That boded ill for anyone trapped in here.

As I stepped across, a boom shook the foundation of the whole structure. "What was that?"

Greydusk searched his stolen memories. "A failsafe. If the enemy breaches these protections, the stronghold falls."

Behind us, magickal light snapped into place, barring our way. It was meant to shield the books from intruders and thieves I had no doubt, but it also prevented us from going back the way we'd come. There was a chance I could dismantle the spells if given time, but channeling that much energy might also fry my human body. Since I didn't want to retreat, I discarded the notion. Nothing would serve but to press ahead and keep looking for my father. I thought it highly unlikely that the mages hadn't left themselves another rathole, another exit.

"Are they running?" Chance asked.

"I suspect so. They need to regroup before they face me." But it wouldn't go better on different ground, unless they surprised me again, and I wouldn't make that mistake twice.

Once I passed the rune of silence, I couldn't hear the destruction behind us anymore. The Saremon might end up killing any survivors we had missed, which spoke to how they regarded their lower classes. If I killed these days, it was purposeful, not a casual result of mass destruction.

A long hallway lay before us, with doors on opposite sides as far as the eye could see. The corridors branched farther out, going left and right; this warren was worse than the prison where they kept their entertainment.

"The Saremon are really into experimentation," Chance observed.

Greydusk nodded, apparently not realizing it was a joke. "They're always looking for ways to add to their abilities. They're not as physically strong as the Hazo, but their aptitude for magick is unmatched."

I raised a brow, and he added, "Until your return, Your Majesty."

Mollified, I strode over the dark tiles. Here, the floor looked like polished obsidian, etched with various runes. I stopped when I realized I could understand them. Skimming, I ignored the irrelevant areas of study, like pyromancy and divinations. Greydusk had stopped too and read the runes alongside me.

"Research?" he guessed.

"It's as likely a place as any to start."

I continued down the straightaway and cut left, as the runes had indicated. None of the doors were locked.

Some stood open, as if the magicians had fled in great haste. Labs showed experiments in various stages of completion, arcane ingredients and odd machinery with sparking wires. I glanced at Greydusk, who wore a matching expression of bewildered awe—and that told me this wasn't common knowledge among the other castes. There were cages full of strange, hybrid creatures, likely bred by the Saremon, though for what purpose I had no clue.

In one room, machines with knobs and levers with piles of copper cables connected to a weird black box emitted a low hum. It was like that for fifteen different rooms with still no sign of my father. Maybe Oz had been lying. *If he dared* . . .

"I've been following the cables," Greydusk said, interrupting my thoughts.

"Oh?"

"I think you want to see this."

I went with him, and I noticed that the cables went from the machinery to the black box, on through the hallways. Then I stepped into the room the Imaron indicated and time stopped. In all my centuries, I'd never seen anything like it. I couldn't even imagine the purpose.

A man hung in a metal framework, those cables plugged into his flesh. At first I thought he must be dead, for they had cut open his chest and filled it with transparent liquid, and where his heart ought to have been, he had a bright, glowing jewel suspended in the solution. In place of flesh, he had glass casement, permitting the ones who had done this to him to see inside his sternum.

"What the hell?" Chance gasped.

That summed up my reaction, too. Even if he was beyond saving, we should cut him down. The compassionate thought surprised me; it wasn't like me to care about the fate of random strangers, but that was my human aspect, I supposed. I wasn't the queen I had been, but any version of myself was better than oblivion.

As I stepped closer, the man's eyelids fluttered open, and I took that first look like a fist in the face. I knew those blue eyes. I knew this man. Oh, part of me didn't. To that part, he was a stranger. But the other part of me remembered his French toast and his predilection for Panama hats. The human half of me surged forth with desperate strength. She had to be in control in this moment, riding the bittersweet reunion. Because I understood its importance, I didn't fight; I fell back, and this time, the shift occurred without pain.

I reached out and touched his face, cupping his bony cheek. If they ever fed him, it didn't show. He had the skeletal shape of one affixed to a cross, a martyr's bones beneath his skin.

"Dad?" Despite Oz's taunts, I hadn't expected to find my father—and certainly not like this. He hadn't aged, though he looked awful. This man appeared to be no more than five years older than me. "What have they done to you?"

His lips moved but no sound resulted. Frustration flashed in his thin face. A copper wire was plugged into his throat and he turned his head slightly toward the knob next to it, trying to tell me something. I clicked it on and adjusted it.

His voice emerged from a speaker on my left, tinny and scratchy. "You have to get out of here before the magister returns."

All Saremon were mages; that wasn't a helpful distinction. "Which one?"

"The others call him Oz, but I don't think that's actually his name."

My hands fisted in impotent anger. "He's the one responsible for this?"

"Yes. *Go*."

"Will it hurt if I unplug you?" I asked.

For the first time, hope dawned on his desperate features. "Hurt, yes. Would kill me. I can't survive outside this contraption." And by his tone, he didn't want to. He wanted to be free like the dearest of unfulfilled dreams.

"You don't recognize me, do you?" It was impossible that he would.

I had been a child of seven when the demons took

him, skinned knees, gapped teeth, and mousy brown braids. My father, Albert Solomon, took a closer look then, studying my face with ferocious concentration. His eyes—so like mine—widened. A pained sound escaped the speaker.

"Corine?" He didn't wait for my confirmation. "You're all grown up. Have I been here so long?"

An eternity for him, no doubt. Over twenty years in the human realm.

"It's me," I said softly.

"Oh God, you shouldn't be here. How's your mother?" The same sweet love I'd remembered between them sparked in his blue eyes now, undimmed by time's passage or the impossible distance between them.

"She died." In as few words as possible, I explained what had happened in Kilmer, the murderous twelve and the terrified townsfolk . . . and Maury. It hurt to relate and wounded him even more to hear. "She missed you until the end."

"I don't know if that makes it better or worse." My father closed his eyes, too late to hide the fat tears that struggled out from beneath his lashes. Whatever they had done to him had not left him too inhuman to cry.

"Does it hurt to talk?"

"Everything does. I don't remember what it's like not to hurt. But it's worth everything, knowing I saved you from this."

I froze. "I don't understand."

"They came for you, Corine. You were the last girl child born of Solomon's line. When your mother and I had a daughter, we talked about the likelihood there would be trouble. So I was ready. I had a counteroffer for them."

That didn't square at all with the laughing, carefree man I'd known, but I had been a child, shielded from all the darkness, until it split my world wide open. "Why didn't Mom tell me?"

"I don't know. Maybe she thought you were too young to understand. Or she was afraid the guilt would cripple you."

"So she knew you sacrificed yourself for me." As she had. Maybe she'd meant to explain it all when I was older, but she never had the chance. At least now I understood why she never wanted to talk about him. In other cases, a woman abandoned by a man called him all kinds of names, but this hadn't been like that.

I just hadn't known the truth. Having just found him, I wasn't ready to lose him, but looking at what they'd done, I didn't think he could be saved. I turned to Greydusk.

"Your thoughts?"

"This looks like a reaping machine," the demon answered.

Chance raised a brow. "What's that?"

He took a half step toward me, his expression unsure. I curled into his side, grateful to be myself for these moments, though I could feel Ninlil scrambling in my head, preparing to resume control. I returned a gentle caress to the back of his hand.

Greydusk explained. "Remember the soulstone I used to open the gate?"

I nodded.

"This is how they're made."

"How long does it take?"

"Fifty years, or so I've been told."

Damn. I didn't imagine getting my hands on one for a quick exit would prove a simple task. Obviously my father hadn't been here that long, so the jewel in his chest shouldn't steal his soul. When we unplugged him, he would just die.

Just. As if that wasn't bad enough.

The queen half of me didn't remember her dad. She'd had one; but after siring a daughter, the father's parental role became less critical. Demons had a longer life span than humans, but they were not immortal. In this fashion, Ninlil always ruled in Sheol, until the archangel summoned us and stole our power. That lingering anger blunted some of my grief. She'd heard of soulstones, of course, but she'd never seen the apparatus responsible for their making. Ninlil also whispered to me that it was possible to use a fresh sacrifice and open a gate that way, but for obvious reasons it wasn't always practical.

Yeah, because *that* was my concern.

"Why do they want your soul?" I asked. "Apart from obvious reasons."

The speaker crackled, reminding me of Shannon, and that made me feel like my father was already dead and I was talking to him through her spooky radio. "They hope that a soulstone created from one of the Binder's line would permit a stronger gate to open between worlds. A *permanent* gate."

"Hope or know?" Chance asked.

My father's expression was like a shrug, though he couldn't move his arms. The agony from being suspended like this had to be intolerable and he couldn't even scream unless someone turned the volume on for him. Rage chilled into a solid brick inside me; this would not stand.

"I won't ask what you're doing here," he whispered.

Yeah. Best if you don't.

He went on, "I'd rather not imagine you trapped as I am, so I'm going to pretend you have a plan—that you came to save me and now you're getting out."

My voice rasped like sandpaper, thick with tears. "That's the idea. Is there anything you want before . . . ?"

He knew what I was asking. "Would you hug me?"

It wasn't easy getting close enough with all the wires, but with some help from Greydusk, I wove through the tangle and put my arms around my father's waist. He was beyond emaciated, thin in a way that meant he hadn't eaten for years. They were using magick to keep him alive—and for that reason I wanted the Saremon dead even more. *They* had done this. Hurt one of mine.

I didn't waste my energy on more mental promises. Instead, I lived in this moment, where I had my father with me. He had no body heat. No heartbeat. Albie Solomon was the next best thing to dead already, so why did what I was about to do hurt so badly?

The embrace went on for a long time, and then he

stirred against me. "I love you, queenie. I couldn't be happier that I got to see you again . . . or that you're the one who will end it for me."

God, I'd forgotten he called me that. The memory tumbled into my head. I was a princess, wearing a pink dress with a frilly skirt and a play tiara. He used to call me Reenie, and that day it became queenie, because of my princess outfit. After that Halloween, I remembered him spinning me around with raspberry kisses on my stomach, and teasing me with chants of *Reenie-my-queenie.* My mother had watched us with an indulgent air. How I wished I could have more of these recollections; I needed them, craved them in a way that seemed more vital than air—but there were no more.

I looked at Greydusk, who seemed transfixed by my pain. Queens weren't supposed to love the men who had given them life. This one did. And I regretted the years I had spent calling him a shiftless bastard in my head. I'd imagined him finding a new family, a better one, and instead he had been here, suffering for *me.*

"Where do we start?" I asked the Imaron.

He went to examine the apparatus, as the answer wasn't readily apparent. After giving me a comforting squeeze, Chance joined him. And while they checked out the reaping machine, my father stared at me.

"All I ask," he said softly, the speaker crackling with his pain and resignation, "is that you make it quick."

"I won't touch anything until they tell me how."

We talked then. Precious, stolen moments. I told him about my pawnshop and my dog, about Chance, who had been my first love and by some miracle was standing beside me still. His eyes grew damp when I told him what I'd done in Kilmer, and he spoke the six words that every child longed to hear:

"I am so proud of you." Only they came with reverb and distortion.

They had taken everything but his loyalty and devotion. My mother had been lucky to share even ten years with this man. And maybe that's why she never went looking to replace him. She knew that quantity mattered

less than quality and that nobody could ever take Albert
Solomon's place in her heart—and that was why she
stared wistfully out from the front porch. Not because
she thought he was coming home someday but because
she knew he never would.

He gave up everything for you.

"I love you," I whispered.

Greydusk stepped to my side and murmured, "I found
the main connection. If you unplug there, he should feel
no pain."

"Dad, I'm sorry." Tears sprang up in my eyes, not fit-
ting for a demon queen, but one who hurt this much
could not help but weep.

"I'm ready," my father said.

"Corine, let me." Chance touched my arm lightly.

For a moment, I wanted him to take the weight. I'd
love to give the burden to him to bear, but then when I
looked at him, I would see the man who killed my father,
not the one I loved. So I shook my head, hair drifting
against my cheeks. I felt like one of those screaming
women of old with a shriek rising in my throat that I had
to swallow down like razor blades. No, better I should be
haunted by my own reflection, for I was used to that.

So many dark choices—and this might be the worst.
But there was none better. At least I could offer him
surcease from pain.

Leaning in, I kissed my father on the cheek, as I had
done so many times as a child. He did not smell of Old
Spice. He didn't have a bowling shirt or a Panama hat,
but he was still the man who held my dreams in his hands
until the day he disappeared. With his blue eyes set in an
ascetic face, he smiled, though his lips didn't move. Then
he sang in a tuneless tenor the chorus from "Fire and
Rain," which he'd always belted out in the shower. The
speaker crackled with the emotion, and I couldn't bear
another moment. As he finished the last word, I stepped
behind the reaping machine, grabbed the cord Greydusk
had indicated and tugged.

It popped free with a spurt of fluid, and I kept pulling.
The Imaron helped me, knowing I was mad with grief

and that I had to get my father down. I *would not* leave him in this place. Chance worked beside me, his face taut with echoed sorrow. Because he loved me, he mourned with me. I wondered how he would feel if we had found his mother in such a state.

But due to his luck, we'd saved her. And I'd killed my own father.

At last I set Albie Solomon free and he fell into my arms. I held him and rocked, tears streaming down my face. He felt like a child against me, thin and small and wasted. His legs resembled matchsticks, arms like pipe stems, and his face was too young for so much pain, borne in my stead.

Chance and Greydusk let me grieve for a while before the demon dared to intrude. "Your Majesty, we cannot remain here. The mages might return."

The queen surged forward then, taking over. I bit off the words like chips of ice. "Let them."

No Way Back

"I'm not leaving him." My tone brooked no refusal.

In response, Greydusk knelt and collected my father's body. The Imaron cradled his wasted form with proper reverence, and the pain ebbed enough for me to rise and lead the way out into the corridor.

Now we needed a rathole.

I had an idea. I toyed with it, wondering if the small creature that felt so ambivalent about me could truly help us. But it was worth a try.

"Put the dog down," I said to Chance.

"Corine . . ." He trailed off. Then he obeyed, kneeling beside the animal with a worried air. "Don't hurt him, okay?"

I wrestled a duality of reaction: anger that he'd dare question anything I did commingled with an absurd sense of hurt that he thought I *would*. With great self-control I put aside both responses to be analyzed later. Eventually I would have to deal with the divergence in my head, resulting from my twin selves—which hadn't merged, but left me with conflicting impulses—but for now the compound was shaking down around our ears, even if we couldn't feel it here in the the sanctum sanctorum.

"I won't," was all I said before I directed my attention

to the animal. Butch, that was his name. "So you're a clever beast."

The dog eyed me skeptically and backed up a step. But it wasn't growling or trying to bite me, which felt like a small victory. Then it yapped. Once.

"That means *yes*," Chance put in.

I remembered that after he said it, as if it was a fact I had learned long ago and since forgotten. "Excellent. If I find something that belonged to the mage who worked in this lab, could you follow his scent?"

Butch pondered and then yapped again. He could.

"Brilliant." Greydusk saw the plan in its entirety, I had no doubt.

In essence, it was simple enough. If the dog could follow the trail, it should lead us to the route that mages had used to escape my wrath. If we found their hiding place along the way, even better. It could end here and now. If not, we left the collapsing Saremon compound and went straight to the palace, where I could issue my first proclamation, hire staff, begin renovations, and organize a proper funeral.

That list daunted even a demon queen—but that had to be weariness and grief talking. I had been born for this role. I had lain dormant in the human's blood, in her soul, waiting for my moment. Once I set my affairs in order, the pleasure in this would return. I didn't permit any doubts to take root.

Instead I took action, ransacking the lab for some cast-off piece of clothing. My efforts bore fruit when I slammed open a drawer and found a dirty handkerchief. It was damp with some unidentifiable fluid and I found some pincers to pick it up, then I knelt and offered it to the dog for his perusal. He sniffed and then sneezed. Whined a little too. I couldn't blame him; it was fiercely revolting.

"Is that strong enough?" Chance asked.

The dog's look said, *Hell, yes. Any stronger and I would die.*

I swept my arm out before me in an inviting gesture. "Lead on. We're right behind you."

The little dog pranced. Part of me found it adorable; the rest of me wondered how it was possible the creature hadn't been eaten. Butch lowered his small head, tail up and twitching with excitement. He sniffed around outside the door and then settled confidently on a path that led back the way we'd come, only at the first opportunity, he hung a left. We'd explored this part of the lab complex, but I hadn't been looking for an exit then. I'd only been thinking of my dad. Later I would replay those moments with him. My heart hurt; it was a caution against love and its shocking weakening, but I did not deny those feelings. Even pain would make me stronger in the end.

The dog led us straight to a hidden passage. This place was probably riddled with them. When I knelt beside him, a breeze swept out from beneath the stone. I felt around for the catch and then a section of wall slid behind the rest.

Though I half wanted resistance, I encountered none. The mages had gone to ground and would strike next from a fortified position. They were smart enough not to want to face me in a dark tunnel with little preparation time. The strongest rituals took time to set in place. That was why I hadn't dealt instant death in the arena.

The hidden passage led us into a plaza across the way, and when I turned, I saw the utter devastation of what had been the Saremon compound. They had shaken it to rubble rather than let anyone else gain a foothold there. It would take a salvage crew weeks to unearth their library, though the magickal shields should protect the books from harm. A host of curious onlookers had gathered to watch the fall of the house of Saremon. They didn't see us emerge behind them.

"Summon the carriage," I told Greydusk. "And take us to the palace."

After handing my father's body to Chance, the Imaron did as I ordered. I watched with implacable resolve as the cube unfolded and he sent the black mist of the Klothod into the mechanism. It wasn't revolting anymore; it was a tool to be used. The demon assisted me into the coach, and we were off before the assembled mob took an interest in our activities.

The city—and the caste checkpoints—flew by in a blur; then the coach stopped outside a massive black gate with barbed points atop the walls. This wasn't a glamorous fairy castle. It was entirely suitable for a demon queen. Time had been unkind, but with a little effort, the villa would glow once more with a dark luster.

"Home sweet home," I murmured.

"You need to disembark, Your Majesty. The magickal protections sealed the place up when you vanished. Only your touch can raise the portcullis."

Nodding, I dropped down to the cobbled street and strode toward the gate, where I wrapped both hands around the bars. "Open in the name of the Once and Future Queen, who is risen."

A shudder rocked the ground I stood upon. Then the bars scrolled backward with a hideous, rusty shriek. I returned to the carriage.

"It knows me," I said with satisfaction.

"As do we all," Greydusk replied. "Even those who oppose you cannot dispute your identity."

The coach clattered over the stones into the courtyard. Behind us, the portcullis lowered on its own, like enormous jaws slowly swallowing prey—an ominous and efficient magick. I approved.

Craning my neck, I took my first complete visual inspection. The structure was Gothic, with crenellated windows, four separate towers, flying buttresses, ribbed arches, and high vaults. In places the dark stone had crumbled away, leaving chunks broken on the courtyard tile. Part of me remembered when this place bustled with those eager to do my bidding, but it was dark and silent now.

No matter.

"Lay him out here," I told Greydusk.

The Imaron set my father's body down gently. Though it would take time and power, I knew a ritual that would burn him to ash, but I needed magickal accoutrements first, much stronger than the white witch herbs in the box my human half had treasured so. Unfortunately, her belongings had been left in a car abandoned on a mountainside. There might be some components left within the castle.

Inside, it was a ruin, and I found nothing salvageable, save a white curtain, which I used as a funeral shroud. With a stub of charcoal, I scrawled my needs on a scrap of ancient parchment. "You will fetch these items for me immediately," I told Greydusk.

"As you command, my queen."

That left Chance and me alone in the dying light, as shadows gathered around my father's body. Yet I couldn't bring myself to leave him. Someone should stand guard over him in death as no one had in life. His sacrifice must be respected.

"Can I hold you?" he asked.

It was proper that he did inquire, even in private, and I craved the comfort of his arms. Such behavior was not regal, perhaps, but there were none to see, not even the quasits, which had stalked our steps since our arrival. Now there was only darkness and silence.

In answer I went to him and he wrapped me up. I rested my head on his heart. "Is this all very strange to you?"

"You have no idea."

"Yet you remain. Such loyalty is a treasure beyond price."

"I'm not altogether sure who you are at the moment," he admitted softly, "but somewhere in there is the woman I've loved for years. That's enough for me."

From the deepest recess of my mind, a whisper came: *I love you too.* The human's joy cascaded through me until it became my own. She was stronger than I'd realized, forcing me to feel what she felt.

"I'm she, but more too."

"Yeah, I got that earlier. I could tell you were different when you came back for us." He ran his hands along my sides, grazing the wound I'd taken in the arena.

I hissed a breath and drew back.

"You're hurt. How bad is it?"

I shrugged. In my natural form, such minor damage would have already healed. I had no idea how this hybrid thing I'd become would handle wounds, though certainly I was frail by comparison.

"I'll survive. He won't." With my gaze, I indicated the white-shrouded figure lying supine on the stones.

"Don't blame yourself for his choices. He loved you that much."

"I am more concerned with vengeance than guilt," I said silkily.

"Ah." From his expression and the way he pulled back, folding his arms, I could tell I had disappointed him somehow, given an unexpected response.

"There will be satisfaction in destroying those responsible." I tried to explain, and I hated the impulse. A consort need not approve my actions; he needed only to submit to my will.

"Do you remember where we first met?" he asked.

The knowledge swam at the back of my head, so far away that I had to sink to retrieve it. "At a dry cleaner's?"

"Yes." His voice went warm and husky with relief. "You returned my keys."

This didn't seem like the time to admit I didn't really remember, experienced none of the nostalgic emotions that colored his beautiful features. I had an attachment to him, but it was an echo of the woman in the back of my head, a haunting of something lost.

His demeanor warmed, and he drew me back into his arms, careful to avoid my injured side. Eventually the dog pushed out of the bag and investigated the courtyard, and then christened a corner of it. *Charming.* We stood like that in silence, mourning the dead, until Greydusk returned.

"It took multiple stops," the Imaron said by way of greeting, "but I collected everything you need."

I nodded, but didn't thank him, and stepped away from Chance.

The ritual took hours. First I deployed the ingredients in proper order, then drew all the sigils, infused them with magick, and etched the body with matching runes using special ink rendered from blood. By the time I finished, I was panting and exhausted. Here I had no secret source running through the stones. Finally, I backed away from the meat that had been my father, and I spoke the command words in demontongue.

The sigils flamed with darklight, incinerating his flesh in mighty bursts. I did Albert Solomon's bravery the honor of not turning away. I watched every horrific moment, each puff of smoke, each breath of ash, until there was nothing left but cinder and char, chips of bone, and a great ruby that had been his heart.

Sorrow crowned me as I bent and plucked it with careful fingertips. It burned with a cold, eternal fire. From this jewel, I would have a necklace made, something exquisite, so I never forgot this moment. My enemies would see it glimmer at my throat and fear my resolve.

"Did you wish to speak a few words?" Greydusk asked.

I shook my head and drew my athame. I pulled the power that wreathed me in sweet darkness and summoned a wind to scour the courtyard clean. The broken moon had risen, shining silver and blood, by the time the breeze died. It was wrong that Albie Solomon's mortal remains should be scattered here, but I'd saved his soul, at least. If there was anything left of my mother, he could find her. The thought comforted me.

"Let's go inside and find a place to sleep," I said.

"I brought food," the Imaron ventured. "I know this is not what you are accustomed to, my queen—"

I moved my shoulders in a careless shrug. "It will be grand again. In time."

"When you have crushed your enemies," he finished.

"Precisely so."

The three of us passed from the courtyard to the darkness within. Greydusk unloaded a few parcels—the food he'd mentioned—and I found shards of metal suitable for my light spell. Soon the room I chose as the least wrecked offered a semblance of cheer in the form of tattered fabrics piled in a makeshift pallet.

"Some queen," I said with a bitter smile. "Of rats and rags."

Together, we ate in a primitive picnic. I didn't wonder about the nature of the meat. It only mattered that it would sustain me and give me the strength to push forward with my plans. Tomorrow, the city would know the queen had ascended.

Greydusk lay down outside the door, and Chance pulled me into his arms, offering his body as a shield against danger. It was an instinctive maneuver, driven by his imprinted instincts as first male, but I appreciated it nonetheless. Generally, chosen consorts were more concerned with personal gain and status. In my long memory, I could remember no one who offered such devotion—and it moved me.

When she sleeps, I wake. But I can't wrest control away permanently. Even those moments with my father were given to me like charity, not a result of my own strength. I can hear Chance breathing beside me. I can't tell him that his loyalty touches me. I can't control my own body anymore. This isn't what she promised.

I'm a spectator in my own life. We're not a new person, joined. We're two opposing forces, fighting for control. I can see everything she does, hear everything she says. But I can't change it. I can't protest.

It's dark here. The weight presses in on me, making me feel small and tiny. I can't move. I never thought I could feel more helpless than I did in Oz's hands, but I do now, sleeping in the arms of the man I love.

In the morning, I woke alone, and I heard voices in the corridor beyond. Chance pitched his words low, but they carried. "What can you tell me about her new . . . personality? Is this permanent? Can she be fixed?"

Fixed? As if I were a defective piece of machinery. Anger rose to an icy point.

"Her Majesty will never be human again."

From Chance's sigh, those were not the tidings he'd hoped to hear. "Damn."

The demon sounded surprised. "You don't find her strength more appealing?"

"This incarnation has a certain ... something. But she'd hate this, if she really knew, if she was herself."

"She made the choice." Puzzlement laced the Imaron's tone.

"Sometimes she does things that are better for other people. You know she fought so we wouldn't be harmed. And at some point in the battle, she had to let the queen in ... or she would've died. I don't believe she would've done that under any other circumstances."

"Be that as it may, it is done. There is no way back from here."

Those words resonated; they felt true.

But Chance didn't think so, apparently. "Really? I doubt you'd tell me even if there was some way to reverse this—to help her. You've always wanted the queen, and now you have her. You're her right-hand man, and she'll step on your throat to give you that special, irreplaceable thrill."

This could easily escalate. Chance sounded like he wanted a fight, and I couldn't afford dissent when I had so few foot soldiers. I made a conspicuous noise as if I were just awakening. Silence fell.

Then Chance stepped into the doorway. "Ready to start the day?"

If he persisted in such informal address in public, I'd have to chastise him. For now, I let the intimacy stand. I gave my first orders.

"Greydusk, issue a formal announcement. The palace is hiring. I will consider all comers, even those with cases waiting to be reviewed by the Eshur. I will accept murderers and thieves, so long as they are entirely mine." I smiled, anticipating the day. "And who knows? Perhaps such minions will prove useful."

"As you say, my queen. What more?"

"Procure suitable amenities at once. Furnishings, art, carpets, clothing. Confiscate all private Saremon holdings ... you should encounter no trouble so long as you bear my seal." I turned, still disheveled from the night, and went in search of the ruined study, where I had once signed proclamations and reviewed proposed amendments to caste law.

My ancient desk had been reduced to splinters, but I remembered where I had hidden my seal from untrustworthy ministers. I opened a rosette in the stonework, where rested at its heart a ring graven with my mark. It had been centuries since this graced anyone's hand. I passed it to Greydusk with proper reverence, and he fell to his knees. Chance stood propped against the doorjamb, watching with a troubled furrow of his brow.

"Rise," I commanded the Imaron. "You chose wisely when you promised to serve me. Your word remains sufficient, now and forever. You are my second, Greydusk of the Imaron caste. There is no station higher, even should I invest you with the mantle of a knight's power."

Greydusk drew in a sharp breath. "You would slay the Imaron knight?"

"If he displeases me or will not swear. Does that trouble you?"

The demon displayed a toothy smile. "If he is foolish enough to resist you, my queen, then I would be honored to assume his role."

"Once you have done my will, send runners to each of the castes. Tell them I will expect them to swear to me in two weeks."

"Yes, Your Majesty."

"Carry a special message to Caim. Tell him he is to attend me at once . . . and that he should bring a gift, lest I grow wroth."

Greydusk inclined his head. "The human girl?"

"Precisely so. No one touches what is mine."

True Justice

My new servants came in droves.

At first, they wanted to get a look inside the castle that had been sealed for so many centuries, and then they stayed, partly for the work and partly for the prestige of joining my court. They were the ragged and desperate, but raising them up would cement their loyalty. It wasn't the poor I needed to fear; it was the rich and powerful who had something to lose.

Through a combination of magick and hard labor, they worked to restore the structure to its former glory, and then decorated, using the goods Greydusk had confiscated from the Saremon. Beyond the gates, the city lay in turmoil, with pockets of resistance from those who truly thought they could repel the tide of change. The Eshur remained neutral, as I'd expected, waiting to see how it all played out before they committed. From the Phalxe I received an emissary and welcome gifts, though I wasn't so foolish as to keep them.

Never trust the Phalxe.

When workers completed renovation of the throne room, I summoned the Hazo knight Caim into my hall. Though there had been no formal coronation, I needed none. I sat on the throne with a confidence borne of birthright, and I watched his approach with a cool, quiet smile.

At length my silence unnerved him, and the enormous demon dropped to his knees on the red carpet that spread before him. "My queen, I beg mercy. The attack on your person was none of my doing."

I let the dread in him build. "Did you return the girl?"

"Yes. She's waiting in the antechamber."

At my gesture, the servant beside me ran to fetch Shannon. I intended to maintain proper decorum, but as the door opened, I pushed upright. My feet moved, and then I was running. I had to see her. This was an imperative beyond politics, beyond all other considerations.

The girl was thin and pale, with dyed black hair tipped in pink. She wore all black, and she looked exhausted. But all in one piece. I stopped short of a crushing hug because some part of me wondered if she'd know me at all, a curious concern, but then her eyes widened, and she threw herself at me. I wrapped my arms around her and pushed out a shaky breath. Absurd, but I could nearly weep. That strong surge of emotion let me take over; the queen protested as I drove her back.

"Are you all right?" I asked.

"You came. I can't believe it. Corine, you don't know what I did—"

"I do, actually. I handled your iPod."

"So you know I'm with Jesse?"

I nodded, hugged her tight. Though there had been sacrifices, they'd been totally worth it to get to this moment. Even the time spent riding as a captive in my own body—*that* was worth it.

Shan asked, "How are we getting out of here? And where *is* here?"

"In due time," I said. "I have your things."

I beckoned the servant and told him to fetch her backpack. Most of the items had stopped functioning—out of charge—but it should comfort her to get them back. That accomplished, I turned and strode back to where Caim waited on his knees. I stumbled as Ninlil wrested control from me. Conflict raged as to how to judge his fate. On one hand, a show of strength might be necessary. If I crushed him for what he'd done in the human realm and his part in holding Shannon hostage, it should chasten the Hazo. But one never knew how the warrior caste would react. Instead of being fearful, they might be roused to rebellion. I tapped a finger against my cheek, studying Caim where he knelt.

"What should I do with you?" I asked aloud.

He dared tilt his face back. The demon knight was a creature of terrifying violence and basest evil—and he feared *me*.

The creature licked his tusks with a nervous tongue. "You cannot suffer me to live, my queen. For what I did, I must be stripped of my powers and destroyed. Otherwise all would take your mercy for weakness."

"Queen—," Shannon started to say, but I lifted a hand, demanding silence.

He was right. I could not begin my reign on a low note.

"Because you were bound when you attacked me, I will permit you to choose your successor."

"I thought it might come to this," Caim said heavily. "I brought him."

"Then let us see it done."

In short order, another Hazo joined us. I could tell he was younger, a little frightened at seeing the knight on his knees. It would be good if he came into his power both fearing me and in my debt for raising him up. That beginning boded well.

"Caim, you are judged guilty of treason," I intoned. "Therefore, I strip you of your rank, your power, and your life."

"So be it," the demon said softly.

He had known he would not receive clemency, I thought, even with Shannon in his care, though if he had hurt her, his end would have been a thousand times as painful. I turned my attention to the other Hazo.

"Are you ready to be invested as the new knight of your caste?"

The young Hazo swallowed. "I am."

"What is your name?"

"Zet."

"Kneel, Zet." Once he did, I continued the ceremony, though it had been so long since I'd performed it. "Do you swear to serve me in all things, to set my will above your own, and obey my commands without question?"

"I do so swear."

I slammed a hand on each of their brows. Instinct, as it came back to me. The power peeled away from Caim at my touch, and my body became the conduit, funneling incredible amounts of demon magick. It occurred to me, belatedly, that there might be consequences from this. My physical form was human and had not been created for such work. Regardless, I held on, even as the connection became painful. Darklight swirled about me in jagged pulses.

Through raw agony, I maintained the link until Caim fell forward onto his clawed palms. New purpose radiated from the young Hazo knight. I turned and demanded, "A blade."

My servant brought one that had been mounted on the wall. "Zet, as your queen, I give your first command. Take his head."

Shannon opened her mouth to protest, but I pinned her with a look that made her step back. Her eyes wide, she gave me room to finish what I'd started. Zet rolled his head on a muscular neck and then took the sword; in one ferocious swing, he cleaved through Caim's throat. The severed head bounced away in a spatter of blood. It was hard for me to remember why I had feared the creature. It seemed so weak and pitiful now.

"Zet, you stand as the new knight. You have proven your strength and loyalty this day. So long as you remain steadfast, your caste need fear no reprisal from me. Soon, I will call upon the Hazo in my extermination of the Saremon."

He dropped to one knee, amid the black ichor staining the tiles. "Your will shall be done, my queen."

"Splendid. You may go."

The young knight turned with new confidence, striding toward the double doors while barking orders to the lower-ranking demons who had accompanied Caim and

Zet from the Hazo complex. Soon the throne room had emptied except for Shannon, me, and the servants already removing the corpse.

"I don't understand what's happening," Shannon said shakily. "You *look* like Corine, but . . . you aren't. Is this another trick? Are you a shape-shifter?"

This was complicated to explain—and she seemed to be the verge of all-out panic. I didn't move toward her. "Send a runner for Chance," I said to a nearby maid.

That calmed her slightly. "Chance is here?"

"He came with me to rescue you."

She scowled at me. "No offense, but this is the worst rescue ever. You waited for them to *bring* me to you and you seem to be in the midst of a coup."

"I'm doing what I must," I said.

A tense silence resulted while we waited. To his credit, Chance arrived quickly. The consort greeted her with a half hug, and she clung to him as if to convince herself that we couldn't both be evil shape-shifters.

"You're safe," he said. "Greydusk said they wouldn't dare hurt you, if they intended to use you to make amends, but it must've been terrifying."

Her head jerked in a quick nod. At once, I wanted to level the Dohan compound; they were the ones who used her as bait. But I couldn't afford to make such a drastic move until after my first court. I needed to assess how many castes would throw in with me and how many would support the Saremon. At this point I couldn't satisfy my personal desire for retribution; it could wait until I consolidated my power. I had a long memory.

"Let's go somewhere more comfortable to talk." I gestured to the throne room, which had been designed to intimidate.

"Agreed." A shiver ran through her, but she followed me toward the study, which was smaller and more intimate.

I chose a seat in the grouping of chairs away from the desk. These furnishings had been taken directly from a Saremon warehouse. Hard not to take pleasure in that. More to the point, this should help set Shannon at ease.

I didn't expect her to take the news well, but she would come around.

After we all settled, I ordered refreshments. Chance sat beside me, his knee pressed against mine. I took more comfort than I should in his presence. I'd monitor this attachment to ensure it didn't become problematic. Once the food and drink arrived, I summarized the situation for her.

"She's kidding." Her gaze cut to Chance, begging another explanation.

"Unfortunately, no." He was no more pleased about my ascension than Shannon was.

Their reactions puzzled me. Why didn't they want a better life? "Things are unsettled at the moment, but once I get the city in hand, it will be magnificent."

Shannon gaped at me. "So that's it. You're not even going to try to leave?"

"Do you know how they opened the gate to get us here?" I asked softly.

"I wasn't exactly in a position to check out the process, no."

"They destroyed a human soul to get you here, Shannon. And then another, when I followed. Do you know what that means?"

"Oh, shit." She grasped the heart of the matter right away. I felt a flicker of guilt at manipulating her this way, since the destruction of a human soul was not, in fact, why I was staying. "So to go home, we'd have to do it again."

"Yes," I said quietly. "No afterlife. No reincarnation. Just fuel for the gate. I'm not doing that again. I didn't know before, when I came through. I do now."

"So you figured while you're here, why not make the best of it?" She tried a smile, but her heart was breaking.

It had just dawned on her. No more dreams. No Jesse. Nothing but Sheol and Xibalba until the day she died.

"I'm sorry. Ultimately I'm the reason you're here. And I wouldn't have chosen this for you."

"Well, you didn't choose it either. You only came because of me—and that means a lot. Obviously I'm not okay with sacrificing some poor bastard either, just so I can go to college and have some kids someday."

I nodded. The human half of me had understood she would feel this way. I'd used that awareness shamelessly, and by Chance's expression, he *knew*. But he didn't comment on my management of the situation. He only stared at his hands.

Shannon went on. "I only wish there was some way for me to get word to Jesse. I'm not sure if you knew this, but he's got major emotional damage."

She went on to tell me things I didn't care about, like how he didn't trust himself because he could be swayed by other people's emotional states and how he feared he'd never fall in love for real, just spend his life in a depressing spiral of serial monogamy. But I listened because I felt I should at least pretend to be like the woman she remembered, even if that person—at best—was only able to whisper from the back of my head. Eventually, she ran out of words and then she cried. I put an arm around her and Chance stroked her hair.

Finally she said, "Thanks for letting me get that out. It's been a really shitty few weeks."

"For us too," Chance murmured.

Shannon nodded. "I guess nobody sets out to get trapped in hell."

"Do you have a moment, my queen?" Greydusk stood at the study door, bearing some papers I needed to sign.

"Of course." I read them over before scrawling my signature where he indicated—not that I didn't trust him, but in all honesty, I didn't. I trusted *no one*. That was what it meant to rule.

Shannon talked with Chance while we did our business, and then I performed more introductions. "Greydusk, this is Shannon Cheney. You are to treat her with all royal consideration."

At first she recoiled, but I hoped she would get used to my second and eventually not view him as a monster. Things were different in Xibalba, and the sooner she accepted it, the happier she would be. Perhaps, in time, I could arrange a marital alliance with the Luren. Shannon would certainly find one of their males physically appealing, and I could appease Sybella with the offering. I had broken our agreement, but I wished her luck in enforcing a bargain that had been made, technically speaking, with a person who no longer existed.

For the remainder of the day, I put aside all business and spent time with Shannon. She ate, bathed, changed her clothes, and then I showed her the palace and grounds. Once the tour ended, I enlisted her help in decorating private rooms that had been passed over in favor of attention to the public areas, like the throne room.

"Seriously? You'll let me have free rein on all of this?"

"Indeed. And I will need another adviser I can trust. I'll create a title especially for you."

"Holy shit. Okay, so let me get with Greydusk."

I nodded. "He'll assist in obtaining all the materials you need."

Because she was young, she didn't realize I had more important matters to attend to. I couldn't spend days entertaining her, and I had to be sure she would be gainfully occupied. It wouldn't do for her to get homesick and cause trouble. She had to stay here, safe and protected, and out of the hands of my enemies.

At my word, Greydusk escorted Shannon to the storerooms, where we had piles of unsorted goods, fresh from the Saremon confiscations. That left Chance with me in the study, and he didn't look pleased. In preparation for an unpleasant conversation, I shut the door and took a seat behind my desk.

"You have something to say?" My tone was dangerous.

"You lied to her about why you're staying, and then distracted her with busywork. Even though you did try to explain, I don't think she realizes how . . . different you are, and when she does, it's going to be a problem."

"What do you suggest?" It wasn't sarcasm. In this setting, with no witnesses, I'd permit him to speak his mind.

He scrubbed a hand through his inky hair. "I don't know. I'm just worried."

"As am I. But what are my alternatives? If I renounce

the throne and devote my life here to doing good works among the downtrodden, how long do you think we'll live? Any of us?"

"You won't convince me your decisions are driven by altruism," he snapped. "Poor you, taking on the whole city for our benefit? Bullshit. You *want* this."

I pushed to my feet, flattening my hands on the desk. Leaning forward, I whispered, "Am I supposed to apologize for wanting things, Chance? You don't."

He stilled, his tiger's gaze locked on mine. A muscle ticked beside his beautiful mouth. Even in anger I craved him.

With measured steps, I approached him and stopped short of a touch. "As I recall, you pursue your impulses beyond what's reasonable. Or do you feel guilty because you still desire me? Maybe even ... because you want me *more*, this way."

"I don't." But there was no conviction in his voice, and he leaned toward me, just a little. Just enough.

"Power's an aphrodisiac. You crave my certainty. Want it straight in the vein."

"No." But he stepped closer, nostrils flaring.

"Don't fight it anymore," I whispered. "Or pretend. Or lie. You've always secretly wanted someone to control you. Make you give everything. That's where the primitive instincts flare. When you growl *mine* and go savage, you need someone who will say it back—and mean it. You've always been searching for the iron fist in the velvet glove."

No. Don't do this to him. He loves me, not you. *Don't fuck with his head.*

I banished her voice with a little more difficulty this time. Silenced her protests.

Desperation flashed in his face—not because I was wrong, but because I was *right*—and I had him. He couldn't resist such bone-deep need. When he bent his head, I kissed him with every ounce of possession in me. Chance swept the desk with feral hands; then it was all heat and teeth, slick, hard friction, wild as a firestorm.

The Court Convenes

Two weeks after Shannon arrived, I held my first court.

I saw her relatively little, but she busied herself with the decorating. When that work concluded, I'd find something else for her to do. Anything to limit the amount of time we spent together; her questions were piercing, distracting, and I had no time or patience for her emotional needs. Chance had stopped worrying about that, at least to me, as I kept him too occupied in my bed to do much thinking. He was wholly mine now, owned in a way few consorts would permit. In the past, I recalled other lovers who had wanted a rival killed or to be raised to the rank of knight. He had no caste, so he never asked me for favors.

Everything was coming together beautifully.

On that day I sat on the throne with fierce anticipation. Greydusk had located a suitable crown—not the original, of course, but it shone with impressive brilliance as the servant announced the knight from each caste. I had been cautious enough to prohibit them from bringing their own guards into the audience chamber, so a muted rumble of voices came in from the antechamber each time the heavy doors swung open. Zet had sent a contingent of Hazo warriors to add consequence—and guard my person. Four of them on either side of the throne made for an impressive display. They did not speak, merely stared with unnerving intensity.

The throne room itself was glorious. The dark tile shone like obsidian and the new hangings added an air of gravity to the chamber. Other artful touches like rare sculpture had transformed the room, and now it was time for me to meet my public.

I was not surprised to see Sybella in the forefront of my first petitioners. This time, however, I looked her in the eye and felt nothing at all beyond irritation at how she had inconvenienced me when I first arrived in the city. She dropped into a low curtsy, her graceful neck bent, and I let her stay that way until her muscles trembled from holding the pose. The balance of power had shifted, and I gloried in the juxtaposition.

"Rise," I said at last.

"Your Majesty." Her smile was tight, but she had dressed for the occasion in her best stamped silk, matched with real gilt on the buckles of her shoes. Her hair was a dark river, intricately twisted, and her mouth had been painted into a red bow.

"I am willing to hear your oath."

Her expression drew even tauter, revealing lovely bones. But then, the Luren were *always* beautiful, so it would be more interesting to encounter one that did not possess sheer physical perfection. I tapped my nails lightly on the arm of my throne, gazing down on her with an impassive expression. And my silent scrutiny made her uneasy. She shifted her weight.

"We heard how you treated Caim." She meant to sound confident, even silkily threatening, but my regard unnerved her enough to unravel her best intentions.

"When he came to this hall, he *knew* how the encounter must end."

"Why do you suppose he did not fight?" Recovering a little poise, she tested me, wondering how powerful I was in such a hybrid form.

"Because I would have annihilated his caste like the Saremon. He showed courage in accepting my judgment, and thus the Hazo prosper." I gestured to the eight in positions of trust at either side of me. Not that I wasn't constantly watching them for signs of conspiracy or rebellion. In the royal house, I was on my guard at all times. It did not make for restful nights.

My reign had barely passed into its infancy. Careless hands would bring everything tumbling down.

"Yes, I had heard you brought their stronghold low." Anxiety flared again before she dropped her eyes, unable to hold my gaze.

Good for me, if she carried word to the others. Destroying the Saremon in the heart of their strength would give the other castes pause. I alone knew I hadn't destroyed every accursed mage—unless the Saremon had come out of hiding to foment dissidence and insurrection. Yet if the worst came to pass, I would deal with it.

"Indeed. As I said, Sybella, I am willing to hear your oath. You harmed none of my party and did not interfere with my destiny." Without further hesitation, she dropped to her knees, and I spoke the words as I had to Zet. "Do you swear to serve me in all things, to set my will above your own, and obey my commands without question?"

"I do so swear," she whispered.

"Rise, Knight of the Luren. I have no orders for you at this time."

One by one, they all came: the awful Aronesti with their wings and stench, the Birsael, the Dohan, the Klothod, the Mhizul, the Noit, and the Phalxe. They swore to me on bended knee, and most seemed sincere, at least in their fear. It didn't mean they would keep their promises. They might all be plotting, using these pledges as a means to keep my suspicions at bay until they could strike in force. But for my personal recollection of assassination attempts, my thoughts might have sounded like paranoia.

I accepted their pledges and dismissed them. No caste would be welcome in the royal palace until some time elapsed and I sent my spies to test their loyalty. There might be more chaos on the horizon, more structural reorganization necessary before I could be content with the strength of my rule in the city.

Heartsblood, the Imaron knight, came last. He was a little smaller than Greydusk, but otherwise indistinguishable apart from the aura of tangible power he radiated. "You have shown my caste great honor," he said in greeting.

He dropped to his knees without being asked. I read fear in his alien face and a silent question. Greydusk had been serving me faithfully since the beginning; would I reward him for that? It was not beyond the realm of possibility that I would wrest power away from Heartsblood and bestow it upon my favorite—a capricious decision, yes, but one worth considering. In ages past, I would've done it without a second thought. I let the knight kneel in terror for several long moments while I regarded him thoughtfully.

"How would you reward one such as Greydusk? He is my right hand."

"There *is* no higher honor," Heartsblood rejoined.

Ah, clever. I decided I liked this Imaron. With five slim words, he intimated that his own station was already lesser than the one Greydusk had attained through his own merits, and therefore an insult to him, should it be offered as a prize. In the same breath, he honored me; the compliment was well crafted—masterful, truly.

Amusement shone in my expression. "You are kind to say so."

"I would swear my oath, if it pleases Your Majesty."

"It does."

He was quick again, this time when he knew the right words without my prompting. Heartsblood trotted them out as if he had been studying, but with every indication of sincerity. When he finished, I said, "On your feet, Knight of the Imaron. I am pleased with your alacrity. In time, I will host a ball to inaugurate this glorious new era. Until then, be watchful on my behalf and report anything that troubles you."

"Do you expect insurgency, Your Majesty?"

Here, I hesitated. While his wit was pleasing, I didn't trust him. "It is always best to anticipate trouble. That way one may be surprised for the better and prepared for the worst."

The Imaron knight flashed a mouthful of teeth. "Spoken like a true queen."

"You will keep your finger on the city's pulse?"

"I swear it."

I dismissed Heartsblood then. Perhaps he esteemed me enough to keep his word on that alone; and if not, then gratitude might do it. I could have replaced him with Greydusk, knowing his loyalty was absolute. Instead, I chose to give Heartsblood an opportunity to prove himself. That might be all the rope I needed to hang myself, but I couldn't rule this city without allies. Some would come through fear, others through respect.

Deep weariness trembled in my muscles. I glanced at the Hazo standing motionless on either side of my throne. They must be exhausted too; it had been a long day—and how *odd* that I would consider such a thing.

"Go to your barracks now," I said. "I am retiring from the public eye. Clear the hall and the antechamber. I'll see no one else today."

Mustering the last vestige of regal dignity, I swept from the throne room and down the hall. Demons on their hands and knees already, scrubbing the tiles to a high shine, lowered their faces so they could see nothing but the hem of my robe. I missed the freedom of the trousers and boots I'd worn on the streets, but since I wouldn't be engaging in personal combat, I bowed to tradition and wore more impressive, ceremonial garb while holding court.

Deep down I hated it.

Some parts of this, I loathed. Unexpected, that. I'd thought once I pulled together the shambles of my court, the painful dissatisfaction would fade. But it hadn't. With a soft sigh, I went to my rooms to change.

The future lay before me, surprisingly bleak and endless. *I don't want to be queen. I want*—the thought was too foreign for me to finish. It didn't even feel like *my* thought. My head ached in the worst way, and I dug my knuckles into my temples. Nausea rose to accompany the pain. I didn't know how long I sat like that, but a soft touch on my shoulder roused me.

My vision was spotty. I turned, wondering what they needed now. "Yes?"

"You don't look good." Shannon sat down across from me; she and Chance were the only ones who entered my rooms without knocking. "Headache? I guess you can't get Aleve here."

"No." And I feared taking a demon remedy. It might affect my human body in some unpredictable way. In time, I would deal with that problem, research reliable magickal alternatives. And I needed to think about the question of aging, as to how it pertained to the three of us. Demons had much longer natural life spans.

"Have you been avoiding me?" That was like her, some distant part of me recalled. Not letting anything get in her way. And I respected her for it.

"Definitely not. There's just so much to do."

But I had been, because I didn't want her to realize how different I'd become.

"Are you sure it's not because of Jesse?"

For a moment I didn't even know what she was talking about. Then the memories filtered through: a tall, lean cop with a cowboy's walk, tawny hair, and a Texas drawl. But I didn't feel much of anything about her being with him. He didn't belong to me. Never had.

"Honestly, I don't mind at all." I dug deep for some memories and the pain in my skull eased. "I was never really with him anyway. Not like you."

"But he was into you. Not me. I just walked into the vacancy."

That sparked a stronger response, a chemical reaction in my tired brain. The pain blossomed into a full shift, and suddenly I was on the right side of the glass, no longer screaming in silence. *Oh, gods and goddesses, I'm me again.*

"There must've been something, Shan. Maybe he focused on me because I was suitable. You're the one he's not allowed to have without people judging."

"I'm nineteen," she said angrily.

With a small pang of surprise, I realized she was. I'd missed her birthday. "I'm sorry about the forget spell. I never meant for it to last as long as it did. It must have been . . . confusing."

Her brow furrowed, as she remembered. "Yeah. There were . . . fuzzy places, where you used to be. I couldn't remember exactly how I got out of Kilmer. Only that Jesse was involved. He said something traumatic must've happened to screw with our heads. That . . . or magick."

"He guessed that?"

Please, let this last. Don't let the queen take me over before I finish talking to Shannon.

"Yeah, but he wasn't sure on the details. I mean, we knew there were pieces missing. But the harder I tried to fill in the gaps, the worse it got. My whole head hurt and it was easier not to think about it. To move on."

That was the nature of the forget fog. It had a little avoidance spell wrapped up in it, so that people wouldn't stare too hard at the holes in their lives. They'd just step around them and go about their business until it wore off. In theory, that was only supposed to be a couple of hours; a day or two at most. It was more of a prank spell than a powerful one. I'd screwed it up royally to make it last two months . . . until she passed through the water gate and was stripped of its effects.

"I understand how it happened and I'm not upset, I promise. You had a thing for him back in Kilmer."

"It was a crush," she said quietly. "But I never expected he'd look at me because you're right, you were so much more suitable."

I smiled at her. "Just because we worked on paper, that doesn't mean it was right. If he'd truly loved me, the feeling would've remained. He wouldn't have fallen for you as soon as the obstacle in his conscious mind disappeared."

"I never thought of it that way."

"In the beginning, I think he wanted to save me . . . and there was sexual attraction, sure. But it was never anything permanent. I wanted to give him a chance because I felt like I should, not because I thought we were destined to be together. I'd been telling myself I wanted a normal life, and who better to give it to me, right?"

"He's not as normal as you think." Furious color touched her pale cheeks, but she was grinning.

There was a frantic buzzing in the back of my head, like a giant fly caught in sticky paper. *Ninlil. Let her see how she enjoys being trapped without recourse.* It felt so good to talk with Shannon. God, I'd missed her.

I don't like it at all, Ninlil shouted. *I have plans.* She pushed, and it was hard to hold her back. But I managed, savoring the conversation.

"Really?" I drawled the word, inviting confidence.

"Handcuffs," she said, smirking.

Maybe it was a cop thing. That *definitely* would not have worked for me. She opened up by inches, telling me what I'd only glimpsed from snooping in her netbook. It was better this way, and by the time she finished talking, she was smiling, relaxed. She believed I was okay with what they'd done.

Then she realized she'd never see him again. The smile died.

"I'm so sorry," I whispered.

"No, don't be. I get it. I don't want to wreck somebody's soul just so I can make out with my boyfriend."

"Once we finish excavating the Saremon library, I'll put someone on researching a way to connect the realms without a gate."

Her eyes brightened. "Like a demon phone?"

"Kind of."

"I'd appreciate that so much, if you could. Just so I could explain."

"You know Jesse. If you tell him where you are, he won't stop until he finds a way here."

"I won't be specific. I'd just like to let him know that I'm one gifted chick who didn't flake on him."

"You think that would be better?"

I considered my father, who I'd thought abandoned us all those years, when it turned out he had, in fact, been taken. Just like Twila said. If I'd known he loved me and hadn't abandoned me, would that have helped? *Yes,* I decided.

She confirmed my conclusion with a nod. "Totally. At

least I can tell him it wasn't my idea to take off. Otherwise he'll always wonder."

Like I did.

"Like I said, I'll put someone on the spell research as soon as I can."

"Thanks. Maybe it won't be so bad. At least you have Chance, right? So what's the scoop there? You back together?"

"Yes." No doubts, no hesitations. He'd proven himself so far above and beyond the call.

"He seems a little sad sometimes."

"I am too."

Shan nodded. "Being stuck here?"

That wasn't the only reason. Better not to explain what I'd done to survive the search for her. The pressure built in my head. I wouldn't be myself—at least not this version—for much longer. The demon queen shoved hard, trying to gain dominance. We weren't united in the sense that we shared a common purpose; it was more like two misshapen halves of a bowl had been fused together, so that stuff slopped over and ran out the sides, and the way it looked entirely depended on the angle of approach. Now the mismatched bowl was spinning back her away again and the cycle left me dizzy.

"Shan," I said softly, "if I seem different down the line . . . it's the strain of trying to keep us safe."

I didn't want her to know how schizo I'd become. I couldn't stand it if she hated me. Or worse, feared me.

"Dude, I get it. I can't imagine what it's like to deal with all those demons, trying to keep them all in check." She shivered. "It's *so crazy* that your bullshit is all that's standing between us and a hideous death."

I hugged her . . . until I didn't know why I was. I had work to do.

Pushing the girl back, I smiled coolly. "It was a pleasure."

"Yeah." Her expression seemed sad, though I didn't understand why. "It was."

The Spell of the Ball

I should have seen it coming.

For all my memories and experience, this was brand-new; Xibalba had changed in my absence. I struggled to build, but whispers came to me of discontent. I listened and nodded, and I stored them away. Certainly I did the best I could to safeguard the palace compound.

On the fourth day after my téte-à-téte with Shannon, I summoned Greydusk to the courtyard. "What do you see?"

The Imaron scanned the area. "Broken stones and decaying wards."

"Precisely. And both represent a threat to our security."

"I'll have a crew repair the walls and the parapets."

"Thank you. With your help, I intend to reinforce the protections."

Athame in hand, I opened to the astral and assessed the eddies of ancient magick. These runes had been laid so long ago that I had no recollection of them. Ninlil first created them, but queens were always named so as to give the illusion of eternity. Purebred demons had long lives, but they were not immortal. Not even demon queens.

"Of course. What can I do?" Greydusk asked.

"These wards are old ... and powerful, even in decay. I need to use you as a source. Are you willing?"

That required absolute trust, as it left both of us vulnerable. I could kill him if I pulled too much magick through him, and he could do the same to me. It was a two-way connection.

"Certainly, my queen."

Though it was possible to form the link without touching, I found it easier to do so through personal contact. And it formed another layer of trust binding us together. One did not seal a palm against an Imaron's without calculating the risk that he would use his inborn drain. The gravity of Greydusk's expression said he grasped the breadth of what we did. The energy came in a sweet, thick surge. I could have done this for days—without a partner—at the Saremon complex. Here, I needed a boost because the stone was inert, not a hidden wellspring of power.

Unexpectedly, the bond also formed an emotional connection. His awe and adoration flowed into me in unsettling waves, along with his magickal potential, but it wasn't romantic in nature. It felt like a worshipper in the presence of a goddess. I exulted in it, but the silent human observer recoiled, horrified by the prospect. She was growing stronger, harder for me to dominate. Soon the girl might be ascendant as often as I, and that would be disastrous for my ambitions. She didn't give a damn about ruling in Sheol.

Hand in hand, we walked to the gates. First, I restored potency to the sigils on the gate, the ones that prevented anyone from entering unless they bore my mark. All of my servants had been interviewed and then tattooed with a magical crest that gave them right of passage. Anyone who came through the gates without my mark died a painful death. Early on, a few had tried, and the weak wards hadn't been enough to end them—just make them wish for a quick and merciful death once the Hazo took them into custody.

More layers of protection against offensive spells. Harmful intent. Weapons. Mind-altering charms. It took the rest of the day to renew the wards, infusing them

with my personal strength. Greydusk was exhausted, as
was I, but I'd been careful. Neither of us would suffer
lasting ill effects from this day's work.

I offered a grateful nod. "Thank you. I couldn't have
done that without you."

A queen never said that sort of thing to a lesser creature. Unquestionably, my human half weakened me, but
it was the sort of softness that roused a reaction of
shocked pleasure in my subordinates. It served to keep
them off balance, at least.

"It was an honor." Greydusk swept a credible bow.
"There's much to arrange before the ball, my queen. I
believe Heartsblood is on your calendar for the mor-
row."

Ah, yes. "I'll be ready for him."

Once I parted from the Imaron, I used my remaining
energies to add a layer of protection to the bracelet Tia
had given me. I knew some demons found it odd that I
chose such humble personal adornment; I was never
without it. Viewed in the astral, the item was layered in
wards, and they were compelling, beautiful, with the
flickering energies intertwined for my benefit. But they
were missing one crucial factor, and I remedied the over-
sight with painstaking care. I wouldn't be surprised by an
offensive spell again.

For the remainder of the day, I read in thick dossiers
about how the various castes were responding to my
rule. Outwardly, the city had accepted my return. Trade
continued, factories produced goods, and feuds ran their
usual courses. Beneath the external quiet, though, dire
and threatening whispers fomented.

Heartsblood was reliable in his reports. "The Saremon bear watching," he told me the next morning in my
office. "I don't trust their quiet. I hear rumors now and
then that they're planning something."

"Do they have sufficient numbers?"

"I don't know. I wish I did."

"Is there any word on who their allies may be?"

He shook his head. "The Eshur, along with their servants the Obsir, stress their neutrality."

That didn't surprise me; they were concerned only with maintaining order. "Did they rule in my stead?"

"No." Heartsblood paused, obviously seeking an analogy. "I suppose it's more accurate to say that each caste territory functions like a self-governed city-state. If there are disputes or laws broken, borders violated, then the Eshur step in. Their judgments are enforced by the Obsir."

"Their power has increased in my absence." In my day, the Eshur attended only to petty matters, too small to be worth my personal attention, and the Obsir, also known as the Hidden, had been *my* enforcers. "Would it be worth my effort to woo the Hidden away from their quiet masters?"

"I think not, my queen. The Obsir and the Eshur have been hand in glove for such a long time. If you fail, it would only weaken your position."

"Truly spoken. You'll come when you have more intelligence?"

"Assuredly." Heartsblood bowed and let himself out of my study.

When the knight left that day, I was uneasy. At length, I pondered the implications . . . and all the data I'd received. In the end, I proceeded as I had in the past—with lavish spectacles to distract the masses. The formal coronation ball would strengthen my power base, terrify my enemies, and introduce Chance as my consort. The plans had been ongoing for some time, and now was the moment to strike.

The day of the ball I spent with my dressers. It took hours to curl my hair just so, apply cosmetics, and tweak my gown so that the fit was flawless. In this game, appearances mattered. I must prove that the Once and Future Queen had ascended and that they could dislodge me from my rightful place when Sheol froze over.

Hours later, I stood in the ballroom with my hand on Chance's arm. He was resplendent in black and silver, his suit tailored to match my ornate gown. I wore my father's heart about my throat—an enormous ruby fit for a queen on a hammered silver chain. Its bloody shine brought out the highlights in my artfully arranged hair. Together, we watched the assembled crowd. The Hazo stood at the perimeter, scrutinizing the guests.

Along with the knights, I'd also invited a mixed swath of important persons, those who had influence within their castes. Some hadn't been born when the archangel stole me from my rightful throne—therefore, they could not look on this frail form and find it lacking in comparison—but I saw flickers of doubt in the countenances of old demons, who had known me before.

". . . pretender," I heard someone whisper.

But when I turned, the crowd was too close and thick for me to make out who had spoken. My nails bit into Chance's arm. In an easy motion, his palm covered my fingers, stroking lightly.

Then he spoke in my ear. "You *are* their queen."

It was enough. I lifted my chin. When the guests paused, I led the way through the crowded ballroom to where Greydusk stood. He too had donned black and silver for the occasion to differentiate himself from other Imaron in attendance. Before the festivities began in earnest, I had two important matters of business to conduct.

"Greydusk, step forward."

The Imaron did so, hands clasped behind his back. We had rehearsed for the occasion, so this should go off without a hitch. "Before these gathered nobles, I do formally commission you as my Baron of the Exchequer, responsible for all matters of trade and finance pertaining to Xibalba. The title shall be hereditary, passing in perpetuity to your heirs. Do you accept this office?"

"I do, my queen. On behalf of my son, I thank you." He sank to one knee, dazed with delight, though he had known this was coming, formalizing his reward for believing in me when I had been a stupid, worthless human of uncertain potential. As our work together had begun with a pledge of faith, I did not ask for the ritual that bound him to his promise; I trusted that his loyalty was absolute.

"Greet your new baron." I stared out over the crowd, registering the waves of hatred and envy.

I'd created a higher rank than knight; now Greydusk, once a lower-class Imaron, had leapt over those older and more powerful. It would goad them—and I intended it to. From their subsequent treachery, I would uncover those conspiring with the Saremon and decapitate them all in one stroke.

From the crowd, Heartsblood began the applause with loud, deliberate slaps of his oversize palms. Part of me thought I should be shocked at the monstrous faces staring back at me. I was at a ball full of *demons*, acting like it was no big deal. Deliberately I shut that voice down, but it was a little harder each time; the human girl gained purchase each time I let her in. Others joined the ovation until the room rang with unwilling approbation. Greydusk rose and accepted his due with a nod.

"Before I release you to enjoy my hospitality, I present to you the king consort, Chance Yi." A rumble of mixed reactions ran through the crowd. I spoke over them. "Thus the succession is secured. There may be an heir on the way, even now." I touched my belly for effect, noting the way Chance tensed beside me. "Now enjoy the party!"

The newly minted Baron Greydusk cued the players at the far end of the room.

When the musicians sounded the first notes, I stepped into the first turn with Chance. The court let us dance alone for a few moments in a gesture of respect and then they joined us on the floor. Tension buzzed along my skin as he spun me. I registered the dark looks and speculative, watchful eyes.

"So," he said conversationally. "At what point did you plan on telling *me* you're having my baby? Oh, wait."

His knife-edged disrespect, laced with anger, secretly amused me, but I leveled on him a stern look. "The queen controls all such matters."

"I'm just a sperm donor, then?" A tremor ran through his hand, where it held mine. He twirled me in time to the music, his face pale. "Is this *really* happening?"

I'd spoil him with such behavior, but I answered anyway, in an undertone, "Not yet. It would be unwise to bring our heir into such an unstable situation. I merely used the possibility as an agitant."

"I can't even follow your train of thought anymore," he admitted, his voice low.

That didn't trouble me. My chosen male didn't need to be brilliant, or even capable. He only needed to be virile and loyal. By comparison, Chance was surprisingly adroit in every respect. He would sire a fine daughter to rule in my stead someday; and perhaps his divine blood would compensate for my human deficiencies.

"Those who have the most to lose will actively strive against a firm succession," I whispered.

That was all I needed to say. He understood my plan and approved it with a quick nod. But he still looked shaken. I might make his head explode if I didn't consult him regarding our reproductive schedule when the time came. It surprised me that I didn't entirely mind. If I'd had such a powerful bond with my consort when the archangel's call came, I might have denied it. I might have resisted temptation. If I hadn't assented in my own destruction and accepted the pull, none of this would have come to pass.

That was my deepest shame. I had abandoned my people for a seductive summons—for a taste of new, intoxicating power. And it cost me everything.

This time it would be different.

The band played on. Drink followed and laughter outpaced the whispers. They had forgotten the glamour of a queen's court. I'd spent an hour in here before the ball, leaving little traces of magick to make the night gleam a little brighter, encouraging frolic and recreation.

Shannon waved to me from across the room; she was dancing with Greydusk, surprisingly enough. At least she had the sense to keep away from the Luren. One of them would have her naked in an antechamber before she knew what he was doing. She looked lovely in a black gown with blue accents. I lifted a hand from Chance's shoulder as he spun me. When we twirled, she left my sight.

"Thirsty?" Chance asked eventually.

"A bit."

Waiters circulated with trays of shimmering golden wine, but I led him over to the crystalline bowl filled with an effervescent red liquid.

He eyed it with skepticism. "What is that?"

With a half smile, I indicated the room, full of monstrous company. Some had wings and horns, odd-colored skin; others looked more or less human, apart from extra bits like tails or claws. And others were more beautiful than any human could hope to be. Such a diabolical assembly—and they belonged to me, one and all.

"Devil's punch, what else?"

Chance laughed quietly. "What's in it?"

"Best not to ask." I recited what had become a running joke with Greydusk.

Before I took a sip, a capering Noit tested it for me. As queen, I had a taster, and this little idiot had volunteered. I watched for a few moments, but it showed no ill effects, apart from the bad manners of smacking its wide mouth and burping. "More!"

"The rest is mine." I took a sip, and the flavors burst on my tongue.

After I drained the glass and Chance sampled it, he swept me back out into the dancing, mostly as a defense against the encroachers who inched closer while we stood idle. I found his protective nature . . . delightful. Other consorts had proven less than concerned about my welfare.

I did not dance with anyone else that night. And so I was in Chance's arms when the hammer fell. The ballroom filled with wintry mist and beneath the fog lurked cold shadows hunting me—oblong smudges of darkness with icy hunger at their hearts. They hated the living and they drank our energy like a fine wine.

I knew who had sent them; I *didn't* know how they had gotten past my wards.

Traitor. The word whispered in my head, even as the guests screamed and fled. A panicked Noit tripped a Luren female in a lavish gown, which tangled about her graceful feet. She fell to her knees and a shade consumed her. Her ivory flesh went blue and then crackled with ice. Soon, it shriveled and went dry like a husk, and when the shade drifted on, it had gained form and solidity. Across the room, an Aronesti took flight, sailing above the crowd toward the doors. A shade rose and swallowed the demon. First came the muffled screaming, and then silence, which was worse.

Quickly I cast to counter the freezing fog, making it harder for the shades to find living bodies to drain. Even demons lived; these creatures did not. They came from someplace darker and colder than Sheol, and that sent a chill straight through my body. The shades were new monsters, ones with which my pitiful human half had more experience than I. The Saremon had sent them; of that I had no doubt.

Warm steam filled the room, confusing the shades. Darkness swirled amid the white, steamy bursts. The guests fought one another to reach the exits, maddened by danger and terror, skills and magick made unreliable by too much liquor. Across the room, Greydusk huddled protectively over Shannon, fighting toward the doors. His body rippled, and then shifted; the Swordwraith took his place, and he threshed the girl clear. My last sight of them came when she turned to lift her chin at me, an acknowledgment that she was safe; then Greydusk changed back and led her away.

"I'm getting you out of here," Chance said.

I was torn. It would send a stronger message if I stayed and fought, but I already had several caste knights, including Heartsblood and Zet, and my Hazo guards battling the invading spirits. Staying meant risking everything for pride. While I weighed the factors, he took the decision from me. He swept me into his arms and pushed toward the exit. The Hazo saw the consort coming and cleared a path with their magickal axes; they didn't seem to care who got in the way of their swings, and at the moment neither did I.

Someone had betrayed me. There was no other explanation.

I couldn't count this, definitively, as an assassination

attempt. Instead, it acted to shake my people's faith in my ability to govern, since I couldn't even keep my own perimeter secure. Really, it was a brilliant first maneuver in a guerilla campaign against me. I admired the executor, even as I considered the best way to eliminate him. I had to find Oz. And kill him.

Kiss Me Like You Mean It

In my chamber, I activated the preventive wards on the
doors. They'd fry anyone who attempted to pass through
without my permission. Butch raised his head and stared
at the crackling gold energy and then yapped at me as if in
question.

To my surprise, I answered. "It's a mess downstairs,
but we're safe in here."

That seemed to be enough reassurance. He went back
to sleep.

The next thing I knew, Chance was kissing me, pas-
sionately, furiously. He drew me against him, hard, his
whole body shaking. For a few delicious seconds, I fell
into his need, before setting my hands against his chest.

"Flattering, my darling, but this isn't the time. We
must—"

"You must *stay safe.*"

Ah. The imperative to protect must be overwhelming
him with sexual instincts. The Hazo, if chosen as consorts,
were prone to such behavior. How interesting—a male
as beautiful and elegant as Chance shared those primitive urges.

"Please," he whispered, pressing hot kisses down my
throat. "Greydusk will alert us when the danger's passed."

"And you propose we make love while monsters run amok in my demesne?"

"Better than fiddling while Rome burns."

"But not by much," I said softly, stepping away.

A visible tremor shook him and he turned to brace his forearm against the ornate carved bedpost. He dropped his face against his arm and compassion sparked, a foreign instinct. For the first time, I saw what I was doing to him. I touched him lightly between the shoulder blades.

"Is it bad?"

He exhaled. "Yes. You consume me. I exist for *you* . . . and I don't even know who the hell you are. *Not* Corine, that's for damn sure."

"I was Corine. And I was Ninlil. Now I encompass us both, although not comfortably so. Does it trouble you?" I hadn't given any thought to his feelings or his state of mind as I went about my business. That wasn't the unusual bit; the odd aspect of this conversation was that we were having it at all.

"It did. Not so much anymore. And that bothers me."

"Because you don't loathe me? In your heart, you told yourself that you love *her*, not me — that you could esteem nothing in a creature like me."

"Yes," he whispered.

"And now?" His reply mattered.

"You know the answer." His face grew taut and desperate. He didn't want to speak it aloud.

"Give me a truthful response and we'll go to bed." Manipulative, certainly.

"I love you," he bit out. "You're the same to me. These days I don't care who I'm talking to, whether you're fierce, ambitious, and powerful, or sweet and soft. I love both sides, and I feel like I'm losing my mind."

"You love me?" Shock reverberated through me. Consorts did not love the queen; they submitted to her will. They obeyed. They hoped for favor.

But love? Never.

Until now.

"Awfully," he said. "Endlessly. It's a torment."

My heart shifted. Softened. The human woman pushed, pushed, until she surged forth, spinning me away.

"Chance, it's me." I touched his cheeks with my fingertips. "I'm still in here. Just . . . she doesn't let me drive very often."

"Corine?" His desperate happiness sparkled like polished diamonds.

"I'm here. I love you."

"Thank God."

Before I could savor his mouth on mine, she shoved me back. This wasn't union. It was a revolving door. *Not* what she'd promised.

The other banished, I stripped him from his clever tailored suit and he tore away the layers of my gown with its spell-enhanced fabric. Once it came down to skin, we weren't gentle. Primal impulses drove him, and I fed that fire with uninhibited response.

Chance kissed me again and again, his hands frantic on my body. He backed me up, one hand curled around my head. Each step pressed us closer with a tantalizing friction. His hard heat drove me wild.

"Not the bed," he growled. "Like we almost did it in Kilmer."

A swirl of memory eluded me and then firmed. Held. *Chance backed me into the bathroom, spun me, and pressed me up against the bathroom door. I felt every inch of my nakedness in contrast to his sleekly clothed muscles. He'd grown even harder since I left. When his mouth took mine, he didn't ask if I wanted it, or if I'd permit it. Heat sparked between us like two live wires and I came up on my toes.*

The wall felt cool against my back when he pressed me against it this time, but I was different now. I was done turning him away. He was mine, and I'd never let him go. I curled a thigh around his hip, then he lifted me. In his ferocity, he was a selfish lover, hard hands on my hips, working in mad, deep thrusts.

I urged him on with nails in his shoulder. In this position, I couldn't move much. He was in control. He liked domination when the protective urge rose—and submission when it didn't. In turn, I enjoyed him tied to my bed, but I also enjoyed the rare sense that I'd lost control.

And then I did. I screamed and scratched, rational thought gone. He arched into me and came in hard pulses that left him weak. Both shaking, we staggered to the bed and collapsed on it. Chance wrapped his arms around me as if he couldn't bear to lose contact with me for even a moment. I'd never permitted myself to bond so deeply with a lover before. He was in my head, my heart, down to blood and bone. Somehow, *her* feelings had become mine. She had gouged out a channel inside me that belonged to him alone.

"Better?" I whispered, kissing his shoulder where I'd scratched him.

Shivers still wracked him, but he smiled at me with eyes gone molten gold with satiation. "More relaxed, anyway."

"Are you sorry you came with her?"

He ran his fingers through his hair as he considered. "No. I can't claim I dreamed of reigning and having babies in hell, but it's not terrible."

I nodded, curling into his arms. "Sheol has its beauties."

"Like you." He kissed the top of my head. "I was so scared I'd lose you . . . and this time, there'd be no coming back from it, no chance to beat the odds."

"You mean because I'd be all Ninlil and no Corine?" That didn't trouble me; he had loved her first, but he cared for me too. He was, truly, an extraordinary male.

"Yeah."

"I didn't want to destroy her. Only survive. The angels took *everything* from me . . . and I had harmed no humans. I seek no foothold there. My subjects come to earth in response to human ceremonies, complete with offerings and rituals!" Even now, the unfairness of it boiled my blood.

"I don't think most people realize that." Chance levered up on one elbow. "Explain to me why angels and demons hate each other so much. They say you fell or something? There was a rebellion in heaven?"

The question distracted me from what might be happening downstairs. Anger lanced through me. "That's rubbish. If there *is* a heaven, the angels have never seen it. They create their own legends, every eon or so, and then update all the manuals."

"There are manuals?" he asked, a brow arched in surprise.

"I don't know. I was being sarcastic. The truth is, angels and demons are descended from the same lineage. They come from Sheol, just as we do. It's not heaven or hell. . . . It's just another realm."

"Interesting."

"There was a civil war, but it wasn't over God or *divine orders*. It was so long ago that even our records are incomplete. I only know it had to do with a question of succession. It was before the first Ninlil took the throne, before the castes formed as we know them. There were only two types early in our history . . . the winged and the walkers. We were more beautiful then too, but once half our number left, it led to inbreeding, and you end up with monstrous creatures like the Noit and the Aronesti."

"What happened next?"

"The demons *won*," I said quietly. "We booted the losers out of our realm to yours, where they went to work interfering with the course of human history. Now they have a new tale, a new hierarchy, but it's nonsense. An ancient *ka*, who calls himself an archangel, organizes their mythology according to his personal agenda."

Chance frowned; I had succeeded in rattling him. "*Ka?*"

"In some old languages, it means *spirit* and that is an accurate enough name for us, what we used to be." It hurt me to remember these things because then I had to consider how I'd learned them. The information I gave Chance had not come to me easily or without anguish.

As if he keyed into my thoughts, Chance asked, "How do you know all this? You said the records are incomplete."

Hard to explain in words, but: "When the archangel summoned me, there was a moment of unity, where I knew him . . . all his thoughts and memories. Some of it stayed with me, after I was wrenched away and he bound me to the Solomon line."

"So you saw inside this . . . archangel?" I could tell he no longer liked the term.

"Yes. He was very old. He would have been a king in Sheol with such power."

Chance nodded. "He might have led the revolt."

"If I ever knew, it was not one of the memories that stayed with me." A half shrug in apology—I was not the queen I had been—but sometimes different didn't mean lesser. Perhaps the kindness that came from my human half permitted me to see things in a new light, and would result in a brighter future for Xibalba.

The light of debate sparked in his eyes. "You're very critical of how the angels interfere in the human world, but how are demons better? So many are just so . . . evil."

I raised a brow. "So are humans. Am I to judge your race on those who prey on children and dismember their loved ones? You have not met every demon in Xibalba. Many are interested only in living their lives. Some enjoy pain. Others craft magickal trinkets. Do you see a pattern?"

A wince revealed that I'd scored a hit. "You're saying demons are like humans, some good, some bad, some neither."

"But I would, wouldn't I? Especially if I'm an amoral, lying she-devil who only wants to steal your seed."

He laughed softly. "A pity I keep ruining the challenge by giving it to you. Why do you think he summoned you?"

More anger, dagger sharp. "He wanted a general for their war against us. They bred among you in the early days and gave birth to the most brutal of their foot soldiers, the Nephilim. Since then, these *angels* have used humans as their pawns. I see nothing good in the way they kill, convicting their victims on blind faith." I shuddered, remembering. "I loathe knowing she shared this body with one."

"I . . . what?" Beside me, Chance froze. "Corine . . . ?"

"Before I woke, she slept with one. You call him Kel."

"I knew about that. *Not* that he's Nephilim. He says he's the Hand of God."

I scoffed. "Those fools are made of empty titles. I suspect the archangels invent them to inflate their minions with false consequence and reinforce their blind faith when it falters."

"So there's no master plan?"

I shrugged. "If there is, I have no knowledge of it. Sheol is old, but so is your world. There are no answers to some questions."

He hesitated, as if unsure whether he ought to ask something. I encouraged him with a nod. "Did she ... did Corine know his nature, when they—"

"Yes. She loves him, you know." Horror rolled through me—hers—in a quiet wave—and her protest echoed in my head. *Not anymore. I love Chance. You're only saying that to make him prefer you.* "That is *not* an affection we share, unlike the one for you."

Chance pushed out a shaky breath, looking as though he'd been punched in the throat. "I'm done with personal questions," he said quietly, eyes closed.

I hate you for this. I ignored her pain and grief.

"*I* love you." I touched his cheek and wondered if he knew that I had never spoken those words before.

His lashes flickered up; they were thick and spangled his eyes like stars. I felt I could stare at him forever and let the city burn. *That*, in truth, was too powerful an emotion. I should love no one person above the city that I ruled. Yet I did. He was the quiet repeating echo at the core of me, the smile within every heartbeat, and my dreams when I slept. The human Corine laughed in my head, delighted she'd given me this weakness.

Then he smiled and my heart nearly stopped. "I see why they fought and died for your favors."

Heat touched my cheeks. "Have you been listening to gossip?"

"They tell stories."

"About what?"

"The old days when you tired of a consort and held a

match in the arena. Scores of demons entered the lists and the survivor joined you in your bed."

"I expect they told you I had my lovers killed once the affair ended."

He nodded.

"It was . . . prudent," I explained, marveling that I felt the need for his understanding. "A consort who has fallen out of favor can foment rebellion among other malcontents, destabilizing entire zones."

"Any man would be bitter over losing you," he said.

I had heard such words before shaped in idle flattery, but this was the first time I believed them. His sincerity sparked between us, and it was terrifying. I had lost myself once; I could easily do so again.

"I love the way you kiss me."

He paused, distracted. "You do?"

"Yes. You kiss me like you mean it. Always."

"I lost a layer of civilization somewhere along the way, I guess, but I'm glad it works for you." Chance went on, not looking at me, "Tell me where this ends. An execution when you tire of me?"

The pain at this mere possibility eviscerated me. I would do anything to prevent it. Kill anyone. Burn the city I loved. His safety might as well be written in runes on my skin; I could never harm Chance.

"Never. You're mine, always. I will bind myself with the ritual they use upon the Imaron to reassure you, if you wish. That way, any actions I take against you would cost my own life. In truth, I'd prefer it that way."

He kissed the tip of my nose. "No, I don't need the spell to believe you. Can't live without me, huh?"

"I can," I said. "I don't want to."

"Me either." He leaned his forehead against mine.

Greydusk knocked then. I donned a robe quickly, dropped the wards on the door, and answered. "Is the estate secure?"

"It is, my queen."

That night should have signified the best time of my life. It should have heralded halcyon days.

Instead it marked the beginning of the end.

All In

Two nights later, the first indication of new trouble came in the form of a terrified Noit servant dancing outside my door. "Monsters," it shrieked. *"Monsters!"*

Since the Noit preferred to communicate in annoying, obscure rhyme, the situation must be dire, even if I didn't have all the details yet. I dressed quickly in my combat clothing—all black—and boots, athame strapped to my thigh. Chance was already pulling his pants on, roused by the Noit and the commotion outside our rooms.

"Report," I demanded of Greydusk as I found him in the hallway.

"The Vortex has gone down."

"What? How is that possible?"

"Unknown, my queen. But the Xaraz have taken the opportunity to strike. They've overrun the Luren quarter and are marching toward the Barrens."

"And the monsters?" Chance asked.

Greydusk replied, "You remember the Gorder? There are worse things in the wastes beyond our walls. Thumpers, magickeaters, wailers. They'll all come without the Vortex to repel them. It will be mass carnage."

The Imaron seemed shaken, looking to me to set the situation to rights, but I'd never even heard of a spell strong enough to disable the Vortex, even temporarily.

Unless . . . "Could it be done if all the surviving Saremon worked in concert?"

"Perhaps," the demon answered.

A link of that magnitude, similar to what Greydusk and I had done in the courtyard, would be unspeakably powerful. Normally demon mages didn't trust one another enough to permit such an undertaking, but when their survival depended on my extermination, desperate times called for desperate measures. It was a bold stroke and one that would end the battle once and for all.

I wished I still felt confident that I would win.

"Have they breached our walls?"

"No."

"Protect the city," I said. "Send a runner to the Hazo. They must fight. It's what they live for, after all."

In earlier times I would have had a trained military to handle this threat, but I was still putting the pieces back together. They'd struck sooner than I expected, and I wasn't ready. My spies hadn't brought me the names of the conspirators, so I didn't yet know who I could trust.

Helpless and blind, Corine whispered in my head. *You are no true queen, only a pathetic echo of ages lost. Let me out. Let me fight.*

This was an odd juxtaposition. Once, it was me, whispering to her as I scrabbled to gain a foothold. Now, I felt tempted to turn the mess I'd created over to her. While I worried, Chance slipped his gloves on, flexed long fingers, and whispered the command word. Flames burst to life around his knuckles—a pure white-blue, unlike the last time.

I glanced at Greydusk. "Does that mean something?"

"The gloves only burn like that for a true king."

Chance offered a crooked smile. "Told you."

That roused a smile and dampened some of my worry. "Did we confiscate anything that could help in defense of the city?"

"No, my queen. You instructed me to focus on household goods."

So I had. It seemed important to get the palace habitable so I had a base of operations. A queen did not beg shelter from her subjects like a supplicant. In consequence, I wasn't ready for such a battle. *Fine.* I'd improvise. My human half was best at that anyway.

I grabbed the Noit running up and down the hall, delighted with the chaos it had created, and slapped it across the back of the head to settle it down. Satisfied that I had its attention, I demanded, "Were you outside the walls just now?"

"Yes, Majesty!"

"And you saw the monsters?"

"Yes, Majesty."

"And where were they? How far away?"

I couldn't cower and let the Saremon wreck the city. There would be nothing left for me to govern. If the creatures had already ruined the Luren sector and were headed to the Barrens, there must be a reason—

"March, march, eat our hearts!" it sang.

"Offer me another poem instead of a sensible reply and I'll eat your heart myself." I meant it, though it would doubtless be black, shriveled, and disgusting. Even if it made me sick for a week, I'd keep my word.

The Noit *knew* it too; the creature sobered. "Apologies, my queen. Sometimes one gets carried away playing the clown."

"Understood."

"The situation is dire. The gates have fallen and the Vortex is long gone. The Noit and Phalxe sectors are burning. There are monsters everywhere. Magick hangs in the air, remnants of heavy spell casting. People are panicked, and they're fighting in the streets. I'm not sure they even know who the enemy is."

"Tell the castle staff not to venture outside the courtyard walls. Dismissed."

The little Noit scurried off to carry out my orders, leaving me with Chance and Greydusk. Before I could formulate a plan of action, Shannon ran down the hall toward us. Her black hair was spiked, standing on end, but not on purpose, and she had dark circles beneath her eyes, as if she hadn't slept well. A pang of regret pierced me. *I didn't want this life for her.*

"What the hell's going on?" she asked.

Greydusk filled her in while I paced. Leaving the castle grounds might be foolhardy if the Saremon were trying to draw me out, but at least this would end. And then I had the answer. *Thank you, human female witch.* A quieter echo: *Thanks, Mom.*

"This way," I said. "Quickly."

"Why?" Shannon asked.

"No time. If you'd rather stay in the palace, it should be safe."

"No *way*. Have you seen the things that live here? No offense," she added to Greydusk.

The Imaron bared his teeth. "None taken."

"I'm with you," Chance said.

"Even if it's a wild, implausible plan?"

He kissed me hard on the mouth. "That's the best kind."

At top speed, I ran through the corridors, ignoring the way the frightened servants dropped to their knees. I didn't have time for ceremonious behavior. The towers at each corner led to the walls overlooking the city square. With the others trailing behind me in various stages of interest and confusion, I dashed up the steep, curving stairs to the top of the wall, where there were a few guards posted.

They snapped to attention on my arrival, stammering excuses, but I waved them off.

"I don't expect you to defend the city alone," I said. "You were hired to keep watch over the palace, and that you have done. Now stand back."

Quieting, they did. I wouldn't leave the safety of the wards without a little leverage, and I was about to summon it. First I built an image of the Gorder in my mind. Then I shaped the spell energies as I had done that first time, outside the city. Energy spindled to life at my core, flickering and wild, like lightning over water.

Then I sliced a hole up high in the glimmering field that protected the castle. Too high for anything but a flyer to reach; it was a necessary, calculated temporary vulnerability. The guards cried out in protest, and I ignored them, along with mutters from Chance and Shannon. Greydusk held his silence, trusting me fully.

With a shout of "*Advenio!*" I released the spell.

Outside the walls, the ground rumbled. My Gorder was in the city, looking for me. I'd suspected that might be the case, as it had imprinted on me like a big pet, and now I would use it to destroy my enemies, just as it had freed us from the magus trap. I stood my ground as the others backed away. They didn't know my plan and for obvious reasons I hadn't shared it.

I couldn't protect them all. The wards would do it in my absence. This city belonged to me, and I would fight for it. Since I had no army, it fell to my magick and me. *So be it.*

When the Gorder stuck its blind head up over the wall, scenting me with its open mouth, I took a running start and leapt from the rampart. I passed through the narrow gap in the field and as I tumbled back, I sealed it behind me, so they could not follow. Chance tried, and he slammed into an implacable wall. His face twisted when he realized my intentions, but I couldn't hear his cries as I fell. I might have managed a levitation spell, if I hadn't focused on closing the wards. I was too close to the ground to have time now.

"Catch me, friend!" In answer, the Gorder snapped its jaws shut, snagging my thigh just before I slammed into the ground. The save hurt, wrenched my back and pierced my flesh, but the creature didn't mean to harm me. It adored me; the feeling rolled off it in waves.

"Down now."

The monster dropped me as gently as it could manage and shivered in delight when I stroked its side. I pictured our mutual enemy and sent it along our bond. Fury sang in my blood as I scrambled up; there was a place to rest where its wormy neck met its lizard shoulders. Gorder hide felt rough and hot to the touch while bumps along its back gave me a place to hang on.

"Ready to fight?" My monstrous mount reared and carried me toward the battle I heard ringing in the distance.

If I encountered more beasts, I might bend them to my will. I had power to spare and it could best be spent on driving an army instead of limited to offensive spells. The ones I'd left behind fell away like smoke in the wind. So did my doubts and fears. Distance became no obstacle with the fearsome Gorder carrying me at such breakneck speed. We raced toward the city gates. First I'd pacify the worst areas and then I'd hunt down the magicians responsible for dismantling the Vortex.

"The queen!" The awed cry went up from those cowering in broken buildings. "Ninlil will save us!"

I will, or die trying.

As I passed, I called, "Get to safety! This will be over soon."

The Noit hadn't exaggerated the threat. Smoke rose from multiple fires, and the screaming increased when I drew closer to the battle. I unleashed a spell to suck the air away from the flames, and they sputtered out. The Gorder ate a demon mage casting from a rooftop, and I raised up on my knees to assess the scene. *Saremon insurgents, definitely.*

A nightmare monster lashed out at random victims, eviscerating them with its swordlike talons. It had black skin and spines all over its body. *Mine*, I thought. The spell took shape in my head, a sweet, soul-stealing magick, and I unleashed it on the Swordwraith. The creature stiffened, its wild rage fighting my mental leash, but I pressed while the Gorder whipped its tail, smashing another Saremon. With a scream, it accepted my mental domination and turned its natural weapons to my will.

Swordwraith and Gorder—my army grows.

But it gave me some indication how many creatures I could hold at any given time. One more would tax my limits. Four would break my mind wide open and unleash those I controlled at the worst possible time. I'd pit these two against any foes, however, so I shouldn't need more.

In short order, the Swordwraith and Gorder threshed through my opponents, leaving the terrified citizens intact. A few at a time, they rose from the wreckage, cheering. Even in the old days, they could not have sounded more glad or grateful. Listening to the welcome shouts of "Ninlil! Ninlil!" I turned the Gorder toward the next pocket of insurrection.

As we moved, the magick purled out of me in trickles. I gauged my reserves and calculated how long I could manage these two beasts. The Gorder, since it liked me, required less output. The Swordwraith fought my tether with each step, draining me faster. In time, I'd kill it and seek a more docile pet.

I went from zone to zone, destroying resistance and putting out fires. After each fight, I grew weaker. More exhausted. But I pressed on, hearing the screams in the night that said there was nobody else coming to save my people. The wreckage ravaged me; nothing so dire had happened inside Xibalba in living memory.

The streets ran with blood, choked with the detritus of fallen buildings. Corpses lay with no one to cart them away, and quasits shrieked and circled, diving to rend and gnaw the flesh. Noit sector, clear. Luren sector, fires out. In the Phalxe part of the city, I collected another pet, and added to my mental burden. The Wailer resembled an enormous stingray made of darkness and malice with a broad, flat mouth that hurled sonic screams at my enemies. They fell after one blast, eyes bleeding. I stopped casting entirely. Taking the wailer for my small army also meant hitting my limit. I could manage no more.

Pain became my constant companion as I swept the streets, searching for the Saremon who kept the Vortex down. I hit heavy resistance in the Mhizul quarter and I ducked low against the Gorder's neck as a fireball exploded on the stones in front of me. The Swordwraith screamed and charged; it was all I could to aim it at the mage instead of the helpless mob fleeing before her.

Its long, bladed arms lashed out, severing the Saremon at the waist. The upper half of the body tilted and fell over while the legs took two more steps before buckling. Blood fountained up, slicking the streets, and the terrified cries increased until the citizens realized the Swordwraith wasn't attacking them. The monsters trembled, tugging fiercely against my mental leash, but I held firm.

"Find shelter!" I called.

As one, the crowd dropped to its knees amid the carnage and bowed their heads. "Yes, my queen."

"Now!"

They did as I bade them, running away toward the city center. The worst of the damage lay closer to the walls, where more monsters gathered. By dawn, I had quieted the last city block and turned toward the broken gates. There, a monstrous army gathered, but they were so wild with hunger and rage that they fought among themselves, just inside the city. My vision turned spotty from the effort of holding my three pets, and I could only send them all a vague order to attack.

The Swordwraith hurled itself into the fray, slicing limbs and veins and keening its vicious delight. The Wailer fluttered over the mass of beasts and aimed a shout that liquefied half their brains. A mob of monsters fell over, all wings and fangs and razor-sharp claws. The Gorder lashed and ate and smashed with its tail while I held on with the last of my last strength.

I must not falter. I must end this. For my people. My city.

The man I love.

Just when I thought blackness would overtake me, the battle ended. There remained only my three monsters and an endless corpse pile. The burning would take days without magickal assistance.

Only one more step. Almost there.

"Find magick for me," I whispered to my mount. "Strong magick."

It stood to reason that the joint casting the Saremon had performed left a powerful trail. The Gorder was blind, but it had other senses. This might not work—

Then it fixed. A shudder ran along its awful length and it leveled two buildings, taking the most direct path. Its speed left the Swordwraith howling with rage, but the wailer kept pace above us, broad wings flapping lazily.

The Saremon mages heard us coming. They scram-

bled from their hiding place like rats, and once they
moved, the Vortex snapped back into place, a swirling
maelstrom of unthinkable power. There were twelve of
them, fleeing before me in desperate terror. The wailer
stunned them, unable to kill through their magickal protections, and I rode them down. My Gorder swallowed
two in a delighted dip of its head, while the others trembled and begged. Their words fell like stones on my ears.

I slew them all.

Afterward, I ordered the wailer and the Swordwraith
to fight to the death.

Their destruction eased my mental burden and kept
me conscious, barely, as the Gorder carried me through
the ruined city. As dawn broke, casting golden light over
the shattered buildings, sorrow weighed on me. Though
I'd slaughtered monsters and killed a number of Saremon, I hadn't seen Oz anywhere.

Which meant he was still out there. Plotting.

He must own a particular madness, one such that he
didn't care what he destroyed if it wasn't his. *If I can't
possess it, then no one will.* It was a brand of evil that
troubled even me, who had once killed lovers as a precaution. I trembled with weariness. Nothing left to give.
But at least I'd kept my word, protected the city to the
best of my ability. We'd rebuild. Hunt down Oz and his
few remaining rebels.

So tired.

"What am I going to do with you?" I whispered to the
Gorder.

There could be no return to its life outside the walls,
but the city was no place for such a huge beast. It had
given up its home and hoard for me when I called, fought
bravely, and I had no suitable reward. The monster
whirred in its throat, delighted with my attention. It destroyed three more half-burned homes on the way back
to the palace, and I closed my eyes against the dizziness.
It got harder to stay on its shoulders, harder to keep the
darkness at bay.

At last the crenellated walls rose in the distance before me, dark stone shining with silver streaks in the

morning sun. It seemed quiet, despite the bodies piled outside. Citizens had thrown themselves at the walls in hope of finding sanctuary, but I was the only one who could have let them in; they'd fried on my protections. That was when I noticed the awful truth: No shimmering field prevented our entry.

At some point in the night, the wards had fallen.

The Running Game

The gates stood wide open. Not broken. As if someone had unbolted them from the inside. They were broad enough for me to pass through, riding, so I nudged the Gorder forward. The giant lizard-worm proceeded with caution, its blind face turning constantly toward a threat I couldn't see.

I sensed it, though. Currents of distant magick warned of imminent danger. With my last burst of energy, I opened to the astral and saw smears of old spells all over the ether. In the courtyard, bodies lay everywhere, but the fighting wasn't over. I charged into the melee—or rather, the Gorder did. These invaders had to be Xaraz; they reflected all demon castes and abilities, and only a handful of defenders remained, most bloody beyond belief, faces blackened with dirt.

The Saremon must have promised the Xaraz amnesty. They fought as if they had nothing to lose. Two Hazo went down the Gorder's throat, but an Imaron slid under its guard. It slapped long-fingered hands onto the monster's belly and began the drain. A shudder went through the enormous creature. *Dying,* I thought.

I had no magick left. As the Gorder shook, I vaulted down. My knees nearly buckled, and my head spun. I ran at the Imaron with only my athame, not because I thought I could defeat it in single combat, but because I couldn't surrender. My one advantage was that the Gorder would recover if the demon broke physical contact, which meant it had to fight me one-handed.

Other monsters slunk closer. By their ragged clothes and shocking stench, they were all outcast. Noit, Mhizul, Luren, Hazo. There were just too many. Without the Gorder, I had no chance to defend the courtyard. If this Imaron turned *into* a Gorder once it completed the drain, then it was over. I struck from the side, but even in a weak, starving state, the Imaron knocked me away in a fierce blow. I was too tired. The other Xaraz pressed, encircling me. Tremors rocked my limbs, so powerful I could scarcely keep hold of my knife.

At least I die on my feet.

Beside me, the Gorder churred in a mournful dying song and its enormous body fell, crushing a couple of Noit. The Imaron's skin rippled; that marked a transformation in progress. I should have charged then, but there were too many demons between us. Right then, they seemed to be assessing the threat I presented; if I took a single step, they'd attack.

It's finished.

Then a blade impaled the Imaron from behind. Dark blood bubbled out from the wound as the sword withdrew. When the demon dropped, Shannon stood in a battle crouch. She flashed a grin. "The Hazo taught me a *lot* of shit while they had me. What did you think I was doing while they held me hostage?"

I had no reply as she whirled into motion. Chance and Greydusk came close behind, and I swayed as they fought. Better that I didn't get in the way. Chance slammed a Noit with his frosted gloves, and the demon froze. With his unnatural strength, Greydusk broke it into fleshy demon chunks with an open-handed blow.

"What happened?" I asked, once they had cleared the courtyard.

"The Hazo turned. The palace has fallen."

That made a horrific kind of sense. Only someone already inside the walls could have corrupted the wards so they failed. "Any idea why?"

Greydusk sighed. "Zet was Caim's son."

"So while he appreciated the promotion, he also bore a grudge."

And so Caim has the last laugh, after all. Cunning bastard.

"But he's clever for a Hazo," Greydusk went on. "From what I can gather, he allied with Oz and they planned a two-pronged attack—"

"So that while I defended the city, I'd lose the castle."

"Yes. I'm sorry, my queen."

Pain suffused me. "By which you mean, we can't win."

"The entire Hazo caste has aligned with the Saremon, and they held their best mages. The ones who went to Vortex were ... expendable."

"Is there more bad news?"

"The Eshur and the Obsir have chosen. Your return created too much chaos. They seem to believe the Saremon are the best chance at restoring order. The Dohan, too, have turned."

I nodded, battling complete despair. "What of the other castes?"

"They are loyal, my queen, but they are not strong enough to stand against the might arrayed against them. They will hide until the battle ends."

That's it, then.

I turned my exhausted mind toward an exit strategy. "Is the portal room still functional?"

"I believe so," Greydusk replied.

At least I had that much luck remaining. I wished I'd paid more attention to Chance when he was talking about how his luck could affect me. It had seemed like such an unlikely consequence of loving him.

"Then that's where we go. Long ago, I had them built in the event of another civil war. We'll retreat to my mountain fortress and consider our next move."

"It will be a difficult run, my queen. The castle is embattled and no route will be safe. We will encounter heavy resistance."

"There's no choice." I held Greydusk's look and saw

he knew this. "If you have any magick in reserve, I can cast, if you're willing to link with me."

"Certainly, my queen."

I took his hand and opened the channel. His strength made mine seem puny for the first time. I'd burned through all my resources. Fortunately he had been more conservative and I took him to half before breaking the connection. At least I no longer felt like passing out.

"I could kill you." Chance seized my shoulders and kissed me with all the pent-up rage and fear I'd thrust upon him by going out alone. I wrapped myself around him and fell into his desire.

When I broke away, I said, "I'm so sorry I scared you."

My apology made him cant his head. "Corine . . . ?"

Not surprisingly, he could tell who was ascendant. Ninlil never apologized for doing what she felt she must.

"Mostly, I think."

Something flickered in his tiger's eyes. "Is she . . . all right?"

"Yeah." I didn't know how I felt, realizing he was *worried* about the demon who had stolen half my brain. I mean, I knew they'd been together, sometimes without me—and I had seen most of it without being able to influence events—but this was—whatever. I put it aside for later contemplation.

Shannon yanked on his arm. "No offense, but this isn't the time to chat with your girlfriend."

"She's right. This way." Greydusk picked a path across the corpse-strewn stones. "There isn't much time."

"We have to fight to our quarters. I'm not leaving my mother's grimoires. Or my dog."

"I thought you'd say that." Chance patted his backpack.

Then I noticed Shannon was already wearing hers. And incongruously, Greydusk carried my purse. Butch popped his head out.

"How?" I asked as we ran.

The Imaron explained. "When the wards went down, I suspected betrayal. I knew we had to be ready to move when you returned, so I ran to your rooms and gathered your things."

"Since then, we've been holding that tower, waiting for you to get back." Shannon pointed at the far end of the courtyard.

"We couldn't defend the palace," Chance added with the salt of regret.

"But you saved *me*. Thank you."

Shannon laughed. She seemed happier than she'd been since she walked into the throne room that first time. "I thought Chance would climb out of his skin. Greydusk had to physically restrain him. He wanted to go look for you after the wards went down."

"We're going to talk about that," Chance said tightly.

With the protective imperative in place, it must have nearly driven him insane. "I couldn't take you with me . . . and I thought you'd be safe here."

"The Hazo have established a base in the throne room." Greydusk cut in. "I'm sure they mean to come root us out of the tower, once they secure the rest of the castle. The Saremon patrol the halls, and there are more Xaraz all over."

"What about the Eshur?"

Greydusk reminded me, "They don't fight, but the Obsir are present."

"Their enforcers." I nodded to show I was with him, but I didn't feel as I had. The roles of various castes were murky in my head, and at the moment I didn't give a rat's ass about the fall of my kingdom. All the magick she'd channeled had burned the queen out. At the least, she'd gone comatose, leaving me more . . . myself.

Unfortunately, Ninlil was the expert here. Not me. It was a blessing that Greydusk remained at my side, as he knew the palace like the back of his hand. The demon skirted the front entrance, instead leading us along the side. We'd try one of the postern doors in the hope it would prove less heavily guarded.

Outside the door lay more bodies, servants in my livery who had been trying to flee. I'd told them to take shelter inside, where they would be safe. My misplaced confidence had ended in so many deaths. The horror overwhelmed me for a moment and stole my breath.

"I can try a cloaking spell," I said softly. "But it will draw most of the power you loaned me. Do you think I should save it for combat?" I glanced at Shannon and Chance, inviting them to consider the question too.

"Save it," Chance finally said.

Greydusk nodded. "We'll have to fight, and there's no guarantee that the spell will work. They may have set up motion-detecting runes inside the perimeter."

"Shan?"

"Dude, I have *no idea.* But I've got this cool sword and Grey was nice enough to spar with me to keep me sharp. So, y'know." She flashed a grin, almost as if she *enjoyed* the insanity that surrounded us.

Well, it *was* a pretty cool sword. I smiled as the demon tried the postern door. Locked. I had strength enough to handle that. Using the spell I'd perfected in the Saremon stronghold, I sent a jolt of magick into the lock mechanism, which snicked open. Greydusk stepped inside first. The palace smelled of charred flesh and burning fibers. They hadn't spared the servants they found. Misery deluged me.

I promised safety and I failed them. That sad whisper came from Ninlil, huddled in the back of my head, but she didn't push. Didn't try to take over. I was grateful for small mercies.

"Shoes off," the demon instructed.

My boots would ring out on the tiles; they had been designed to make me sound imposing. That ran counter to our aims now. As much as possible, we needed to run undetected. There was no way to avoid fighting entirely, but it made sense to conserve our resources as much as possible. When I pulled off my boots, Chance and Shannon did the same. Greydusk wore no footwear, so soon we were good to go.

"Which way?" Part of me knew, but Ninlil was silent and distant, lost to despair. She had never failed like this before.

Neither had I—on this scale—but I was used to life kicking me in the teeth. My personal soundtrack could be that Chumbawamba song. The chorus rang in my head as I followed Greydusk, who answered by moving forward. Shannon and Chance fell in behind me. I tried to glean more about this mountain fortress, but the Ninlil half of my brain wasn't talking. *It's probably crumbled to dust and infested with monsters.* This silent taunt drew no response.

Fine. I'll do this without you. Crazy, but I missed her. She had been part of me for so long that her withdrawal left me with a hole inside. Sometimes I'd hated her fiercely, like when she taunted Chance about my loving Kel, but just as my love had become hers, her pain became mine.

"We have one advantage," Greydusk whispered. "They will not expect you to return and fight your way to the heart of the castle."

"They probably think she's gone," Chance agreed.

"Seeking more allies?" Shannon sounded steady. Fearless, even.

She'd come so far from the scared kid on the bike, desperate to get out of the town that meant to sacrifice her for being different. God, I loved this girl. A trauma like this would've destroyed anyone else, but she took it on the chin and rolled with it. Maybe Kilmer had a reason for pride after all. I hoped I got a chance to tell her how amazing she was. A frantic escape didn't offer the right time for emotional talks.

Light of foot, I ran behind Greydusk. He cut through little-used corridors that connected abandoned parts of the castle. Soon I was helplessly lost. If he betrayed me now to save his own life, I had no defense. My stomach tightened with fear; he might be leading us into a trap. *No. I don't believe that. If he was going to do that, he could've just summoned the enemy to the courtyard.*

For a good while, the coast seemed clear, though shrieks and sounds of combat echoed through the halls. No defenders remained apart from us, so this was just the enemy slaughtering the helpless. Xibalba would suffer with Oz on the throne, for there was no question that was his goal.

The rooms Shannon had decorated with such pains-taking care lay in ruins. Wild hands had rent the fabrics and set random fires. No rhyme or reason to it—just destruction for its own sake. Her expression revealed that this hurt her as much as anything had since she first realized she probably wouldn't see Jesse again.

Wish I could fix everything for you, Shan. But it's all so fucked up.

Greydusk stopped us once and I pressed up against the wall, listening to my heartbeat. A troop of Hazo tromped past us in the next room and took the adjoining hallway. The Imaron was uncanny in his ability to gauge such things.

"You're sensing them, aren't you?"

He inclined his head. "It's a simple matter to taste eddies in the air."

"For you, maybe," Shannon muttered.

Chance asked, "How close are we?"

"Our course has been circuitous," the demon replied. "I was afraid the direct route would draw too much fire."

"That's not an answer," Chance pointed out.

Weariness drew Greydusk's voice tight. "Halfway, provided my memory serves. I've only gone past the portal room once."

Belatedly I registered the demon's uncertainty; he wasn't positive we were going the right way. It must suck to have so much weight on his shoulders. Maybe I could help ... I had been there, long ago, but the details were fuzzy.

Ninlil, can you tell me where we are? Where do we need to go from here?

Silence.

I guessed I was on my own. *Poor Greydusk. Poor all of us.*

The Imaron scanned, striving to recall our next turn. With somewhat less surety, he led us to the left. This part of the palace hadn't been restored yet, so there were loose stones and broken tiles. The floor showed long years of neglect.

Good. Maybe they won't look for us here.

That was a long shot. If I was Oz, I'd search every inch of this place. Fortunately for us, the stronghold was a warren. In the time it took him to cover all that ground, we might get away. Hope fluttered inside my chest, as Greydusk found the connecting corridor.

Our luck couldn't last, of course. In the next room, we ran into a squad of Saremon—six strong—and as soon as they saw us, they began casting.

Pretty, Pretty Pain

The fireball slammed the floor in front of us and I dove backward. None of Ninlil's reflexes now, just my own clumsiness. I did have the echo of spells she'd cast, however, and I brought the power to bear. It wasn't enough to drive all the enemies out of the castle, but maybe, just maybe, I could defeat the ones trying to stop us from reaching the portal room.

The magick buzzed in my head, but I felt no pain. I sent the spell out my fingertips and dropped the confusion on them. Three of them shook it off, as their shields were stronger; these were among the best the Saremon had to offer. It wouldn't be that simple, unfortunately. And before the ones I'd caught could launch spells at each other, their companions slapped them with a cleansing charm.

Shit, they were ready for us. They'd been studying my methods.

"Oz is waiting for you," one taunted me. "You'll never survive this."

"Neither will you," I answered.

Before the Saremon finished casting, Chance, Shannon, and Greydusk closed to melee. She didn't have her radio, but unlike me, she showed no hesitation about physical conflict. Her swordwork looked strong to my inexperienced eyes; it was certainly better than the mages were used to, and the Saremon found it difficult to focus on casting while fending off physical blows. She skewered one as Chance set fire to another. The mage ran, slapping at his burning robes; then his fear became screams of agony as his flesh melted in the magickal fire that could not be extinguished until all fuel was consumed.

Greydusk drained a third, hopefully taking all his energy along with his knowledge. I wasn't clear on how that worked without Ninlil whispering advice, but she wasn't talking. That left three, even odds. A tall horned Saremon mage prepared a spell, but Shannon hacked off his fingers before he could complete the gesture. His cry interrupted the effect, and Chance finished him.

The sounds of battle alerted more enemies. Footfalls pounded in our direction and I spun. Combat might not be my forte, but I did have assets. Quickly, I pricked my fingers and used my athame to draw a rune behind us; then I fed power to it until a shimmering wall sprang into being. The Hazo, drawn by our battle with the Saremon, slammed into it en masse, which would've been funny if I wasn't so worried.

"You'll have to take the long way around," I yelled.

I spun in time to see Greydusk eviscerate a fifth with a Swordwraith's natural weapon. The partial transformation impressed me, but there was no time to admire my companion's skill. Only one Saremon remained; she tried to run, but Shannon took her from behind with a slash across her hamstring. The demoness went down.

"Don't kill me," she begged. "I was only following orders. I can help you."

"At the first sign of trouble, she'll turn," Greydusk said.

I knew he was right. But maybe I could get some information first. So I did something dreadful to this cowering female; I gave her hope.

"Possibly," I allowed.

"I'm Oz's right hand." It was clearly an empty boast.

I pretended to believe her. "Are you? Prove it. What's his true name?"

The Saremon female laughed with a touch of hysteria. "Nobody knows that, except Oz's mother, and he killed her two centuries ago to keep her from talking."

"Nice," Chance muttered.

"So far you're not telling me anything worth the risk of letting you go," I pointed out. "I don't want excuses. *Dazzle* me."

Her brow furrowed. "He plans to kill you and take the throne himself, now that you've opened the castle. He'll restore order in the city and everyone will be so grateful, they won't care if he has royal blood. He thinks power is enough."

"That's probably true," Greydusk said.

Shannon shrugged. "So? That's not news. And I don't see how it helps us."

I gazed down at the wounded Saremon on the floor. She wrapped her arms around her knees, drawing them to her chest as if they could protect her. Her horns were tiny, barely there amid the tangled mass of her black hair. I wondered if that meant she was young, and then I cut the thread of that thought. I couldn't feel sorry for her. In my place, she would've killed me by now.

"That's information we puzzled out on our own. I need to know where Oz is, where he's left the most troops."

"I'm not sure where he is now, but he was upstairs, ransacking your quarters. He's looking for something that belongs to you."

In reflex, I touched the red jewel at my throat. This was the only thing I'd taken from the Saremon stronghold. *Oz must be after my father's heart. But why?* Greydusk offered a shrug, as if he shared my curiosity but didn't have the answer.

"Troop movements, then?" I prompted.

"Oh. Well, the Hazo have been divided up. They were stationed in the throne room, but now he's got them patrolling. The Xaraz are in the kitchens. I don't think they were ordered to do that, but they're scavengers at heart. They're just looking for stuff to eat and steal. I don't imagine they'll fight very hard."

Remembering the rabble in the courtyard, I agreed. "And your cohorts?"

"We have orders to find and slay you."

I sensed that was all I'd learn. A nod at Greydusk conveyed my intent, and the Saremon panicked. She fumbled for a spell, any spell, but fear made her clumsy. The Imaron moved on her—and when I gave the order for her execution, I wasn't the queen of Xibalba. I was only Corine Solomon, making another bad choice for the greater good. Yet when Grey broke the mage's neck, it didn't feel good at all.

"We have Hazo after us," I said, ignoring the awful weight in my stomach. "I blocked them, but I can only do that two or three more times before I'm done."

"Then we'll be fast." Chance took my hand.

Shannon was already moving. "Let's go. I don't much care where, but we can't stand around."

Butch yapped in agreement. Mostly he cowered in my purse on the demon's shoulder, but he agreed we had to put some pep in our step. Then he went back into hiding. I hoped he wasn't permanently traumatized, but at the moment I was more worried about finding our escape hatch than about my dog's mental health.

The Imaron closed his eyes, as if visualizing the castle layout. Too bad Shannon couldn't get on her netbook and call up Google Maps. The absurd thought put a desperate, exhausted smile on my face. I hadn't thought of such a thing—a *human* thing—since we arrived at the palace. With effort, I set it aside. Later, I'd deal with the weirdness of having someone else drive my body around like a smart car.

"Hurry," Chance urged.

Greydusk opened his black eyes and flashed a look that said he wasn't helping, but he set off nonetheless. Behind us, the shield I'd set flickered and went down. It didn't have the power or lasting potential of a permanent ward. I could throw blocks in their way—that was all.

Hope it slows them down long enough.

The Hazo couldn't know the castle as well as Greydusk did. Hopefully that would work to our advantage. Shouts echoed through the corridors, most useless and faraway. The next one made me think the warrior caste had closed enough that they might have gotten behind us again. I had to keep them there.

"I'll catch up," I called.

I didn't know if they heard me. *Doesn't matter.* While the others kept moving, I stopped to drop another block. Another slash to my fingertips for extra power; the other cuts had coagulated, and they burned like hell when I sliced them open again. These scars weren't like the ones I gained handling charged objects.

Set, shape, strength. I worked as fast as I could, my heart hammering in my ears, and then I saw ten Hazo thundering down the hall at me. The wall went up just as they charged it. One popped through, a second split in half in a grotesque explosion of guts, neatly sheared by my magical barrier. Demon innards splattered all over me, and I almost puked, except I had bigger problems.

Namely this giant, enraged demon whose pal I just tore in two.

Its ursine features twisted with rage, the tusks rising and falling with each breath as if anticipating how good I'd taste. "You killed Caim."

No disputing that.

"He accepted my judgment," I said quietly. "You dishonor his bravery with such betrayal."

"*Do not* speak to me of honor, half-breed filth. You are no true queen, and we will cleanse your stain from this land."

While he spoke, I shook with exhaustion and backed up. This confrontation flashed me back to Peru and how helpless I had felt with Caim. Only this demon didn't have a harness for me to read. And I certainly couldn't beat the Hazo in hand to hand.

Its great size telegraphed its attack. I stumbled back another step, intending to run, but my feet slipped in the demon guts, and that mishap saved me. The brute aimed a vicious blow at my head; since I was already falling, I took only part of the hit to my face, hard enough to slam me back five feet into the opposite wall, where the hall bent left. Blood spurted from my nose. If I'd taken the whole force, it would've snapped my neck.

As it was, I landed hard, ears ringing. The Hazo charged. Instead of beating me to death, as I expected, it lifted me by the throat. Its giant fist tightened, cutting off my oxygen. Fruitlessly, I kicked, but I couldn't connect. My motions grew jerky, spasmodic, like death throes I had seen in so many other creatures.

So sorry, I thought. *About everything.*

My vision went black-speckled, and the pain seared me from the inside out. I lost consciousness for a few seconds and woke when the pressure eased off my neck. I fell then, and the Hazo roared—because it had a sword sticking out of its thigh. Shannon removed it with a jerk and used the wall to propel herself out of range.

I lay dazed, unable to process anything for precious seconds. The gulps of air I drew into my tortured lungs felt like the whole world. Beside me, Chance came in low and hard, his strikes lightning fast, a maddening flurry of fire. With each blow, the Hazo moaned its anguish as the flames licked over its hide. The stink of live, burning meat filled my nostrils, and then Shannon sliced it from behind.

A clever stroke. With its spinal column severed, the Hazo fell. Not dead but dying, and in absolute agony. These weren't invulnerable like the summoned knight had been. We were on its home ground and it lacked the magickal protection Caim had owned in Peru.

But there were so many more hunting us. It had taken two on one to bring this Hazo down. Too many more fights like this one, and— No. Best not to consider the worst, even in my head.

My arms felt like cooked noodles. I tried to push away from the wall, but I couldn't get up. No strength. Chance lifted me, wanting to shake me, no doubt, but my cheek was so swollen I couldn't see out of that eye; I looked too pathetic for his wrath. Instead he cradled me against his chest and beckoned to Shannon.

As he ran, he demanded, "What the hell did you think you were doing?"

My bruised throat felt as though speaking would kill me. I forced the words out anyway in a hoarse rasp. "Slowing them down. Watching our backs."

"Yeah? And who had *yours*?"

"You and Shan," I whispered. "Like always."

He held any further castigation because Greydusk met us halfway. His sharkish features drew tight with worry. "How badly are you hurt, my queen?"

"Please don't call me that. It's Corine." Such an effort to push the sounds out. "You should go. Save yourself."

The demon shook his head. "You may not be their queen, but you are mine. I will never forsake you."

"*Tell* me it's not far," Shannon said. "This is fun and all, but I'd like to make our big exit now."

"One more room, I think. Possibly two." Grey sounded unsure—just what we needed to bolster morale.

I touched Chance on the shoulder. "I can walk now. My legs are fine."

Overstatement. The bite where the Gorder sank its teeth in to save me from falling throbbed like fire. Might be infected, but it wouldn't help to whine. My face and throat were fucked up beyond all recognition; I turned my head in order to see the left side of the hallway.

"Are you positive?" Chance asked.

"Yep."

As he set me on my feet, the rest of the Hazo troop found us. Nine of them. Four of us—and a terrified dog. I'd faced some shitty odds in my life, but this—this was something else entirely.

What spells do I remember? I had a big blank spot in my head. I didn't remember my mother's magick. I had relied on Ninlil for so much, gotten comfortable with her natural knowledge, and now I was fucking helpless. Dead weight.

"Shannon, stay back," I begged.

She gave a nervous laugh, holding her sword in a defensive stance. "I'm not charging *them*. I'm not crazy."

"Stall them," Greydusk said.

Chance moved in front of us protectively while I cast another ward. *My last.* This I remembered because I had been drawing runes all the way through our retreat, but I couldn't recall any other wards to save my life. Maybe this one would.

The demon's skin rippled as he shifted; he had fought the shades in Swordwraith form. Hopefully it would prove effective against the Hazo too, who threw themselves repeatedly at the shield, trying to break it down with brute force. They couldn't circle around; this was the rear part of the palace and there were no other paths. We would pass here, or we would die.

"Retreat around that corner," Chance ordered. "It'll help me focus if you're not in danger."

I glanced at Shannon, who nodded. Out of sight, we huddled together. She put an arm around me and I leaned in, shaking. Her heart beat too fast as the shield fell. I could tell it had by the combat noises. Screams, blows, madness. I willed it to be over, for Greydusk and Chance to prevail. I had no magick left, or I would have fought beside them.

At last Chance called, "Corine!"

I limped back the way we'd come. Found nine Hazo corpses in a gruesome pile. To my horror, Greydusk lay on his side, blood leaking out of a terrible wound. Shannon sucked in a sharp breath.

Ignoring my own pain, I knelt beside him. "Let's get you up."

"The portal room lies just beyond those doors. . . ." He gasped, one long fingered-hand flexing with the pain. "I . . . fear I will not be able to finish this task."

"Bullshit." Tears prickled in my eyes, and I dashed them away. "Oh, God, Grey, *don't*. You said demons don't have an afterlife. I can't—"

"You treated me as a man of honor from the beginning. With you, my queen, I was free. That is worth dying for."

And then there were three.

My Sweetest Downfall

For long moments, I knelt in guilty silence.

"There were too many. They're so fucking big. Strong. I'm fast, but with five Hazo trying to eviscerate me, I just couldn't dodge them all. I got tired. And he threw himself in front of me."

He didn't need to tell me why. I knew. *Because you're the queen's consort.*

"He died for you—to please *me*?" Raw anguish scalded my spirit.

"To save you from pain."

"I should have told him he wasn't just my minion or whatever. That he was a friend too."

Shannon put a hand on my shoulder, and for the first time I noticed that our gifts didn't spark off each other anymore. We hadn't touched much since the Hazo gave her back to me, and I couldn't recall when it started. The sinking in my stomach told me I wasn't human anymore, but despair had to get in line behind my grief.

"He knew," she said softly. "Why do you think he stayed with you, fought so hard? Demons aren't known for their altruism."

No, they weren't, and the fact that we'd found such a good soul here, of all places, made me wonder about the stories I'd been told. I didn't know what was true any-more. I wanted to cry but there was no time.

It didn't seem right to leave him, but Chance was cor-rect when he said, "I need both hands free to fight."

"Give me another minute." Laying my hands on Greydusk's brow, I whispered to him in thanks and affec-tion. Maybe the Imaron had been right; there was noth-ing left of demons after they died, but I spoke the words for myself.

Then, with great regret, I picked up my purse—which Greydusk had gone to so much trouble to save for me and checked on Butch; he was terrified but whole—and then slung it over my shoulder. My heart ached as I limped away from Greydusk's body. His loyalty shouldn't have meant giving up everything for me, but he wouldn't want us to die either. I squared my shoulders, pressed the fear down, and led Shannon and Chance toward the final door. Tears stung my eyes; I stepped through, partly blinded by them.

The room was massive, full of imposing statuary in weird, demonic shapes, molded arches, and a fountain in the center. Along each wall to the right and left there were mirrors twice as tall as a man, not made of glass but of hammered silver. Magickal lights hung around the pe-rimeter in ornate sconces, and I noticed four shadows at the far end that didn't come from the marble statues.

Then the spell hit us.

It tingled in a familiar way, but my bracelet deflected it. Tia's gift broke into rusted metal shards, falling from my wrist. I recognized the feel of the snare spell and whirled, dashing the tears from my eyes. *Oz.* From his appearance, times had been hard; his robe was ripped and stained. Unfortunately, he also had a Hazo and a couple of Saremon minions as his honor guard.

We were so fucked.

Need two hands free to fight. As one, we dropped our belongings, but I was careful with my purse.

"Hide," I ordered the dog.

Chance and Shannon sprinted for the lesser threats. I

guessed they reckoned if they could kill the other mages quickly, it would limit the amount of magick flying around. Oz didn't waste time. He slammed another spell and ice frosted the place where I'd been standing. I wasn't anymore. I rolled behind a huge statue, stifling a moan at how it aggravated my injuries. If he couldn't see me, he couldn't target me.

The Hazo roared. I peered around the stone thigh and saw the enormous demon charge. Chance rolled under the attack and came up with fiery fists to punch the first Saremon. He didn't need to kill him with one blow. The flames leapt to the mage's robe, and once the arcane fire started, there was no way in hell the demon could focus enough to cast. He ran, screaming, slapping at the fabric to no avail. Which left three.

Shannon stabbed the second Saremon while Oz aimed another spell at me. I ducked out of sight, racking my brain as to how I could help with a bad leg, one good eye, and little magick left. A shade sprang up behind me and I had to find new cover before the thing touched me and sucked all the life out of me.

I ran out into the chaos of combat; the Hazo chased Shannon, who hadn't managed to kill the second Saremon. The first lay dead in a smoking pile, and Chance had turned his attention to the second mage. It made sense to deal with the enemies who died most easily, but it showed a cold, menacing side of him that sent shivers through me, even as I appreciated his expertise. The mage, however, took a page from my book and ran like hell away from Chance. Which at least meant he wasn't lobbing spells.

"Watch out for the shade!" I croaked, but it was enough, loud enough that Chance and Shannon registered the threat.

Then inspiration struck. I dug deep in my memory, fighting past the layers that had belonged to Ninlil and found what was truly my mine—and my mother's before me. I drew my athame and angled my head; if I was fast, I should be able to get this spell off before the shade reached me. My hands shook as I pulled the weak, thready bits of power remaining to me. They were like magickal cobwebs, clinging to my mind. The slash of darkness radiated cold, sweeping closer and closer as I shaped the spell, spindling the power until it reached sufficient mass.

With a final twirl of my athame, I released and the Hazo went blind. Shannon gave me a grateful nod and I ran from the shade with as much speed as I could muster. Exhaustion hammered at the back of my eyes, burned in my muscles. *I don't see how we can win this.* But we'd fight, until there was nothing left.

The enraged warrior demon charged blindly and slammed into a wall. Impact knocked it down, but I couldn't watch for long. Oz had summoned the shade to deal with me, so it hunted me relentlessly through room. I kited it, but I had no damage spells to use against it. Ninlil had been the queen of those; my mother hadn't used her powers that way.

Come on, I screamed silently. *Wake up. Greydusk is dead because you're a coward. Don't let us die too.*

Oz was casting again. He had to be tired as well, but he still had tricks up his sleeve. I dodged away from another icy burst, conscious of the shade closing the distance between us. If my throat hadn't hurt so much, I'd have trash-talked him, but apart from the blind Hazo growling with rage and beating the hell out of a statue, the room was more or less silent.

Shannon slid up beside me, breathing hard. Her blade gleamed red from where she'd slashed the mage. "Do we honestly have a chance here?"

"Yeah," I lied. "Watch out!"

Then I relocated again in a slow, lopsided gait, leading the shadow away from her. How the hell could I kill this thing? While I maneuvered I kept pillars and fountain between Oz and me, frustrating him. Finally he shouted, "Give up, Binder! I'll be kind. Think of how much we could learn from you."

"Like you did my father? *Fuck you.*" At first I wasn't sure my damaged voice carried to him, but his answering snarl said it did.

Shannon took the second mage down. Busy fleeing from Chance, the Saremon didn't even see her poised with her sword. She chopped him neatly across the middle; she lacked the strength to cleave, but the gut wound dropped him, and Chance finished him with a single punch. The mage's face . . . melted.

At last, the demon queen stirred from her grief. She looked out from my eyes and saw the shade, the Hazo preparing to charge, and Oz deploying another spell. Her reflexes took over and they saved me from a bolt of acidic darkness. I dove wide and the energy hammered a statue behind me. The great stone beast sizzled and fell, breaking into chunks that smoked and flaked into dust.

"Chance, take the shade," I ordered. He'd dealt with them successfully before, using his gloves. Fortunately Oz couldn't summon and control more than one; his reserves must be running low also. Otherwise we might not win this.

Suddenly I was sure we would. I had a battle plan, one that was hers, and mine. Ours. She was back, and I was stronger. The imperative filled my head. This wasn't defeat; this was an obstacle, nothing more. We'd kill these two pretenders and then retreat to heal up and regroup at my mountain fortress. In time, we'd return. Without Oz to lead them, the other castes would fall on their knees. I'd break the back of the resistance here and return triumphant. Even my pain and weariness lessened.

"Shannon, distract the Hazo."

She cut me a look as if to say, *Are you crazy,* and then I nudged my purse on the ground nearby. Butch popped out of the bag.

"You too," I told the dog. "Run around. Bark. Make some noise. Don't let the big monster step on you."

Butch crawled out of my bag, quivering, but his ears went up and he bounded away, his tiny, fierce yip sounding. I couldn't watch how Chance was doing against the shadow. Head down, I ran for Oz, as fast as my bad leg would carry me. I wove around the statues and columns, ducking and rolling away from his spells. They came slower and slower, more time between them. He was tired, and I'd finish him.

Athame in hand, I charged and he fell back. "You're not strong enough—"

His empty words died as I sank the blade into his side. His eyes widened when I realized what I was doing. Not a killing stroke, but a draining one. The demon blade served as a conduit, and I forced the last flicker of my power in through the weapon and latched on to the magick he had left. Then I pulled with every ounce of will.

He screamed and scrabbled frantically at the athame, but his strength faded as I suctioned his energy. Dark, tainted magick unfurled in my veins, revitalizing me. I held him pinned until his eyes fluttered shut and he sagged to the ground. For good measure, I cut his throat in a decisive slash and then I spun back to the battle in time to see the shadow explode into icy fragments at Chance's hand.

Butch circled the giant Hazo, yapping ferociously and nipping at his toes. If you've ever seen someone try to step on a cockroach and fail—well, yeah. Despite the dire situation, I smiled. From behind cover, Shannon threw chunks of stone at the beast. The blindness was starting to wear off, but the demon didn't have complete peripheral vision yet. Chance whispered the command word for fire, his gloves obeyed, and he flanked the Hazo smoothly.

He unleashed a flurry of blows, searing the creature's hide. This Hazo took longer to catch fire because of its scaly hide and lack of clothing. And this one, as I viewed it with my witch sight, was layered in protective runes, courtesy of the now-deceased Oz. Unfortunately, his wards didn't die when he did. I set to unraveling them, but it was slow going.

Shannon saw that Chance had the demon's attention, dropped her rocks, drew her blade and rushed into battle. The Hazo swung by reflex and caught her in the abdomen. The blow sent her spinning back and she hit the ground hard.

I abandoned my work on the protections and ran over to see how badly she was hurt. "Shan?"

"I'm fine," she wheezed. "Well, maybe not *fine*. But I'll live. Help Chance."

I nodded. "Butch, get out of there. He can see you now."

The little dog leapt away, bounding in and out of piles of debris. I drew on stolen magick to craft a dark, insidious curse. The demon queen wouldn't permit any harm to her beloved; and when Chance took a claw in the side, utter rage filled my head.

With a snarl in demontongue, I unleashed hell upon the Hazo. From the moment my spell hit, its blood bubbled in its veins, growing hotter and hotter with the fury of hellfire, until steam leaked out its ears, its eyes cooked in its head, and ichor ran out its ursine nostrils. The demon screamed in anguish, and Chance sprang for the final blow. He whirled in a snap kick, followed by a hammer-fist strike so fierce it crushed the demon's nose back into its skull. It fell back with a heavy thud, and clouds of dust swirled around us.

"We did it," Shannon said in a tone etched in disbelief.

Chance nodded. "Now let's find the portal and get the hell out of here."

Exit, Stage Death

"First I look at your wound," I corrected.

He grumbled but let me peel away his shirt. It was a bloody rake, but not deep. The blood had already clotted, leaving a messy slash along his flank. I hated seeing the damage, but it wasn't life-threatening.

"How am I?"

"Gorgeous. Amazing. Mine." I raised up on tiptoes to kiss him. "And you'll be fine, albeit with some interesting new scars."

"You've got some too, now."

"Other places besides my hands." I only had the flower pentacle there now. "Does that mean I'm a real warrior?"

"A veritable badass."

Yeah, relief was definitely making us loopy. I drove back the awareness of the price Greydusk paid to get us this far. Images of the Imaron haunted me. He had been a true friend from the first, even when I had been frightened of him. From the beginning, he behaved with honor. I didn't deserve his loyalty or his sacrifice. Ninlil, the demon queen who abandoned us in our hour of need, deserved it even less.

Shannon turned with a worried look. "I hear the next wave coming for us."

"Right. I'm on it." I limped over and closed the door, and then in quick, practiced motions, I set the barrier in place, using most of the magick I'd stolen from Oz. "We can't afford another fight. We're all injured and I have no more juice."

"Agreed. Which portal do we take?" Chance paced away from the door.

From outside came the unmistakable sound of a Hazo troop. After four blows, it splintered and they slammed into my field. With dawning fear, I saw there were twenty of them. There was no way in hell we'd win that fight. We had as long as my shield lasted to find the portal and bug out of here.

"Butch!"

The dog popped out of hiding, tail wagging so his whole body looked like it might tip over. He cocked his head. Yipped once. *Yeah?*

"Great job."

He lifted his muzzle at me, just about grinning, and his enthusiasm was contagious, despite the circumstances. I said to the others, "Grab your stuff."

Following my own instructions, I got my purse and put Butch in it. He settled in with no protest, so I guess he'd had enough excitement, tormenting the Hazo and all. Twenty demons watched through the shield with malevolent eyes, waiting for the moment when our time ran out.

That's not happening, bitches.

Ninlil directed me to a mirror on the far end of the hall. I double-timed it over there with Shannon and Chance close behind. It didn't look like a portal, but I don't know what I expected, either. A glowing red pool of light? The demon queen had known, but her knowledge didn't feel like mine anymore. Her disappointment had forced a gap between us, as if we were two separate beings again; she'd crawled into a corner of my mind and gone ominously silent. It was different than it had been.

"Is this it?" Shannon asked.

"Yeah."

Chance canted his head. "How do you activate it?"

"Shh. I'm asking."

They both stared at me as if I was crazy. Ninlil drove me to step up and set my palm on the glass. *That should do it.* Only nothing happened. It remained a flat silver surface with no way to pass through.

"How long is it supposed to take?" Shannon sounded scared.

Yeah, twenty Hazo waiting to remove our heads would frighten anyone. A thrill of terror wormed its way down my spine, curling into my kidneys. I repeated her question in my head and received blank puzzlement.

"It should work," I said. "It only requires my touch."

Chance made a muffled noise. "Oh, God."

"What?" I turned to him.

"I think Nin means *her* touch. But you're not her . . . at least not in her body."

I gaped at him. "But the gates opened for me. They knew me. My energy."

Shannon offered, "Maybe the portals are more personal. . . . They had a physical component factored into the spell."

"So we came all this way for *nothing*?" Frustration boiled in my veins.

Without waiting for an answer, I limped along the wall, touching each silver mirror to see if any of them responded. Nothing. Just more flat metal.

"We're going to die," Shannon whispered.

Her gaze fixed on the shield. I saw that the energy had started to thin. In a few more minutes it would be down entirely. Tonight, riding high on triumph, the Hazo wouldn't care that Oz was dead. Zet might figure he could take the city for his own, the first warrior king. I saw the end, then, and I clenched my fists in utter rage.

Then Ninlil offered the solution. The knowledge rose, fully unfurled like a rose; in my head, I saw it with perfect clarity. She didn't want to do this. Neither did I. But it was better than the alternative.

At least the ones I loved would live.

"There's another way out," I said softly.

I closed my eyes, making peace. In the end, I would

have done what I set out to do: rescued Shannon from Sheol and Chance would get out safely. They should live, if I couldn't. Perhaps that would count for something. If there was an afterlife, I hoped they wouldn't punish me too harshly for the things I'd done. I always had valid reasons for my bad choices, but there was a saying about hell and good intentions.

Either way, it was time. There was nowhere left for us to run.

I cannot come with you. It was the first time she'd spoken in a while, other than flashes of insight or intuition. *When you leave this place, it will mean my death.*

What're you talking about? You're part of me. I wasn't exactly excited about bringing her back into the world with me, but the defeat had weakened her. I didn't expect to be riding shotgun in my own head anymore. Oddly, I was the stronger one, despite her ancient soul and her great power. I had more experience being knocked down and getting back up again.

When the archangel summoned me, he placed a geas on me. I can never return to the human world as a living creature. He cursed me to survive only as a parasite on the Solomon line, dormant until one of your lineage returned me home. Here in Sheol . . . this is the only place I can exist now.

Chance had told me about a war between demons and angels, and how according to Ninlil, the angels weren't even necessarily the good guys. Even if she was telling the truth, I couldn't let it affect my decision.

I do not tell you this to change your mind, Binder. The queen sounded sad, weary beyond belief. *Only to prepare you for the pain.*

Pain?

"What?" Shannon nudged me, breaking my communion with Ninlil.

No matter how I tried, I couldn't raise the dark lady again. She'd gone back into isolation in my head, where she could wallow in failure. I strode over to the fountain, knowing I couldn't explain the solution to Shannon and Chance. They'd never let me do it. With a growing sense of resignation, I put my hand on a palm print etched into the stone of the fountain's rim. The water bubbled merrily, hiding the grim purpose this artifact served. Not even the demon queen's most trusted advisors knew why the palace had been built here, or why this water feature must never be removed.

I knew.

With my other hand, I raised the athame to jab it into my heart.

But I'd forgotten Chance's speed and his preternatural need to protect me. He caught the blade as it hovered millimeters from my chest.

"What are you *doing*?" he demanded.

The shield faded more. In less than a minute, it would be gone. The Hazo roared in preparation for their victory.

I spoke quickly. "This isn't just a fountain. It's also a gate to our world, but you know the price. It requires a soul to open. That wasn't a problem for the demon queen, back in the old days."

"Hell, no," Shannon snapped. "I'd rather die with you, fighting, than let you kill yourself for me. That shit's not on. I wouldn't have had a life without you anyway. They'd have gutted me in Kilmer."

"Shan, no." Tears streamed down my face, and I fought for the athame, keeping my palm in place. "Let me do this. Let me make it right. The two of you can still get out safely. It's my fault you're here in the first place."

"Give me the knife," Chance said softly.

"No."

We struggled as time ticked away. He was stronger. First he shoved my hand away from the point of contact. There was an indent where a soulstone could be inset, but a living being worked as well, if you weren't squeamish. Sobs choked my damaged throat as I lost ground. My fingers slipped on the knife.

"It has to be this way," he said desperately. "Look at how your luck's turned since we've been here ... the trouble in the city. Maybe the portals would've worked if I hadn't come with you. It's all because of me, love ...

and I can't be without you again. It almost broke me last time, but you're stronger. You'll be all right."

"No."

I wouldn't be. I'd rather die here with him. We'd go down fighting. Greydusk's broken body haunted me. He'd given his life so I wouldn't have to live without Chance. That couldn't be for nothing.

Chance wrenched the athame, and with my fingers beneath his, he rammed it into his chest. "Take Shannon and go. Live for me."

"*No.*"

It wasn't supposed to happen like this. *I* always meant to be the sacrifice, to pay the hidden toll. I'd known this journey wouldn't be accomplished without cost, but it should never have been him. He was special, born of Yi Min-chin and the Japanese small god, Ebisu. I remembered the story he'd told me about his parents and the cherry blossoms, and for a brief second, I smelled them in the air instead of the coppery sweetness of his blood.

The pain stole his voice. For a few seconds his lips moved without sound. I leaned toward him, resting my face against his hair. It slid like black silk against my cheek. Then his words came, softer than a whisper. "This isn't the end, my own. Have faith. Even death will not keep me from you."

He tried to lean forward, to hold me one last time with the arm not resting on the palm print, but he collapsed against me. I cradled him, the hilt of the knife between us, digging into my chest. *It should've been me. Should've been me. Never you. Oh, Chance.* I brushed my lips against his. His breath barely puffed, but he returned the kiss. Tears burned behind my eyes. Trickled out from the sides like salt in a wound.

The first Hazo pressed through the doorway. Charged. The rest would be on us soon. No more time, no more, no more.

I didn't want to believe he'd taken a mortal wound, but I saw the placement of the blade. Desperate with rage, with grief, I screamed as I never had before, past pain, past sanity, and I pulled the knife out, but it was too late.

His red, red blood gushed over the rim of the fountain and into the water. A shuddering shock wave of magick exploded out from the water, tinting it crimson, as I remembered from the first time I passed through. The water gate formed in an unnatural swirl overhead, and Shannon pulled me toward it.

I tried to carry him with me. I *tried*. But I wasn't strong enough. My leg buckled. His body fell against the fountain. The stone that had been my father's heart flared bright as sunrise at my throat, and a flare of heat staggered me.

The Hazo thundered toward us.

"We have to go," Shan shouted, "or this is for nothing. He died for *nothing*."

Weeping and blind, I dove through the gate and howled as half my soul ripped away.

Collateral Damage

The gate dumped us in an alley—a one-way trip—it must have snapped shut behind us, leaving the enraged demons to maim Chance's corpse. I fell in a boneless pile, still clutching the athame slick with his blood. His sacrifice. I hugged the blade to my chest and wept in bitter, wracking bursts. On some level, I knew I had to get myself under control—that if anyone spotted me crying with a bloody knife in my hands, it would mean trouble.

Bad trouble.

For Shannon, I had to get my shit together.

But I *couldn't.* The tears wouldn't stop falling, and then I felt her beside me, arms going around my shoulders. She rested her cheek against my hair and stroked my back as if I were a child. Now and then, Shannon choked back her own sobs as if she knew it wouldn't serve any purpose for us both to lose it. She was so damn strong.

Oh, Chance, no. Not like this. I can't live through this. I can't.

"He loved you," she was whispering. "So damn much."

The words meant to comfort only made it worse. I'd never wanted him to love me so much that he died for me. *There was so much blood. . . .*

Stop. With imperfect self-control, I fought the anguish down, even though I had never been this broken. First my father, and now Chance. It was too much; I could not bear it. I leaned like so much rubbish against a broken brick wall. The darkness of the wrecked building loomed behind me, and from this angle I could almost see the other side, could almost touch what I'd lost. A great yawning hole echoed inside of me, as if I'd had more than my heart ripped out in the last thirty seconds. I was ... empty. Incomplete.

I sat away from Shannon and brushed the damp hair away from her cheek; it was sticky with sweat or tears or both. "Are you all right?"

"No," she said, her voice thick. "He shouldn't have—"

"I know." I didn't say he'd done it for me, for *us*, but she understood. I'd asked the question of myself before, but now I had my answer. Sometimes the price of survival was too high; I had been ready to die beside Chance, but he'd inflicted upon me a role ten times harder— making me fall in love with him again and then forcing me to live without him.

"We'll make the most of his sacrifice." Using my thumbs, I wiped away my tears and blotted my face on my sleeve.

I glanced down to see how bloody I was, and then I realized the black I'd preferred as the demon queen didn't show the stains. The fabric simply swallowed them, as if it hadn't happened; he hadn't died. Shaking from head to toe, I pushed to my feet, and then offered her a hand. Together, we were strong enough to survive anything. Even the unthinkable. Even *this*.

Fortunately, Shannon had gathered our things before pulling me through the gate. Otherwise, I'd be injured, exhausted, brokenhearted, and stranded wherever we were without any recourse. I couldn't think about Chance. Had to focus on one minute at a time, one heartbeat. Thinking about the future was impossible. With effort, I turned my mind to practical matters. After taking my purse from Shannon, I opened it to hide the bloody athame and Butch popped out.

"You made it," I said in relief.

The little dog sniffed me with puzzling suspicion and

then licked my cheek, kissing away my tears. At least I still had Butch . . . and Shannon. For now.

First order of business was to figure out where we were.

I picked up my belongings from where Shannon had dropped them—all I had left of Chance—and spun in a slow circle. The buildings were old, shoddy brickwork and rickety fire escapes clambering up the sides. Across the way, bright graffiti had been sprayed all down one side, but it was in a different style than what I'd encountered in Mexico City. Plus, the air was cool and damp, the sky overcast.

"Where do you think we are?" I asked. Not because I expected an answer, but because I thought she needed the question, giving her a reason to separate from the trauma and think of something else.

I could do it, one minute at a time, but I had never wanted those minutes less.

She took her own inspection and then shrugged. "I'm not sure. Nowhere I've been before."

"Let's find out."

I strode from the alley onto a narrow street with vans and cars parked untidily along the curbs. The shops were small, with advertisements posted in the windows for products I didn't immediately recognize. But all the signs were in English, which limited the options as to where we'd ended up. I noted the faces of passersby, a good mix of colors; we'd landed in an interesting, culturally eclectic neighborhood.

"England." Shannon grabbed my arm. "It must be. Look inside the cars."

The steering wheels were all on what would be the passenger side in North America. Given the other clues, I agreed with her. "Good eye."

Chance brought me here once. Memories of that trip pelted me like small, fierce knives: laughing in the rain, a kiss on the stairs leading to the metro station, and the posh shop where he bought me frangipani perfume. Those memories became diamond-hard in my heart because nobody who still lived in this world could remember them with me. Mine alone.

Alone. I could die of that word, a cold so deep it became fever.

"I can't believe he's gone," Shannon said huskily.

I couldn't either. But he'd said, *Even death will not keep me from you.* Perhaps those had only been words to drive the grief away, but I'd cling to them. I'd look for him. Find him again, somehow.

We strolled in silence, Shannon distracted by the new sights and me numb. People stared at my bruised and swollen face and then hurriedly swung their eyes away, as if abuse might be contagious. The street market we passed reminded me of the ones near my shop, and a wave of homesickness swept over me. My gaze lingered on the variety of goods, though we had no local currency. People milled and bickered. Now that we were in the throng of shoppers, the prevailing accent was a dead giveaway. I wondered how Shannon and I looked, if we seemed like exhausted tourists or whether people thought we belonged.

"I should find a phone," she said softly. "Call Jesse."

It was a good idea. As we walked, I glanced around and didn't find one. Pay phones had just about gone the way of the dinosaurs since everyone carried cells these days. Mine was a paperweight, though; there hadn't been any outlets in Sheol.

"We might be better off buying a travel charger."

She nodded.

A few blocks down, I went into a small electronics store. The man behind the counter looked up from a magazine. He was tall and thin with a crop of ginger hair that looked as if he hadn't combed it in a week, and his face was covered in freckles. He greeted us with a broad smile and a thick accent. "What can I do for you, ladies?"

"My cell phone died. I'm looking for something to juice it up quick."

"An instant travel charger, eh? What model have you got?"

I checked. "I have a Nokia."

As I recalled, she'd left her phone at Jesse's house, so she didn't have one in her backpack. Yet thinking about them together roused fresh grief. *Not* because I wanted

Jesse—because I'd lost Chance. Shannon interpreted my expression correctly; she looked so sad and tentative that it broke my heart. Which didn't take much doing, as it was already smashed into tiny pieces. But I didn't mean for her to feel she had to hide her happiness or walk on eggshells around me.

So I asked, "Where's yours again?" My tone was teasing, for the benefit of the man behind the counter, but it gave Shan the proper message.

It's all right. Really.

Her smile bloomed. "I have a Samsung Infuse at home. It was a gift from Jesse."

"So you could stay in touch better while he's working?"

The sweetness of it was so Jesse Saldana. Shannon was a lucky girl, but I didn't have even a whisper of regret that things had turned out this way. At least she had him, waiting for her to come home.

I didn't. The man in my life, the one with the infernal luck, had died for me. Good fortune wasn't enough to save him; or rather, he wouldn't let it. After so long in Sheol, I needed a cleansing, but I didn't know any practitioners here, and likely none of them would help out if they got a good look at me with their witch sight. Plus, I swallowed a scream at the idea of erasing any part of Chance, even the bad stuff. I wanted to keep him close; I wanted to *remember*. Anguish boiled up in a hot rush, filling my eyes with tears again, and I blinked them away as the clerk sorted through his inventory. He didn't react to my bruised face, which I appreciated.

"Here, I think this will do," he said eventually. "You can use it up to four times, though that'll depend on the battery size."

Mentally crossing my fingers, I gave him the prepaid Visa card I carried in case of emergencies. Without Shannon's cool head, we'd be really bad off right now. I didn't have a bank account, and I'd changed dollars to pesos as I needed it from the briefcase Escobar had given me. In Mexico, it was easy to live that way. Nobody blinked if you paid your bills in person and with cash. In fact, most people did.

He ran it with no questions asked. "Do you need a receipt?"

"No, it's fine. Do you know of a good hotel or a bed-and-breakfast nearby?"

The young man offered a sympathetic smile. "Had a run of bad luck, eh?"

"You could say that." His kindness, after everything we'd been through made it harder to keep my composure. Maybe it had something to do with how battered I looked; men wanted to save women, even when it wasn't possible.

He thought for a moment, then named a place. "My cousin stays there sometimes when he comes to town."

"Thank you." I took the charger. "Would you mind jotting down the address?"

"I'll do better than that. I won't send you over to Amhurst Park unless they've rooms available. Give me a mo." To my surprise, he went to work on the laptop open nearby, checking on a reservation for us. "You'll want a twin, en suite, I'm guessing. Americans don't usually like sharing bathrooms."

"Please," Shannon said.

I exchanged a look with her, and she was smiling. How . . . unexpected. After being with demons, I'd almost forgotten people could be nice for no reason.

"You're in luck. Can I help you with anything else?" he asked gently.

Was my face tearstained in addition to beaten the hell up? I wondered. It was the only explanation I could conjure for his continued willingness to assist us.

"If you know of a currency exchange, that'd be everything."

"Let me check." He played with the laptop a little longer and then said, "There's one on Moorgate. I've never been, but I can print you some directions."

"Thank you." Maybe I *wasn't* covered in Chance's ill luck anymore. It was possible the gate had stripped the effect from me, just like the results of the forget fog I'd cast at the house outside Laredo fell away from Shannon.

"My pleasure. I was just surfing anyway. It's a slow

day." He handed me a sheet of paper with some instructions.

In the grand scheme, using his laptop for us didn't amount to much, but considering how fucked up I felt, how broken, it might be the difference between getting through this day and surrendering. With a quiet wave, I stepped back onto the street. First thing, I cracked open the battery and plugged in our phones.

Next, using the directions, I navigated the route to the currency exchange, which involved one train and some walking. I exchanged the dollars and pesos I had on me for British pounds. It amounted to £150, which I hoped would be enough for a room. Shannon had all of twenty-four bucks in her backpack, and she converted that too—around fourteen pounds and change. I could give them my prepaid card for incidentals if they insisted. I hoped the clerk hadn't sent us to a pricey, upscale place.

Until I got hold of Tia and asked her to wire some money, I couldn't afford to splurge on a cab, so we walked ten minutes to the Kentish Town West station, took the overground toward Stratford, and got off at Hackney Central. I was bone-tired, and my injuries throbbed. Four minutes later, we reached the hotel. If the guy at the electronics store could be believed, shelter waited for us. Here, I could rest and make plans.

Figure out how to survive.

But I don't want to.

With desperate determination, I drove that voice out of my head. The brownstone looked clean and respectable. Inside, it was a budget hotel, no bells and whistles, but they took my cash and gave us a key. In the morning, I'd worry about passports and how the hell we were getting home. The ones Eva had cooked for Shannon and me were sufficient to pass land border scrutiny between the U.S. and Mexico, but I didn't think she had the skill to clone RFID chips to fool the scanners. Which meant we'd have to apply for passports at the embassy and go into the system, unless a better alternative presented itself.

At this point, I couldn't imagine what that would be.

The Endless Unknown

Our room was clean, with a tiny private bathroom. Twin beds took up most of the space, and they were covered in black and white plaid. With a sigh, I set down my backpack and got out Butch's water dish. I filled it from the tap and put it down. I had no kibble for him, but I needed to rest before I went back out.

From her expression, I could tell Shannon wanted to call Jesse, so I handed over the phone and stepped into the bathroom to give them some privacy. I splashed water on my face, cleaned up as much as I could. Unfortunately, even with the door closed, I could hear her side of the conversation.

"Jesse, it's me." A pause. "Yes, Corine found me." More silence. "I'm in London." He had to be tearing her a new one, and she sniffed in response to whatever he was saying. "No, it wasn't like that. I promise I'll explain everything when I'm home. I am safe, though." A longer break—I sensed the warmth of her reaction to his words. "I know. I'm sorry. But I'm glad you knew before I called. I promise I got on the line as soon as I could." And then, "Yes, I love you too."

Their conversation lightened from there. "I have my laptop, so I'll be online in a little while if you want to talk more. I can't burn all Corine's minutes."

She talked to him for five minutes more, laughter in her voice, and I hated her in mute silence, my head resting against the bathroom door. Not because she'd taken Jesse Saldana from me, but because the man she loved might be across the ocean but he was still in this world with her. She would *see* him again.

So will you, I told myself. *He'll find a way. He keeps his promises.*

I couldn't believe it wholly, but how I wanted to.

Then Shan knocked, and I didn't loathe her anymore, because she was my best friend and little sister combined; she was Shannon Cheney, and her life was worth suffering any pain. Even the unthinkable. Even this. I'd made my choice when I went to Sheol after her. Humans didn't venture to the demon realm without paying the price; Chance remitted my ransom willingly, and the ache of that would never abate.

When I opened the door, she hugged me hard, without speaking; then I stepped back. I mustered a smile.

"Jesse said we were gone a month."

I couldn't begin to process that. It had seemed longer, a lifetime. So I focused on our mundane needs. "Yeah? Interesting. Stay here and set up, okay? I'll buy us some things. Watch Butch."

He yapped twice in protest. "You want to come with me?"

One yap.

"Fine, but you can't walk unless I find you a leash."

He gave me a look, but when he hopped into my purse, I figured he was okay with the terms I'd dictated. I cleaned out the bloody athame and things from the demon world that had no place in this one.

With Butch in tow, I limped down the stairs and out the front onto the street. I got lucky with a pet store a few doors down, and I bought Butch a small bag of food and a leash. That made him happy, as he stretched his legs. Eventually I located a Tesco, where I bought us cheap T-shirts, some snacks, an AC adapter for our devices, and two travel kits with miscellaneous toiletries. Nobody said anything about Butch, so I guessed they were used to purse dogs, even here. On the way back, I stopped at a place called Noodle Express, where I ordered Vietnamese spring rolls, king prawn pad thai, and ngay tho. They made the food fast and I returned to Shannon with a sense of utter exhaustion.

Conversation was sparse; we ate while she IM'd with Jesse like I'd once done. I had no reaction to their relationship apart from minor happiness, which was all I could manage. Afterward, we showered in shifts and went to bed. I dreamed of Chance dying, over and over again. I felt his mouth on mine, the desperation in his eyes as he sank the blade into his chest. When I woke, my chest felt as if I were dying too, but I hid the pain beneath a tired smile.

Yesterday's emptiness felt more profound. On impulse, I grabbed my athame and whispered, "*Fiat lux.*"

Nothing. I tried to pull my mother's power. There was no tingle, no heat, no pain. I suspected my use of demon magick had sealed those pathways, and I was no longer a poorly trained witch; any magick that remained to me would be demonic in origin. I didn't know if I could still use the touch, but I didn't care enough to test it.

I have to call Min.

My hands shook as I input her number. When I heard her soft *hello*, I lost it. "Min? Min, I'm sorr—"

"I know," she said, her voice raw with weeping. "I already know. He's with his father now."

She cut the call, whether because she couldn't talk or she blamed me, I didn't know. I stared at the Nokia in my hand, and then squeezed my eyes shut. *No more,* I thought. *I can't bear it.*

"What now?" Shannon asked eventually.

Haunted, I raised my head. I wished she had her radio with her. Chance hadn't been mortal. Not entirely. And the gate required the full strength of a mortal soul to open, so what happened when a demigod gave himself over to it? Surely he was bigger, stronger, than a normal human spirit. I wouldn't believe there was nothing left, not even in the afterlife. He had been the son of Ebisu, for god's sake. That had to count for something. If Shannon had her radio and tuned in, she could find him, and I could hear his voice again.

I'd know, at least, that part of him had survived the transition. For now, however, I had to concentrate on our current predicament. Using Shannon's laptop, I checked on how complicated it would be to get a passport—when you'd never been issued one. Research indicated there would be all kinds of bureaucratic red tape, awkward questions asked. It wasn't like I could tell the embassy that I'd slipped into London illegally via Sheol. I didn't look forward to dealing with all the complexities of modern life.

Unable to face that just yet, I called Tia, who answered on the fourth ring. Belatedly, I realized it was probably the middle of the night at home, if it was morning here. "*¿Que paso?*" she demanded in a worried tone. "*¿Quien es?*"

"It's Corine," I answered in Spanish.

"Are you all right, *mija*? Did you find your friend?" *No. And yes.*

Aloud, I said, "I need your help again. Can you wire me some cash?"

"*¿Donde?*"

I reached for the laptop and found an agent who could receive payments, then gave her the information. "There's money in my room—"

"I know," she interrupted. "It will be hours before Western Union opens. Will you be all right until then?"

"I should be." We had enough for another night here, but only that. "You can wait until tomorrow to go. I won't be able to pick up the money before then anyway."

"I'll take care of you. Don't worry." It was comforting to hear her voice, under the circumstances.

"*Gracias*. I'm sorry I woke you. I should have waited to call." I paused, feeling like I had something important to tell her, but my mind was heavy, tired. "Can you get my passport? It's in the—"

"Lockbox under your bed." She knew *everything* that went on in her house.

"I'll need it later." Though my fake passport wasn't

good enough to get me out of the country, it would permit me to pick up the wire transfer.

"*Sí, claro*," she said. "I will go to FedEx as soon as it opens. And then I will go to Banamex tomorrow."

"*Gracias por todo*. Feel free to take whatever money you need—for whatever reason." Then I remembered what I meant to tell her. "Your bracelet saved my life."

"I knew it would," she said with satisfaction. Before I could question her, she cut the call.

I handed the phone to Shan. "Ask Jesse to overnight your passport and radio."

We couldn't travel by rail or ship without ID, and I wasn't sure if the fake driver's license in my wallet would stand up to scrutiny by international authorities. This measure would serve as a stopgap solution while I figured things out. If need be, we could rent a house or a flat while we were here. Tia could send small, multiple payments easily via wire, until I had a respectable nest egg, a buffer against disaster.

Don't think about Chance.

Shannon nodded. "My phone too, while he's at it."

The day passed in a blur. I got more cheap takeout, walked Butch, and rented the room for another day while praying Tia would come through. Faith sustained me; she'd never let me down yet. On schedule, the package from her arrived first thing in the morning. I studied my passport—the one Eva had made—and wondered how Chuch and Eva were. How the baby was. They seemed so far removed from this life, this crisis. I missed them, but they were better off keeping their distance from me.

I didn't want to tell them about Chance. During the long wait, Shan brushed and braided my hair. She talked about her plans. Trying to distract me, I know, but the pain kept time with the beating of my heart, so it pulsed in my blood. Eventually, she wrapped her arms around my back and rested her chin on my shoulder.

"Thank you for coming for me," she whispered.

That drew me out of my self-imposed distance. I turned and hugged her. "Of course. You're my best friend."

We cried together then, as we hadn't given ourselves time in the alley. Reaction set in. Everything we'd seen and lost. She was the only person in the world who knew what it was like in Sheol. At least we still had each other. My nose ran, my eyes swelled, and her sobs rang in my ears.

"I feel old," she said finally, easing back to wipe her face with her forearm. "Like, ancient. Jesse used to talk about the age gap between us, but between the kidnapping, the time with the Hazo, your rescue . . . I feel like I lived a whole life there, you know?"

"I think maybe we did. It seemed longer to me too." A month, Jesse had said.

No, Shan was right. It had been a lifetime.

Exhausted from the emotional catharsis, we napped. I didn't mean to; it just happened, and I dreamt of Chance again. This time without the blood. This time I saw him in the spray of cherry blossoms, where his father fell in love with Min. He was smiling. Beckoning. I woke smiling, my feet on the floor. Only there was no sunlit orchard waiting, just a cheap rented room and Shannon asleep on her side.

Tia called my cell, startling me. "The money should be there, Corine."

I thanked her and went off with my cooked passport and my dog, hoping for the best. An hour later, I returned with two thousand dollars, and Shannon was signing for her package down at the front desk. It was large and bulky, due to the antique radio. My heart literally skipped a beat, and then steadied. Her ability drained her, but fortunately, we had snacks in the room, so I could ask Shan to use her gift without feeling guilty.

I *had* to know.

Upstairs, she unpacked the box and found more than she'd requested. Her radio, her fake passport, some clothing—T-shirts and underwear mostly—her phone, which ha'd a picture of Jesse Saldana as the wallpaper when she booted it up, and a prepaid MasterCard. As a cop, Jesse would know it was illegal to send cash via FedEx, so he'd tried to help Shannon as much as he could without knowing the specifics of her predicament. It had to help, just knowing she was safe.

"I already know what you're going to ask," she said.

I produced the adapter, plugged the radio into it, and then connected it to the wall in confirmation. "It's killing me. I can't sleep, can't do anything without knowing. I *dream* about him, Shan." My voice broke.

"It's okay," she said. "Let's do this."

She clicked on the radio that let her summon and talk to the dead. At once, a chill swept through the room, so strong I saw my breath. I tucked my hands beneath my arms as I folded them and waited for Shannon to work her magick. I'd seen her in action before, but it had never mattered so much.

"Chance, Corine needs to hear from you."

Like always, she fiddled with the tuning dial as the tension rose in the room, until the hair on the back of my neck stood on end. It felt like fingers stroking, stroking, and a shiver ran down my spine. At 1122 on the AM dial— also Chance's birthday—the static resolved. I bit down on my lower lip.

"Are you here?" Shannon asked. "Chance, can you hear me?"

Those fingers stroked down my nape again. The radio spoke in a hauntingly familiar voice: *"Even death will not keep me from you."*

The gem at my throat blazed with heat—and this time I wept tears of joy.

DEMON CASTES

Aronesti—the Snatchers. They feast on the flesh of the dead, and when summoned will often manifest in cannibal killers. They are winged, humanoid with withered features and terrible claws. Most likely, they gave rise to the Harpies of legend.

Birsael—the Bargainers. They are the most commonly summoned demons. They love making deals with humans; they thrive on mischief and misfortune. In Sheol they are shape-shifters and can take whatever form they desire.

Dohan—the Drinkers. These demons can be summoned only via blood magick. They require a sacrifice, and can be bound to enhance a dark practitioner's power. They appear human, apart from their unusual eyes. On the rare occasions when they passed into the human world corporeally, they gave rise to vampire lore, as they subsist on human blood.

Eshur—the Judges. They do not respond to summonings of any kind. They are outside the other castes and sit in judgment of their peers. The Eshur cannot be bribed; they are emotionless and bound to duty. They are tall and thin, blue-skinned, with vestigial horns.

Hazo—the Warriors. They can be summoned only to sites where great battles have taken place. A human possessed by a Hazo spirit becomes a berserker, incapable of stopping short of dismemberment, impervious to pain. The Vikings perfected a rite that guaranteed possession by a Hazo, and by all accounts, the warrior enjoyed a symbiotic relationship with his demon—the only known circumstance in which the possessed does not lose all control of his or her form. In Sheol they are enormous, red-skinned with black shoulders, ridged skulls, and faintly ursine features. They have fangs that are almost tusks and razor-sharp talons. They favor heavy weapons, are fiercely aggressive, and can be gated if sufficient power is expended at the summoning site.

Imaron—the Soul-stealers. Honorable. Law-abiding. They have the ability to drain skills, thoughts, experiences, memories, all the way up to life itself. If an Imaron drains a victim, only a husk remains. They are gray-skinned, with narrow skulls, double rows of teeth, and a distinctly alien appearance. It is not possible to discern gender via visual inspection.

Klothod—the formless legion. These are the only demons that have no physical form, even in Sheol. They were cursed by King Solomon to live solely as shadows. If a demon is summoned from its physical form and remains in the human world too long, it is possible for its physical body to die, at which point it becomes a Klothod. This is the only circumstance in which a demon can change its caste, but it takes centuries for the summoning-stasis magick to go inert, permitting it to occur.

The Knights—high-ranking individuals who command in Sheol. Each named knight comes from a particular caste, ruling over the rest of the demons in a functional oligarchy.

Luren—the Tempters. These are the most beautiful of all the demons, preternaturally seductive. Their skin is more burnished; they do not grow body hair. They possess pheromones to tempt their prey and feed on sexual energy. They are rumored to have Nephilim blood—meaning that they are the result of interbreeding between demons and angels. They respond only to summonings involving sex magick, and will not possess an unattractive host. The Luren gave rise to legends about incubi and succubi.

Mhizul—the Miserable. They feed on all negative emotions, their favorite being despair. Their appetites reflect in their appearance, as they have the look of wretched lepers, with pale, peeling skin, yellow eyes, and long, dirty nails. They are the lowest of the low, even more despised than the Klothod. In summonings, they respond to practitioners who have suffered a recent loss, not any particular type of magick. Often a summoner who is clinically depressed finds himself unable to summon any other type of demon because the Mhizul find the call irresistible.

Noit—the Dark Brood. These demons are like evil children. They are small, no more than four feet high, and have skin that varies in tone from pale to brown, with shadings of green in between. Their heads are oversize, eyes protuberant. They thrive on mischief and misfortune as much as the Birsael, but they do not bargain. A Noit, once summoned, will do whatever it can to wreak havoc for its summoner, choosing the worst possible interpretation of any order or request. A host possessed by a Noit demon may be diagnosed as a manic depressive who never falls into the depressive stage. Oddly, they love cats. These demons gave rise to the lore regarding brownies and gnomes.

Obsir—the Hidden. These demons do not respond to summonings. They serve the Eshur, investigating crimes within Sheol. Other demons find it difficult to describe the Obsir because it is hard to hold on to the memory of an encounter with them. It is known that they exist, but nothing else has been recorded, other than their notes pertaining to various trials.

Phalxe—the Liars. They are of average height and build, pale-skinned, rather innocuous-looking, like bald humans. These demons thrive on deception and confusion; they are inveterate manipulators who have supernatural powers of persuasion. Great con men who pulled off the most improbable scams and Ponzi schemes have often been possessed by a Phalxe spirit. In Sheol they are always plotting something, but the other castes are wary of their schemes. To summon a Phalxe demon, the practitioner must soak aloe in black cat oil for nine days and then perform a specific rite. On manifesting, the Phalxe demon will promise practically anything in hopes of getting the caster to break the binder before an iron-clad agreement has been struck. Only a fool trusts a Phalxe demon.

Saremon—the Progeny. These demons are descended from Solomon's line through humans who interbred with demons. They are humanoid in appearance with extras like fins or spines or horns to show their more interesting lineage. They rank fairly high in the caste system, just below the knights and the Eshur. They seldom respond to summonings and can be called only by a practitioner who carries some of the Binder's blood. They are largely uninterested in events in the human realm and are committed to developing their own arcane powers. For obvious reasons, magick users covet the guidance of the Saremon, who own the greatest collection of spells in existence, the fabled *Bibliotheca Magus*.

Xaraz—the Outsiders. This is not a caste in the sense that it encompasses a certain type of demon, but in the sense that they have all become outcasts. If a demon is judged guilty by the Eshur, he or she loses all status and becomes Xaraz. These demons, therefore, may have once belonged to any of the other castes, so their appearances will be varied. They are driven from Xibalba and are not permitted inside the city. Instead, they dwell in shanty-towns populated with other exiles. On closer inspection, one notes the evidence of their crimes magickally scored into their flesh. They are the most wretched creatures in Sheol.

AUTHOR'S NOTE

For obvious reasons, the cocktail Corine had at the ball is more exotic than the real Devil's Punch. I thought it best to preserve the mystery and not reveal the ingredients in what she was drinking. She was in Sheol, after all. However, here's the actual recipe if you want to knock one back after finishing this book.

Ingredients:

> *2 oz. tequila*
> *1 oz. orange liqueur*
> *1 oz. Limoncello*
> *1 oz. sour mix*
> *dash of orange juice*

Preparation:

1. Pour the ingredients in a cocktail shaker with ice.
2. Shake well.
3. Strain into a sour or highball glass.

ABOUT THE AUTHOR

Ann Aguirre is a national bestselling author. She has a degree in English literature and a spotty résumé. Before she began writing full-time, she was a clown, a clerk, a voice actress, and a savior of stray kittens, not necessarily in that order. She grew up in a yellow house across from a cornfield, but now she lives in sunny Mexico with her husband, children, two cats, and one very lazy dog. She likes books, emo music, and action movies. You can visit her on the Web at www.annaguirre.com.

Read on for an exciting excerpt from the next
Sirantha Jax novel,

ENDGAME

by Ann Aguirre
Coming in September 2012 from Ace Books.

This is not a love story.

It *is* my life, and as such, there is love, loss, war, death, and sacrifice. It's about things that needed to be done and choices made. I regret nothing.

It's easy to say that. Harder to mean it. Sometimes I look back on the branching paths I took to wind up here and I wonder if there was another road, an easier road, that ends somewhere else. Yet it all boils down to a promise.

That's why I'm on La'heng, after all.

After six months of appointments and following procedure, I'm ready to tear my hair out. Instead, I sit obediently outside the legate's office, as if this meeting will turn out any different. The Pretty Robotics assistant monitors me with discreet glances, as if the VI has been programmed to see how long people will wait before storming off in a fit of rage. So far, I've been here for four hours. I hear a door open and close down the hall, and I recognize the legate as he tries to slide by me.

It *is* around lunchtime, so I push to my feet. "How lovely of you to make it a social occasion," I purr, falling into step with Legate Flavius.

He's been assigned to deal with all of our appeals, which makes me think he pissed somebody off. His favorite tactic is avoidance, but since I've caught him, he can't dismiss me without calling for a centurion to eject me from the premises, and I have a legal right to be here. In fact, I have some grounds for a discrimination suit since he made an appointment and then refused to honor it, something he wouldn't do to a Nicuan citizen.

"Come along, then," he says with weary resignation.

"Where are we going?"

"There's a place nearby that does an excellent salad and they have truly superior wine. None of the local shite."

Fantastic, so he's a snob, and he thinks nothing on La'heng could be as good as what they import from elsewhere. I make a note of that and walk beside him, mentally lining up my arguments. He makes polite, strained small talk on the way to the restaurant, which is atop one of the towering structures nearby. The floor rotates slowly, granting a luxurious view first of the harbor and then the governor's palace in the distance. Jineba, which is the capital city, shows no trace at all of La'heng influence or architecture. Rather, the buildings are like Terran trees whose rings reveal their age. Jineba is like that, only you can tell how old a structure is by the architectural style and which conquerors designed it. The Nicuan occupation has resulted in a series of colonial complexes, where pillars and columns mask the modern heart.

The penthouse dining room shares that quality, and there are La'hengrin servants instead of bots. They take our orders with quiet humility, and I loathe their subservience because someone has sent them to work here. It wasn't a choice, and they don't receive wages. Whatever the nobles call it, this is slavery.

Legate Flavius orders for us without asking what I want. To a man like him, I suppose it doesn't matter. Once the niceties are attended to, he steeples his hands and regards me across the white-linen-covered table.

"Make your case, Ms. Jax."

"Under the Homeland Health Care Act, ratified by the human board of directors in 4867, the natives of

La'heng have the right to the best treatments, including but not limited to experimental medications. Carvati's Cure ameliorates damage created by widespread exposure to RC-17." When we seeded the atmosphere with a chemical that was meant to keep the La'hengrin compliant, we didn't factor in their adaptive physiology. It's been centuries now, and the effects linger still. "Therefore, the Nicuan council actively prohibits a treatment that will improve quality of life for the La'hengrin, which is unlawful according to article thirty-seven, codicil—"

The legate sighs faintly. "Yes, you've inundated my office with claims about your miracle drug. Unfortunately, you haven't passed licensing through the drug administration. As I recall, there have been *no* trials. What kind of monsters would we be if we permitted you to use the La'heng to test your product?"

The kind who make the La'hengrin your slaves, like the ones you have at home.

I grind my teeth, holding the retort. "We applied for permits to begin trials three months ago. They were denied due to lack of residency requirements."

He smiles. "Ah, yes. You must achieve residency on La'heng before you can expect to receive the rights that come with citizenship."

I want to come across the table and punch him in the face. Instead, I bite my inner lip until I taste copper. The pain focuses my anger into a laser.

"I applied for citizenship," I say carefully. "And my request was denied."

The unctuous smile widens. "I did see that. Your unfortunate past makes you rather ... undesirable, Ms. Jax."

"Excuse me?" I bite out.

"First, Farwan Corporation charged you with terrorism—"

"Those accusations were entirely baseless," I snap.

"As if the business with Farwan wasn't questionable enough, your military career ended in a rather colorful fashion, did it not? To wit, charges of mass murder, dereliction of duty, and high treason."

"I was acquitted. It's illegal to deny me citizenship due to crimes the court judged I did not commit."

"Hmm," he says, feigning concern. "Well, feel free to appeal within the Conglomerate courts. Since we are, at least in the tertiary sense, subject to their laws and jurisdictions, if they deem that our denial violated your rights as a Conglomerate citizen in good standing, then we will certainly reconsider the decision."

He knows that will take turns, damn him. Turns to appeal the rejection. Turns to get another application approved. Then I'll have to start over with the permissions to initiate drug trials. They're trying to kill the resistance with blocks and delays.

Assholes.

Holding my temper by sheer willpower, I say, "So you allege that you're denying progress with the cure for the good of the La'heng."

There's that awful, hateful smile again. "Certainly. We take our duty as their protectors very seriously."

"Sure you do." I shove back from the table and stalk away. There's no way I'm spending another minute with this jackass, now that I know it's a dead end. In the past six months, I've met countless petty bureaucrats who get off on jerking people around. Nicuan is full of stunted dictators who have secret dreams of being the emperor, and so they rule their tiny department with an iron fist.

Vel's waiting for me at home. I take public transport to get there, and then walk some distance as well. We're off the beaten path for obvious reasons. As I trudge the last kilometer, I reflect that Vel can try. His record might prove harder to block, as he doesn't have my tarnished reputation. He was a bounty hunter known for his compliance with all regulations, and then he commanded the Ithtorian fleet to great personal acclaim. But it's so fragging disheartening to think of starting over.

And maybe there's no point.

Loras thinks this is a monumental waste of time, but he let me do it while he puts other plans in place. Rebellions aren't born overnight. They foment over time with careful nurturing, and while I waste my time with Nicuan officials, he's working other angles. By the time I give up the whole thing as untenable, he'll be ready to move. In a way, I'm his stalking horse. While they're screwing with me, the nobles won't expect problems from any other quarter.

"How did it go?" Vel asks when I walk in. He gets back from flight school before I finish up my work in the city, and it's nice to have him waiting. He's over two meters tall, covered in chitin, with hinged legs, and my mark on his thorax, a character that means grimspace in Ithtorian. His side-set eyes and expressive mandible no longer seem strange to me, though people on La'heng sometimes stare if he's out of faux-skin.

"For shit," I mutter. "Who I am is actually working against us. Or at least, they're using my past to block my petitions."

"I am sorry, Sirantha."

When we first met on Gehenna, Vel had taken a job to retrieve me for Farwan Corporation. He slid into a friend's skin, and figured out a way to get me to willingly go to New Terra with him. That could've end badly for me. Fortunately, Vel was as honorable a bounty hunter — as he is in every other regard — and once he realized the Corp was using me as a scapegoat, he became my biggest ally. Now, he's my dearest friend ... with nuances of something else, maybe, someday. But he doesn't look for promises any more than I'm looking to make our relationship more complicated. His mere presence defuses some of the tension and frustration that comes with the territory. He's always supported me, believing the best of me even when I screw up, even when I don't deserve it.

I shrug. "Loras warned us it would be like this, but ... I'm not used to such abject, consistent failure. I keep thinking I'll stumble on the magic handshake and get somewhere with these assholes."

He crosses to me and runs his claws down my back, more comforting than it sounds. "It is unlikely."

"I know."

My mouth sets into a firm line. "They'll regret it. Someday."

"You gave them a chance to do the right thing. They are more interested in maintaining their own luxurious lifestyles. I shall not care when we raze them to the ground."

His quiet assessment of their prospects makes me laugh, partly because of his calm tone and partly because that day seems so far off. But I'm capable of playing the long game, as Nicuan will discover.